flip city

f!ip city

a novel

ROSSJAMESD/KPaulyMD/Rm3H
Admit:6.1.1970/DOB:10.15.1955
Med:Tofranilpm150mg/1:24

linda burrows

RARE BIRD
LOS ANGELES, CALIF.

RARE BIRD

THIS IS A GENUINE RARE BIRD BOOK

Rare Bird Books
6044 North Figueroa Street
Los Angeles, CA 90042
rarebirdbooks.com

Copyright © 2024 by Linda Burrows

FIRST TRADE PAPERBACK ORIGINAL EDITION

For more information, address:
Rare Bird Books Subsidiary Rights Department
6044 North Figueroa Street
Los Angeles, CA 90042

Set in Warnock Pro
Printed in the United States

Cover Design by Robert Schlofferman
Interior Design by Hailie Johnson

10 9 8 7 6 5 4 3 2 1

Library of Congress Cataloging-in-Publication Data available upon request

To Marilyn Sidran, finally
"So that's the story."

Some people are at odds with the world
and they become serial killers

and others become artists.

—Jayne County

Stay not, be gone. Live, and hereafter say
A madman's mercy bid thee run away.

—*Romeo and Juliet*
Act 5, Scene 3
William Shakespeare

Author's Disclaimer

Flip City takes place in a fictitious world in a different Chicago that doesn't exist in true life. Readers whose experiences in situations similar to those depicted here may argue it never happened like that, and they would be right.

FORWARD

"Quick Joey Small" is stuck in my head, if I kill myself now, that's my reason. Not the wasted feeling that smothers this place or the meds that fog everything up. Not my transistor radio either, or tonight's Hit Parade, which *is* pretty depressing when bubblegum pop songs get played. Before I could switch the radio station the orderly snatched my transistor away. So the last verse I heard repeats in my brain rhyming over and over and over. About Joey Small who went over the wall. Enough to drive *any*one batty.

It's angel who stops it, the downward spiral, his calm steady voice taking over. «purple haze, gimme shelter, whole lotta love» he says, naming tracks from new albums I'd choose to play if I were the deejay or home. Or could just change the station, if I had my radio back.

I tell angel I don't get how sane people do it, sleep through the night without music. And he says, «it's only been forty-five minutes» And I go, well it feels like forever to me. And he goes, «well it's in your shrink's office. go snatch it back»

The night nurse lets me in when I knock on Pauly's office door, she's easily flattered at the hint of a smile from me. She wants to know why it was taken away, when I say I just want my transistor back, my earphone, and my 9-volt battery. She pulls my file from a locked cabinet and opens the folder. Her eyes tick-tock down the page for a moment then rise and tick-tock over me. Barefoot and aware of these dorky pj's, I cross my arms tight to my chest.

She sits sidesaddle on the edge of his desk. "Did Dr. Pauly say it's okay?" she asks, skimming his notes for the answer. I say I don't know, I'm not talking to him. "You're not talking to anyone," she says. Which isn't completely true, I point out, I'm talking to you. Can I please have my radio back.

"You can't close yourself off by listening to music twenty-four hours a day. You can't get well without opening up, James," she says.

I don't want to cry but I feel it coming. «tell her the truth jamey tell her why»

"It's the only thing that makes me happy," I say.

Her eyelids flutter, her glance flicks away from my face and my vandalized wrists to the handwritten words on my chart. "Doctor's notes *do* say your sleep meds may be adjusted. As necessary." She winks like we're friends and she's breaking a rule for me. She lets herself into the pharmacy locker with a ring full of jangly keys. I have to cup my hands over my ears.

She's left my file open on Pauly's desk, all his detailed notes about me, his ass-essments and de-structions. Which are mostly like scribbles in some foreign language, French or Spocktovian, who knows. But then—it's like shock—my dad's name tops my chart, *Jeffrey David Ross* pops off the page to punch another hole in my heart. My dad's signature, I freak out to angel, my dad signed the paper, what for? Blinking to read it but the letters are wrong, like they zapped out the part of my brain that could tell an A from an L or a Z.

«it's a consent form» For what? angel deciphers the scribbled message into plain English for me. «electroconvulsive therapy» he says. «ECT»

His voice floods my head now, his wise words that know what to do. «you can't stay here» and he's probably right but the night nurse confronts me, untangling my fingers out of my hair, lifting me back to my feet. She gathers the pages scattered all over the floor. An orderly appears so there's no fighting anything now, his menacing presence or her night pills I swallow from a little paper cup. And I can already hear it, what Pauly will say in his shrink voice he thinks is a comfort. That he sees me improving every day even if I won't do my part. Well, he has to say that, like proof to my dad he's worth all the bucks my dad pays him. But there is no improvement, just stronger drugs. And the absence of anything sharp.

The orderly escorts me down the hallway, back to the private white room. He waits till I'm back in the bed under covers. If I get out of bed or this room before morning he will strap me down, that's his warning. I'm just watching him check out the rest of my stuff, as if there's more he can take. The new *Creem* magazine or *Tiger Beat*, Snickers or *The Catcher in the Rye.*

Angel is sick of it. «go over the wall» he says. «quick jamey small go over the wall» Then over and over, bringing it back, the gnawing rhyme of that song. I pull the pillow over my head. «before morning comes and they come to restrain you» Which gets me on edge despite these night meds and warm blankets. I can't sleep or ignore him.

The orderly is helping himself to the room, I can hear him from under the pillow. I keep still, hardly breathing, and pretend I'm knocked out, just waiting for him to be done. Hearing pages I left on the dresser top flip, a sketchbook that's blank and those jumbo

Crayolas that roll off and snap on the floor. Drawers slide open and shut, my stuff ruffled through, till the scuff of his shitkicker boots move away, his footsteps retreat down the hall. The whole time I'm listening, angel keeps singing, «quick jamey ross go over the wall»

I've got no reason to even listen to him, I know angel doesn't exist. Despite what my dad says, or Dr. Pauly, I don't think I'm crazy, pretending he does. I'd just rather not be alone.

«**hurry**» **he warns** me the moment the orderly's gone. So I dress in the dark with my heart gearing up, new boxers and socks, Levi's cords and a T-shirt, a long-sleeve flannel and shoes.

«and your jacket»

That's true, I might need a jacket and grab it.

«go jamey jamey go go»

It's scary though, like the edge of the world, when I step from this white room back into the empty ward.

«nobody's watching. they'd never expect a good boy like you to take off»

One foot, then the other, in silent white high-tops, I sneak down the sanitized hall. But angel is right. There's no one in sight, no night-shifted nurses or brawny dis-orderlies, just wisps of their laughter and pot smoke behind me drifting from Pauly's office door. And its soft distant light that's making the polished floor glow.

Passing dark rooms with no locks and the doors kept wide open, like animal dens, that's what I'm thinking, all the kids in here caged by their nightmares.

«don't think» angel tells me. «just go go go go»

Faster then, through the dark dayroom, past tables of bored games and incomplete puzzles. To the NO EXIT fire door with The Oaks Manor crest on a sign with a warning: ALL GUESTS MUST

CHECK OUT THROUGH THE LOBBY. Pressing ka-chunk on its metal latch and stepping out into the night.

Stars twinkle hello in the vastness above, unmoved and timeless, but I'm lickety-split across the Manor-cured grounds, past their fountains and benches and flowerbeds, through the thick leafy hedges that hide the surrounding brick wall. Laughing too, despite the panic alarm sounding loud in my head and quickening the beat of my heart. Inhaling big lungfuls of fresh air and freedom, like some new happiness drug I've found. Which would be enough if they stopped me right now, to get through the night strapped down. But nobody does. So I'm jumping to grip the concrete lip high above and pull myself up the wall, a knee, then one foot, to the top, tumbling over. Like a thrill ride almost, where your stomach drops out in a floating moment, knowing you're going to fall.

part one
angel

1

Loud clanging bells explode in my ears, clearing the meds from my head and waking me up to the day. To crossing gates closing and red lights flashing, a train pulling in all massive and noisy. CHICAGO & NORTH WESTERN, its yellow and green passenger cars take over the whole station platform. Commuters pile on or off, the conductor leans from a doorway in a blue uniform and flat-visored hat, he calls out the name of my suburb.

"River Hills!"

I sit myself upright, shove my hair back from my eyes. When did all these people get here? It was pretty much deserted before sunrise. But now cars change places in parking lot spaces to drop people off or pick them up at the curb. Suburban white husbands, and black cleaning ladies, and teens my age acting cool. On the platform they all blend together though: the help in their aprons and pressed house dresses, the men in their suits with hats and briefcases, the kids dressed like hippies in tie-dye and faded patched Levi's.

But none of them are Gary yet, coming to get me. I called him collect from the train station payphone. *No sweat, meet you there,* he said.

Pacing the curb, I'm excited to see him, Gary Spanier, my best friend since sixth grade. Well, my "partner-in-crime," if you believe what my dad said, Gary's no real friend at all. *A real friend has your best interests at heart, a real friend watches your back. Even your imaginary friend is better than Gary.* If my dad had to choose, he'd rather I hang out with angel instead. As long as I stay on strong medication. As long as I stay in The Oaks and get well.

The Oaks *Mental* Manor.

«the oaks is a mind game, who needs that place anyway, not you» angel says. «you're not crazy» Ha, that's pretty crazy, my imaginary friend says I'm sane. So doubt fills the cracks in last night's twisted logic that made walking away the right choice. *Consequences, consequences,* like a shrinkology session, art or group or talk therapy, where you hear Pauly's voice all calm and controlling, with questions he sets like a trap. *And how does walking away fit into our plan to achieve mental wellness?* he'd ask. And my dad's disappointment, whatever I answer. What therapy frees you from that?

Slipping out of my Levi's jacket, the morning air creeps up the cuffs of these plaid flannel sleeves, chilling my skin like an ice bath. It does calm you, though. Ice water.

I tell angel, I honestly have no idea what my dad will do this time he finds out I split. I won't go back, though. I already made up my mind about that.

«no sane person would. you got out, your dad would've done the exact same thing, so how can you be crazy» I tell him I don't know, I'm just glad he survived despite all the meds and shock therapy they tried, angel's the reason I'm even alive, I don't think I'd be here without him.

Still, my teeth chatter. Trying so hard not to think panicked thoughts, but I'm bombarded, unable to stop them. Like the all-night escape from The Oaks just to get here and how quick they could do it by car. Once they know I split and start looking, they won't have to look very far. They'll notify authorities and gather paperwork and send an APB over the wire. *One-Adam-12, one-Adam-12, be on the lookout for James Daniel Ross, fifteen, white male, five foot six, blond hair. Last seen in pj's and five-point restraints.* Then squad cars with sirens scream through the streets and searchlights circle the sky. And dogs, maybe even. Big dogs. German shepherds or bloodhounds on my trail. If they catch me, they'll commit me back into The Oaks. Or send me back to jail.

Railton. I quickly shake that nightmare out of my head, release a deep breath, relax my tense shoulders. Close my eyes to the gray skies and the herd moving by in a blur of mostly suburban white faces. *Mooo* fills my head now. Ha. *Mooo,* like my big brother Tommy joked once, riding the train downtown to the Loop, taking me with him to my dad's high-rise office. Mooo. Holding my hand through the herds of commuters. Holding my hand so tight.

The platform fills and empties three times, three trains come and go, and still I'm sitting here, left foot shaking, right foot up on the bench, waiting for Gary, my partner in crime.

But talking to anyone now sounds so hard. What do you say, really? Even the misfits and mental defectives wanted to know, you'd think they wouldn't, living at The Oaks with me the whole summer. Between gin rummy games where all the heart cards are missing, replaced with Clue cards or Monopoly, *The Knife in The Hall* or *Get Out Of Jail Free,* even they found some reason to ask me. "You're the boy on the Sugar Sprinkles box?" Like if they had a box, they wouldn't be mental.

```
ROSSJAMESD/KPaulyMD/Rm3H
Admit:6.1.1970/DOB:10.15.1955
Med:Tofranilpm150mg/1:24
```

I want it off me, this retard band, my wrist tagged like baggage or something that comes with instructions. Pulling at the plastic, the unlockable snap, trying to take it off, rip it off, slip it over, but my palm's too wide.

«maybe if you had a sharp» angel says.

It's not who I am though, or ever wanted to be. A boy with a shiv, a boy who even knows what that is, kept handy in a hidden hem, tucked up a pantleg or under his pillow, ready to fight or kill. A boy who would ever need something like that. And it hits me, I don't have any meds, where am I supposed to get meds?

«maybe you don't need any meds»

I'm suddenly dizzy, The Oaks' dinner last night churning the back of my tongue. I have to get up, stumbling into the station, past the two wooden benches, the vending machines for Refreshing Drinks and Cigarettes, the lone ticket window, and into the MEN's restroom door. Chicken fried steak or coq sans vin, I barely make it into the stall before upchucking it all in the john. But I don't feel better, even taking deep breaths, which sort of works when they won't give you your meds.

Try to rewind myself, back a few years when everything still seemed so normal, but my head's so messed up I can't even remember what songs used to play. So I wish more than ever I had my radio back.

Shake it off, my dad said. Stand tall. Be a man.

I don't look like a man at all, though. More like a mannequin in new fall clothes, tan Levi's cords, navy T-shirt, tan, navy, and white plaid flannel shirt, white PF Flyers. Like a department store ad in the Sunday newspapers. **Back-to-School Class of 1971**. Look, it's Jamey Ross. The boy on the front of the cereal box.

«maybe you could go back to school»

Rip a paper towel from the jaws of the dispenser, mop myself off, and drop it on top of trashed coffee cups, punched train tickets, and discarded newspaper headlines. More about the Vietnam War. **BODY COUNT ESCALATES**. More horrible things. Why would anyone want to live in this world? I'm not even kidding, I don't see the point. Of therapy or getting well or anything.

«maybe if you had your pepsodent»

Which starts a laugh somewhere deep inside, thinking about toothpaste. Ha. Like that's all you need, a sparkling white smile and your life will be all right.

"Gary!" I recognize him immediately, even with the mustache he's got now. Gary Spanier, so cool at school or wherever you're with him, Friday night social dancing, the record store uptown or just toolin' around River Hills. Gary and me, jamming at his house like rock stars or something, hacking out "Purple Haze." Gary, who set me up with good times and parties and Mandi Maroney. Gary, who's sixteen and licensed to drive now, he rattles the keys in his hand. The second I see him everything's better, so I'm glad I lived and last year's over and who needs angel when I get to hang out with Gary again.

Except he's not alone.

I start to shake when I see her. When it hits me, they could've erased her, one massive brain shock, and z-z-zap! Mandi Maroney's out of my mind forever—God, what if they had? He's holding her hand, she's dressed like the cover of *Seventeen* magazine, real mod with thick bangs and mascara. She looks as grown up as my big sister Laura, she's beautiful, she's got white go-go boots on, earrings like peace signs, and a blue polka-dot trench coat. Well, it is sort of overcast out.

Gary grins like he's happy to see me. "Hey-hey," he says. Holding the door for her coming inside, his hand on her back, so I follow behind when he guides her past me to the vending machines. He opens his wallet and buys cigarettes, and signals I don't have to pay. He gets Mandi a coffee and me a Coke but she's already got me all wired, sitting so close her pink bubblegum popping sprinkles my cheek.

Mandi Maroney! like my best dream come true, and now with me again on this same wooden bench where we once sat together last summer. "Mandi, hey," I hear myself say. The lamest two words ever spoken.

But she smiles anyway. "Hey-hey," she replies, like a private joke or the key to a kiss we once shared. *Juliet*, that enters my head now, the verse where Romeo sees her and goes, *Oh, but if she knew she were.* She does know though. She traces a finger around the heart I carved in the armrest last year. Her initials and mine, **1969 MM+JDR**.

Heart pounding, opening my heart, not something I planned to do. But I can smell her Heaven Sent *eau de parfum* and a rush of emotion wakes up inside me, wanting so bad to be Romeo. *My lips two blushing pilgrims ready stand.* To touch her hand and, you know, make it real. *To smooth that rough touch with a tender...kiss.* Which is all wrong as soon as I try it.

"Jamey!" Mandi jerks back and it's like instant zap! ECT of the heart.

God, I'm so stupid! Anyone normal would know she's with him, the evidence is easy to see. One, she's got on his ID bracelet, two, it's his name engraved in the band. **G A R Y**. The silver chain rattles when he holds her hand, three. My best friend + Mandi, that sums it up, minus me.

My head fills so buzzy with *eau de stupid* I'm wishing this wasn't real.

Her glossy lips purse like a cobweb just brushed them or maybe her coffee's too hot. Looking for clues in her eyes but she won't look at me, she looks at Gary instead. He's big now, not skinny like me, how we both used to be. Like rock stars. More like a guard now or orderly, all muscle-necked and wide shoulders, hair trimmed so adult. And the mustache, my sister wrote me last April she saw him with that. But nobody told me he's with Mandi Maroney, who once stole my heart and kissed me alone in her bedroom.

The next breath doesn't come, I can't breathe.

"Jamey, look, it's not me, okay? It's my dad," she says, in a tone like she thinks I might break. "He thinks you're a homme fatal, or something? I don't know. He is so weird." She circles her eyes at how weird, twisting her face up all goofy, making me smile if I think about that and not what she's saying. "My dad said I can't see you anymore because you're like Romeo. And that doesn't end well."

I cough up this Coke, practically choking, like I forgot how to swallow or, or live.

"Jesus!" Gary slaps my back like he knows how to stop you from dying but I twist away from his touch. He backs off, lighting up a Marlboro, shaking the match out, he turns, dropping it in an ashcan.

"Sorry, sorry," Mandi says, God, almost in tears so I just want to say it's okay but she gets up and goes to his side so I don't. "I just thought I should tell you in person, that's all."

"You okay?" Gary asks, me or her I'm not sure, but his arm wraps around her blue polka dot shoulders, smoke flows from his mouth when he speaks. "You still wanna go to your grandma's?" he says. "Because we can drive you wherever." So I guess he's talking to me.

I can't even picture that though, going *wherever* with them together. And where Wherever would be.

Gary pulls at the hairs over his lip and nods when we're passing the payphone outside. "Oh, *that's* where you called me from. Collect," he muses, head bobbing like he's just figured some mystery out. I nod and tell him I'll pay him back, I forgot to bring any money. This familiar grin smears across his face, pulled from the back of English lit class or detention hall, or just toolin' around River Hills. "I swear, Jamey. Your old man is still the biggest living asshole on two feet."

Dread fills me, I don't want to hear it and look straight ahead, at the parking lot, at the cars and a shiny red Stingray Corvette, at the park-like suburb beyond.

"Don't be pissed, man. I just wanted to ask you if it's cool to bring Mandi, that's all. So I called your house. And, man! he flips *out* on me—the whole goddam third degree thing. Shit, so I go, what is this, am I on trial here? I just wanna fuckin' talk to Jamey. And he flew off his goddam nut, accusing me of God knows what."

I turn away, but the panic seed's already planted. *They're coming for me.* Thinking how they're preparing it now, rubber sheets, unbuckling the leather cuffs, plugging in the electric shocker. The smell of it. "D-did you really say that word?"

"What word?"

"The F word."

"*Fuck*, yeah." Gary grins. "And I told him I always thought he was an asshole. Because what kind of a fucking lawyer can't keep his own kid out of jail? And he hung up on me. So it just proves my point."

Bad idea, another bad idea, see, here it is again, bringing Gary into it, why'd I do that? Stupid stupid stupid. And worse, Mandi, prettier than memory, softer and better and smart enough to obey her dad and make the right choice. Crammed into this cramped red Corvette, his dad's new Stingray, two doors two seats three of us, no way to escape any of it, ninety mph gunning past every car on the highway. Perched on my lap, she's pressed against me, her trench coat, her mini skirt, her hair fresh with herbal shampoo. But I get no reaction because everything's broken, I can't blame medication for what I can't do. **The Oaks Manor *Institute for Adolescent Wellness*.** But I'm *not* well. Even tucking the hospital band up my cuff, she still sees the tattletale scars.

"God!" Mandi jumps, spinning around, her hip bumps the dashboard, her back blocks the windshield, there is no place farther to go.

Gary shouts, "Sit down, Maroney!" then, "What'd he do?" so her tailbone digs into my thighs and he's able to see out the windshield. An accusation, actually, that's what it is. Like I did something crazy to her.

"He slit—*both* wrists?" Mandi gasps, it's a horrible thing, I realize that.

Electric Ladyland ejects with a poke from his finger so there's nothing to block out his voice. "Jesus, are you mental?"

So forget breathing normal, prescriptions, hospitalization, therapy, ECT. Screaming fills my vacant head, HELP ME, ANGEL. "No, I, I just…really missed you guys."

"You tried to *off* yourself? Oh my God, Jamey!" she spits out. "My dad was right—that's not romantic, that's psycho!"

"I'm not—" Grasping for words and the door handle, I pull up on it desperate for release. Let me out let me out let me out. "I didn't do anything—"

"Well, you pushed Ratachek through the cafeteria window," Gary says, with maybe a chuckle. "I mean, everybody in the whole school saw."

She punches his arm. "It's *not* funny, Spanier! God! Ratachek almost died—"

Snapping the 8-track back in, I turn it louder, loud as it goes, "Crosstown Traffic" filling the Corvette and my ears, crank down the window filling my eyes with the blurry city passing by. I don't know these Chicago streets at all like Gary does, which exit you take to my granma's apartment or where's a good place to park. Just the three of us all scrunched together in two bucket seats, electric guitar licks soaring, Gary flooring the engine, it roars underneath with the power of 370 horses. But *nothing* excites me. Good times are old times, I want them back but you can't hold on, there is no cure or apology, one dumb mistake and the good things're gone forever.

Mandi shoves the door open and leaps off my lap to the curb. Shuddering, her arms clench her trench coat, she paces impatiently in high-heeled white boots. Brownstones and big leafy trees line the street.

"Which building's your grandparents' again?" Gary asks. He's double-parked, if he gets a ticket for this then whose fault is that? He wouldn't even be here if it weren't for me.

I recognize their apartment building, the three-story yellow brick one.

He creeps the 'Vette forward till Mandi on the curb fills the rearview mirror. "I shouldn't've brought her," he says. "Sorry. Don't know what I was thinking."

«yes he did. he's no real friend at all»

My foot finds the curb but Gary holds me back, his hand pinning mine to the console. So hope flickers a moment he might prove angel wrong and choose me instead of Mandi. But his hand moves away, his mouth opens to speak, then instead shakes his head and starts over. "So what did Ratachek do, anyway? He try something funny with you?" Asking like it's his job to know and my obligation to tell him.

Heat flushes my jaw. Truth, the whole truth and nothing but. Turn away, look out the window. Not at Mandi, at nothing at all. "I went back to his class to ask for a hall pass. But he had this other kid in there, like on his lap. Touching him and stuff."

"Touching what, like his dick? Really? What kid? Come on, Jamey. What kid?"

Shake my head, it's not his business, but he insists, what kid? Who? So I just go, "This kid Kyle," and it's instant regret, letting the name out, instant regret I answered, or ever woke up this morning at all.

"You pushed Ratachek through a second-story window because of Kyle Bodie? Jesus, Jamey! You got yourself locked up over a faggot? What for, man? Aw, hell. Jesus!" Gary's fist pounds the steering wheel. "Railton, what was that like? Kiddie jail, right?"

Shaking my head, 'cause none of it matters, and he knows that too. What happened last year in the cafeteria stairwell when Ratachek tried to stop me from telling and tripped. I caught my balance breaking out of his grip, but Ratachek went through the plate glass.

"Rattysex, man. Fucking homo." Gary stares at me for confirmation so I have to look down at my hands. At the hospital band.

Tofranilpm150mg/1:24

I almost ask, did Rattysex try something funny with you? but I already know his answer.

"Man, you really did a number on his face. You seen him?"

It hits me I can't say anything to Gary except "hey-hey" anymore. I push myself out of his dad's sporty car. "I have to go see my granma now."

"You're okay though, right?" He fiddles with his key ring, the Playboy Bunny on a chain. He nods at the scars on my wrists and the hospital band. "I mean, they let you out and all."

I don't tell him they didn't, he already thinks I'm mental. Approaching Mandi Maroney one last time but she pops another bubble and sidesteps around me, two or three steps and she's taken my place in his dad's new Corvette, so I turn the other way.

To my granma's house.

2

There's a tiny patch of perfect lawn squared off with a low picket fence that's easy to just step over. So I do, turning away from the revving Corvette to the yellow brick entry and glass-paned wood door. The rumbling engine fades, rounding the corner until I can't hear it anymore.

A shriveled old man hobbles out the front entrance, croaking at me, bony finger accusing, "Ey! Schmuck! It's a fence dere! It's a sidevalk! Vhatza matter vidt you?"

Which shakes me, you know, just to face disapproval and what happens next if my grampa's upstairs? Hoping instead, Granma Hannah's up there, I'll do whatever she says to, I swear, I already made up my mind, and quick before I change it, I slip under the arm of the pruny old man holding open the heavy paned door.

Inside it's quiet, the foyer's a sponge absorbing all sound. Like a church or library with solemn dark wood and the smell of wax polish my grampa's been using since probably before I was born. *Rabin Rosenberg* on their mailbox buzzer, but I don't buzz it. Quickly taking the stairs up two at a time or three, I don't touch the gleaming banister and barely mess up the vacuumed pattern on the ancient carpet at all.

At the third floor the staircase ends so I'm at the top looking down at the mosaic foyer below. Feeling ghostly and strange, like I'm floating almost, not part of this world or any world now, unsure if I ever was.

Knocking on the apartment door, jiggling the gleaming brass knob, my skin goes all prickly and cold like I've broken a rule, *Rule #14*, the one that reads, *Don't get your hopes up.* 'Cause what if this isn't Granma's building or even her street? And I messed up completely, my memory shot, I'm not sure who'll answer the door.

But then, "Who is there?" sings through the peephole in my granma's lyrical voice.

It's my favorite, the French toast she makes me. The bread's the thick yellow Jewish kind all butter crispy and powdery white with sugar, not like the rubbery half-slices they give you at Railton, something I'd rather forget.

"What else can I get you, dolly?" she asks. A melon slice, a bowl of rice pudding, a pink bakery box filled with sweet rolls. A tall glass of ice cold choco milk too, so I'm glad angel knew to come here.

She sits down at the dining room table beside me, leans her chin on her palm so petite you just know she was a knockout when she was young. A symphony plays on her ancient Philco. It's Stravinsky, the broadcaster's smooth voice announces, "The Firebird Ballet Suite" from 1945. My granma sighs. "It wasn't helping, that hospital?"

I tell her all the puzzles there have missing pieces. You could be there forever and never be done.

"Oy, sweetheart. Nothing's forever." She brushes my bangs back where they catch on my lashes, she does that with no warning and plants a soft kiss on my forehead.

"They don't let you listen to music," I say.

"Oh my. That's simply barbaric, isn't it." She smiles, she loves me, she understands. "I'm afraid that is not how your father will see it. Do you think it was wise to leave?"

But it's not her question or even *your father* that's freaking me out. "When does Grampa get home?"

We both turn to look at the grandfather clock then at each other and break from the moment, laughing. She says, "I'm not worried about Grandpa, tatalah. I'm worried about you."

I tell her I already promised I won't kill myself. I add, "I'm not a liar, you know."

She used to believe me. Now she nods her head slowly, more like she's scared to say no.

Choke down emotion, I don't want to cry. "I was thinking maybe I could sleep in the cellar and then when Grampa goes to work come upstairs and we could hang out together and then I could go back down or someplace else when he gets home. He never even has to know I'm here. God, even my dad wouldn't have to know."

"Grandpa Rabin is retired, sweetheart."

"Oh."

"Today, he's at shul, but tomorrow? I don't know."

"Well, forget that then, I already know he hates me."

"No, dolly." Her embrace pulls my cheek to her apron, it smells like vanilla and roses. "Believe me, that old grizzly, he's a teddy bear inside."

She slides the plate closer to me, the French toast then choco milk and tucks my hair behind my ears. It's long but she doesn't tell me to cut it.

"Jamey? Let's call your daddy, all right?" she says. "Together, we'll call."

The sting of betrayal hits hard again. 'Cause I saw his signature on my chart in Pauly's office. *Jeffrey David Ross, Atty at Law.* "Uh-unh, Granma. He signed the paper, he wants them to do it to me again. ECT—" I push away from her, wishing she could just see that torture room, Electroconvulsive Therapy, I know she'd agree in a heartbeat.

"Shock treatment, z-z-z-z. Like, you know, like..." I have to stop for a moment to calm down and not cry.

«just explain it to her» angel says, «she's on your side»

"Like for mental cases," I say. "You know what that feels like? Like I'd rather be dead."

Her eyes flash with pain or memory. "No, kinehora, no."

"He wouldn't care anyway if I was."

"Oh, dolly. Of course he cares. He wants what's best for you. The same as he does for Tommy and your sisters."

"He wants me in an institution, Granma." Pleading almost, don't make me go back there.

She nods, slow and distant. "You scared him, Jameleh. You scared us all. You chose to take your *life*. Oh, sweetheart." She's brushing back my bangs again, dabbing these tears with the hem of her apron. "Perhaps this Oaks Manor place will help you both heal. I know in your heart you want this, too. I hope you'll give it another chance."

I'm shaking my head no no no the whole time. "All he's gotta do is say he wants me to come home. Why can't I just go home? I could take those same meds there. Do the same stupid puzzles. Drool all down myself in front of the TV."

"He needs to know you're safe, sweetheart. In a safe place where no one can harm you."

Well, he's a little late! almost screams out full of anger and hate but she's on my side angel said, so I swallow the words with a bite of sharp toast that scratches my throat like a blade. Swallow hard but nothing goes down. Not even the chocolate milk, it just comes spilling out through the chip in my teeth, dribbling on her lace tablecloth and down the front of my clothes. "Sorry," I'm hearing myself say now, sorry. I can't do it anymore, be normal or hold myself up. "It's just like I thought at Railton. I don't belong in this family anymore."

She's quiet and bows her head a few seconds then looks up again. "Would more medicine help? Such sad thoughts go away when you take it, don't they?"

I shake my head. "It just gets me all…like a non-person. You know, like a TV show or something and all I can do is sit back and watch."

"But if Uncle Shelly brought you more, you would take it?"

So I almost wish Uncle Shelly would show up right now, with his white doctor coat and stethoscope, and his black bag of miracle cures. A Band-Aid, a lollipop, a reassuring smile. "If you tell me to."

"Please, dolly. Take it. Take whatever you need from this world to live a long and happy life." Her fingers brush my cheek and she places a kiss like a crown on my head. "But first? Take a bath." She gives me a hug and a big pink fluffy towel from her closet.

The first photo I see when I wake on her pillow is when I was ten in the *Sears Christmas Wishbook 1965*. In a black tuxedo and high-top sneakers, blowing on a saxophone, shiny hair flying. Like if there was sound to it you could hear me wailing, but no, if there was sound you'd hear nothing at all. I can't play sax or anything else, except maybe play dumb, play with myself, play like I'm sleeping when Granma comes into the room.

She balances a folded stack of clothes on her forearms, slides the whole pile in a drawer. She believes I'm still sleeping, well, maybe not, I have no idea what she believes about me anymore. That I'm messed up. She leaves my shoes, she leaves her bedroom, she shuts the door quiet to not disturb me. Too late. It's a different picture filling my head now. Of fish swimming toward the claws of a grizzly preying for them on the shore.

Grampa is a fisherman, he likes to fish, I don't. In the trunk of his Lincoln Continental there's a folding chair and tackle box. A ball of live worms in an old pickled herring jar. They squirm and wriggle but you have to do what he tells you, prick the barbed hook straight through the belly, like popping a blood blister. He pulls off the road wherever there's fishing to see if they're biting and gets out his rod. You have to sit quiet so you don't scare the fish, even catfish and crappies, the ones he throws back.

Worm my way out from her pink quilt cocoon, the cool air finding my skin. Stepping out of Granma's warm bed onto her soft bedside rug, wishing Grampa didn't have to live here.

On the dresser there's family portraits and in picture frames hung around the room. The Grampa one with his fishing rod, I turn his picture face down. My cousins, my uncle, us—I mean Tommy, Laura, me, Bethie. Rarely my mom, except as a bride with my dad at her side. Mostly my dad, in a sharp tux or dress blues or cap and gown, like some handsome hero you'd stand to applaud. A groom or Marine or summa cum laude.

Wipe tears off on the cuff of this white Arrow shirt, damp from my hair and cold, wrap it around me tighter. It's one of my grampa's cotton dress shirts, starched from the cleaners, the tails drape my knees, the shoulders droop halfway to my elbows. Looking through wet bangs at the familiar faces framed on the dresser top or smiling at me from the walls. Tommy with his Eagle Scout badges. Laura the queen of the prom. Roly-poly Beth on horseback or in tutu and ballet shoes. Pretty boy Jamey, suddenly a stranger I hardly recognize, I don't remember taking these pictures at all. School portraits, studio headshots, and stuff you wouldn't think people frame, cereal ads or labels off baby food jars, flattened boxes of Sugar Sprinkles, department store catalog spreads. Some with his mother on magazine covers, *American Family, Women's Day, The National Science Review.* "Is Ritalin© the Wonder Drug?" He flirts with you in every shot, baby toddler preteen saxophone player. Medicated wonder.

There's no recent pictures though. The last one's from over a year ago, modeling Sears Doub-L Tuff jeans.

I turn toward the door when Granma comes back. Knock-knocking this time like a wardrobe assistant with my clothes neatly hung on wood hangers. She lays them out on the pink quilt. "Grandpa's downstairs, dolly," she whispers, combing a part in my hair with her fingers and tucking it behind my ears. "He's on his way up. Hurry now and get changed." She shuts the door gently behind her.

Getting changed. Into the same boxers and socks and tan Levi's cords, but looking brand-new again. Tie the white PF Flyers on my feet. Put on the T-shirt and the plaid flannel. Navy, tan, white, my mom made sure everything matched. Like that's most important for mental ward wear.

Pick up the Levi's jacket. Granma washed and pressed it all. So my dad would just say I'm burdening her now too.

Sit down on her bed when I'm dressed, trying so hard to wade through the muddle. It's true I am mental, I never could think, as far back as I can remember. Dyslexic, distracted, defective, unable to put two thoughts together. Like if you said, "Don't open her drawer, James," I open the drawer. "Don't take her prescription," I take the whole bottle, pop off the cap, two Percodan, then one more that's three, from my palm to my mouth, gulp it down. See?

Take it, Jamey. Whatever you need. Granma said that. Her pills in my pocket. What else do I need? Something sharp. A knife or a scissor, but her jewelry box just has old lady things, like brooches and hatpins and pearl earrings. In her sewing basket though, there's a scissors—a *real* scissors—its keen blades wide open against my scarred wrist. One snip, that's all, between plastic and skin, and the hospital wristband drops into her bedside waste bin.

From her bedroom I can hear Grampa's growl "harrumph!" and a few grumpy words that slip through. "Hijackers," "hippies," and "Nixon's henchmen." Waiting for my name but it's not mentioned.

I straighten her pink quilt over her bed, smooth like you have to at Railton. Push my bangs off my face with this soft flannel sleeve, smelling so laundry soap sweet. Twist my hair in a tail I tuck down my collar inside my flannel and hidden. Try to put on a catalog smile but none of them fit and what am I selling anyway?

Deep breath. Open the bedroom door. Dreading to face the grizzly, but I'm already grounded ashore.

Keep in the shadows of the hallway, sneaking like 007 or a peeping tom. Grampa's back is turned to me, hulking and hunched over. Granma takes his wide-brimmed black hat and prayer shawl, all silky white and blue knotted fringe, she puts them away in their old world wardrobe. He gives her a perfect red rose. She closes her eyes and smells it, hugging him. Her eyes peer over his black-suited shoulder, all sparkling and happy. "Mmm...heaven's perfume, you see?" Granma pulls away from him and brings the rose to me.

I wish I knew the magic words you say to be invisible. Because he casts his eyes like fishhooks and impales me.

"I should have known, when Izzy Feldman said some faygelah hippie trumped all over my lawn," he says, and looks at Granma. "What's he doing here?"

I can't smell her rose or heaven or anything, and just turn away. Trump to his front door, trumping away from him. It's so hot, but I'm putting my Levi's jacket over the flannel shirt anyway. Reaching for the doorknob with shaky hands, trembling badly like being plugged in before they throw the switch.

"*Nothing*, he's doing. I made him a little breakfast to eat," Granma is saying, combing my hair back with her fingers. "He's a good boy, Rabin."

"Good? He runs from the hospital, sick in the head! Like a criminal, this one! And a meal you give him?" But what she gives doesn't matter, he likes to prey on me. "Can't you ever do as you're told?" he bellows. And then at Granma, raising his voice. "Again you're meddling, Hannah! In what you know nothing about!"

She turns from him, her hand on my shoulder stops me. "Come, Jamey. Let's call Daddy now."

"Bah! The police you should call! Not Jeffrey!"

"You hush!"

But he doesn't. "God forbid, he should hurt a person again, or worse!"

"Worse is a grandfather speaking such words to a grandson!" Her words all Jewish or German chase him grumbling into a different room. But still I can hear him cursing "the schikse," which means my mom, and "Ross," *harrumph!* cursing my dad's last name too.

Granma's hands cover her mouth like someone who's just seen a trainwreck. So I'm left with regret, they were happy without me, I don't belong here and why'd angel tell me to come? Well, except Granma's French toast, I don't regret that.

Her paper-thin grip squeezes my shoulder then slides down my sleeve to my hand, slipping my fingers away from the doorknob, her lips to my hair. So her coffee breath is the perfume I smell. Maxwell House, she once told me, the richest kind. Like Zsa Zsa Gabor and the Hollywood movie stars drink.

"I have to go now," I say. "Just let me go."

"Where, dolly?" Her mouth sort of curdles attempting a smile. "Where will you go?" She doesn't stop my hand this time when I turn the doorknob.

The deadbolt clunks! and unlocks. "I don't know."

"One favor, promise Grandma?" She empties her coin purse, tucking a ten-dollar bill in my pocket, filling my palm with loose change. Then clutches my hand to her heart to her lips. "Please. You'll call Daddy." She kisses my knuckle and lets go.

3

I'm thinking about my granma's life and how she made it through. Grampa and drugs. Protection and Percodan, well, it says right on her prescription label, "for relief of pain."

Lifting the receiver from the payphone hook, I clench it between my shoulder and jaw. Drop a dime in the middle slot, hear it clink and rattle into the coin box, till the dial tone hums in my ear. Traffic noise rumbles outside this phone booth, I have to muffle my other ear while I dial. I'm nervous about calling and who'll answer the phone, I don't want to hear my dad angry. But even if...waves of warm Percodan already float through my veins.

It rings a lot. Nobody answers, and angel's all «ha, all that worry for nothing»

Well, it's Saturday. My dad's tee-off is at like seven I think, and my mom's got her errands to run. Car wash, dry cleaners, beauty salon, pharmacy.

Someone picks up. There's the shuffle of the receiver lifted from its cradle, the last harsh *br-r-r-ring* in my ear. Then agitated prima donna breath. Beth breath. Which is a relief.

"Good morning, Ross residence." Talking like a secretary, she pretends like that sometimes.

"Beth—"

"Jamey! Are you coming?"

"What?"

"Home! *Bandstand*'s on, David Cassidy's the guest star and guess what? He's wearing a Monkees shirt!"

"That's, that's, that is pretty crazy."

"You missed Rate-A-Record, but hurry up, we can still learn the new dances together."

"Well I—I...Can't Laura?"

"Uh-unh. She snuck out with gross Roger. God, Jamey, she's in almost as much trouble as you. How come you're not home yet?"

"Is Tommy there?"

"Big duh! He's at college. Jamey, how come?"

Big duh. "Well is—is Mom around then? Or, or Dad."

"No, they went to get you! I told them like fifty times you didn't run away, just wait 'cause you're on your way home. 'Cause you are coming home, aren't you?"

A truck goes by, the ground and my shoulders rattle. Beth is on the phone. My little sister. It's nice to hear her voice. "I don't know, I...I was thinking I could, you know. Get a job and, and maybe live someplace else."

"Oh. Well, where?"

Swallow it back, the flavor of pain relief. Check my flannel chest pocket, the one you'd keep cigarettes in, and take out Granma's orange plastic bottle.

"Will they let me visit you there? I'm *pract*ically thirteen."

Pop the white cap, tip it till I catch one in my palm. But the receiver slips, pinned between my ear and shoulder, it slides down this clean hair and denim jacket, dropping out of my grip. I save the yellow pill, though. Pop it in my mouth. The receiver flails on its silver cord like a fish out of water.

Look around for some or even better, choco milk, this Percodan caught all nasty on my tongue. But it's just a gas station phone booth, cars pulling in, pump jockeys scurry to wash their windshields, check oil, fill 'er up, exchange cash, then they're gone. And there's Beth faraway, just a little mouse voice dangling so disconnected at the end of the telephone line, talking to my knees, which is funny.

"Jamey, are you there?"

Laughing at that, how disconnected I am. But then I taste how bitter it is and whip back my neck gagging it down, a glob of saliva and Percodan.

She's supposed to be a nurse, a very proper nurse, but her tight white uniform and Barbie Doll body are not like any of the nurses who ever stuck a needle in me. It's just a soap opera on one of the TVs displayed here, but still, I'm watching how the doctor pins her to the operating table, all octopus arms and groping hands, trapping her into a kiss.

She gives up struggling, well, I can understand that, how you'd just go vacant and be someplace else. So I'm glad when this other nurse walks in on them and gasps all melodramatic. The organ chord soundtrack grows loud and crescendos till *General Hospital* fades from the screen to a charging white knight on a steed with a lance, zapping everything clean. "Stronger than dirt!" the jingle goes, and he's pointing his lance right at me. So I move out of the way.

Every TV set's on, lined up side by side to compare the skin tones and color. Too red or too green, holding my hand up passing the screens, ha! it's me that needs readjustment. A game show surrounds me with audience sounds, cheering and shouting and jumping around. Excited contestants risking it all for what's behind Door Number Three, sometimes a clunker, a donkey, or a brand-new TV. *Let's Make A Deal*, I've watched that a lot, then a rerun of *I Love Lucy*.

It's when I decide to leave. I like Lucy, I'm just not in the mood. If this was The Oaks I'd go back to my room.

They won't hire me to work here either. The lady said, "Try again at Christmas, we employ a lot of extra hires at Christmas," but Christmas is four months away and what if you need money now? The TV sales guy's glad I'm leaving. He's not mean or anything, shaking his head at the soap opera, saying something about the nurse being the doctor's long-lost daughter and the one he's kissing is married to some surgeon who went off his nut and is in the mental ward upstairs. And I look up at the ceiling but I already know it's just comfy new mattresses they don't let you sleep on and the Personnel Department up there. Then I realize he means upstairs in the soap opera hospital. Big duh. So I turn around, toward the department store escalators, taking the one going down.

My dad's office is in one of these skyscrapers, way at the top where the windows sparkle like constellations above the whole cityscape. Empty, I'm hoping, with everyone gone for the weekend. The address it's at, well, I can't remember the street name to even ask for directions. In my mind, though, I know what it looks like, the missing puzzle piece I could probably match if I turn the right corner. The heavy brass revolving door you use to go up there, the whoosh of it sweeping debris out of the lobby back to the street. The ancient guy guarding the visitor's desk in his uniform and hat, signing you in with your name on a badge. "Master Thomas Ross" typed for my brother, "Master James Ross" typed for me. The turnstile arms ratchet you through to the elevator lobby, OFFICES OF BROWER, SIMON, & ROSS, A LAW PARTNERSHIP. You press twenty-four I think or forty-two, your stomach drops out on the ride to the penthouse suite.

I wish I knew which street you take or corner you turn to find it. W. Adams, Van Buren, Wacker Drive, or Randolph, you could be wandering around forever. With no map or memory nothing's familiar, like I've never even been downtown before. So I wonder how the explorers knew where to go, Lewis and Clark and Ponce de León. To discover the fountain of youth or the Mississippi River. I just want some place to sleep.

A safe place where no one can hurt you, that's where my dad wants me to stay. My room is safe, thinking about that and the last time I slept there. Almost a year ago, if you can believe that, and how everything was the last day. Red plaid bedspread and stereo speakers, my albums and electric guitar. Well, the empty case for it anyway, my dad took my SG away. And now Laura's snuck out, so she's probably grounded, no phone, no friends, no TV. Laura's in almost as much trouble as me.

«not remotely possible»

Poor Laura, though, if that means she gets placed too. I doubt he'd do it to her, but what if? I'd tell her don't come home at all. We could just go someplace else with gross Roger, I wouldn't care if she's with him. An outlaw partnership. Laura, Gross Roger, and me.

It's the light-bulb-over-my-head thing, thinking how cool that would be, to get our own place, Laura would dig that. I have to squint it's so brilliant, the bright glow of genius, I think. Rounding the corner into its radiant glare.

BUS-BUS-BUS. Flashing the bustling city dusk like a welcoming blue neon flare.

4

The bus station's busy with people coming out and going in, every light blaring like an open invitation. So I follow behind them going inside, searching with radar eyes for a telephone and a safe place to sit.

Yellow arrows point the way to the terminals underground, down the escalator, down into sudden warmth and mugginess like into someone's gym locker or old shoe. The lights flicker kind of greenish and dull so your skin looks diseased and it smells rancid down here like a cafeteria table or the rag they give you to clean it.

Feeling Granma's money tucked deep in the front pocket of my cords. Walking slower, past ticket booths with posted fares and destinations. PEORIA, ST. CHARLES, KANKAKEE, RAILTON. Wherever, Illinois.

Scruffy bums in newspaper blankets sleep in chairs that have TV sets locked to them and a coin box. There's chips and candy in the vending machines but my stomach's so keyed now I don't think I could eat.

The people settling in here, you wonder where they come from, greasy and unwashed and not speaking English, which is probably illegal in River Hills. Old croakers all alone guard garbage bags filled with ratty belongings. Why do they even bother? Pushers and pimps huddle in corners all dressed like a part for a TV show. *Dragnet*, I think or *Hawaii Five-0*.

My gut starts to warble, feeling suddenly ill. The harsh smell of piss lurks in corners and doorways, or maybe it's the cleanser they use. I can't even breathe just passing by MENS, so forget that, I can wait till I'm home.

«home?»

Chills shimmy my back. God, why'd I say that? But it's true, it's the only place I want to go, not listed on any of their destinations or the fare to get there. The price I'd have to pay.

«the oaks mental manor. for as long as they want to hide you away. forever, maybe»

No, 'cause Laura will know a good place to stay. A hippie commune in San Francisco or Berkeley. Then Laura and me could hang out with Tommy when he doesn't have classes or on weekends, and go with him to rock concerts and frat parties or sit-ins to protest the war. So it's Laura's number I want to call, my big sister Laura, with her private line and Princess phone, her room full of albums and posters and incense.

I try to ignore what he's saying, this shadowy man using the payphone. I'm next in line but he brushes past, gold teeth flashing beneath a purple hat. He tips its feathered brim at me, mumbling in a language I don't understand. He hands the receiver to me.

Huddling small as I can shrink myself, squeezing in, my nose practically touching the holy metal partition all scratched and scribbled with nasty words and telephone numbers. Dialing my sister, thinking don't mess up don't mess up, fumbling to steady my finger in the "P-R-S" hole. Circle it around to the metal hook then let it go *click click click*ing back to "0." And again, six more times, dialing each number. Strangers lined up behind me lean in with ears perked to hear every word. So I know my skin is flushed and I'm whispering when the phone's finally answered, when my big sister finally picks up. "Laura? It's me—"

But it's my dad's stern voice that blasts my ear. *My dad*. "Roger! What did I just tell you?"

Choking down my own spit to answer. "Wait, I—I didn't—"

"She's seventeen years old and you're twenty-six, twenty-seven? You call here again, so help me God, I'll see you prosecuted for statutory rape. Am I understood?"

He's thinking I'm Roger on Laura's line, he's threatening Roger to protect her, but only for her, not for me, not *ever* protection for me. "I thought you said you couldn't do that. You said—"

"Jamey?"

"—you said even if I say the truth—"

"My God, where are you? Near Grandma's? Stay there, I'll come get you."

"You said to just forget it happened. You said it would just make everything worse."

"No, I said I wouldn't risk putting you through that. Not just you—Mom, all of us—Grandma, Grandpa, the ad agency, the advertisers, the clients. Believe me, that's not something we want to make public."

"But how come if it's Laura you—"

"This has nothing to do with Laura. It's different for girls. It's not as repugnant."

Repugnant. So that twists my brain. "You think I'm repugnant?"

"I think you should be asleep in your private room at The Oaks Manor. Not setting off the fire alarm, for God's sake, and running off in the middle of the night."

"You signed the paper, how come, you didn't even ask me, why'd you do that?" Although thinking back, I don't remember any fire alarm at all.

"Listen to me—"

"I don't wanna be locked up my whole life for therapy or shock treatments, why do I have to?"

"Calm down, son."

Son. A word feeling better than Percodan calming my heart. Calming down.

"It's not 'your whole life,'" my dad says. "Where are you calling from?"

Looking around to describe where I am to my dad. On the phone and talking to him, I'm his son. "At the, um, the bus station, the Greyhound one, downtown. By the, the TV chairs and all the telephones and MENS, the men's john, and the guy with a big purple hat—"

"Jamey! Listen to me! It's important you don't speak to—to *any*one there, do you understand? Grandma said she gave you ten dollars?"

"Grampa came home and he yelled."

"I know, I know. Forget about Grandpa. Everything's going to be all right. But you have to stay calm. Do you think you can do that for me?"

I nod, I know he can't hear that.

"Jamey! Are you listening? Here's what I need you to do, all right? Buy yourself a snack from the vending machines—Fritos, a candy bar—see if they have chocolate milk—and just sit and watch TV. I'm leaving the house now, I'll be there in an hour. So I need you to be waiting outside at eight thirty. Do you understand? Wait by the Randolph Street entrance. But don't talk to anyone, Jamey. Don't even smile. Not until we get you home."

Home. I don't hear what he says after that, just purse this smile and hang up the phone.

I shove folded pages of old newspapers away and sit down in one of these plastic chairs. They've got rows and rows of plastic chairs, orange and yellow, all scuffed and dirty from random strangers sitting here every day. Ha, each one leaves a little dirt behind.

«your dad said he's taking you home» angel says. So I almost crack a smile.

I put a quarter in, the mini TV flutters and wakes. Not adjusted right but I've got no idea how to stop the static or the kill count on the screen, the Vietnam map with arrows and bomb bursts and stacked body bags, I can't watch that. Turning the dial to a better channel, 2, 5, 7. But it's just more gory stories I don't want to hear in some news guy's monotone voice. "...*the unidentified remains of an adolescent male found today in an Uptown dumpster...*" Not worth a quarter at all.

At least it doesn't smell so awful outside, the stagnant night air with hardly any traffic to stink it all up. Watching the street for my dad's baby blue Mercedes, anxious when it doesn't come. Other cars do. Pulling up to the BUS-BUS-BUS station entrance, picking guys up, late arrivals I guess, and whisking them away to their destinations. Their dads, friends, families maybe, taking them home.

I have to sit down, my legs feel all hollow and wobbly. Lowering my back on the grimy brick wall settling onto the gritty sidewalk. A handful of stragglers passes by, sailors and hippies or college guys, preening and posing and puffing smokes. They hang out at the curb or the bus station entrance, then disappear in the city shadows under the elevated train tracks. Some of them get in the cars.

This one kid tips his Cubs cap like a gentleman at me and asks to bum a smoke, but I don't have any and he jerks his hair from his eyes and nods. Like we've got that in common, blond hair and no smokes.

He's looking up, his jaw gaping open at the skyscrapers soaring above, scratching his head like a tourist or someone who's lost. "Bet that's the tallest building in the world," he says. It's not, but I just shrug, not talking to him.

"Bet they got lots of jobs, right? First thing Monday, man? I'm gonna get me one. Working in that building, at the wa-a-ay top." He's probably my age or maybe sixteen so I'm about to ask, you know, like what job that would be. But he's looking down his nose at me, at my Levi's jacket, my flannel chest pocket, and the orange plastic bottle it holds. Granma's prescription bottle. "What's that?"

"What?"

"*That*," he goes, and with a swoop of his hand, it's not in my pocket anymore.

Standing is like lifting concrete, I'm slow to get to my feet. And he's already snapped the white cap off, the bottle tipped to his palm, his palm popped to his mouth. He shows me the yellow pills on his tongue and gulps, then shows me his tongue with no pills. I lunge to snatch the bottle back, but a horn honk-honks!, my heart skips with relief—*my dad's here!*—the Cubs cap kid steps out of reach. Except it's not my dad's car so any smile I had for my dad disappears.

A red pickup truck's parked at the curb, engine humming and headlights bleaching us white. The driver unfolds from behind the wheel, expanding from the front seat like a sponge. So you wonder how he fit or will get back inside. His silhouette looms in the bright headlights, flashing light-dark-light-dark when he breaks through the beams, approaching. Around the front bumper, up the curb to the sidewalk, in a plaid Pendleton jacket like Gary's or a lumberjack wears, one of those red and black kind. He hikes up his blue jeans, his belly hangs over his belt.

"Either of you be interested in earning a few extra bucks?" His voice low and hollow from a big barrel chest, his eyes hidden behind dark glasses, his loose jowls pasty in the harsh light.

The Cubs cap kid turns with a quick glance at me like we're partners in crime or something. I'm about to shout, *Give me my meds back right now!* but angel stops me.

"Me! I would!" the Cubs cap kid says, raising his hand, and the lumberjack nods and opens the door so he scrambles up into the pickup truck cab.

"What about you, kid?" This lumberjack guy's all smirking like Gary looking at me with another bad idea.

I shake my head, stepping back. Well, he's a whole lot bigger than me and it's nighttime and he's got sunglasses on. Wiping the sidewalk grit off my cords, I try to ignore him. Keep checking the street for my dad.

The lumberjack guy checks his watch. "Gotta be on-site at sunrise, my crew's a little short. Easy work, five bucks an hour. How about it? Even throw in breakfast." His size XXL hand finds my shoulder, I twist out from the weight of it, stepping back again. He kind of grins, though, at me for this one quick second, even worse than his touch. I step further away, still feeling the heat of it creep through my clothes. Stumbling back, ouch, into—

"Hey! Stand back!" An accusation, a voice of authority, I'm shaking my head, I didn't do anything, but he nabs me, this Chicago cop does, a really short cop, not too much taller than me, in his blue uniform, leather jacket and cap, shiny badge gleaming. I snap away, surprised to free myself so easily, rubbing my shoulder where they both touched me.

"Is there a problem here," he says, not really asking.

Don't talk to anyone, but this one's a cop, I think you have to talk to them. "I—I'm just waiting for my dad, that's all." «sir» angel reminds me, *Rule #8: Be respectful*. But "Sir" squeaks out so shaky and unsure, I wish more than ever my dad was here now, or anyone else. All the stragglers have scattered and gone.

The cop swings a thumb toward the lumberjack guy. "Right. And this is Daddy?"

"No, sir," me and the lumberjack guy say together. The lumberjack guy nods over his shoulder at the red truck. At a decal on the window, **West Suburban Law Officers Association Member 1969**, and the Cubs cap kid waiting inside. "That one's with me," he says, and flips open a wallet, showing the cop his ID.

The officer nods and looks at the decal or maybe the Cubs cap kid. "Appreciate the support," he says, then looks directly at me with impatiently beckoning fingers. "Drivers license or ID."

But The Oaks wristband's gone now, snipped off, thrown away, their plastic hospital ID. So I could be anybody, I can't prove I'm James. I shake my head, not speaking.

"Right. Ya got no identification. Is that your story?" The cop has handcuffs out like a punch you don't see coming. A lump of dread fills my throat I don't think I can swallow.

"He solicit ya, sir?" the cop says. "Offer services in exchange for payment?"

Like a duet we both answer "Yes, sir," accusing each other, the lumberjack man and me. Except they exchange knowing looks man-to-man like a handshake or game I don't know how to play.

"Punks," the lumberjack goes, shaking his head, chuckling. "How dumb and stupid do they think we are?" He leans casually against his red truck, aiming a wink at me, like it's all just a joke, *little man little dick*, or something like that with a rude gesture the cop doesn't see.

The cop shoves my shoulder, knocking me back, handcuffs gripped in his fist. "How old are ya anyway? Huh, blondie? Christ all mighty! What t'hell's wrong with ya—you're a good-lookin' kid, you got screws loose or something?" The squeal of the El train rounding the tracks overhead obscures his words and whatever he's saying, "no self-respect" and "it ain't safe for ya out here" with the agony scream of metal on metal braking to stop at the platform above. My hands block my ears but his voice muffles through like a warden or principal you have to listen to, "ehhh, for your own good, kid. Let juvie deal with ya."

I shudder the scream out of my head and try to make sense of what he just said, sorting his words like a diagrammed sentence. *Subject / Verb / Direct Object.*

"Let's go," he snaps. *He / pushes me toward / a squad car* parked behind the red truck and barks at the lumberjack. "Sir! Move the vehicle along or I will ticket and tow ya!"

The lumberjack uprights himself off the truck sort of defiantly, his eyes on me the whole time. Clearing his throat, his voice rumbles under his breath. "Yessir, Officer A-hole."

But the cop turns on me, his grip like a wrench twists my hand up behind me, pinning my elbows and crunching my wrist bones together. Before I can think, cold steel bracelets bite my skin, locking my arms bent wrong and painful against my back.

I'm wincing. "Wait, I didn't do any—ow..." moving my arms kills so bad I stay still. "It hurts, take it *off*." But he doesn't, even when I stumble and practically fall. "Please take it off...my dad's coming, I swear, he's a lawyer, he said to wait here."

"A lawyer," the lumberjack says, as if that's impressive.

The cop scoffs. "Good. Let 'im pay off the judge."

Twisting from him to see if my dad's here, pulling up in the nick of time, so this cop will be sorry he picked on me, reprimanded, demoted, no medal on his chest or bonus at Christmas. That's what you get, messing with the lawyer in the baby blue Mercedes. No phone, no friends, no TV.

"It's too tight," I complain. But the uniform cop shoves his hand into my back, plowing me toward the squad car. Away from the lumberjack folding himself back into the red truck. Away from the Cubs cap kid getting breakfast, a job, and five bucks an hour. Away from the red truck leaving the curb to blend with the flow of traffic. Away from the Randolph Street terminal entrance and towering sign flashing, BUS-BUS-BUS.

His hand on my head dunks me into the squad car back seat. Slamming the door and locking me in so I'm no longer outside, waiting. My forehead bumps into the caging before me, my elbows behind me scream out, falling against the hard vinyl seat. One huffing breath, then two or three, settling into the pain. Hurry up Dad, replays in my head, hurry up hurry up hurry up. The cop talks in ten-code on a two-way radio, but only static replies. Ha. *Officer A-hole.* Numbers glow on his dashboard display. *20:22* clicks to *20:23*. Looking back, but there's nothing outside the window to see.

Above, the dark skyline. Behind, the empty street.

5

My dad never came, my dad isn't coming, it's just words Granma said because she had to say something, *he only wants what's best for you,* words that aren't true because he hates me.

It's so cold sitting here my nose goes numb and my teeth keep chattering. I can't stand up or lie down, I'm handcuffed to the bench, the chain stops me. With no clock and bright lights on, my eyes tear and burn, I'm hours past tired with weak floaty arms and knees crossed so tight, holding myself to not pee. Huddled in the corner of this lockup cage like The Most Repugnant Son In The World.

«go to sleep» angel says. So I do.

Just like a lawyer, his pen's busy scribbling words the judge says on a lined yellow pad, taking detailed notes about loopholes and statutes and planning out strategy arguments. It's what lawyers do, think two moves ahead like a chess game with *checkmate!* already mapped out in their heads, and he's been appointed my lawyer. Law *guardian,* not lawyer. Law *student,* like Tommy, I think. Sitting with me across from the judge at this regular table in this regular office, not like a courtroom at all.

The judge peers up behind tiny square glasses hung from the tip of his nose. "Don't slouch before me," he says. In my head that's the argument between angel and me. Why should I show any respect?

«maybe he'll let you go home»

I sit myself up in this hard wooden chair. Feet flat. Shoulders back. Chin high.

Their words volley regardless. "The statute allows a peace officer to take into custody any child whose surroundings are such as to endanger his health, morals, or welfare," the judge states. "Clearly, the respondent meets that criteria."

"With all due respect, Your Honor, you've got to be realistic. It's 1970." The law guardian grins, like *Check!* "Most of these hippie types live in the street. I don't see where any criminal behavior was established." *Checkmate!*

"He's fifteen fucking years old, counselor. I'm not going to release him to the streets. In view of what I've got before me, he's going to be remanded with the privilege of parole to a responsible adult."

«ah, remanded» angel says, but I don't even know what that means.

"Your Honor, he was detained on the pretense of a solicitation complaint. I would ask for dismissal on that."

The judge turns to me. "Let me ask you: Is it your usual behavior to be out after dark in a known pick-up area where undesirables ply their trade? And by undesirables, I am referring to boys—young men—who engage in lewd acts in exchange for payment."

Lewd acts? Why would he even ask me that?

I shake my head, but my mouth's dry and gluey so half the words stick to my tongue. "My dad said wait there. To take me. Home." My teeth chatter, slouching again, I look down my chin, holding it high doesn't matter.

"Home is River Hills, up in Lake County, is it? When I call Lake County Juvenile Court, am I going to find a probation violation? Or anything else you'd like this Court to know?"

My mind blanks, a thousand pinpricks crawl over my skin, I can't think or reason out anything, it's just *quick jamey ross went over the wall* and how everything bad is my fault.

The law guardian is writing and doesn't object, the judge scribbles something down, too.

"All right. Can we refer this to DCFS." He thumbs through paperwork, shaking his head, then peeks through his specs at me. "Unfortunately for you, court will be in recess for the Labor Day holiday. So you're going to be held over until...Wednesday, it looks like. Yes. Wednesday. Let's see what Lake County sends over. I truly hope Dad takes you home."

The judge rolls around the table, it's not what you expect to see, either. A judge in a wheelchair. Waving his hand, the judge wheels out of the office. The law guardian stands, opens his briefcase and drops in his yellow legal pad. So just for a second I see all the notes he's been writing.

MILK & PEAS. That's all it says. Curly-Q doodles fill up the rest of the page.

In this dream Mandi's with me, soft skin and fresh linens, her chest pressed to mine so our hearts beat together and it's my name ID'd on her bracelet. *Doest thou wish to kiss me?* she asks like Juliet in the Shakespeare play. Her mouth moves to mine with a flickering smile, *her lips two blushing pilgrims ready stand*...the ache to be touched bristles the dark with excitement.

Don't stop, Mandi, don't stop

Kissing her, but it's not her cheek, it's Cleveland's face, zitty and oily and orange, Lowell Cleveland, holding me down in the rhythm of his rustling bunk, crushing me so I can't scream. I can't get away from the nightmare of him. I can't. Even if I'm sleeping some place safe, even if he's still locked up, far away at Railton. Panic breaks me every time, coating my throat with the flavor of him and canned peaches, salty and sickly sweet. Cleveland's hot whisper in my ear, *Relax, little Angel*. It's the magic of angel who makes Cleveland's face become Mandi. Her smile, her touch, the way she once kissed me. Soaring me over the top.

«it's okay to feel good» angel assures me, as if that makes a *lewd* act okay. Shuddering repugnant out of my head, as if you could ever erase it.

Moaning, my right hand's gone numb cramped beneath me on this uncomfortable bench. My whole self numb actually, waking up now to a dull, ugly ache.

It's freezing here, they took my jacket and flannel, my nose sniffs with cold and I'm shaking. Huddled in my same slept-in clothes, my head pounding, not feeling rested at all. Even with an extra blanket. Gray cinderblock walls, gray all around, the same gray unchanged so I'm not even sure if it's morning.

"It's juvenile custody, kid. It's not supposed to be the comforts of home," that's what the guard said when I said I can't sleep, the lights are too bright and the ceiling stains here give me nightmares.

I asked him politely to please let me go, he said no. Wednesday's the day they said I'd be held till, but Wednesday's already been here and gone, and no one, not even my dad when I called him can say how much longer I have to remain. Another few minutes or...or months.

My nerves don't stop trembling, just thinking of how long.

Till Monday. That's what the guard informs me now. Last Monday was a holiday, he says, which messed the whole docket up. Which triggers the switch of *I deserve this* and strips away anything hopeful.

"I haven't had drugs since I got here," I say. "I'm supposed to take drugs every day." Sliding my back down the wall to squat on the floor, but even rocking myself doesn't help anymore. I need something, anything to take me away from this place. Drugs medication music or a sharp. Or an angel who really exists.

He brings me a Snickers and another thin blanket.

Later a tray of supper slips in, like feeding a dog, that's how I know it's dusk outside or maybe four thirty. A carton of milk, lukewarm and waxy, I don't even open this time. A sandwich on white bread with crusts that are already stale. I think it's the same tray from yesterday, the same square of plastic American cheese, the same circle of greasy pink meat in between, all seasoned with saltpeter, Cleveland once told me, so you won't get horny or full. Which is pretty much halfway untrue.

What am I going to tell my dad? So I don't have to go back to Railton or The Oaks. 'Cause I swear if I had a kid, I'd rather ground him all day up in his room than waste him away in some institution. Then I'd clean up for my mom, do the yard for my dad, like a work crew at Railton, I could do that. Pull weeds on my knees and scrub toilets with my toothbrush. They wouldn't have to pay me, either. Or my allowance. Or anything.

Excuses like chess moves play out in my head, but I already know how useless they are. Just one look from my dad and I lose.

"Party's over, Ross. Time to go." The guard unlocks the door and hands me a bag with my warm flannel, Levi's jacket, and laces. He waits till my Flyers are tied and I smooth out these stained grubby cords, standing up shaky to face him. Watching him chain me, my throat goes dry, my wrists locked to my waist and restrained. It's the rules, he says. I don't complain, moving before him out of that cell, I'm glad just to see different walls. No rush of freedom stirs the stagnant air, though. It's hardly like freedom at all.

He walks me beside him, his hand cups my elbow, down the echoing hall. Catcalls shout out from the lockup cages, a whole zoo of perverts and lewd undesirables. *Cutie-pie. Baby-cakes. Sweetheart-come-here-I-got-a-big-boner-for-you.*

He stays at my side like my own private bodyguard, following the yellow stripe on the floor. Escorting me through a backstage maze to play the Auditorium Theatre. Past roadies and groupies that call out my name, that's what I'm pretending, I'm Jimmy Page, Hendrix, Morrison, Iggy Pop. It's a sold-out show, SRO, I hear the roar of the crowd. Till we turn down this hallway lined both sides the whole way with the same office door, office door, office door where the guard suddenly stops, his hand on this one office doorknob. With a wire-reinforced window all baffled and unclear as my head.

His key clicks the lock so the chains fall away, and he nods. "Your folks made the effort. You show some respect. Everybody goes home happy."

My folks? Twisting away, to see him grin at the shock shooting through at "your folks" just like that with no warning. On the other side of the door.

6

The office is already thick with emotion when I step inside, so it's not easy to think or breathe, hardly. Feeling so spot-lit, their eyes focused on me—slept-in clothes, uncombed hair, reeking of lockup and grayness—so I want to turn away and fix it quick, fix everything. But this black lady stands up, in a brown dress and pumps, her hands on the back of this one empty chair where she wants me to sit. But I don't.

My dad stands, too, less than three steps away, in a classic three-piece charcoal suit and polka-dot necktie, and my mom, all Coco Chanel, in pearls, plaid jacket, and matched pencil skirt, her hair polished into an upsweep. Not polka-dots, though, when I blink my eyes dry and focus. Little white Snoopys pattern his tie. Like the Father's Day gift I gave him one Sunday when I was his son in sixth grade. Why would he choose that tie to put on? So my mind goes completely blank.

The law guardian's sitting across from my mom, the chairs arranged in a circle. Wearing a suit and clip-on tie, smelling of English Leather. I'm not even sure if he's the same guy. God, I don't want to be here.

My dad holds his arms out open to me, just standing there, waiting. Like here's where I hug him and drop to my knees all thankful with endless apologies. Except I'm not grateful or sorry to him about anything at all. Anger burns raw just seeing him here, and my mom, well, not her, she's beautiful, but the moment to hug her is gone. So

I'm hugging myself instead. *Where were you!* I almost spout, but my mouth's like sandpaper and nothing comes out.

"Shhhh," she says softly, so I don't have to talk. "I'm here now, James. Daddy, too."

Like I don't see him or something. His sharp suit, gold cufflinks, trimmed sideburns, Italian shoes. Dorky tie. He looks at the case-worker, MS. LETICIA POOLE on her name tag from the State of Illinois Department of Children and Family Services. Judging her scuffed pumps, her Afro, her plain shirtwaist dress, then turning to me, his eyes piercing blue and expressionless.

"You said eight thirty," spits from my mouth into his face. "Well, you're a little *late*." Not aiming for my mom, but still she's hit too so I feel like dying and wish she stayed home.

"Take a deep breath. And sit down," he says, completely unfazed. "I understand you're upset. Believe me, I'm angry too. I should've been notified you were detained, the moment you were brought in." His eyes sort of flicker with injustice or maybe remorse. "Mom and I had no other option but to wait until we were called into court this morning." He leafs through a court file before passing it on to the law guardian, who slips it away in his briefcase. With a handshake that lingers as they exchange words, my dad thanks him.

"But they gave you a safe place to sleep," my mom says. "Daddy made sure..." She stops talking when I look away.

The law guardian passes the guard at the door, who opens it, letting him leave, you can see who my dad would prefer for a son when my dad turns stone-faced back to me. So I sit down, feeling stupid, that's what it's like all over again, hating myself, my left foot so shaky even rocking won't calm it.

My dad's chair scrapes closer, he's talking to me, words that circle my ears like mosquitos. How he was there at eight thirty, how he searched the bus station for over an hour, how he drove through the

Loop until well after midnight, how he's sat by the phone around the clock since last Sunday, how he hasn't had any sleep.

«well try sleeping in lockup and not get a bath for a week!» angel snaps or maybe it's me being bratty who says it. Maybe I'm glad he didn't sleep 'cause of me.

"Last week on the news a boy was found murdered. We didn't know where you were and honest to God, Jamey, we feared the worst. Thank God the police finally called and confirmed they had you in custody. Thank God, the murdered boy wasn't you." An *onslaught* I have to swat out of my face or cover my ears with both hands. He's got NOTHING I want to hear. Except the words he hasn't said yet, *I'm sorry come home.*

Ms. Poole bends to my eye level like she's peeking in. "Can I get you a drink of water, James Daniel?"

"Can I just go home," I say.

Flipping through a folder, she looks up for a moment, one hand on her hip, one ankle lifts so the heel of her pump clumps on the floor. "Due to the nature of the complaint, and the fact that the Lake County Juvenile Court terms have been violated, probation has been revoked at this time. He's going to be remanded into custody."

My mom is crying. "Jeffrey? Don't let them take him." White gloves muffle her mouth, blue eyes flutter like a sandstorm, she catches her balance on tiny doll feet. So I just want to hug her and say I'll be better, but my dad hugs her first with both arms around her, one hand gently rubbing her back.

"He's broken probation, Elle. And he's got this, this homo—" So my head jerks up at that word, shaking no, no, no, and how wrong he is, but he's pleading with her like I don't hear him or matter at all. "— sexual solicitation charge, trying to sell himself—"

What? "No, un-unh, Mom! That's not true, I didn't try to sell anything. I was waiting for Dad but he didn't show up, how is that my fault?"

"You were doing so well at The Oaks," my mom says. "What happened? Dr. Pauly said—"

"They *zapped* me, Mom, shock treatment, you know what that's like?" Man, how stupid! Of course she knows. She's probably the reason they did it to me. She lowers her head, twisting a soggy lace hanky in her lap.

"I don't wanna be a zombie," I say. "No sane person would, no sane person would *ever* hang around and let them do it again." Despite being the worst son in the world, I'm not like my mom, clinically depressed, I just have a few things to work out. Which is such a relief to realize, I barely hear what he yells next.

"You don't *get* to run away! You don't *get* to decide where you'll serve out your time! Do you realize how you've jeopardized your future and possibly any litigation against the state? How do I defend my own son's continuously delinquent behavior and yet argue for his release? How many times can I apologize to the court on your behalf?"

The guard takes a step then two toward my dad, one hand on his gunbelt and the cuffs it contains, so I wonder what that picture would look like framed. Jeffrey D. Ross in chains.

Ms. Poole clears her throat. "If you would, Mr. Ross? Let's sit down. Can we agree on that?"

"Excuse me, *Mizz* Poole," my dad overrules her. "The Oaks Manor has the best adolescent psychiatric program on the north shore. My brother's on the board—Dr. Sheldon Rosenberg—he's head of Pediatrics over at Mt. Sinai downtown. One phone call and we'll have my son off your caseload and continuing the court-approved treatment he so obviously needs."

So I'm shaking my head, no. no. no you said *home*

Her glance slices sideways, cutting him off, turning her question to me. "James Daniel? Do you feel you're no longer suicidal?"

I fold my arms to my chest, both wrists tucked away. "It's just how angel got me out of Railt—"

"No 'angel!'" My dad interrupts, jumping to his feet. "Ms. Poole, this is ridiculous. My son's delusional and needs professional treatment. Before 'angel' and Railton become his excuses for further destructive behavior—"

"It's a mental hospital," I tell her.

"It's a residential facility. For emotionally disturbed adolescents," he says. "They were helping you."

"I don't want any help."

"It's the choice an intelligent person would make."

"Yeah, and it's not my choice."

His voice raises again, not out of control but almost. "Is *this* your choice?" Gesturing, his arms circle this room, this whole county building, Cook County jail, juvenile lockup, and where they keep perverts downstairs. I fold my arms and slam back in this chair because it's so obviously not. "Because that's exactly where you're headed if it is."

Sharp words spit from me like poison darts. "Is this my trial? 'Cause I want a better lawyer if it is."

Hard, fast, flat, and smack! his palm cracks across my face. Ducking from him and the unjust handprint screaming on my cheek, I didn't do anything, I didn't do any thing, not even aware anymore of them hustling him out, the assassin, before any more damage is done. My mom, too, I see her red heels turn, hear the swish of her silk stockings rush for the door.

Rocking, I can't stop it, screaming in my head like a plea like a prayer, I JUST WANT MY LIFE BACK. THAT'S ALL. JUST GIVE ME MY FUCKING LIFE BACK.

part two
rand

7

A million thoughts like shattered glass flash crazy in my mind, like little windows to brilliant answers, all moving too fast to grasp or understand. So I want to say wait! and have everything stop, rewind the tape and be back in that room. Only, let my dad hug me this time and agree with whatever he wants, *I won't solicit homos or anyone, ever,* get down on my knees and beg. But the guard and Ms. Poole are escorting me through the passageway maze of this government building, all dingy and dim with despair and not air when you breathe.

Wading between them upstream through chaos, no one seems happy to be here. Uniformed men in suits with holsters or briefcases ready, the abused and accused and everyday people who just look out of place and confused. Trying to not see the faces that pass me but still searching, I realize, for someone familiar, lawyers or law partners, the lobby doorman to say, *Master James Ross? You don't belong here! Come, let's get you home.* But mostly my dad, that's who I want to turn back and see chasing after Ms. Poole and me.

The guard corrals me into a room with a whole group of youthful offenders. They clutch folders with labels like TRUANT, DELINQUENT, or WARD OF THE COURT. Like mine, in my hand is the file she gave me, you have to carry your own. ROSS, JAMES DANIEL. MINS.

The few benches in here are already taken so there's nowhere but the floor to sit down. And then when I do, I have to scoot over to let a deputy through, handing out hot dogs from a wheeled silver cart.

"Just in time for lunch," Ms. Poole chimes like a tour guide, like how lucky I am to eat it. A gray rubber wiener steamed in wax paper on a soggy white bun. I'm so hungry I actually take one.

All these criminal guys, I don't want to know them, what crimes they committed or why. But this one kid's quick hand in less than an eye blink snatches the lunch from another kid's palm. The kid plump and clueless moves in slow motion lifting his palm to his open mouth then sees his hot dog is gone. He turns in a search for someone to accuse, weepy eyes, pouty lips, plump pillow butt like a target now. *That's what you get, baby-cakes*, I would tell him, for holding it out like an offering almost. Practically giving it away.

Looking down at the scruffy floor, so glad this unruly hair hides my cheeks flaming red to even think those words, *pillow butt baby-cakes*. Planted in my head now, lewd pervert thoughts. So I'm frantic for some place to spit it out, this rubbery lump so soggy and awful on my tongue. In its wax paper in my palm, then scuttle on my knees to this huge trash barrel to dump it. Ms. Poole nods her approval, like I'm so well-bred not to spit up on the floor.

What's next, angel? But angel doesn't come, only panic, I messed up again even worse. Desperate for fresh air but there is none, it's just heavy with hot dogs and sweat. Trying to not throw up, but repugnant is hard to keep down.

"I can't live in jail," I tell Ms. Poole, I know she's listening. I don't know the words to make it much plainer.

She readjusts the court folders stacked in her arms. Her eyes lock on mine, her head cocked, like she's peering under the hood of a car, figuring out why it's stalled. "You know, sometimes emotions get the better of us and we say hurtful things we don't mean. You imply he's not a good lawyer, he suggests you're incompetent." Which triggers tears and I quickly turn away, toward the door. The door to the hall. The way out.

"None of which is true," she says.

Still, she won't let me go.

"I know you're disappointed. However, I do agree with your father, juvenile detention is not appropriate in your case. I'm hoping DCFS has a bed for you. I've spoken to the judge—"

It's when tears come, I don't know, for all this, I guess. The judge, MINS, a DCFS bed, gray hot dogs, the pillow butt boy, my mom and my dad who don't want to let me come home.

"I'm sorry," Ms. Poole says. She checks her watch. "The van usually picks kids up at four."

Nodding, I'm belting my arms around myself. She takes the folder from my hand, adds it to the top of her pile, juggling it open. Licks one finger to leaf through the pages, lots of pages. What a waste, is what I'm thinking, whoever had to type all those words in the spaces.

She takes out one paper and hands me the whole folder back. "Let's see if we can't get you back on your medications at least. Agreed?" Her hand on my shoulder, pat pat pat, then it's gone, she's out the door and lost to the chaos streaming by in the hall.

Agreed. Feeling so floaty like I'm leaving myself and I don't know if I can get back.

"Cool, man, medications. That's how I do time."

Looking up at him, the one talking to me in a voice from *The Beverly Hillbillies* or maybe the backwoods like Huckleberry Finn. The one who stole the baby-cake's hot dog. The thief.

I stand up, blinking quick, hide all emotions away. "I'm not doing time," I hear myself say like I'm listening to somebody else.

His lip turns up in a snarky smile, he's the same size as me. "Me neither. I jest come fer the free lunch."

Which for some dumb reason makes me laugh.

He laughs too, and takes my folder, jerking his head for me to follow, one dark greasy cowlick springs over his forehead. His face is a splatter of bad teenage acne, all picked at and painful to look at. He's got on this cool black satin baseball jacket, though, with a red letter A in a yellow halo embroidered across the back. *The California Angels*, it says.

I admit I'm not thinking when I make the decision to follow the thief to the door. Out of the MINS corral, not looking back, slipping behind him into the hall. Trying to keep pace with the solid clump-clump of his cowboy boot heels, muddy and worn, the yellow flash of the halo and red letter A on black. I try a few times to catch his attention and snatch my court folder back, but he keeps one step ahead out of reach, weaving between people as if we're unseen or supposed to be leaving now. Stealing away from the youthful offenders, from the van that gets here at usually four. Farther and farther away, moving quickly in disbelief. Hallway to stairwell to hallway, on the heels of a hillbilly thief.

Rounding a corner, daylight explodes, sun rays burst through from the windows above, flooding a massive lobby. Looking up, there's a rotunda at the way top ringed with a biblical mural, the scales of justice in a heavenly cloud. The hillbilly kid doesn't notice or slow down, weaseling his way through the crowd.

Double glass doors open and close, close and open before me, all busy with people coming and going and going and coming. Beyond them, there's daytime and downtown Chicago. Above, even better, real clouds and blue sky. I follow the Angels jacket right through the lobby, I follow his cowboy boots clump-clumping outside.

The Loop rises around me like a vacation postcard, GREETINGS FROM THE WINDY CITY. Sunlight glints off steel and glass making me squint just to see. It's warm with soft breezes that still smell like summer. I open my arms like hugging the sky, turning with eyes closed, feeling giddy. Thinking, ha, there's the joke, angel! or maybe the punch line and chuckling out loud how easy it was, to just leave.

The hillbilly waits on the courthouse steps, his face all screwed up like *What's funny?*

I just shrug. "Nobody stopped me."

"Nobody cares, most likely," he drawls.

Which is hard to shrug off. But still. I look back at the double doors to the lobby and the bustle of people maybe coming for me. "She—she went to get my medication. I should probably go back."

"Never go back, man. Always go forward," he says, one finger in the air like a philosopher or something. He checks the label on my folder, ROSS, JAMES DANIEL. MINS. *Minor In Need of Supervision.* He holds up the first page like a proclamation. "'It was *all* a turrible mistake,'" he reads. "'Case diss-missed.'"

"Wait, does it really say that?"

"Hell if I know. I don't read." He stuffs the whole folder in the trash can behind him, then slaps his hands clean with finality and a big dopey grin. "Let's see if we can't find yew some proper medications. Agreed?" he goes, just like a caseworker.

He doesn't believe me so I stop saying no and denying it ever was me on the cover of *Rolling Stone.* "Who are yew again?" He crosses not with the light so taxi horns wail in a crazy blur missing us by inches and a city bus. "Man, I know I seen yew around somewheres."

I don't say, well, on baby food labels, Sears catalog pages, or maybe in the cereal aisle, I just tell him I'm James, but he squints like

I'm kidding. We're crossing a park, he jumps benches like hurdles and laps a quick drink from a fountain. "James Mins," I go. "Like it said on my file."

He just chuckles and goes, "Right, right, most likely," like there's something else making him smile.

Neon reflects off the glass all around us, bottles and jars, the pharmacy cases, flashing in my eyes like rainbow lightning, YϽAMЯAHꟼ on the storefront window and the xЯ signs. You don't need a prescription for most of these ƧᎮUЯᗡ, you can be your own doctor, just read if your symptoms are on the label. Scratching my head at the millions of labels. For fever or heart pain or MINS. So panic tingles my brain, what if my folder's been found in the trash and they're coming to supervise me again? Mizz Poole in her brown pumps, hot on my trail.

Looking at this hillbilly, Rand. It's his name he says when I ask him. Durrand Jennette, the name of a hillbilly thief. Getting me meds I *most likely* need.

"Pharmaceuticals, man." Rand laughs. "Which one's yer cure?"

I mumble, I'm not sure, Tofranil-PM or Thorazine, maybe. Or Ritalin, I've taken that most of my life. I pick up another bottle, another dreary label gray with tiny words. Bufferin, or something benign like that. Then put it back. It just gives me a headache to read.

"Why don't yew go'n ask the drugman?" His wide zitty grin with rotting buckteeth nods at the pharmacy counter, where the pharmacist stands like a wizard almost, all kindly and wise, with wispy white hair and a skullcap.

The pharmacist nods hello.

I sort of smile back, ready for my refill and gathering the right words to ask. You know, the right information—last name first, date of birth, home address. And what do I confess to that?—when his face twists to look behind me.

I swivel to see—at my back like a shadow is Rand, hidden by me I realize and out of the pharmacist's sight. Still, I catch the quick flick of a Buck knife in Rand's fist slit open a plastic bag of balled cotton, stuff a fluffy white fistful in his black satin pocket, and why would you even want those?

"Can I help you find something, young fellow?" The pharmacist asks. Me. So at first I'm hearing *young felon* not "fellow" because that's what this is, a robbery. Rand's crouching low and behind this one counter, jacking a cabinet open, ransacking drawers where the locked drugs are stored, he's made me his partner in crime.

"No, well, I'm, I..." Fumbling for other words now, like a cover-up or guilty alibi and not what I intended at all. "I—I just needed something like I had before, like the brown ones, I think Tofranil? Or the yellow, maybe Percodan. Or just Ritalin or something, because I still..." It's when this hillbilly Rand pops up at my side, one brotherly arm drapes my shoulder.

"He wants the magic ones." Rand winks at me. "Ain't that right?"

The pharmacist all suspicious looks at me but I'm not sure I understand either and I'm asking the same question he is. "There's magic ones?"

Rand leans over the counter into the pharmacist's face. "Bar*bitu*ates, man! See, all's yew gotta do is give 'em to him," Rand sneers, raising his knife to the pharmacist's throat. "And, poof! Jest like *that*—" He snaps his fingers and a whole handful of penny Bazooka disappears from this bowl by the cash machine into his black satin pocket. He opens his empty palm like it's magic. "We're gone."

The pharmacist slams Rand's fist flat, *whomp!* just like that, pinning the knife to the counter, faster than Rand can react. "What are you, the Manson family?" Pulling a gun from thin air, he aims it point-blank at Rand's forehead then wags it at us like a finger. "You—" he goes, pointing the barrel at me, I step back, and there's sweat you can see, beads of sweat on his round pale forehead. "Coming in here like a decent young man, shame on you! Peace and love, I thought hippies stood for, to protest the Vietnam War. Not fer-caca dope fiends and lowlife thieves."

Rand swears and yanks his hand free, two fingers raise in a V for the peace sign then just one middle finger, so his fist turns and I don't believe it, he's flipping the pharmacist off.

The gun in the pharmacist's hand pokes forward and Rand jerks like a scaredy-cat back. "You've got two seconds to put what you've stolen down on this counter," the pharmacist says. "Two seconds." Behind the register his other hand lifts a receiver, one finger dialing the rotary phone.

"*Peace* on yew, old man," Rand says, stepping rapidly backward toward the door, but "peace" sounds like "piss" so I just want to ditch him or say he's sorry, but he's quicker than I am, snagging my sleeve, Rand drags me outside the store.

In his jacket, there's more. When I snap from his grip to go back and apologize, he opens his jacket to all these things, cotton balls, colored party balloons, packaged syringes. Bazooka bubble gum. He drops the wrapper without reading the comic and pops a pink piece in his mouth. And he's pulling pill bottles from his waistband and pockets, rattling them in the streetlight before me, four bottles, I can't see the labels. He spills pills like candies into his palm, all different color combinations.

"Abracadabra," he says. "Pharmaceuticals, man. Yer choice."

So I reach to pick a red one then a yellow. A half-blue-half-red or a white. I'm not sure what they cure.

Rand knows. "Reds are devils, whites're loads. Blues're goddam angels from heaven."

I take a blue one. He chuckles like a madman, head cocked and nodding. "Angel!" he proclaims. "That's who yew are, man! Nice to do business with yew, Angel." A siren wails blocks away or maybe around the next corner. Rand turns to split but before he takes off, he dumps four more blues in my hand. I don't wait for the siren to get any closer. I take off running *forward* to keep up with Rand.

It's just blackness, pure and thick and safe, but I'm leaving it now, awakening out of Rand's heavenly blue ones. Becoming aware of the world outside, activity humming around me. Movement, I guess, from the land of the living. Which is a surprise to realize, I just slept a whole night uninterrupted and I'm not waking up in a cell.

Open my eyes to the leather back seat of somebody's luxury car. *Cadillac*, Rand said. *Good vee-hicle to crash in* like he knows. Rand's in the front seat, I can hear him sit up, pill bottles rattle, the strike of a match, the smell of sulfur and cigarette smoke fills the car. The sound of his door latch when he gets out, the tinkle and splash of his piss on the parking lot wall. Sun spikes through the windshield stabbing my eyes like a good morning alarm. I pull my jacket over my head and drift back to sleep in the dark.

8

I'm sticking like glue to Durrand Jennette, weaving through crowds of denim and tie-dye, long hair and love beads, fringed suede and leather, all milling outside the Syndrome arena. Keep my eyes peeled for someone I might know, my sister maybe or Gary and Mandi Maroney. But it's crazy with people and I get too distracted, the night air electric with rock 'n' roll magic, this rush of excitement takes hold. Bass and drums and the crush of the crowd, my whole self swept up in amplified sound, plugged in to rhythm and wailing guitar, drawing me in like a magnet.

A *million* times better than a 9-volt transistor with one puny monotone earphone.

But I don't think Rand even cares what band's playing, that's not why he's brought me along. Doing business, hawking his drugs, he hustles the street and parking lot, exchanging pills or pot or whatever he's got in his black satin pockets for money. A lot of money, way more than the price of a ticket. Which is the only reason I'm here.

"Teeckets?" Rand laughs. "Hell, Angel. We don't need no steenkin' teeckets! Jest turn around..." he turns and waits till I turn too, "...and walk backways through the exit, man, and presto-chango, yer in." Which makes like zero sense to me but I do it anyway, walk backward with him to the exit gate, maybe five or six steps, where this fat hairy guy in an EVENT STAFF vest stops me with a hand on my sleeve.

"No hand stamp, no ins-n-outs, man," he grunts. Man. So we both hold out the backs of our hands, Rand and me. In Rand's there's two joints but they're instantly gone, and the doorguy stamp-stamps both our knuckles.

Rand chuckles, amused at the inky mark stamped on his skin. A purple smiley face. "Fuckin A," he declares leading the way when the doorguy signals us in.

"HELLO, CHICAGO! ARE YOU FEELIN' ALL RIGHT?"

It's like plunging right into the deep end, a huge roar goes up, sweeping us into a human sea under a kaleidoscope galaxy of colorful clouds above. Huge swimming shapes rainbow the ceiling, exotic smoke fills my lungs, thundering waves of music drown out conversation and all other sound. Heart-pounding drums and galloping bass pull me along to a song that's familiar, but even on tiptoes I can't see the band or the stage, we're in the way back of the hall. All I want is to get closer but Rand lights up and steers me away through the packed bobbing crowd. He shouts, "Weed, speed, whatever y'all need!" passing the joint to people who toke it and pass it around back to me.

Wanting to say you get 2+6 for doing this, two weeks in isolation plus six weeks added to your time. Wanting to feel ALL RIGHT! more than anything now. And it goes through my head: blue pills or brown ones, weed or meds, what difference really, I bet even a judge would agree. So I close my eyes, take a hit off his joint, and hold it inside till my head opens up so there you go angel, fly free.

Jim?

That long-ago name lazily wafts in the crazy smoke hazing my brain.

«jim» It's what Ratachek called me. Jim.

Like proof he's my friend.

Jim! when you step in his class to ask for a hall pass but the first thing you see is some kid on his knee and the snap of his hand moving off the kid's lap to casually brush back his hair. *Have you met Kyle Bodie, Jim?*

Shake the nightmare out, it falls from my right ear I think and goes scrambling like a ferret into the shadows. «good riddance to jim» Yeah, and all the bad things he let happen to him.

I'm dizzy standing up and it's awkward to walk but I think it's because I haven't been eating that great. Trying hard to remember how I got here. With Rand in his black satin jacket, the California Angels. Gone now, he's gone. Where'd he go?

Push my way through the crowd, brushing hands off and offers of pot pipes wine bottles even a tit I can't believe it just all suddenly pink and round and exposed in the smoke and din, or maybe not, when I turn and it's just blurred hair denim and strange laughing faces distorted and blending together. So I'm thinking I better sit down a minute and where to do that 'cause I'm wobbly and nauseous and there's the EXIT to step outside on one empty stoop in the alley where I guess I could sit or lie down. But I don't know. All of a sudden my forehead is hitting the asphalt.

The noise scares me, like my head's splitting open, all hollow sounding and mushy, like a pumpkin smashed. It's not, but when I open my eyes, I can't get up. I'm just collapsed, lying here, too twisted to move.

Brick walls surround me like a cell with no roof, just open to let in a cool evening sky. Stars twinkle and blink and the moon glows above, small enough to fit in my hand. With astronaut footprints and the American flag. Reaching for it I can't reach it. Lie against the alley brick. Close my eyes to the deluge or delusions of crowds rushing by. Slipping away, spinning down down down. Ha, like a toilet flushed. Or Alice in the rabbit hole. Waiting to hit bottom. Or someone to catch me.

Hands brace my back as if I could stand but instead I melt back in the asphalt. Strong hands with thick arms in black and red plaid. A lumberjack Pendleton jacket just like Gary had when we were best friends last year. "Hey, hey," I hear myself say. "Can we go to your house and order a pizza?" His mom still likes me, I think.

"Hungry?" His low voice rumbles, sounding so adult. "Sure you are. Teenage boys are always hungry," and something about a red truck. I tell him I can't get in trouble anymore or ever be locked up again. His face above me, maybe not. Dark glasses, double chin, small lipless mouth with no mustache. Pockmarks, not dimples. Not Gary's Wayfarers or side-swept dark bangs and cool grin. No smile at all. Familiar though, I've seen this face—but the features twist all distorted, changing like smoke in a breeze. Poof! Changing into the uniform of a Chicago cop with his ready baton, his badge shiny, black leather, and handcuffs. No no no. No cops. Please.

But officer—Shaking my head with no strength to speak out or even stand up on my own. Shaking it all away, these millions of people flashing past like a View-Master clicked through on high speed. Click-click-click-click-click or a metronome. Till it's just Rand with his buckteeth, bad acne, and black satin jacket. Calling me "Angel" and saying he's taking me home.

"Are you taking me home?" That's what I ask when he says he knows a warm place we can crash. He hustles me through blurred city streets and the mist of a light midnight rain. "'But, Occifer,'" Rand mimics me, practically choking on laughter.

A squad car wails past just when he says that, siren blasting and slicing right through my brain. Heads turn to follow, concert-goers college kids or criminals, who knows, when more blue-and-whites zip by. *We Serve And Protect* with a star on the door and roof lights flashing blue lightning on the storefronts and into the sky. Rounding the corner into an alley, Rand grabs my jacket, holding me back. Cop shadows flutter before us like moths looming large in their flashlights or the headlights of squad cars. Scrambled radio voices beep and volley the brick alley walls, surrounding a dumpster, like trash dumpsters you pass all the time in this city. Except this one stands solo in the wandering circles of light.

There's two cops in the dumpster, one standing tall and handing some shapeless dark thing to the others around him. Something wrapped in brown plastic. Somebody retches, you can hear watery puke splat the ground.

Rand pulls me away, in the opposite direction. Balls, he goes, I go what, he goes balls somebody's balls in a brown plastic bag so I'm gagging that down, following Rand, looking back at the flashing lights every few seconds till we're blocks away and there's no more police lights to see.

We're in another dark alley, I can't look at the dumpsters that line the brick walls, all of them suddenly scary to me, but Rand walks right by them and heads toward the street where a broken-down beater is parked. So at first I think it's to another car vacancy, a free back seat back street motel. But he passes it too, and checks in instead to a FIRE EXIT door, battered and rusty and wedged open an inch by a beer can crushed in its jamb. We slip through the crack into absolute blackness and an echoey loud conversation. Forbidden words I don't think I hear right muffle the air, then clearer when Rand parts these thick dusty drapes. He grabs hold of my sleeve, leading me into a dark musty theater. Triple-X skin flick, that's clear. Sexy soft sucking and four-letter sighs.

He's right. It is warm in here.

Rand pulls me along, stumbling up worn carpet steps to the empty back row. When I plop down beside him into a seat, the cushion's so worn I sink halfway in. Dull fleshy motion is blown up before us on a theater screen twenty feet high. Dicks lips hairy slits glistening pink bits so mostly I keep my eyes down. "How do you know it was balls?" I whisper.

Rand's face ignites eerie white in the flame of his lighter. Taking a hit, he muffles a cough and hands this small metal pipe to me. "The cop said, I heard him, man. It was some kid's gentles." He chuckles. "Bagganuts."

I take a hit off his pipe, its magic takes over, melting gentles and bad things away, melting me into myself really mellow. And it hits me: there's nowhere I'd rather be. Oh. *Bag o' nuts*, ha. Rand passes the pipe back to me. In his eyes I can see the projected film light, the gross scene reflected off the theater screen twice. Bound hands and legs spread wide. I can't watch that.

My eyes adjust slowly instead to the shapes in the blackness. Scalloped rows of seats mostly empty or topped with heads or hats sunk low, shady figures ducking in, slinking out. If I move in this seat there's this same squeaky noise like insects all around us.

"Five bucks a hand job," Rand whispers. "Jest go down and set next to one of 'em." When I shake my head, he chuckles. "Zero does it all the time, man. He's crazy."

I can't find any words to answer. Rand springs to his feet, his voice low. "Gotta meet my man," he says, and poof, he blends into the dark and he's gone.

I kick crap away under the seat, crumbled tissues and gross sticky things. Kind of creeped out that Rand's left me alone. Keep my hands to myself not touching the armrests. Not touching anything. Spacing out. Letting go. Slipping far from myself. Someplace warm. Someplace nice. Someplace safe.

Something jolts me awake, like an instinct or angel that danger is near. A shadowy figure whisks up the stairs, looming larger and larger coming up here then slinking down this last row of chairs and taking Rand's seat right beside me. He shakes out his head, flicking a black shock of hair from his eyes, sniffling back a cold or pneumonia, rubbing a finger on his nose and buck teeth. Flickers of color from the big movie screen shimmy over his black Angels jacket. He doesn't say anything, nodding out. It's just squeaking seats and the warbled moans of actors or perverts filling the warm movie house.

I don't really like it, being a tourist attraction. That's what Old Town is like with these cars trolling Wells Street, gawking at hippies or snapping their pictures like a stop on a sightseeing tour. They shout from their windows, "Hey, slob, getta job!" "Keep on truckin!" "Beautify America—get a haircut!" slogans or insults, who knows. Rand shoots them all the finger.

It's when the acid kicks in. Slowly at first. So I'm blinking my eyeballs, as if I doubt what they see. Piper's Alley, all narrow with head shops and windows in colors that glint and sparkle. Reaching for Rand, my hand leaves a trail in the air when I move it, from me to the ruby red "A," a fiery gem on his back. "Too late to jump off this train," he's saying, but his words slow way down like they're playing at thirty-three rpm.

HEAD LAND glitters above and Rand ducks inside, me too, my liquid hand ripples in his satin black back. Incense surrounds me, nag champa, I think, the scent of my big sister's bedroom. Her lava lamp and tapestries, lace and leathers and the faces of strangers whose secondhand clothing's for sale. Battered old Levi's and wavering shirts made from American flags. Flickering candles and eerie black lights, knives in display cases Rand points out, "serious knives," and all kinds of pipes, even hookahs. Posters of rock stars digging this scene, Dylan and Hendrix whisper to me, The ZigZag man and *ZAP! Comix*, peace signs and LOVE shines in big Day-Glo letters. *"Man, it's all chocolate milk,"* Jimi says.

"Jamey?"

And my sister.

Decked out like a hippie in cotton-soft Levi's and a tangerine-tangy paisley-print blouse, with some hippie cat's arm wrapping her shoulders. He fades to white as she looms closer. Hugging me, the paisleys are butterflies and flutter away in a wispy ballet through the ceiling. She's telling me something, *"We miss you and wish you were home, even Daddy,"* but her lies are hot bullets that sting as they're piercing my chest. *"Laurie, back off,"* the hippie cat says and she breaks apart into shards of radio static. *"Rah-ah-ger, that's my-hi bay-bee bruh-ther,"* *"Give him space, love,"* he says. And I'm trying to warn her *don't let him misplace you* but it's slower than honey to drip from my tongue. Too slow to reach her before she reloads. *"You-are bray-aching ow-er hearts, Jay,"* and she's shot me down to the ground.

9

I'm laughing at how spongy the sidewalk's become. How fast Rand can walk when I've got cement soles weighing me into the ground. How my shoes just sink deeper with each heavy step, I feel like I'm two hundred pounds. It's the red ones. Rand's pharmaceutical red ones. Ha.

One lonely bus bench haloed in streetlight calls my name like a heavenly psalm. *James! Come lay your weary head down.* But I get this feeling if I lie down I won't be getting back up. Not panic though, and not so horrible like you might think. More comforting, really. Like relief or believing in God.

«do you believe in god?»

Yeah, you sort of have to, don't you? You have to believe in something.

«i believe in you»

Just hearing those words lightens the weight more than any therapy or drug. Knowing that he'll stand by me no matter what. I'm suddenly exhausted and just want to crash, I think I could sleep for days. With room service and a chocolate mint on the pillow, DO NOT DISTURB on the door.

But there's no WELCOME! or SLEEP HERE JAMES signs, no money to get a hotel. I'm just face-to-face with night in the city, all locked doors and alleys and trash. Trying to teeter under the streetlights and walk a straight line on my own, but I need solid walls and storefront windows just to stay upright and not fall. Clinging to my reflection there or his, figuring this out.

I realize I do that a lot, say *he* meaning angel or *you* meaning everyone else. When it's always been me. *Dissociation*, that's the word they put in your file. From shameful things mostly too hard to admit to. Not as an excuse for further abuse like my dad said.

Mustard yellow, ketchup red, white light burns your tired eyes like high noon in the night. Stumbling past the fast food counter down a little hall, then going in the door marked MEN with its picture of a cartoon king on a cartoon burger throne. Not feeling much like MEN at all. Feeling pretty small and alone.

Flip the faucets full force, water pounds into the sink. Pump the soap thing twenty times for a few grains of gritty pink powder. Dunk my head under, warm water thunders my ears. It's like scrubbing the city out of my hair, watching the murky suds circle the drain and swill down. Wishing I knew a safe place to sleep where you wake with your face on a pillow instead of waking up damp with morning dew and crawly bugs on the ground.

«they have hot cocoa here»

Shivering before the mirror, my jacket, my flannel, even my cords, wet from my hair dripping now. Pull down on both sides of the white band of cloth that loops through the towel dispenser, but it's stuck at the end of the roll, dirty with handprints and grime. Still, I duck my head under and ruffle my hair dry, mostly thinking of hot cocoa to drink.

The dining area is pretty much empty, I'm the last one in the ORDER HERE line. The blaring-lit menu above is so bright it holds back the night for the final few stragglers and me. I count thirty-eight cents from my pocket. Twelve, that's the cost of French fries, ten for hot cocoa, how much for tax, I don't know.

This bag lady is paying or trying to, tattered and old, her BO assaults you just getting in line. I mean, really bad. So I'm about to tell her, just go into WOMEN and wash in the sink, or even the toilet. But she suddenly turns, all mad dog and yapping, at this strange guy behind her, his fingernails polished and impatiently tap-tap-tapping the counter. Which is pretty obnoxious, actually. But she explodes, blasting the world with curses and quotes from the Bible at the top of her lungs. So I don't tell her anything.

"Oh God, help us all and Oscar Wilde," the strange guy says, rolling his eyes.

Odd duck, that comes into my head now, somebody once said that about somebody else, my brother maybe, no, my uncle. Talking at dinner one Sunday at Granma's about a patient I heard him say, "A real odd duck came in today." And I wondered what that must look like and pictured a strange guy then, a lot like this strange guy now. I know he's a guy but his thick hair's dyed yellow and coiffed on his head like a wig, his eyes lined with black and mascara. Wide nose and full red-colored lips but he's not very dark or maybe it's because of his makeup.

He hefts a huge bag on the counter. Purse, I mean, actually. To go with his mink-collared coat and high heels. Odd duck, you know. The bag lady takes her coffee and funk outside to a shopping cart towered with junk. So he's finally next. The odd duck. He fans sour fumes of stink from the air and faces the Place Order Here chick.

"Welcome to Burger King. Can I have your order?" she recites like a part in a high school play.

"You may," he says. "A Whopper with cheese, doll. And fries— *fresh*ly Frenched, please. None of those pitiful geriatric spuds I see aging under that warming light for God *knows* how long. An orange pop—small, please. A few extra ketchups would be di*vine*." He fills her palm with change but it's like she misses it, her eyes catch mine, her cheeks mottle all suddenly aflame.

Coins clatter and bounce off the white tile counter, she ducks below chasing them on the floor. The odd duck raises his brows at me but I don't think I did anything wrong. She straightens up, punching the keys on the cash machine but still all distracted, glancing up every second then down. "Oh. Oh. God. Sorry. Um…" Freeing her curls from under the old lady hairnet she's wearing, she smooths the loose tendrils in place. *DING!* the cash drawer shoots open, she counts out the coins in her palm. "Do you have twenty-eight more cents?"

"Twenty-eight?" This odd duck checks his purse and fur pockets. But I guess he doesn't.

I slide these coins from my cords pocket over the counter. They click on the cracks between the white tiles. One quarter, three pennies, exactly.

They both stare at me.

A real odd duck came in today.

She sweeps up my change, sorting the coins in their till compartments, smiling the whole time and blushing. Shutting the cash drawer with her hip, she slides his order slip down the counter then turns her wide smile to me. "Hi. Welcome to Burger King. Can I have your baby?"

Your *order*, or maybe she said something else. The odd duck still staring, not blinking or breathing just frozen in his high heels. So it's awkward, facing them with empty pockets now. I kind of shrug at her, I know she's all flushed and flirting with me. But I've got nothing to give her, just this last dime, clicking across the counter tiles, pushing it toward her. "A hot cocoa?"

"That's all? You sure?" Smiling, she raises a finger and turns to the machine that makes it, HOT COCOA 10¢. She pokes the red button, it starts *whrrOOooOOSHsh* filling a cup with steaming brown water. "Whipped cream?"

When I nod she shakes up a canister and *whrOOshes* a swirling white peak on top. Then plows the cup across the counter to me, and my dime, too. She goes, "On me, man. It's cool, giving that weirdo your money."

Really cool. So I give her the dime back, she circles her eyes and brings me another hot cocoa. But when I'm leaving the Pick Up Order Here window, the weirdo taps my shoulder. I just keep walking, a cup in each hand, and take a seat in a booth, like I've got everything that I need.

"Mind if 'Weirdo' joins you?" The odd duck rolls his eyes, and giggles. He hooks his coat on the edge of the booth, adjusting himself on the opposite bench till he's directly across the table from me. His hair's bleached, I think, and cut short on the sides so his pierced earrings show and these blotchy dark hickies bruising his neck. Love marks, or whatever my mom told my dad when Laura got grounded for that.

He pushes his tray so it's under my nose, his Whopper and fries, driving my empty gut nuts.

"Help yourself, doll," he says, his hands flutter over his chest. "I rarely eat before work anyways."

When I shrug, he nods at his supper, insisting he's counting calories and would I please help him stay on his diet. So I slide a hot cocoa cup over to him and take a freshly-Frenched fry. Its crisp grease bursts hot between my teeth, tender inside and salted just right like the best French fry in the world. Which just makes my gut growl hungrier. So I don't take his Whopper, well, it wouldn't be enough, and it's got tomatoes and onions.

From his handbag he gets out a small stationery set, pops the cap off of a purple ink pen and starts writing. Swirly handwriting on lilac note paper, the cheap kind you get from a five-and-dime, not boxed with a ribbon and an embossed monogram like my mom's. Just a spiral pad in a plastic pack with lilacs printed all over the cover and a pocket inside with matching envelopes. He tears out the top sheet, slipping the note he just wrote in an envelope and sliding it over the table to me.

"I will pay you back, doll. Scout's honor," he says, saluting three fingers to his forehead. He takes out a lipstick and reddens the shape of his mouth. So I look away and not at his note in my hand.

I stand up. "I'm not a doll." That's all I say, stepping around him, his lilac and lipstick and odd duck hair, downing the last drop of warm cocoa. On the way out the door, though, I open the envelope, stepping back into the night. Stopping to read his swirly handwriting under the Burger King light.

I.O.U. 28¢

Forever Yours,

Donald

Donald. Ha. I'm laughing at that, *odd duck*, you know, so I'll probably always remember his name.

10

Maybe because I don't have a jacket, I left it somewhere I don't know, but my nose won't stop dripping. So I'm sniffling a lot, feeling heat off my forehead, burning eyes, sore gummy throat if I swallow, it's easier to just spit in the street.

THE ALL   ARCADE

THE   NITE ARCADE

THE ALLNITE ARCADE in blinking red neon that lights up the night like a circus. Inside it's high volume, pinging pinball, blaring rock music so loud it's distorted and hard to guess what song. Wrecked or reckless packs of street kids, greasers, bikers, and hippie freaks, all mixed together like crashing a party without invitations or chaperones. Then three of them in a speed-blur flash, circle me like a tribal dance in army surplus, a fat red coat, a black satin jacket with a red letter A on the back.

Just seeing Rand, I feel instantly better. But he turns away, shouting to me as he goes. Something about zero and they'll be right back. And I shout "What?" which just gets lost in the din, and then, "Wait!" plowing my way after him, through this swirling maze of big top madness and finally the quiet outside. But too late. I don't know which way he went.

Turning at first back inside the arcade, but what if I miss him, so I wait near the corner phone booth out front. Guys like pigeons flock around, hanging out, smoking, swaggering—soliciting, I realize—drugs or rides when cars pull up. Like a taxi stand. Only you don't see any taxis.

Solicitation. It's against the law but nobody here's getting busted. And I wonder, who *are* these guys? The undesirables, ha. This one like an Apache catches me staring too late to break my gaze, he steps so close I can see his pinpoint eyes. Mumbling so I don't hear his words exactly, something about "selling your junk" that makes him chuckle.

He's got white jeans and a suede shearling coat like the Marlboro Man in the magazine ads, on the billboards, and TV commercials, only worn out and grubby, his hands hidden deep in its big side pockets, pacing the curb in black Beatle boots all cool like a rock star. Gary had those but the heels are high so my dad said no, you can't get them.

He stops at my side again. "Holy Christ, another fuckin' baby," he mutters. His hair tangles out from a red bandana tied around his forehead like Tonto or Jimi Hendrix, lopsided grin, eyes glassy from laughter or being stoned. "What's it, some kinda national nanny holiday?" He snickers. "No one's minding the nursery, man. Alla fuckin' babies have escaped."

I shrug, sneezing. Wipe it down my flannel sleeve, the cuff sort of crusty. "Yeah, well, where'd you escape from," I say through chattering teeth, not believing I'm even talking to him at all.

His head bobs once. "Fair enough," he says. He grins, stepping backward off the curb in his high-heeled boots, turning into the street in front of a barreling Mac truck, a fast one you think will stop, but no.

THUMP! White jeans tumble, flipped up in the air, then *THUD!* On the street before you can breathe, *WHOMP-WHOMP!* Front and back tires mow him down to the pavement. White legs and tan sleeves rolling over and over for one surreal moment then to a stop in the street. The Marlboro guy, twisted and broken, twitching all crazy and mumbles silent, a growing black puddle on the asphalt beneath him darkening his hair and bandana. His eyes stare wide open blankly at me, like laughter, still grinning. *Fair enough.*

My heart's pounding so loud and alive, I want to hit rewind and stop it from happening—wait!—and for maybe an eye blink all time stands still.

Then curses and shouts volley the street, red dots of lit smokes arc the darkness, long eerie shadows break the harsh Allnite light. They spill from the curb so the street quickly fills, to come to his rescue, start CPR, or just see. They tug at his tan suede coat, its pockets, his high-heeled feet. But the Marlboro guy doesn't get up.

«there's nobody here who can help him»

Shouting, arguing, shoving, elbows shoulders knees fists, I slip out from their midst and back to the sidewalk, trembling badly. My knees fold, taking me down to sit on the curb, shaking as if I'm plugged in, I have to cover my ears from their din. The whole pack like barking coyotes dividing a kill, Rand the loudest of all. Then standing before me with his bucktooth grin and his arms piled high with the grungy Marlboro Man coat, and he's handing the coat to me. Durrand Jennette, the thief.

He sits down at my side, takes a drag off a smoke that he passes to me but I'm too shaky to even hold it. He chucks off his own broken cowboy boots in the gutter and puts the Marlboro guy's black Beatle boots on his feet. They're worn out a lot worse than the boots he was wearing but he looks up at me like it's instant Christmas. He nods at the coat with a gesture that says, *Put it on.*

"What?" he grunts when I don't respond.

"It's a dead guy's coat," I say. I can't stop shivering, holding the mangy coat to my chest. It's warm.

Rand shakes his head like I'm nuts. He pulls the coat from my arms and drapes it cape-like over my shoulders. Just the weight of it warms me, blocking the wind out and chills. But still, loose gunk in my chest tickles my throat so I can't catch a breath or stop coughing.

"Jesus, Angel. Yew oughta take better care of yerself. Here. Yew kin owe me." He opens his palm to a nest of blue pills. But I'm coughing too bad to take anything. Rand dumps them all in the Marlboro coat pocket.

He jumps to his feet, fists balled in his black satin pockets, stomping around in his new Beatle boots, then into the Allnite Arcade. I turn away but the image remains, the moment of impact and the sound. Dead now, he's *dead*, I don't know his name, I'm wearing his coat and I'm warm.

I get up on shaky legs, make my way through the lingering crowd to the phone booth at the corner. I won't give my name, that's what I'm thinking, just call the ambulance and split. It's dark and empty, but the second I step in and pull the door closed, the overhead light flickers on. So I'm suddenly lit like a window display, posed in a dead guy's warm coat. Still, my jaw chatters crazy, from no sleep, I think, or maybe no drugs, and the dead guy maybe alive in the street. Hurrying up, dialing "0," which takes like five rings till the operator answers, then it's hard getting words out at all. "This…this guy just got killed, hit by a truck," I say. At the Allnite Arcade, that's where when she asks "the location of the reported incident." I think he's maybe already dead, I say, but I don't know. Do you call an ambulance for that?

"Stay on the line." Her voice sounds small and far away. "Are you the party at fault in this incident?"

"Me? I didn't—" But what if I did? He was talking to me and got hit by a truck—and turning, I look out the phone booth's dirty glass walls where the crowd is breaking apart. Like show over, The End, there's nothing else left to take.

The phone to my ear's gone silent. Waiting, I can feel Rand's pills all tangled with threads and grit in the seam of the clotted wool pocket and then remember how creepy, a dead guy's pocket, and pull my fingers out.

"I have a unit on the way," the distant voice returns to my ear. "Please remain on scene and identify yourself to the responding officer. Would you like me to stay on the line until—"

I hang up the phone and step out from the booth back into the cold like a slap.

Flipping hair from my eyes, untangling the pills from the pocket fuzz, I think I could swallow with no water. Checking the other pocket, feeling slick square packets like wrapped rings of candy, slipping one out to see.

Trojans. Shove it back in the pocket but deeper, as deep in the seam as it goes.

Looking up, a red pickup truck glides to the curb, blocking them all from my view, all these guys soliciting or whatever, with nowhere else to go. My hair sticks to my lashes all teary in the wind, I have to pin it back with my fingers to even see who's at the wheel. In a red and black Pendleton jacket, that big burly man is looking at me. The lumberjack guy. And my first thought, why is he here?

A windy blast off the lakefront shudders my bones or maybe the chill's from seeing his face. **West Suburban Law Officers Association**, that's the decal on his window. *The responding unit*, like a cop or maybe plainclothes detective, with a police radio in his dashboard. So he can call in his report on the Marlboro guy or maybe he already did. Or *me*—it hits me like swallowing ice cubes. He could call in and bust me right now. Fifty-one-fifty, escaped mental patient, probation violation, lock him away, case closed.

«stay calm and sound sane»

He leans across the front seat to the passenger side window, and rolling it down, beckons me. "Come here, kid," he says. Loud radio static crackles inside, and a woman's voice, all tinny and dull, drones from a dashboard speaker. *"Code two, one-fiver-two Montrose, ten-fifty-four. Possible deceased. Ten-twenty-three...check the arcade."*

I shake my head no, with MINS like a stamp on my forehead, he's got to see that. Turning away, I point where it happened, just up the street. The crowd mostly gone and no ambulance siren. "He's right over there. The Marlboro guy." It hits me to not say "Marlboro," I'm the guilty one wearing his coat. "The guy that got killed."

His grin freezes, his small squinting eyes stare directly inside me, like reading my whole MINS file. "What guy would that be?" he says.

"I...that's why I called. He got hit by a truck and he's, he's just *dead* over there."

"You called?" He glances over his shoulder but not where I pointed. He switches off the radio, the static dies. "Hit by a truck? Gotta be pretty dumb and stupid not to see that coming."

I shrug, thinking it's true what Rand said, nobody cares. Not even an associate law officer, when you'd think that's his job, to notify the family or the next of kin.

"What're you doing out here? My guess is Daddy never showed up," he says.

It hurts, what he says, like a gut punch, but it's true, I wouldn't even be here, except. My dad doesn't care.

"That's rough, kid. Your old man letting you down like that." A shake of his head, a click of his tongue.

Twinging, my mouth goes all sour like sucking lemons or before you cry. Flip my hair back, wiping stuck strands and wetness away. Bite my lip and shrug.

He tips a pack of cigarettes through the window at me, one shake so up pops a Kool. At first I don't take it, I'm warm in this coat, keeping it closed if I don't let go. But then I do, taking a smoke, and he flicks on the flame of a lighter.

"That's what you told Officer A-hole at the bus station, isn't it? You were waiting for your old man, as I recall." He kind of laughs, but not really.

I lean closer to light it, taking a drag, but it doesn't work, I don't know, it's like solid ash down my throat and I can't help coughing, all dizzy and green, not getting air in at all.

"Careful there. Force me to perform mouth-to-mouth." He chuckles like a friend and not someone mean. "And let me tell you, it's been a while since I saved a life." He's still smiling, but not like a joke when my eyes and lungs clear. "Hell, that was you down at the Syndrome, wasn't it? Passed out in the gutter. The *sin*-drome." He winks. "I thought as much. Like to party, do you?"

"Are you following me or something?"

A distant siren grows louder and closer. I turn in its direction, but his hand reaches out from the cab, beckoning again but for this cigarette. He takes it from my fingers, takes a long drag right on my germs, then stubs it out in his dashboard ashtray. "Look," he says. "Get in out of the wind. We can talk about it over a burger and coffee; how's that?"

The red door of the truck's cab pushes out so I have to step back up the curb when it opens. It's a pretty big step to climb up and his hand extends out to help pull me. It's oversized too, like a catcher's mitt. "Come on, kid, my treat. Get in and shut the door already."

I hesitate, because he's a cop or a lumberjack, because angel or something won't let me get in the red truck.

"Jesus Christ. I'm not gonna bust you. Is that what you think?"

I shrug, yeah—when someone shouts from the street. "Hey! Burger King!" and I swivel to see this Olds Toronado glide to a stop. So at first my heart jolts—I *know* that car, God, it's Ratachek's car, cruising the street for lewd ratty sex—or sent by my dad to come get me, God, my dad wouldn't send Ratachek, would he?—but then, no, it's not Mr. Ratachek at all. And my speedy heart calms at the beaming face leaning halfway out the passenger window, the thick bleached hair and ladies' fur collar, wide nose and makeup and perfect white teeth. Odd duck Donald, waving and calling me. "Doll!"

"Well? *Doll.* Go on," the detective or lumberjack directs me. "Those are friends of yours, aren't they?"

I don't know the driver at all but I nod. "Yeah." So I jump away from the red cab and the lumberjack cop, stepping back into the gutter. Then scurry around the bed of his truck to the open door of the Olds Toronado. Odd duck Donald folds his seat forward, and I settle into the back, sinking deep into heated buttery-soft black leather luxury. Despite the old croaker guy behind the wheel eyeballing me in the rearview. Despite the radio playing some tragic opera in a shrill annoying voice. Donald closes the door turned halfway around, all beaming like instant Christmas. And I can't help smiling back at him, happy to just have the choice.

part three
donald

11

"It's not much, but it's home," Donald says, when we're out of the warmth of the Olds Toronado and heading up a broken sidewalk. Pulling a key from his purse, he unlocks the front door of this ancient four-story graystone from like before the Great Fire or something. Behind us the Toronado glides from the curb and disappears into the night.

"Who was he?" I'm following Donald over the doorstep and asking because the croaker guy driving hugged him good night with a whisper and lingering kiss.

Donald wipes his shoes on a floor mat. Leopard print heels, actually, I guess to match his leopard-print dress. Looking at me, he pushes the foyer door open. "Oh," he says. "Just a friend."

I trip on a missing tile or the jagged ridge left behind, I catch myself before he does. He's all apologies—"Sorry, doll, sorry," and "Are you all right?"—but I don't need him to rescue me or even ask. Moving down this tenement hallway, all musty with age and old wood, a smell you can taste when you swallow. The floor's swept clean and there's wall sconces on, but my dad would call it a slum.

Keeping this thick coat locked at my throat, my arms closed around me. I know I'm sick, like a fever with chills down my backbone, a headache, and eyes burning even in the dim light.

A door at the end of the hallway flings open, and I jump when the head of Medusa juts out, all snaky gray hair and hissing at us. "Who's there!"

"Just Donald!" he calls out.

And me coughing hard again and again so loud the Medusa steps out in the hall, a crooked old lady with fiery eyes and a prodding cane. Donald stops at this one door, his palm raised like a street sign at me, one of the yellow signs, caution.

"Who's with you!" she screeches.

"A friend, honey, if that's okay with you," Donald answers.

"No, it ain't okay! This ain't no bathhouse, you keep your nasty business out of here!"

"Mind your own nasty business," he mutters, then sings, "Bathhouses have hot water!" in opera falsetto to her slammed door. "Still not fixed!"

Looking at me, he giggles. "She's nobody. Just the landlady. *Miss*-manager." Wiggling his key in the doorknob like a secret handshake, he gets it unlocked. But it doesn't push open with the weight of his shoulder. Jiggling the knob more, he lets out a sigh, then *WHAM!* kicks it so powerful with one high heel, not like a girl at all. He straightens his coat and his hair from the effort. "Welcome to paradise," he says.

Opening the door, a calico's whiskers nudge at his ankles, mewing softly. His finger moves to his lips, whispering, "Shhh, no pets allowed," and shuts nobody out behind us.

He hangs his fur coat in the closet when you first get in the door and offers to take mine but I don't give it up. It's cold in here and dark, with hunched figures lurking in the shadows. Or maybe just lamps and big furniture. Donald starts the radiator so this smell like burnt toast fills the room. I don't move from the doorway, keeping my grip ready on the doorknob.

He steps around a couch or some big bulky thing, clicking a lamp on, a red-shaded one. So this whole room glows suddenly warm like a campfire, all rose-colored and cozy.

Dark wood trims the window and purple walls. A plump violet sofa faces the room leaving a hall space behind it. There's overgrown plants and ferns that gleam silver in the moonlight that floods through a white drape on the window. Floor cushions and rugs, bookshelves like a library, candles, and a beaded curtain. It's not like you'd think in here, not like a slum at all.

The strands of beads rattle when Donald parts them, stepping inside a little kitchen alcove with a pint-sized refrigerator and two-burner stove. He spoons cat food from a can into a bowl, then flits plant to plant all over the room with a jar full of water, sprinkling each one.

"Can I make you a hot cup of tea? Sorry—no cocoa. But! I've got Roastaroma. It's carob. The *health*-food chocolate." When I don't say anything his shoulders sag, he holds his arms open like a plea. "I feel I'm Miss-Dreadful-Hostess-of-the-Year-Award here. Won't you at least come *in*?"

Swallowing a lump of whatever, my throat burns so severe when I do. I take one step maybe two from the doorjamb into his room. It's warm. "All this stuff's yours, huh."

Twirling, his arms spread like parenthesis, including it all. "All this precious stuff."

It's just one room, with a closet behind the couch when you first come in, and a bathroom. That's where he is now. At the sink, his back to me through the open door, filling a pot with water, then a few steps to the kitchenette, he strikes a match and poof! a ring of blue flame lights the burner.

He turns, shaking the match out, pointing out the sofa, the shelves, the books. "Goodwill. Goodwill. Alley. Salvation Army. Church bazaar, alley. A friend found the paint in a dumpster, isn't it just too divine? Lavender, the outrageous color, perfectly lovely and com*plete*ly queer. What do you think? Too trash," he giggles, "or not trash enough?" Flipping his wrist, he wiggles his manicure under my nose. I duck back from his red polished nails.

"Who, your friend in the Toronado?"

"No, not my-friend-in-the-Toronado." He plops on the sofa, crosses his legs, hikes his dress up his thighs in a pin-up girl pose. "A *non*paying friend. I do have a few of those. And *I do* wish you would please come in and sit down." He pat-pats the purple cushion beside him so I have to look away. From his makeup, his perfume, his dress and bared thigh. Turning to leave but then what? I can't think beyond turning the doorknob.

"I disgust you, don't I." His voice sort of sags when he says it. He pulls the hem down to cover his knees.

I close my eyes when I swallow, my throat hurts so bad. The pills in my pocket, the blue ones from Rand, I doubt I could get one down and almost ask him for help. Water or an IV or something.

"Have you ever met anyone like me?"

I shake my head so clogged up like drowning. When I open my eyes, he's still here. The purple and everything.

"What about the queers down at the Square? Do they disgust you?"

I get no choice except to listen to him in his apartment with no radio to tune him out or TV to watch instead. Even if I don't know what he's talking about, even if I don't want to hear what he says. Even if I'm sick and just want to lie down and not think. It's his house and I can't say be quiet.

"Well. Call *me* Curious Yellow because they sure as hell disgust me. Not to be crude, *but*. Cheap front seat zipper sex and leaving cum bags in the street? They give gals like us a bad reputation."

Why is he including me? I don't do any of those things, why do I need to say I don't, it's not his business even if…it's not his business about me at all. Holding the wall, it's not straight either, the whole room warped, the whole world. "I don't even know what you mean, 'the square.'"

"Market Square? Honey, it's where you were hanging out. The whole block. From the Burger King and that all-night chicken arcade to the tacky little diner on Lawrence. The Fresh Cup. The park, too. God *knows* about the park."

Words float from my mouth, faraway and not mine. "They didn't seem queer to me."

He clicks his tongue loudly. "The difference between us and them is we're honest enough to admit it. Oh!" He springs up and around the sofa to the stove and pours bubbling water in two cups with a flowery towel around the pot handle. Steam billows, fogging the window behind the white silk.

Spinning in my head, this hopeless dizzy feeling washes over me. Like falling with no safe place to land, so I'm thinking I'd have been better off just going in the red truck with the undercover cop.

"The sofa opens into a bed." Donald sits and bounces on it, petting a cushion like a cat.

I quick wipe my eyes, not wanting to cry or let him see, sniffing it back. "I'm not sleeping with you," comes out. Turning for the door, the whole room turns with me. I could take all the blue pills and go find Rand or sleep in the theater or an unlocked back seat.

"I meant, if you need a pillow to cry in," he says.

"I'm not crying." But it's real hard to get the words out. Twisting to look at him, the room spins like a carousel too fast to focus. When I do, it's at the crushed look on his face. "I don't think you're disgusting," I say, but it barely scrapes out. "I don't think anything. I just have to lie down." His sofa, his bed, the floor at his feet, what difference. He moves over so I can sit, just enough. I squish against the armrest farthest from him. Sinking in deep, it's instant relief. The whole weight of me lifted and drifting on lush purple velvet. It's nice to be cushioned and not fight myself just to stand. A relief like surrender.

I untangle them from this coat pocket, three blue pills. Lean over the tea cups all set on a doily like a party my little sister would have for her Barbies and Ken and me. Popping all three in one painful lump going down with this throat-soothing tea. Roastaroma or whatever. Fall back. My head like a bowling ball sinks in soft purple. Soft neck, soft spine. Soft eyes, if I closed them I could sleep forever and ever.

"All I can say is, if I looked like you? I'd clean myself up, find me a sugar daddy, and live first-class all the way. On the lake. Yachts. Caviar! Winter in the islands. You're a heartbreaker, doll."

Doll. From deep in the purple, anger escapes. I can't lift my head or talk, hardly. *You're breaking our hearts,* Laura said. But it's my mom's face that does it, brings up raw tears. Looking in at me from the ICU hallway, shaken, heartbroken, afraid.

I shouldn't have cut my wrists on her birthday. I shouldn't have cut my wrists at all.

"So you're on the street because...?" He doesn't wait for an answer. "You hated living under their rules. They grounded you. Beat you. Abused you? They're dope fiends. Satan worshippers. Moonies! Or...worse?"

Covering my ears with both palms. I don't want to hear him, I don't care what he says or how rude it is, I don't want to talk about it. Not to my uncle or Dr. Pauly or anyone.

"Born-again Christians?" Donald says in mock horror. *Born again,* as if that's the worst of all things. When starting over from day one sounds good to me.

I let my hands drop to my thighs, looking at him in his dress, his heels, and mascara. "I don't fit in anymore," I say. My eyes burn so raw these tears are soothing. He jumps up alert and hands me a Kleenex, but I don't want to be nursed, not by him.

"So it's all *your* fault. It's because of something *you* did. Because of who you are. Honey, that ballad's bullshit and you know it."

"Never mind, you don't know."

"*I* don't know?" His hands on his hips, his neck sways but his thick bleached hair stays in place. "Believe me, doll. I know."

Maybe he does. It's hard to look at him though and not cry. "I wish I was like you, so it doesn't bother me, but I..." The words choke in my throat. "I just feel so..." *ugly*. What am I doing here, I don't know, I've got to go. I pull myself out of his sinkhole sofa, stand up heavier than ever, teetering on rocky feet to his kitchen where there is no kitchen sink so I leave this empty cup in the bathroom, go to his door. Chills frost my scalp straight down my spine, weepy eyes blind me with headache pressure. My hand on his doorknob, my knee shaking. Where do I even have to go? Nobody cares. Nobody. Just *you're a heartbreaker* like that's all that matters.

I let go of the door and let Donald steer me inside.

When I'm out of his shower and step from the bathroom he's draped across the sofa like a movie starlet, all lacy chiffon and see-through, in a cloud of dime store perfume. He is a he. I look away from his lap.

"How we feeling, doll? Better?"

Maybe even human. I pull this damp towel tighter around me, I won't wear a negligee and I've got nothing on underneath.

He's only got cornflakes for dinner, dry with no milk, Ayds diet candy, and pink mush he feeds to the cat. I can't eat anyway, it's late, I'm sick and too downed out to digest even spit. "Don't call me that. 'Doll.' I'm not a doll."

He flickers like a broken film. "Fine. Then who are you?" He pops another Ayds and sips his tea. It's this other kind now.

"Why do you have to know that?"

"My goodness! I'm not with the vice squad for heaven's sake." He plops down across from me at the far end of the sofa, just sitting there like in a Halloween costume, dressing gown, negligee, and ruby slippers.

I tell him I'm James—James Daniel Ross—which feels more like a lie than a secret.

Donald smiles. "Good tea, isn't it? Chamomile, it'll settle your stomach. It was used in the olden days to cure monthly discomforts." He laughs. "The curse. Honey, let me tell you, I haven't had a bad period in *years*." I can smell his Noxzema when he leans forward. "That's a joke! My God, James Daniel Ross. Your sense of humor leaves a *lot* to be desired."

It feels weird, hearing him say my real name, like I'm naked and can't hide anything now. Well. I am naked.

He suddenly claps his hands. "What's my favorite joke, you ask? Man rushes up to a lady on the street and says, 'Lady! Quick! Call me a cab!' 'Okay,' she says. 'You're a cab!'" He's laughing tee-hee-hee with his knees jerked to his chest like an appendix attack or the funniest joke in the world. "Oh, come on, James Daniel Ross. It's *funny*!"

God. He reminds me of someone so much, and it's not Gary or Tommy or even my sister. For one thing, he's queer, he admits he's like that, he's always felt like a girl. He's not bothered by it or ashamed at all. "You can either deny it and be a miserable bitch your entire life or just accept who you are and be happy." He's got his cat cradled in his arms now, he scratches its head when he talks. "Honey, I've been down the other road and let me tell you, I'd rather live on Happy Street. So I told my daddy, well, I figured he either loves me or he doesn't but *I* certainly wasn't going to be celibate *my* entire life just because he's hung up, you know?"

The cat's eyes close, you can hear purring, low and content. "Anyways, so I told him. And do you know he didn't say one word? Just picked up and walked out the door."

He gets up, puts the cat on my lap so at first I don't know what to do. There's a fluffy little creature standing on my gut. Donald clears the cereal dishes, still talking above the trickle of dishwater at the bathroom sink. "And when I came home from school? There were all my things. Strewn every which way on the front curb like trash. Like *trash*, James! He didn't have to destroy my things, you know. That's just plain *path*ological."

The cat's spine arches hard and defiant against my palm, the tail snaking between my fingers. Tiny velvet paws press through the towel into my thighs, the bottoms padded like Beth's ballet slippers, stepping so soft on my gut. It tickles and when I titter the cat jiggles up and down, giving me this goofy look. So I can't help laughing out loud.

The faucet stops, I can hear him stack the dishes in the shower stall. "*That* wasn't supposed to be funny," he says.

My fingers scratch the soft fur between its ears like Donald did, and they twitch, his cat stretches out in an open jaw yawn, then curls up heavy and warm on my lap. I swear to God the cat smiles. "Donald, look."

He dries his hands on his apron, unties it, leaning in toward his cat. "Aww, Babsy, you've found a new friend, haven't you, yes, yes, you have," he says. His fingers reach down to my lap so I jump but no, it's just to pet his cat. He's not stupid, he already sees how mental I am and cautiously pulls his hand back.

"So. Anyway. Tell me about James's daddy." His chin's hooked on the back of the sofa close to my ear. "Let's see...Mr. Ross. Dashingly suave. Boyish good looks. Still blond but with a tidge of gray at the temples. Blue eyes and a Robert Redford smile. Mustache?"

I shake my head. No mustache.

"Unshaven, with rough, calloused hands. He can rebuild a carburetor, unclog a drain, and takes his son hunting on weekends." He points one finger like aiming a gun.

Shake my head. "Not hardly."

"Mr. 'America, Love It Or Leave It,' he despises hippies and thinks draft dodgers are pinko fags."

"He's not like that either."

Donald's eyes light up. "He *likes* pinko fags?"

"He'd love you, Donald. Probably a lot more than me." I say it sarcastic but it's probably true. Well, maybe not love, but I don't think my dad would despise him. Like at the riots two years ago when the Yippies took over the lakefront, fighting police in the city streets so we couldn't go visit Granma. And Tommy asked him if he'd defend the protesters that got busted. My dad said it depends. He'd defend draft resisters and conscientious objectors until this illegal war ends. But he'd be damned if he'd defend any dropouts or potheads who don't take care of themselves. That's what my dad said.

But I don't say that to Donald. I just say, "He's a lawyer. A good one, I guess."

"So he expects you to be a lawyer too?"

I'm thinking, ha! that's a joke. "Well, my big brother is, he's at, um, you know. Law school."

"Uh-oh. So how long has big brother been in therapy?"

I sit myself up, spooking the cat, she jumps to the floor bristling my cooties away. "Un-unh, not Tommy."

"Believe me, honey. He will be."

He never even met Tommy, he doesn't know what he's talking about. I can't picture Tommy talking to those shrinks at all, Dr. Pauly or Glasser. Or to Donald either. He never would. "Well, not unless the Eagle Scouts have a merit badge for it."

Donald laughs. "They don't," he says. "So the Ross boys grew up pretty well-to-do then."

I'm thinking, Yeah. On the lake, yachts, caviar, winter in the islands. But I just shrug. "We always had enough cornflakes, you know, for dinner."

Donald rolls his eyes. "So what's he like?"

"He's just, regular. With a varsity jacket and crew cut. Not like me at all."

"I meant your daddy."

"Oh. Well, I don't know, he's...he's pretty big and really smart—"

Donald sighs, flips his apron over his shoulder standing up. "Oh, so you're little and stupid?"

Just hearing that, it's like a gut punch or revelation. "Maybe it's the truth."

"Bullshit, and pardon my French, James. *All* our fathers fucked with our heads, one way or another. My God, it's the male curse." He clicks his tongue, pulls out his lilac stationery pad, and shuts himself in the bathroom.

Donald stacks the cushions near the window and opens the sofa into a bed. It takes up almost all the space in this room so it's awkward now with no place to sit or even stand, hardly. He unfolds flowered sheets, shaking them out, and makes up the bed like they do in hotels. Then slips under the covers, pats the empty space beside him and holds something out across the mattress to me.

It's another lilac envelope. It's addressed *JAMES DANIEL ROSS*.

"What, should I read it now?" I start to open it, mostly to stall getting in bed beside him. He's snuggled into a ball with his back to me, his face buried deep in a pillow and hopefully already dreaming.

I unfold the lilac stationery, kneel into the lamplight near his arm. My skin next to his looks sickly or dead, like the color you'd pick for a ghost.

Dear James,

You're welcome to stay here as long as you like. No (heart) strings attached. Please know I would never violate your trust and you don't owe me a thing.

Love, Your Unconditional Friend,

Donald Griswold

Emotion wells up from somewhere inside and relief, just knowing I can stay and don't have to pay or even do anything except sleep. I slip it back in the envelope, crumble it to fit in my hand. I try to move like the cat, not shaking the mattress or waking him, and slide myself under the sheet. Donald turns off the light.

12

Everything You Always Wanted To Know About Sex* (*But Were Afraid To Ask) by David Reuben, MD. There are underlined words that catch my eyes when I flip through the pages, I can't help reading those.

Facts, I guess, or the rules everyone who has sex ought to know. Like *Don't have sex with anyone you wouldn't willingly share your toothbrush with.* But I don't have a toothbrush, so. *Don't marry a hooker.* Well, I'm not getting married. *The size of your dick won't determine her pleasure.* Who is she, that's what I want to know. *Mature men don't masturbate.* Ha, I guess I've still got a long way to go. And then **Chapter Eight. Male Homosexuality.** *Faggots will never be happy. See a shrink if you need to be cured.*

I shut the book. I never wanted to know about that.

Donald's not here. He was gone when I woke, his side of the sheets cold and empty. But putting the book back on the shelf where I got it, this other title catches my eye. On a cover I've seen somewhere before. *The Sensuous Woman* by "J," all dog-eared and slobbered so I wish I had gloves just to touch it. Jeez, Donald. Then I remember, it was in my mom's bookcase. In her bedroom, but it's my dad's bedroom too, so I feel like an outlaw just opening the cover.

Paragraphs jump out when I flip through the pages, sentences underlined in purple, and highlighted words I didn't even think it was legal to print. So I doubt my mom ever opened the book, I can't imagine her reading those words, or wanting to. About biting men on their buttocks to give them an erection. About nice people who copulate anally each day and nothing bad or even unpleasant happens to them.

I shut that book, too.

But who bought the book? It bothers me thinking of her or my dad at the bookstore in uptown River Hills. Debby Schulman at the register ringing it up, reading the title, putting it in a Schulman's Bookshoppe paper bag. Giggling at school, passing around gossip or a note, *Jamey's mom bought* The Sensuous Woman! so by lunchtime the whole school knows. My mom taking the book to him in their bedroom at night or reading it first under their matching duvets. Making her bite him or biting him first.

God, it's my *dad*, it's my *mom*.

Disgusted repugnant what's wrong with me? My mom would never do that, my dad wouldn't, or maybe they would. Nice people copulating anally. Shuddering those pictures out of my head, I get up, stick *The Sensuous Woman* back on the bookshelf between *Christine Jorgensen* and *Wuthering Heights*.

Out the one window it's just the alley you see, wind blowing trash and a trash bin. Two people walking, nice people, they look nice to me. Touching each other, then lewd without clothes, God, I wish I didn't open that book.

Anally copulated by nice people.

It's what the report said, the medical one from the surgical staff at my uncle's hospital. Except not the "nice people" part, it said "multiple transgressions." Still, my dad blames me, like it's all my fault, what happened at Railton that made suicide the only way out.

"Happy Hump Day, James!"

Donald's all smiles when I wake, unwrap myself out of this blanket cocoon, and sit straight up on the sofa. Sun streaming in like golden praise warms his whole purple palace. "Hump day?"

"Wednesday! Oh, my goodness, call Ripley! Baby smiles!"

I do because I thought *hump day* meant something else. He's got the coffee table set up with choco milk, toast, even flowers. So I'm smiling at that, and his eyes wide with delight at some secret he's hiding behind his back.

"Ta-daa!" He laughs, and holds up a familiar cereal box. Sugar Sprinkles. "Tell me that isn't you, honey. Oh, I *knew* it! It *is* you!" Amazed or amused that it's me on the front of the box, he's going to get it framed he says and brings me a pen to sign it. "Apparently you forgot to mention how famous you are!"

Shaking my head, I deny it. "I'm not, though. The boy on the box anymore. That was before."

"Before? Before *moi*, perhaps," Donald says.

I shrug and turn the box around. *Hey Kids!* it says. *Free Inside! Secret Spy Decoder Ring!* I tear the box top apart and the wax paper bag, plunge my hand deep inside. Sweetness explodes like a spray of perfume, which isn't the smell I remember. I fish out the ring in its cellophane wrapper and gather the cereal that's spilled. "I never actually ate these before."

"I don't believe it, Mr. Ripley," Donald says, and points like proof at my face on the cereal box and the spoonful of colorful puffs I look way too excited to eat.

"They were glued to the spoon with spray fixative. It smelled like chemical bananas." I suddenly don't want the ring anymore. I stand up, leaving it on the table. "Anyway, sugar messed up the drugs I was on, so."

Donald looks at me like a secret he's just decoded. He splits the cellophane wrapper apart and reads the instruction paper. He writes something on his stationery pad, then rips it off in a strip he folds into the ring's secret compartment. He snaps the two parts together, the decoder into the green plastic band and gets down on one knee before me. "With this ring I thee wed," he says, but it's weird because he's not really joking, and when I don't take it from him, he whispers, *You don't love me.* He admires the ring on his own wedding finger instead. "Someday my prince will come," he sighs.

"I'm sorry, I just, I'm not...I'm too young to get married." *And I'm a boy*, but he knows that.

"Let me at least be your manager, James. Please? Please-please-please?" His hands clasp at his chin like a prayer, standing up. "Don't look at me like that—you'll see! Believe me, ye of little faith. Lest you forget, I have *many* friends in this town. We'll start with laundry, a new coif. And headshots. A new look, a new you, a new ingénue!"

He moves trinkets and keepsakes and pictures aside to display the autographed box on a shelf. "Is there anybody we can go to for *fund*ing? I mean, how about Mom? Big brother? Grandmother or an ex-girlfriend? My God, a boy as beauticious as you, there must be fans *fawn*ing all over."

"My granma gave me some money before."

Donald's smile grows larger. "*Loaned*, James, and we'll pay her back. We'll just have to call her and arrange for another loan," he says, then counts on his fingers. "First, we'll do laundry. Next, a visit to dear Andrew at Sassoon. And for the final touch: a session with John Frederick, my *fabu*lous photographer friend. Good headshots are *every*thing, James. Believe me. Once you're cleaned up and rid of this scraggly mane, sweetheart, there'll be no stopping us."

God, he makes it all sound so easy.

FLIP CITY

I'm swinging my legs off this washing machine waiting for my clothes to get clean. Donald's sitting next to me, reading a story out loud from *True Romance* magazine. "Mama, Why Didn't You Teach Me to Say No?" There's other people in here, it's pretty far from his apartment and we had to take the train, but he likes this laundromat best he says because it's kept so pristine. It is pristine. It's a better neighborhood, he's right about that, but it just makes him stand out even more.

He's got makeup on like Marilyn Monroe, a beauty mark, lipstick, and powder. I've got this Marlboro coat buttoned up to my neck and no shirt underneath. I'm wearing his slacks, which don't really fit 'cause he's bigger than me and they're ladies. I mean it's not real obvious, but it feels weird, with the zipper in the back, which Donald insisted you can't really see. He's probably right, nobody cares either way, but still. I refuse to wear any of his blouses.

Watching my clothes tumble and spin, I tell him about NYC. The photo shoots there and meetings with ad men and staying in fancy hotels. How well they treat you and take you around in taxis or town cars to galas and premieres or the top of the Empire State Building. And everything's covered so you don't need money, not even for tips or a Coke.

Donald throws me a skeptical look. I say I'm not joking, Donald. You'd love it.

Later, these two guys come in, and I can see they're real queer, the way they hug each other and carry on, Donald and these two guys do, so I'm thinking how perfect he'd fit in New York.

"So *I* said, 'oh, honey. It's *not* homophobia. *Every*one hates you'—" One guy says, and they all three have a giggle fit over that. I turn toward the notices on the bulletin board instead. APT 4 RENT and city ordinances, *Use of slugs in coin-operated machinery is punishable by law.* A xeroxed flyer of some blond guy's happy face. HAVE YOU SEEN ALLEN?

I hear Donald say I'm a child star, which is so far from the truth, I'm shaking my head no no no the whole time, wishing I never had told him. But he's already dragged me into that conversation, calling me doll, like he owns me now, like how Cleveland called me angel, pretty much. Except he's doing my laundry, he's taking care of me, and he said he won't touch me, no matter how much he giggles at the lewd remarks of his friends. So I guess he's not like Cleveland at all. Still, I'm glad when his friends finally fold up their laundry and go.

"Are you scared, Donald?" Because it's what his friends were going on and on about, Halloween and what they're gonna go as this year, Sonny and Cher or Squeaky Fromme. And scarier stuff, about a psycho killer, a real one, not a costume either, and about their friend on the flyer who went off to do dates two weeks ago and nobody's seen him since. So that's why I ask Donald, because it's how he gets money. "Like when you get in their cars. What if one of them is him, the psycho killer? I mean it's probably not, but what if?"

Just thinking about it I shudder the heebie-jeebies away. But Donald flips his hand all cavalier in the air. "Honey, I do anything and everything. Even the dishes! He'd have no reason to kill me."

I try to agree, to stay calm. "If I was the killer, I wouldn't."

He smiles, his eyes sort of sparkle when he does. "How incredibly *kind* of you, James."

Watching him, I don't understand it at all, why he'd want to do this, I mean be so openly queer. It doesn't bother him either, the sour way people look at him. Well, he says, after your mother abandons you and your father throws you out, what other people think doesn't much matter. "Don't worry about it, James. If you're gay, that's fabulous, if you're not..." His brows raise with a sigh. "Don't listen to what anybody else says. My God, especially me."

"Well. You're really nice."

"Well. You're really nice," he says.

But I'm shaking my head.

Donald opens the dryer, checking the last load if it's dry. "You think you're so horrible because you think your father thinks you're so horrible. Pardon my French, but who the hell *cares* what he thinks? I certainly don't." He pulls out my shirt, and winks at this white lady with her wire basket of folded towels. "*She* certainly doesn't." The lady steps back as if he's contagious or something.

I shrug. "I just don't want him to hate me anymore."

"Honey, that's his hang-up," he says, helping me out of the Marlboro coat. I'm bare-chested underneath and he can see how cold so he hurries up, helping me get into my dryer-warm T-shirt and flannel. "The sooner you tell him to fuck off, the better you'll feel. And isn't that what matters?"

But I'm shaking my head, knowing there's no way I could ever say those two words. No way. And ever be his son again.

Donald laughs though. "Not to worry. I'll get you and your daddy back together. If it's the last thing I ever do. Scout's honor," he says, with the three-fingered Boy Scout salute.

13

MARSHALL FIELD'S & CO. FALL SALE
Hand-tooled Authentic Western Boots
By Acme. Sizes 6 1/2–13
Reg. $32 Sale $24.99

Oh, they're beautiful. The drawing of them fills the whole newspaper page so you see every detail, hand-tooled black leather with white Western swirls stitched up the sides. They cost $24.99, they come in my size, and you can pay with your Marshall Field's charge plate. It's what I wanted when I turned thirteen and they asked me. I said, "Cowboy boots." My dad ruffled my hair and said, "But then you'll need a pony and a ten-gallon hat," and Laura and Beth said, "Yes yes yes!" to the pony not the hat. But I didn't get any of it. My dad said it's not something boys wear unless you're in a rodeo or it's Halloween.

The cat jumps up on the purple sofa, nudges her way to my lap, crumpling the *Chicago Sun-Times.* The paper's old from last month I pulled from the litter box stack. And I don't have my mom's charge plate anyway. So. Goodbye, cowboy boots. Goodbye.

ROCK STAR Two words snag my attention.

FOUND A little headline under the comics and horoscopes.

DEAD Pull his name closer, so close it jumps up and punches my heart.

It's so hard to read about, but I have to, like the thirstiest kid in the world gulping dry words, but it's not enough and they don't tell you more or what you really want to know. That it's a lie. Not that he asphyxiated on his own puke. Not that he died all alone. Not that he's been dead since September 18 and I didn't even know the whole time.

I have to look away, but still *Jimi Hendrix* burns like a Polaroid flash in my eyelids. His name next to **Found Dead**. Reaching out for Gary or a telephone to call him but there is no phone here, there's no safety either from bad things you wish you didn't have to know or could stop from happening but you can't.

«happy birthday jamey»

Happy birthday, angel.

«what do you want for your birthday?»

I want to start over again. Is that cool with you?

«how about cowboy boots»

Tears come. Now I've gotta be sixteen, but I'm not ready at all and just want to say wait wait! let me straighten fifteen out first, I can't just leave fifteen still so messed up. But I don't know who to tell that to.

I'm curled up in the front seat of this rusted-out Cadillac, no tires, no engine, no radio. Just cracked upholstery dotted with burns and ankle-deep trash in the floor wells. Cigarette butts, empty bottles, crushed cans, tossed needles, fast food wrappers and bags. Trying to sleep, resting my head against the window frame where the glass is half broken and gone. Not sleeping either, just lying here not making a sound. If I keep still and don't cough maybe no one will find me.

Drug addicts, drunks, detectives, doctors, my dad. Donald's dates. The D people. So I'm keeping quiet.

Rock Star Found. Dead.

Trying to think on other things, try to clear *Dead* from my head.

Lay back and watch the universe. The sky is brittle with the coming of winter so condensation clouds every breath. Stark moon high above shining down, like a spotlight on every mistake.

Staring at the scars in my wrists, healed as they'll ever get. Knowing what it would take to open them again. I don't think I have what it takes. I don't think I ever had it.

Sadness is fine, Dr. Pauly said. It makes us empathetic and human. But not depression, not all the time. *Let's see if we can't make you happy again. Bite down on this and count to ten.*

Something touches my hair and I jump, whacking my head on the door frame. I curse out loud, but then see it's Donald, his face at the window, full lipsticked smile and beaming.

"Don't scare me like that," I say.

"My guest has departed, so..." he says, lifting my hands gently away to check my whacked skull, as if he could fix it or make me all better. "Come back in if you want to." His pink polished nails walk like cat paws over my palms to the scars. "I want you to." His smile sags and sobers, his gray eyes soften and fill. "I've been in that dark place too myself and I..." He looks down at his knees then up to the moon and returns with a smile for me. "I hope you found a way out."

I shrug, because it isn't past tense, it's still dark and what if there is no way out? "I did it on her birthday. My mom's birthday," I tell him. There's more. Tons more, but that's all I say.

"Honey, we hurt those that love us most," he says, which hurts just hearing him say it. "I wish I had someone who loved me that much." His hand circles the air like he's erasing that thought. He leans in, his arms wrap my shoulders and I pull away, but his soft kiss brushes my forehead. "I'm glad you're here," he whispers. "Happy birthday. James Daniel Ross."

"Did you try on the top?" Donald calls out from the bathroom. It's this satin blouse he's draped over the sofa, green, red, and yellow like a traffic light blinking, and not something you wear on your birthday. I shake my head, don't make me put that thing on. Thinking of a nice way to tell him no, I wander into the tiny bathroom and sit down on the closed toilet lid. On this crocheted poodle cover he got from some dumpster or church bazaar.

"What happened to Jimi?" Donald asks, saying *Jih-may*, like Hendrix does on the *Smash Hits* cassette.

"He's dead."

Donald rolls his eyes. "I meant, why did you turn off the tape? I thought you said he's the best guitar player in the world. Fine, remind me tomorrow to find the receipt. We'll exchange the cassette, that's all. Have you heard Babs' new album? *On A Clear Day You Can See Forever?* Oh, it's to die for. Absolute happiness."

So I roll my eyes now. But his head's tipped back looking in the mirror, carefully stroking on blue mascara making his eyelashes grow.

"What if you didn't put makeup on?" I say.

He dip-dips the wand in the tube thing. "Oh, how dull a diamond I would be."

"No, Donald, I'm serious."

He looks at me, the wand like a pointer your teacher uses to point you out to the class, how stupid you are or not paying attention. "Honey, we all can't have Twiggy lashes like yours."

"No, but you do it every day, dress up like a chick. So what if you didn't, just this one time for dinner."

He stops the wand mid-air, ready to stroke his left eye. "Would that make you happy?"

"It'd be the best present in the world."

"Better than Jimi?" And when I shrug, he goes, "Better than cowboy boots?" He nods at the drawing from the newspaper ad. Cool black cowboy boots, if I had the bucks or my mom's Field's charge plate, that's what I would get.

Donald twists the cap closed, drops it into a pink makeup case and takes out a jar of Noxzema.

Feeling so cocky, sort of triumphant, with Donald beside me walking down these city streets like friends. Except for brown penny loafers he's put dimes in instead, he's dressed mostly normal in a starched white T-shirt and pressed 501 jeans. But he's Donald, so it's more like a scene from *Rebel Without A Cause*, the Levi's cuffed and his red jacket worn collar up and unzipped like James Dean. His hair's combed back with Aqua Net into a greaser DA. But he's got on no makeup at all so he looks like a guy, and that's 'cause of me and my birthday.

DOREEN'S FRESH CUP DINER
coffee 10¢ ~ free refill

The waitress sets a plate of fries down, licks the end of her pencil, scribbles across her pad. She rips the page off, slaps the Guest Check upside down on the table. Plants a ketchup bottle from another booth closer to the plate. "Don't eat all the ketchup, boys," she says.

"'Boys.'" Donald's plucked brows bounce high on his forehead when he laughs. Smiling, freckles sprinkle the bridge of his nose, cheek to cheek. His gray eyes and concentration go back to this letter he's writing so secretive like always, with one arm fencing off his words. I'm not trying to read it either, I'm just kind of sitting here across from him in the booth, drinking hot cocoa he paid for, trying to ignore everybody else in this place. It's like if your eyes meet any of theirs, they think it's an invitation to get in your face.

At the counter they order whatever they want, breakfast or pie for dinner. But it's just a decoy, I'm not that stupid, I can see how they do it, the dance they move to, the desperate old men and the destitute young ones, entering alone, leaving together.

Every time they do the bell above the door jingles and Donald looks up, he grins or chuckles to himself then ducks his nose back to his lilac notepaper. Writing, writing, writing. I don't really want to know but I ask anyway. "What're you writing now?"

"A love letter to your father."

"What?" Reaching to grab it, but he snatches it back so I can't. "Donald!"

He just grins, twisting away from my snatching hands, folding the pages all precise into a matching lilac envelope he seals with a lick, keeping the letter out of my reach. "Did you call your Grandma Hannah yet?"

"Okay, my granma's 'Hannah Yet,'" I say. He looks at me, face and freckles all twisted up so I go, "That's a joke, Donald Griswold. Man, your sense of humor leaves a lot to be desired."

His pen flicks my arm, his grin breaks so wide and pretty shaking his head. It's weird that I should even think that about him, pretty, and with no makeup either. Really weird.

"Well, call *me* a cab," he says, smiling. "Did you *telephone* your grandmother yet?"

Granma Hannah, God. It's so easy when he says it but to do it, I don't know if I really can. I grab again for the letter he's written but he twists so my hand knocks the decoder instead, breaking it off his Secret Spy ring. Not on purpose, but still, regret fills me. I don't think he's taken it off since he got it. He fiddles with it in his fingers, snapping the ring back together. The letter unfettered lies on the table.

"You always write letters, huh, instead of just talking to people."

He leans closer. "Words disappear, once you say them, they're gone." He taps the sealed envelope with his purple pen. And that ring. "But see? Write them down and they exist forever."

Jingle-jingle. A flash of denim and a somber wool overcoat slip out the door. So I'm glad to have Donald blocking that out, watching Donald instead of the dance.

Jingle-jingle.

"Did I tell you I was in therapy for absolutely *years*, James? Dear Lord. They wanted me to confront the people who've screwed me up. Well, I certainly couldn't do that, I mean, could you?"

I shake my head, there's like no way I could and stay sane.

Donald agrees. "So they suggested I start by writing letters. When I'm feeling hostile, write a letter to the person who made me angry. When I'm feeling helpless, write to someone who's hurt me. When I'm in love, write that down, too." He's doodling on the cover of his lilac pad the whole time he's talking, and it's my name he's writing, over and over and over. *JAMES JAMES JAMES.*

"And you really mail them?"

"Oh, my heavens, no." He sighs and smooths his hair back with his fingers. "No. But it's helped me so much, I quit therapy altogether."

"Just from writing it down?"

But his eyes and wide smile are past me now and when I follow where they connect, I can see it's with this lumber-jacketed man seated at the counter. Recognition frosts my spine, it's the man with the red truck and police radio—law officer or detective. His sunglasses sit on top of his head, he's staring right back.

At us.

At *me.*

This creepy feeling stirs inside rising up my throat, and I turn my back, facing Donald. "Don't I get to read it? I mean, if it's like to my dad—"

But Donald tucks it in the pocket of his red James Dean jacket, lets his wrist fall limp at me. "You'd never let me mail it."

He's probably right about that.

"Well, well, well." The voice overhead, low and familiar so I know if I look up I'd see that detective towering over us both. "What a surprise," he says. "Wow such a sweet kid like you." Or maybe *street kid,* maybe that's what he says, *How much for a street kid like you.*

I don't look up. Donald does though.

My first thought is to like deny everything but then I see Donald's all smiles and it's when I remember, oh yeah, Donald is queer, he probably likes when men say that to him. So I slink down lower in this booth and out of their scene. But Donald leans toward me, not even whispering. "Ten? Twenty? Fifty. Enough for those cowboy boots, too."

Fear freezes like ice in my throat, looking frantic at Donald, shaking my head. "Shh, Donald! Don't say that! Don't say anything," I sort of hiss at him. "I think he works undercover."

Donald just grins. "Honey, don't we all?" His brows bounce on his forehead, he looks up at the detective, his fingers drumming his lower lip. "And from the size of things..." Donald stands slowly, eyes like paintbrushes swashing over the detective, head to crotch. "Well, hello, sailor," he says, checking that out. "Fifty. Minimum."

The detective's hand lands on my head though, like a huge rubber glove on my hair. "Fifty? How about that, kid? Hell, I'm coming over here to continue our conversation, maybe even buy you dinner. And your swishy boyfriend here tries to sell you off for a lousy fifty bucks."

"Uh—*excusem-moi*?" Donald's hand flags in the detective's face. "Major Miss Communication here? Not Angel, sweetheart. *Moi*." His palm thuds flat on his own chest.

"Fifty? Is that all you're worth?" The detective whistles in disbelief, shaking his head, his hand drops to the back of my neck embracing my shoulders. His face leans so close I can see every ruddy pore in his nose. "What're you doing, hanging around with queers and hustlers? You're better than this, kid. My job offer still stands. Five bucks an hour and your own room. How dumb and stupid do you have to be to pass that up?"

"What job? James? Your own room? You *know* each other?" Donald like a mother hen pecking away with questions. I just sink lower in this booth, trying to think what he's talking about, a job, five bucks, my own room, but places and conversations get jumbled, when did he offer me that?

I look away from the detective, wanting to just leave. Forget cowboy boots, forget birthday cake, I'm not hungry for dinner and just want to go home.

«home?» Well. To Donald's home. With Donald.

Donald whispers across the table through megaphone hands. "Sugar daddy, James. Sugar daddy! If you don't want him, I do I do I do I do!" His hands clasped and begging under his chin, so I almost laugh.

"You can have him," I say, and start to get up but too fast and whack my thigh on the edge of the table, so I'm stunned holding it, stuck getting out of this booth. I bet it's a bruise too, I can already feel how tender. The detective backs off.

When he does, Donald steps out before him all suddenly coy, one finger tracing a line from the detective's collar straight down. Over his shirt buttons, thick Playboy belt buckle, down. Grabbing a handful of the detective guy's nuts.

The detective jumps, I've never seen anyone jump like that, no grown adult before, I swear, if his big lumberjack boots weren't tied to his feet he'd have left them behind on the floor.

It's pretty funny, and it's not just me laughing, it's these other guys too, the hustlers or queers, the waitress, the men on the stools at the counter. This whole Fresh Cup Diner, cracking up.

Except the detective. He swears low and rumbling under his breath, eyes sharp with anger. He snatches Donald's arm, shoving past me so hard I have to stop myself tumbling over.

Donald raises his brow with a goofy smile, brushing against me, and *Z-Z-ZAP!* A static shock jolts from his hand to mine like a live circuit connected. It's so unexpected, I swallow it back, thinking, *oh God what was that?* and hoping Donald didn't notice.

"Well. Call *me* a cab," Donald says, his eyes sparkling electric with a giddy grin ear to ear, hesitating a moment with me, maybe two. Then he's yanked practically out of his penny loafers, the detective's plaid sleeve around Donald's shoulders, sweeping him up like a partner he's chosen, escorting him across the diner to the door.

"Cab!" I call to his ducktail. Donald giggles delighted with a happy glance back, then they're gone.

Jingle-jingle.

14

First thing: "Thanks so much for the *Smash Hits* cassette," that's what I'm going to say. I don't think I even properly thanked him and I feel bad about that. I don't really want him to return or exchange it, that's not why I ejected the tape. It's just, I wanted Jimi Hendrix *not* to be dead, but I guess Donald's right. Dead or no, he's still the best guitar player in the world, if I think about all the great music he made and not how depressing he's gone. So that's the first thing I'll say. *Thank you.*

Except it's been three days and Donald still hasn't come back.

Panic fills me, not so much from hunger, but from nightfall again, I'm all by myself, there's no one familiar, it's cold, and I'm tired with no place to crash. Crazy thoughts fill my head, like where would he be instead of with me? Probably with someone who's loving him back. Wearing his ring and frilly things, and touching each other in bed. So I don't know what good "thank you" would do, when I refuse to do any of that.

Walking slow, mostly backward, in case the red truck pulls up or some old croaker's car, and Donald gets out of the front seat. With money for supper and head shots and new cowboy boots, ready to start managing me.

A boy as beauticious as you, Donald said. *There must be fans fawning all over.*

I push open the door in this corner phone booth, latching myself inside, and heft open the *White Pages*, chained in a black binder sleeve. Heavy with pages, millions of fans, everyone probably who ate Sugar Sprinkles or shopped from the *Sears Christmas Wishbook*.

Flipping through, everything sidetracks me. Running my finger down endless gray listings, names pop into my head, names of people I used to know who maybe would let me stay. Like Spanier or Maroney. Or Bodie. Kyle Bodie, if he thought he owed me or wanted to thank me and maybe tried looking me up—am I listed? So I look up myself, which I know is crazy because it's my dad's house, even if I still lived there, it would list my dad's name, not mine. I know Laura's unlisted, I think my dad pays so she's not in the directory. There is a listing for James Ross though and I'm thinking on dialing the number. Except what would I say worth accepting the charges?

Cleveland. His name pops into my head. Asshole Cleveland, and still, I flip back from *R-O* to *C-L*, singing it to myself, the alphabet tune from kindergarten of all degrading things. *C* after *A-B*. *L* after *J-K*. And still it takes forever to look up his name. *C-L-eveland, Lowell*.

Cleveland. His parents would answer and have to say, "Lowell doesn't live here because he's a rapist. We raised a rapist. We brought a rapist into this world. Would you like to leave a message?" Then what would I say? And why would I want to? Nausea fills my chest.

There is no listing anyway, not for Lowell. Just *Cleveland, A.,* and *Cleveland, Bernard,* and *Cleveland Bros Glass & Hardware.*

Headlights pull over the second I push the phone booth door open, before I even stick out my thumb. A new Country Squire station wagon stops at the curb with fake wood side panels and a luggage rack, like you'd see in River Hills. Not an unmarked cop car or someone who'd bust you for curfew. Not a croaker ride with Donald inside, either.

The driver leans to the passenger seat, unlocks the button, pulls up on the handle to shove the door open, it falls back, he curses and catches it before it can latch. He's all smiling in a suit and tie, a briefcase, and the *Chicago Daily News* on the front bench seat. "Where ya headed?" he asks me, and pats the vinyl beside him.

I don't have an answer. I wanted to stay at Donald's.

«home, just say you're headed home»

I shake angel away, but sort of stumble off the curb, tripping smack against the fake wood with my shoulder. Ow. Holding the pain, catching my balance.

"Steady there, steady. Been out partyin', have ya?"

Partyin', like that's a career you get paid for, so I almost laugh. Passing headlights blind my eyes like camera flashbulbs so I'm blinking my vision back. I tell him, "Home. Like Uptown." I'm thinking that's where Rand hangs.

"Hop in," he says. A flurry of newsprint flutters into the footwell, the briefcase tossed over the seat. He smiles when I get inside, readjusts himself for driving. Cigars is what it smells like when I shut the door and breathe his air. Cigars and armpit sweat. It's tropical in here, like one hundred degrees, the heater turned all the way up.

«you could hike it. stick to the side streets you won't get hassled for curfew» Except this guy stopped and I'm already inside, it's late and I don't feel like walking. I push back my hair and slip out of the Marlboro coat.

The driver nods as soon as I'm sitting and pulls from the curb, merging with traffic to the corner stoplight. Exhaust fumes waver in a sea of red brake lights till *ping!* the light changes everything green, my Levi's cords, the dashboard, the colors of my flannel and skin, the headline under my feet.

TEEN FOUND DEAD IN DES PLAINES RIVER

«the des plaines river that's nearby» so an inkling of panic starts humming inside at the driver beside me, his shaded face in the dark stark as comic book art, black, white, green. He smoothly spins the wheel with one lime hand. His other hand loosens his belt. Unbuckling it, why? and unzipping his fly. Green money, a five-dollar bill drops on my lap.

Shaking my head, my cheeks burning. "Wait. I just want a ride. That's all."

"Yeah?" He flicks the signal on, turns into a corner Sunoco, to let me out, I'm thinking. But he passes right by the pumps to the back of the station. Lights off, so it's all instant blackness and floating shadows, passing a trash hopper and stopping against the alley brick wall. He shifts the gear and shuts off the engine so silence takes over the car.

Dead Teen Found. HAVE YOU SEEN ME? Maybe Donald's queer friend on the flyer.

«you're not queer. just tell him he made a mistake» The crumpled five in my hand damp and sweaty. I choke out some words, any words. "Wait, wait. I—I'm not what you think." How stupid that sounds.

"What do I think?" he says.

My heart racing, I don't want to know, avoiding the headline below and the movement in his lap. Outside the window it's solid brick, like a punishment you get, On The Wall. Where they make you stand till piss warms your pants then they step up behind you and kick out your feet so your teeth hit the shower room floor. *I want to go home,* that's all I said that time too.

Reflected in the window, his gaping boxers and fist jerking off in his lap. His words faraway, I refuse to let in, jumble like alphabet soup, *suck* and *swallow* and loudest of all, *stupid,* I add that myself. The metal scrapes brick when I yank on the handle to open the door. I can't open the door. *Stuck.*

All of a sudden his hand hooks my neck and he's shoving my face to his dick. *No no no I don't want to!* but my lips rub against it for one awful moment, I jump back and *WHACK!* my elbow twangs into the steering wheel. A shockwave shoots through, elbow to wrist, and *splat!* just like that his load squirts my shirt and my hair—I snap from his grip, my back slamming against my coat and the door. Cradling my elbow and rocking.

"Hit your funny bone, didja?" He grabs my numb arm and clenches my collar, pulling me to him again.

"Let me *go*—" with a swift kick, my foot off the floor, to his forearm, his hand, then hard as I can, kick his jaw. His head bumps his window, his grip gone. I scramble up on gangly legs, front seat into the back, landing bam! with my knee on the hard edge of something, a tire iron or crowbar on the floor. I'm grappling to unlock the back door button but he yanks half my hair like a weed he's pulled up, my fingers can't loosen his grip. I grasp the crowbar instead, so sharp-edged and heavy, it takes both hands to lift up and hold steady. Raised and ready to swing or let fall, all set to crack open his skull.

His hands spring open letting me go, he shields his head with both arms. "Jesus! What the hell's a matter witch ya?"

"I'm *mental*," I say, but gravity takes over, the crowbar swings down toward his head. He ducks to one side so sparkling shards fly when it shatters the window instead.

I raise the crowbar again, lifting it to the ceiling with both hands. He cowers, "Don't kill me!" blubbering under folded arms. "All right, all right, you little prick! Go! Just go!"

Hate fills my fingers, this urge surges through me to punish and maim him and smash his head in like a Halloween pumpkin—

«stop» angel says. «just stop»

I drop the crowbar to the floor. Yank up on the door handle, the door swings away, swinging me with it out in a free fall for one detached moment. Then crash landing on sharp alley gravel and glass shards that cut into my knees. The Marlboro coat tossed out next to me. The grumble of his engine roars to life, his car taking off in a red cloud of choking exhaust, tires spitting stinging debris. Scrambling to stand up, grabbing for something, anything, a brick, and grunting to wing it right through his window, crack open the back of his head—

«stop» angel says. «just stop»

Flip both faucets full force with shaky hands in the BK restroom. Water pounds out, splashing the basin and spotting this mangy suede coat. Hate hits me hard, nothing's changed, nothing's changed! Eight months at Railton, it's just all the same, all broken glass and regret, slamming Ratachek through a window and now this perv guy with a crowbar in his own car so who's the psycho then?

«you didn't kill anybody»

You stopped me! Or I would've, what if I had? I wanted to angel so bad! Oh God, I deserved to be sent away, Grampa was right, Mandi's dad and everybody in the whole school and juvenile court, the honorable Judge C. F. Horton, "Probation revoked!" Throw out the key and lock me away with rapists and chains forever.

«you did the right thing»

How is that right? He'll just go pick up some other kid now— God! What if he's the killer? What if that was really the guy and I got in his car, angel, why did I even get in his car? I'm so stupid, so dumb and stupid, I messed up again, I never think right. I'm no good at this game, I lose every time. I'm never going to get better! Why would you even want to be with me? Why would you still hang around?

«because I love you»

Well, it does, when he says that, it does calm me down.

Scrub my palms, my hair, my face and lip where it touched him, my flannel stuffed deep in the garbage can. Trying so hard not to retch or think, *because I love you* echoing in my head like a reason to keep breathing. But repugnance is all I see in the mirror, a criminal, a mental case, a queer. And Rand, like proof I'm disgraceful, steps in behind me. Rand, not saying a word.

I give him the crumpled green five from my pocket. He gives me more heavenly pills.

There's no one here to let me in, nobody answers the door. I'm thinking I shoulda took all of the pills instead of just three or four. Waiting for Donald on his front stoop for I don't even know how long, huddled into the grubby Marlboro coat, clenching the collar tight to my throat, my head muddled with bad thoughts and fog. Till finally finally finally this waddling woman with a flock of brown children unlocks the entry door. I get up, stumbling to follow behind them, through the mailbox foyer and stairwell door. They head up the stairs, I head down the hallway to Donald's. Rap my knuckles soft at first not wanting to disturb whatever he's doing with his date or sugar daddy.

"Donald?" Knocking harder so the sound finds the little kitchenette, the closet, and bathroom shower, even if it's cold or just a trickle, his books, his plants, his sofa bed, I want so bad to be in there. His flowered sheets. The cat you can hear inside mewing like crazy.

"Can I just talk to you?" Hit the door again *WHAM!* my palm flat to the wood then my fist, harder, which echoes all down the hallway. The door at the end of the hall swings open and the Medusa pops out like a Jack-in-the-Box, which spooks me.

"You sick people!" She screeches, finger pointed. "I see what goes on! You tell 'Mr.' Griswold, he can take his nasty business and the whole damn lot of you straight to hell!" Shaking her keys at me, she retreats, then pops out again. "And tell him to feed his damn cat!" *BAM*, her slamming door rattles the walls.

My back against Donald's door, sinking down it like a slide. Huddled on his welcome mat, flowery like his sheets or a Mother's Day card, covering my ears, not wanting to hear myself beg. "Donald, please don't do this to me," pressing my palms hard as I can but the words spew out anyway like pukey peach slime thick in my throat. "It's okay," that's what Donald wants me to say, the two words he's been waiting to hear since day one. Swallowing *okay* like a terrible secret, shaking my head no, no, no. Mumbling, "You can violate my trust now. Or violate whatever you want."

But the door doesn't open. Just crying mew mew mew and no answer.

part four
hannah

15

"Untitled"

(Boy with No Shoes), 1970, barefoot on hardwood

There are paintings here worse than me, I tell her. I've been
through every gallery, Byzantine, Arms & Armor, the Renaissance,
Modern Art, it's not just all portraits and still lifes. There's death
and destruction, disasters of war, medieval tortures, even X-rated
stuff pretty much, framed and displayed, wall after wall after wall.
Pillaging soldiers, the Spanish crusades, French brothels, and
Christ crucified in thousands of ways. But I'm the one they point at
and whisper about, I'm the one they don't want to look at and tell
her to escort out.

"Where are your shoes?" She wants to know. "It's cold outside,
did you walk here without any shoes?"

Looking down at my feet, I wasn't thinking if anyone would
notice. "It's warm here."

She smiles a lot more calmly than me. "Let's talk in my office,
cool?"

I nod, cool, because she's the first person who listens when I say,
you can't leave your shoes out to dry they get stolen still sopping wet,
but I did have their free coffee and that was good but not very hot.

She's got a red blazer and security badge, one hand on my
shoulder guiding me toward the main stairway.

The atmosphere is kept perfect in here, they've got tiny meters in clear plastic boxes on the wall of each gallery space. There's hidden alarms and red blazer guards keeping the art here secure and protected. In the art institution. A safe place where no one can harm it.

You can't sleep here, it's for priceless things, I can understand that, but still. She nods and asks, "Did you get separated from the people you came with today? You seem to be lost."

"I know," I say. "It's scary all alone, I don't know what happened, I had things worked out pretty much I thought." The truth swarms around my ears, twitching my eyes and unsteady hands, how lost I am. "I admit what I did was not the right thing, all delusional and shameful like my dad said, like someone repugnant he wouldn't want to ever live in his house. I just want to get it straight in my head what I am and what I am not, I was working that out and trying to get clean but my coin got stuck in the washing machine."

"There wasn't a manager at the laundromat to help you?"

"It was a slug, I used a slug. I didn't have a quarter."

"Ahh. And you didn't want to get in trouble for that."

See, she understands so I know she's a person I can talk to. "I can't believe all the people crowded around *La Grande Jatte*. Like that's the painting they all come to see. But there's tons of much better art here. *The Old Guitarist* or Rembrandt. Even the haystacks and ballerinas. My granma loves those."

"Ah," she says, "the Impressionists," so I nod and say that's what I once got my little sister for Christmas. *The Star*, that's Degas. Well, a print of it anyway. From the gift shop. Framed for her room.

Going down the grand stairway she says to be careful, hold onto the railing, she thinks she can find me some shoes. "Is Grandma here with you today?" she asks. "Perhaps we can find her, too."

"Well, I looked in antiquities, she wasn't there."

She smiles, I made her smile. "You could be a docent here—you know a lot about art," she says. She walks me right past the crowded line at the coat check counter, down a little corridor, she opens the STAFF room door. "I'd need to know your name, of course. For your security tag."

"I probably need my meds first, though. Not these blue ones I've been doing, my granma already said that. I need to be medicated. And my tooth got chipped," I bare my front teeth, "so it would depend on the dental plan."

"I see." She smiles. "It's a great dental plan. Very comprehensive."

Her teeth do look good. "I wish I was better at life. I wish I knew how you do it without messing everything up."

"Shh, shh," she says, guiding my hands away from where they rip tangled knots from my hair.

She's got lunch that she gives me, PB&J cut in two triangles wrapped in wax paper, Fritos, three Oreos, and while I'm eating she picks through a big box of Lost & Found stuff. A knit cap, mittens, red high top Flyers some art student left in a locker. A big art student, I guess. A lot bigger than me. They flop like clown shoes on my feet.

But when I'm decked out in it all she admires me like her own work of art. "We're friends now, right, Angel?" she asks. Angel, that's the name that I told her, sometimes it's too hard to be James. "Let's find Grandma's number and give her a call, how's that?" she says, taking a phone book out of some drawer and plopping it down on her desktop.

She turns the desk phone toward me. I don't move though, just stare blankly when it hits me what happens next.

"Angel?" Her palms teeter like the scales of justice. "What's worse? Grandma coming to get you, or sleeping alone on the street?" She hands me the receiver like there is no decision to make.

Flipping the pages to Grampa's last name. *R-O-S- Rosenberg*. He'll probably always be pissed my dad changed it to Ross. What if I switched my name back? James Rosenberg. He can't hate me if I do that.

Dialing, I mess up, my fingers're thick and the dial's too heavy. So it's good she's not watching, she's stepped out for fresh air or, or maybe her break time. I'm glad she can't see how retarded I am, redialing it over three times.

BRRIIING. I don't give Granma a chance to say no, this storm in me rising and ready to blow. It does when she answers, her small voice polite and "Hello?" It blasts out before she hangs up. "Granma, it's me, it's angel, don't hang up okay, I'll probably kill myself or some other dumb thing."

"Jamey?"

Chills through me, it's her. It's really her. I did it. So I want to scream out loud I did it. See, Donald? Who needs you anyway. Your letters and lies about phone calls tomorrow. I'm almost smiling. "It is, it's, it's, it's Jamey."

"Where are you, dolly? Are you at the hospital?"

Dolly, so another knot tightens my chest. And *hospital*— "What? No, wait, you can't tell my dad. Please please please, Granma, promise you won't. You can't tell him. You can't say it's me to *anyone*."

"Dear God, what happened?"

I tell her I just need to get money. I don't have any money.

"Where are you, Jamey, can you come over by me? You come to Grandma's right now."

"No, but I can't. I can't do it."

A moment of silence. "Then Grandma's coming to you, tell me where."

It's a trick, another trick. She's got other people there, Grampa I bet, my uncle, my dad, even Pauly. So at first I'm not going to but then terror builds of nightfall again and what happens next? So I do. I'm thinking, meet her outside, it's the smart thing to do, where there aren't any walls or red blazers. "In, in the park, Granma. By the Art Institute. You know, like when I was little. But just you, okay?"

"Wait there for Grandma, Jamelah. By the statue of the little fisher boy."

My granma's coming to give me money. God, my granma loves me so much.

My head's finally calm with the magic of blue pills and memory snapshots of when I was at her apartment. She washed my clothes. She made me French toast and her own bed to sleep in. She likes having me in her life. She's not ashamed or grossed out at all.

Donald should meet her, they'd hit it off. Even if he is colored and wears ladies' clothes, she won't care. She knows how to get through life. She knows how to get along with everyone.

But walking to meet her is hard. These lost and found shoes slip off my heels even double-knotted, they flop on my feet and make me go slow or stumble, so I'm glad hardly anyone's around to see. The few people that are walk hurriedly by like they've got some place urgent to be. It's just squirrels in the park pretty much, romping around like it's recess, and pigeons strutting in flocks on the ground, or gathered on all the park benches. Till something unseen makes them flutter their wings and take flight. They leave pasty white splatters all over the seat slats like abstract expressionist art. *"No Place to Sit"* 1970, park bench with bird shit.

I forget for a minute where I'm even going and why did I come to Grant Park. «granma is coming» angel reminds me she wants to see me. «wait by the statue» he says.

The water's turned off at Buckingham fountain, it's just a pool of litter and dead leaves. There's silver glints that aren't dimes or someone's lost diamond, just tossed bits of foil or pop can pull rings when you swish your foot through the debris. Cigarette butts, faded bus schedule pages, *The Chicago Seed* free press, and Jesus Saves! flyers, which are kind of depressing to see.

The four sculpture children, like friends cast in bronze, pose in the centers of their own concrete ponds. *The Fisher Boy* frozen perfectly still like the game of "Statues" kids play. Except whoever calls "unfreeze!" has gone away, so he's stuck here forever holding a fish.

Perched on the edge of a concrete bench, I keep the Marlboro coat clenched to my chest, blocking the wind that creeps through my T-shirt. I'm glad for the knit hat, even the shoes, and mittens that don't really match.

"Jamey?"

When I look up, my granma's face caves, every wrinkle digs deeper aging her five years at least. Foreign words like religion spill from her lips tinted red. "Oy kine-ahora..."

I don't get up from the park bench to greet her. When she bends down and hugs me, I hardly feel a thing.

Her smile wavers looking at me or from some sour taste on her tongue. "What are you doing to yourself, tatalah?"

It's cold even in the sun. My scabbed knees peek out stringy holes in my cords. The hems drag pretty ragged and worn. "No, well, I got medication just like you said."

She scrubs dirt off my face with her spit on a hankie. I pull away. "I just need some money, that's all."

Her hand juts out for mine. "Come with Grandma," she says, like when I was little, like she's taking me with to visit the Rembrandts, the miniature Thorne Rooms, and to feed the ducks in Grant Park.

But her voice lowers, more somber than happy. "I believe you when you talk about suicide, Jamey. And it scares me."

A brisk wind flaps her colorful scarf like a flag of distress or an SOS signal for the Coast Guard or Grampa to come to her rescue. "Granma...I'm not gonna do that." Downs are protection like deep icebergs that only let weightless words bob to my tongue. Just barely. "I already promised. Don't be scared."

"Sweetheart, you need help."

"Drugs help. You said to take them, that's cool. You told that to me, Granma."

Her brows droop with worry, she clasps her purse tight to her coat. "Come back to Grandma's. We'll eat a little something. We'll make hot cocoa."

"But then Grampa or, or my dad'll spit in my face."

"No, no, kine-ahora. You don't know that."

«oh yes kine-ahora you do! she must think you're stupid and easy to fool»

Squinting up, looking at her. It's hard, though. Makeup so fake, faker than Donald's even. Red misshaping her lips. Circles of rouge mar her cheeks more like bruises. She shakes her head slowly. Her eyes cloud, all foggy and dull.

I try to get up but it's like I'm a statue. The Retard Boy, ha, cast out and stoned. "I thought you loved me anyway. Even if I flunk math or mess everything up. You don't make me feel shitty like I'm wasting air."

"Oy, Jameleh...You need nice winter clothes, new boots, a safe bed. Let Grandma help you. Please."

"Oh...I..." Pushing myself away best I can off the bench. My arms and head heavy though make me sink back. My neck numb against the shitty concrete slat. "My friend Donald's gonna get me new boots. And a new coif..." I smile at her, she's my granma and she's here. That's something, angel. She's here. "He wants to be my manager, Granma. And like...manage me."

"I'd like to meet your friend Donald very much."

"Yeah, but you can't. He went to..." Thinking about where, I'm not sure. Someplace first-class. That's what he said. Like Hawaii or the Virgin Islands. So I'm almost laughing, thinking about that. The *Virgin* Islands. "I can stay with him when he gets back."

She nods with arched eyebrows like a sad cartoon. And tucks loose hair gently under this knit hat, I didn't know was over my eyes. I pull away. "I don't have money. I thought you might maybe gimme some. Like before."

"How much, tatalah?"

Seeing this old weathered granma so unfamiliar. Do I even know her at all? Her purple wool coat and matching cloche hat, an old-fashioned brooch and antique pearl hatpin. She lowers her head, pokes through her purse and everything precious tucked safely inside. She asks for promises. "Promise you'll call if you need munnier anna maabaa..." Her voice tiny, tiny as a little mouse. She gives me her money.

A chill rattles through me or maybe the wind's picking up, colder than ever from the North Pole, whipping in over the lake. It flutters the dead leaves, scattering trash and whatever it touches, birds, old ladies, words, and promises. Except the stoned statue children. Holding their poses they don't even shudder.

16

I know what Rand means when he asks "How yew doin," not really a question like your doctor wants to know, more like a test to see what you've got, more money for pills or a reason to take them, *amobarbital sodium* or whatever he said.

He asks if my boyfriend ever came back, and I say Donald isn't my boyfriend. He checks out these new winter boots I've got on, the only promise to Granma I probably won't break. From the Men's Footwear Department at Marshall Field's, from the newspaper ad at Donald's. Black leather with white stitching, pointy toes, and raised heels that make a solid *clump* sound with each step. Even though they cost half the fifty she gave me. Even though they're most likely the reason Rand cares, *How yew doin'*, like new cowboy boots are proof I'm doin' all right. Even though I'm all sneezy and can't catch a breath or see him too clearly, through watery eyes and wheezing, I think I'm allergic to Rand. Nobody moves to slap my back or offer a cure or hot cocoa, none of these street boys or drug addicts do. They just mutter, "Whoa, man, stay away from me," and move far from my germs to the gutter.

Except Durrand Jennette. "C'mon, Angel," Rand says. "Before yew freeze yer damn halo off."

He knows all the shortcuts through back alley fire escapes, between buildings and busted fences. Rats through a maze, that's what it's like, bypassing the city through shady neighborhoods you'd never want to exit from the highway. And the seedy hotel he takes me to, I follow him inside, feeling my skin crawl to be here. Past a fingerless desk clerk caged in dense metal grating. Up a wide, musty stairwell, three steps at a time. Ignoring bad smells, distant crying and yelling, darting cockroaches, and mystery stains, following Rand like I'm Helen Keller.

The hall he turns down is empty and cold where a window's blown out at one end. He opens the first splintered door on the right, smudged up so bad I can't tell what color, and enters the room without knocking.

Everything flashes popsicle orange from the HOTEL sign outside the window, revealing skeletal figures each time the neon flicks on. They surround Rand the moment he steps inside, all shaky and sick with chalky skin, unwashed and sour, folded bills clutched in their fingers.

I keep my eyes lowered, ha, as if that would set me apart.

It's quick, how they do it, like a handshake almost, trading their cash for these knotted party balloons Rand slips from his pocket, then scurrying off with their stash like squirrels. The room clears out in maybe ten minutes and Rand kicks the door shut after the last junkie goes. He pulls a Marlboro hardpack from his black satin pocket and plops down on a bare queen-size mattress. It's the only furniture here, aside from this big cardboard box full of rank-smelling clothes.

I shift in these new boots where the stiff leather cuts into my toes.

Rand dumps the pack out on the warped hardwood floor between his legs splayed before him. It's not cigarettes spilled out with the lighter though, and I step in closer to see. A severed spoon, eyedropper, wadded gray cotton, tie-off, and syringe. And two of those knotted balloons. One red one, one blue.

Drips from the eyedropper puddle the powder he's dumped from the blue one into the spoon. A stir with the tip then the click of the flame from his lighter beneath cooks it like gravy or Nestlé's Quik. He draws all the liquid into the syringe, till there's none left in the spoon. Then flick-flicks it twice with his fingernail and squirts a quick spurt in the air.

I'm about to ask, where'd you learn how to do that? but he's handing the shot to me.

Crazy *crazy* so loud in my head, angel is pleading with me. For all the times when I needed him, this time he says he needs me. He won't survive if I'm not alive, he won't survive the first shot. He knows if I do it I'll never come back. «don't kill me like that» he cries.

It's angel who wins the argument, he's always been stronger than me. I'm not like Rand, that's what I argue, and I swear I won't ever be. But angel is right, one shot wouldn't be enough, and neither would two or three. It scares me how easy just pushing my sleeve up would be.

I step back. "I...I just want the blue ones, Rand."

"Love them blues," Rand mumbles, chuckling at nothing or maybe at my argument with nobody he can see.

«what's worse?» angel asks me, but I don't really know. I'm not good at judging worse things. Go back to my dad's and whatever his plan is, or go mental alone on the street?

Go home, give up, turn myself in. Strap me down and sedate me, electro-convulsive therapy, that's what I *most likely* need. ECT, therapists. Rules and restraints and the right medication. My real family. My real name. My real life. So I can't remember, why did I even leave?

Everything's blurry, the reasons and horror. Thinking I could do this on my own and didn't need their therapy at all. I could heal myself if they left me alone, but I don't think that's happening.

Rand's Beatle boot kicks my brand-new Acme's. "Nice boots," Rand says, the syringe clenched in his teeth. Hunched over, he rolls up his sleeve.

Dry my eyes on this gritty wool cuff, turning my back, leaving Rand with his drugs, and clumping quick in new boots out the door. Down the hall and hollow dark stairwell, this knit hat pulled low. Past the manager's cage, across the lobby, bursting into the light of day. Shuddering the argument out of my head, hurrying toward home, come what may.

But I can't go back as ratty as this. If I'm going to go back at all.

17

A smell like old people or the clothes they once wore hits me the instant I step in the secondhand store. GOODWILL INDUSTRIES. Even the air's already been used, so it just makes me queasy to breathe it.

A handwritten sign says "HALLOWEEN!" in black marker on a rack packed with used clothing a hobo would wear or a hooker or maybe a clown. Old corsets, bashed-in hats, mismatched suits, baggy pants, so angel laughs, «who do you want to be?» Ha, so I go, James Daniel Ross, which rack's got the costume of me? But I really don't know, I'm not even kidding. My mom buys my clothes and everything else, filling my closet at home and The Oaks. But I doubt she'd ever come here. Not even to donate stuff I won't wear, like if it's outgrown, or dorky, or a style from last year. She just leaves it all in garbage bags on the curb for Goodwill to pick up.

«maybe your old stuff is in here somewhere. maybe you can buy your stuff back»

So I start looking around for something familiar I used to wear. Or Tommy's old clothes, I'd even wear those, his chinos or Wranglers or varsity sweaters. I keep my arms folded though. Creepiness bristles my skin just touching the used stuff in here.

The boys' clothing rack is way in the back, not separated by aisles or even a sign. Just boys' shirts all mixed up 6x to 16, it's a guess what size even fits me. Solids, paisleys, florals, stripes. Holding a madras one up to my chest but I don't know if it's the best choice. Like what my grampa would snipe at my mom if I wore it, because she's a Gentile and does nothing right. "Like a shaygets she dresses him," or "in torn dungarees yet," proof that whatever I do is her fault.

Against this one wall there's white short-sleeved school shirts, and a whole rack of black chino slacks or dark blue. Well, forget that, it's not the uniform so much or the crests on the pockets, *St. Thomas Catholic, Immaculate Conception, Sacred Heart*—my mom doesn't want me wearing short sleeves. But this one collar label, Arrow Shirt Company, sticks out from the rest. I grab the hanger and tug it free from the rack.

It says JAMES in the crest, *ST. JAMES The Lesser*. A white long-sleeve school shirt with my name on the chest pocket in gold and blue thread. A straight Arrow Shirt just like Grampa would wear, or somebody who shops at Sears.

I drop the Marlboro coat to the floor, slip into the new schoolboy shirt. Well, it's new to me, that's what I'm thinking, crisp cotton stiff from the cleaners. *My* new shirt with long cuffs that cover my wrists. Flipping the collar down under my hair, I run my hand over the slack rack. Find nicer pants, too, blue school uniform ones, from St. Paul's or Bernard's, size 28. Perma-Prest, so they won't ever wrinkle.

Put the blue chinos down on the counter. The old lady cashier smiles like a granma or somebody kind, with gray hair in a bun and an apron. I pull out the torn lining from my cords pocket, spilling what's left on her counter. It's only thirty-five cents but she smiles all grateful like it's thirty-five dollars or something.

So I smile too, and ask if there's a fitting room or someplace I could change. Her thin hand on my new crisp white sleeve directs me, to a faded red curtain draping a doorway on the back wall.

Soft rays of daylight streak through the curtain when I push it aside and duck into the backroom it hides. Between shelves stacked with dishes, encyclopedia volumes, weird kitchen gadgets, I change out of these cords. I have to sit on the floor to tug these new cowboy boots off, and the moment I do, it's like instant relief. Bubbled blisters sting my toes and the skin on my ankle's rubbed raw.

You just burn a needle to sterilize it, to pop blisters without getting infected. Like the merit badge in the *Boy Scout Handbook* my big brother earned for First Aid, and he never got sick or gangrene. It's probably what I should do. Except I don't have a needle. Or a match.

There's masking tape on the shelf, which I tear off the roll with my teeth and stick like Band-Aids on my ankle and blisters. And there's voices close by outside the curtain, silhouettes ripple on the red fabric, a triangle of daylight spears through. Icy drafts waft in from the opened back door. Fresh wintry air, like welcome perfume.

Hurrying to get dressed before the voices come back here, buttoning the shirt to my neck. Tucking the tails into clean schoolboy chinos, I don't have a belt, that's okay.

In a cracked wardrobe mirror, I look pretty normal with no rips in my knees or stains. I can't read my name, the letters all jumble, but I like knowing it says JAMES. I'm not sure what to do with the clothes my mom got me, the T-shirt and torn Levi's cords. There's no garbage can, but then why would they need one? They can just stick a price on it. 5¢ or 10.

Pulling the faded curtain aside, I'm about to ask, but I stop. Because I know the voice I'm hearing now, low and rumbling and familiar. The voice of the man in the red truck, the detective. The voice that took Donald away. "Hell, you ladies treat me so well, I may have to stop by more often."

Swallowing a lump like school paste, stepping out before the plaid lumber jacket.

His chin rises and the detective grins, looking down at me behind those black sunglasses. "Well, well, well," he bellows. His whole self fills the opened back door so there's no sneaking past him. These two old cashier ladies act like they're flattered, they flirt for attention, cocking their heads just like hustlers. His beefy fingers lift the shades from his eyes to his forehead. "What're you, on your way to confession, James?"

I'm thrown off completely when he calls me by name. "P-pardon?"

"Come here, James. Come on." Pushing on the Goodwill back door, back-stepping outside to the alley parking lot, this detective beckoning me and calling me James now, how come? This fear I'm about to be busted, for what I don't know, breaking probation, running away, or this stolen tape wrapping my toes?

«whatever he wants, that's his reason»

But who told him my name? Thinking on that. The Greyhound Bus cop, Ms. Poole from juvenile court, or maybe Doreen at the Fresh Cup Diner? Or Donald, the last time I saw him.

«maybe he just read your shirt»

I slip deeper into the Marlboro coat, clasping it closed, hiding my name on the pocket. Squinting up at him in the sudden brilliance of the sun.

"Looks like you're dressed for church, kid," he says, holding the door open for me.

"Or a mental institution," I say. That just pops out.

His sunglasses sit on top of his head, he grins, squinting back. "Is that a fact."

Gravel crunches under my boot heels, wiggling my toes but still it cuts, the bite of the tape digging deeper. "How come you're here?" It's all I can think to ask.

"Got a little donation to drop off." He winks. "You in a hurry? I could use a hand. That is, if you can spare a few minutes before the men in white arrive."

What he says makes me smile because I have lots of minutes, I have all the spare time in the world. And it's my time to take, at my own retard pace whether I'm alone on the street in Uptown tonight or I'm back in restraints tomorrow. So when he tells me he'll pay me to unload his truck, there's no reason really to refuse. "Five bucks," I tell him.

He offers his hand and I shake it.

It's not his same truck, not the red Chevy pickup, it's more like a two-door with a regular front seat and a truck bed stuck on where a back seat would be. A maroon El Camino. With **R. Hunt, Sr. & Son Construction** in fancy white script on both doors.

"Handsome little muscle machine, eh?" He's patting the hood like a good dog. "Style and power," he says, pointing out all its features, 8-track, A/C, super sport auto tranny, 454 V-8 under the hood. "Plus utility for hauling a payload." He nods at the payload in back.

I unload these full trash bags all by myself from his truck bed into the Goodwill back room. He doesn't help, just stays inside joking with the Goodwill ladies, their bodies shriveled and spotted with age but flirting no different than chicks at my school or friends of my sisters. The detective is digging on it you can tell, charming the old raisin ladies. They smile at each brown plastic bag I lug in, thanking me for the donations, mostly ladies' stuff, dresses and skirts or nightgowns. Some briefs and boxers mixed in too, but who would buy those? It's gross just to see them. I deny it's my stuff but they clasp their hands anyway, God-blessing me for my charity. Bringing God into it now. So I'm thinking I don't want to be paid after all. Because where's the goodwill in that.

The last bag full of shoes is heavy and awkward, a high heel or thick sole split the brown plastic and I have to go back out for a few that fell through. A high-heeled boot, a tennis shoe, a penny loafer with a dime. Like Donald did so I guess it's a fad or cool thing you do and Donald wasn't so clever.

«or maybe this is his shoe»

The detective's in the doorway, his back to me, still chatting. I'm standing outside, the shoe in my hand. Donald's shoe, maybe.

«go ahead just ask him»

"Whose is this?" I say, so both their heads turn, the lady who took my thirty-five cents and the detective. Staring at me like I just broke a law so the words choke out guilty. "It...fell out of the bag."

His brows raise, he takes the loafer from me like a foreign thing, inspecting the sole and inside. For a name, I'm thinking, or some form of ID, but no. He plucks the dime out, hands it to the lady. "There's a cup of coffee right there for some poor bum," he says and chucks the shoe in the trash bin behind him.

"God bless you both," she says, dropping the dime in her cashbox and smiling all grateful at me. "My, my. Doesn't he look handsome in nice clothes?"

The detective's arm encircles her shoulders like a meaty shawl. "Like an angel," he says, leaning back in approval at the clothes I've got on, these blue school chinos and Arrow shirt. "Rare to see these days. Kid his age dressed for Sunday School."

"Oh, come now, Richard, not that rare." She picks a stray thread or blond hair off my sleeve. "Thanks to donations from St. James Parish. And charitable Catholics like you."

His cheeks flush for maybe one moment. "I do what I can," he tells her. "Some of these punks, though. Going straight to hell, even dressed like choirboys." He winks at me when he says it.

"Oh, I think Our Lord would disagree," she says, patting his hand. "There's good inside each of us, so Jesus teaches, if we just dig deep enough."

This detective—*Richard*—smirks. "Might pray for a bigger shovel then," he says. His big meaty hand lands on my shoulder, with a quick nod at me. "Five bucks. Are we cool?"

18

There's a black satchel taking up most of the floor well at my feet, so I have to sit straddling it, one foot on each side. Riding in the detective's El Camino. **R. Hunt, Sr. & Son.** *Richard.* Giving me a ride to my granma's.

"Richard," I say loud over the rumble of the 454 V-8. "That's your name."

"Hunt, kid. Mister Hunt to you."

Mr. Hunt. *Mister*, not *Detective*, so I don't know if that's true. But I like calling him Richard. It sort of evens things. "You really thought I was going to confession?"

"Boy, was I off." He guffaws, more like a clown though and not 'cause he said something clever. "Mental institution, aren't you a little overdressed for that?"

"Yeah, well. I'm going to my granma's first."

Turning his head, he's looking at me and not at the road. "What, no *tux*?" He's trying to be funny, I realize that, but it's true if they had one I'd probably be wearing it now. Ha, a Goodwill tux and what good will that do. He checks his watch. "She expecting you for dinner?"

"She's not expecting me at all."

Out the window the city passes in a blur. Blurry people, blurry park, the whole city out of focus, the whole world. I have to look away, down at these cowboy boots so stiff and killing my feet, I'm just glad I don't have to walk. Wipe at a scuff already marring the new black leather.

I'm suddenly missing those floppy red high tops. I chucked them at Field's and what if I went back to get them? I can't stand it and yank this one cowboy boot off, the worst one, with a double blister biting my baby toe and the tape gnawing raw through my ankle.

Richard looks away from the road again, all casual like he's not even driving. At my bare foot on the seat with peeling tape and ripe blisters ready to pop.

"What's the matter, new boots?"

I nod, rubbing the raw skin on my toe. "I promised my granma. So."

He nods. "Well, you look like a choirboy. Grandmas love shit like that."

"Not grampas, though. Well, not my grampa." Not really wanting to put it back on, wanting the other boot off. Smoothing out the Goodwill fabric, these blue chinos, this white shirt already wrinkled and getting sweaty just thinking of Grampa. "I just want to look normal."

"Normal? Normal people do not look like you, kid. Believe me." He's popped those sunglasses back on so you can't see his eyes or know where he's looking. "Quit picking that. You want to infect it?"

When I shrug, no, why would anyone want an infection, his lips purse, he shakes his head. "Jesus Christ, let me look at that." With one hand sharply spinning the wheel, he veers out of traffic into a tight parking space at the curb.

Next to a cemetery. A wrought iron gate topped with pointed daggers like a horror flick or something medieval. Headstones inside, towering ones like statues of saints with the names of the dead carved in capital letters. Like how important they were but dead anyway and locked behind gates forever.

Words come out in a coughing fit that makes my eyes water. "You never said whose shoe it was. Or all those clothes, where they came from."

He faces me expressionless, like I didn't say anything or was talking to somebody else. "Where's that med..." Reaching for the black satchel, he leans across my lap between my knees. Snapping the satchel open, ruffling through the guts of it, scooping stuff out. Duct tape, Vaseline, alcohol but not the kind you drink. Kool cigarettes. The weight of him heavy and uncomfortable, his thick barrel chest digging into my thighs, his XXL hand searching the satchel an extra long moment. There's a red cross on its side like a doctor's bag, not a real one my uncle would carry, more like a doctor on a TV show. Marcus Welby, MD, Ben Casey, or Dr. Kildare.

"Romilar." He finally sits upright dropping a bottle on my lap. "Take a few swigs of that. Really. It'll shut that damned cough of yours up."

Romilar, it gets you goofy if you drink it all, like with Gary my best friend chugging it down before school. Goofy or sick and suspended. It stains your tongue too so there's no denying who you were with when you drank it. The other red-tongued guy. Not really your best friend, either. A partner in crime, not really a friend at all.

I have to wrench the bottle open with my teeth, the cap's stuck on so tight. He reaches to do it, I turn away though and get it open myself. "Donald's got shoes like that. Penny loafers but with dimes."

Richard chuckles. "A bit light in the loafers, is he?"

I shrug, I don't know why but it's suddenly not something I want to admit. "He got in your truck. The red pickup one. So I just want to know where he is." Gulp some of this liquid, thick cherry syrup that burns your sore throat and softens the back of your neck like hard liquor.

"You check Market Square or the park? Queers get busted every night down there."

"He went with you though."

He knocks the pack against his palm popping a cigarette up. Grips it between tight lips and lights it, then shakes the match out, winding the little vent window open, and flicking the matchstick away.

"Let me tell you something, James." Smoke puffs soften the words leaving his lips. Thin, angry lips, hardly lips at all. "I admit, once in a while, I'll do one of you punks a favor, a fiver for a favor. Hell, you're out here doing it anyway, might as well be me as the next horny schmuck. Where's the harm?" He twists in his seat, his belly rubs into the wheel when he does, pointing his cigarette at me like a smoldering finger. "But don't you ever pull any of that sick homo shit on me. Understand? I've got no tolerance for it. None what-so-ever."

Shaking my head, that's not what I am so why would I or want to be? "I'm not like Donald, Richard, I swear. You can even ask him, I don't want to be like that at all."

He nods once, handing the smoke to me. "Good."

"Except when you, you know, pick up those punks, you're not queer, I don't get that."

"'Except when,'" he snaps. "Look, a blow job's a blow job, who the hell cares who's going down on you. Some kid, your wife—Donnie Whoever—I don't care, I'm telling you, you're a guy, you're gonna get off."

I feel my face flush and take a drag. I don't cough this time, the smoke fills my whole self more calming instead. Even if you're not queer. Passing it back to him, wondering if it's okay to ask, since we're sharing a smoke like friends. "Except aren't you a cop? Like an undercover detective or something?"

Richard scoffs. "If I were an undercover cop, would I tell you? What would be the point of that? Think about it."

"Oh. That would blow your cover, huh."

His index finger taps his forehead, like, *now you're thinking*.

Chuckling, I go, "A blow-your-cover job," but I think that's the Romilar talking. Drinking more, it's soothing going down, the smooth bottleneck hole too small for my tongue. My head feeling heavy against the back window. Outside, there's headstones with dead bones below. Breaking the suction, my tongue pops from the bottle with a sound like a kiss.

"Jesus Christ," Richard says.

"Donald did that to you, huh, a blow job?"

He takes a last drag, stubs the butt out in the ashtray. "This fag Donald and you got a thing going or something? An attraction?"

"He's nice to me. I just want him to be okay, that's all." So at first I'm thinking, the park, I could probably just go look there tomorrow, or Market Square. If it's where they hang out, his friends and all, like the ones from the laundromat, they'd know if he got busted or maybe that's where he is. But then no, it's not where he'd be because his plants are dying, his cat was crying, and what about me? "He went with you the last time I saw him, so."

Richard looks at me sharply, grumbling, the fuckin last time when was that, could be anywhere by now, Fire Island for Chrissake, or goddam granny's house for all he knows, fine, if it'll make me quit asking he'll do a little digging, see what he can find out.

But he *should* know, he's a detective, maybe not like *Dragnet* or any detective I ever met, but still. He's got a police radio and knows what goes on. Market Square and the park and people like Donald he pays to get into his truck. A blow job's a blow job. Just thinking of that—Donald with Richard—and chugging this medicine bottle. Feeling it warm me, spreading all through me inside. My neck to my gut, down my arms, numbing my fingers. My crotch. A lot to my crotch. Remembering Donald. His limp wrists, pierced ears, and perfume. His polished nails, lilac letters, hairless skin. His freckled smile. His silky nightgown prodding into my back.

"Sit still," Richard says, "this isn't going to hurt." He grins. "Much."

But it's hard sitting still on his vinyl front seat with my right foot cupped in his palm. He's dousing these open blisters with alcohol, which makes me jerk my foot from the sting, but his hand like a vice grips it solid. Ow-ow-ow, I go, in mostly a whisper.

"I'm a trained paramedic," he says, like an argument almost, but I've got no reason really to doubt it. Big gob of Vaseline like snot on his finger he slathers into these blisters with a wad of tissue he wraps in duct tape like a bandage. "What's the matter, the Goodwill out of socks?"

I sort of mumble I wasn't thinking about socks, when he pulls my left boot off.

"Thinking about the loony bin?"

I shake my head, not believing he'd even want to know what I'm thinking about at all. "Just, do I look normal enough. You know, for dinner."

"Right. At Grandma's house," he says.

Richard doesn't think I have too much to worry about. "You look respectable," he says, turning the street corner where I point, in this familiar city neighborhood, onto this familiar city block. So my blood quickens and it's harder to hear his words. "Frankly, I'm a bit impressed with you myself." He nods when I look at him, not believing he just said that. I impressed him. "Hell, you keep yourself nice. The new boots, clean clothes. Tucking in your goddam shirt. Even your old fart of a granddad's got to approve of that."

Their yellow apartment building's wedged between brownstones the same as the past fifty years. *Don't Touch The Banister. Keep Off The Grass. Respect Your Elders. Do As You're Told.* So despite Romilar and new cowboy boots, clean pants, and tucked shirt, my heart sinks.

"Let me out here," I tell him. There's a moment of hesitation at first, like, no, he's not letting me go, and do I even want to get out, but he swerves this maroon El Camino to the curb and stops. So I open the door.

"Wait a minute. I owe you for that job, don't I," he says.

I shake my head. "S'okay, it's for charity and stuff."

"Hell, I said I'd pay you." He doesn't move toward his wallet, though. Just kind of grins but not really. "I'll owe it to you, how's that. I. O. U." His finger draws the letters in the air.

Even before I reach the front door, this old foreign guy blocks the way, like a dog catcher or border patrol, you can't slip by. Trumping up the walkway beside me, it's Grampa's neighbor, with his cologne of BO and Bengay. I sort of duck from any onslaught-to-come, I remember his curses and accent.

"Acht, the boychik returns, knock on vood!"

Ignoring him doesn't do any good, he grabs the heavy front door and opens it like he's a doorman. So I have to acknowledge that. I nod and say thanks.

"Such kvellingk over you Rabin vould do," he says, rolling his eyeballs and rapping the doorjamb twice. "A magazine! A cereal box! Sears and Roebucks! You vould tingk Einstein he's braggingk you are."

"Me?" Shaking my head, he's got the wrong boychik or grampa. Kvelling or whatever.

His bony grip clamps my coat sleeve, holding me still to speak confidential. "These days, Godt forbidt I should ask, 'So? how's the boychik?' He says notingk. Notingk! Vhat did you do, eh? To bringk such shame to Grandtpoppa?"

He stands in the way so I can't shoulder past him or go in the door to the stairs, the polished banister, three carpeted flights to Granma and everything happy up there.

"I'm just here to see Grandtmomma," I say, looking past him to her waiting hug and approving smile at these clean clothes and new cowboy boots on my feet.

Even through the thick suede and wool lining, I can feel his grip squeeze my arm. "Your grandtmomma Hannah? Already she's home? From a stroke yet, kine-ahora?"

I stop walking, moving, thinking, and turn back to him.

"Your lips to Godt's ears," he says, blowing a kiss toward the sky.

So my hand's to my mouth and my ears grow big. "What—what do you mean, from a stroke, what stroke?"

"In the bloodt a stroke gets you. A clot, Godt forbidt, to stop everytingk. In the midtle of the night such a terrible thingk. Rushingk to the hospital they took her."

His words are a sucker punch that blanks everything out except stars swirling dizzy before me. And a hole in my gut to throw everything up, Romilar and the best of intentions. "What?"

"Oy, such a commotion! Vidt the flashing lights and the sirens you vouldn't believe. For miles you could hear, goingk down Lawrence the whole vay yet to Mt. Sinai."

Breaking away from his words and creepy claw on my arm, in the direction where his bony finger points. Down Lawrence. Turning that way, trumping out the heavy door, trumping right across the lawn before he can curse me, *Gotdam hippie schmuck! Vhat you do!* I don't care. Just repeating in my head with every bandaged step, it's not fair it's not fair it's not fair.

And it's gone, Richard's El Camino, not left or right when I look frantic both ways from the curb. So this panic's for someone, my sister my brother a teacher or doctor to be here and say what to do, visit my granma or take me to see her. Someone real who cares, well, Donald's the one, but where is he now? Richard said check Market Square.

I don't recognize any of them and you'd think that I would after weeks living down here, the ones who say "Hi," or "Hey, Angel." I don't know them or how they know me, like waking up in someone else's life, *his* life, the desperate one, where hustlers and homos approach him like best friends and drug dealer junkies call him Angel. But no one's seen Donald or knows where he is and angel says check his apartment.

Past the Arcade, turn at the corner. Ten blocks, turn left, two more past the neon Hamm's beer sign. Cut through the alley to the back of his building, but then—no. *Everytingk* stops.

Seeing it all, tossed purple cushions, scattered paperbacks, *Stranger in a Strange Land* with my bookmark still in it, *Valley of the Dolls,* and *Christine Jorgensen.* Broken shelves painted purple. Purple sofa end-up in the dumpster, its bed frame splayed wide like a screaming metal jaw. The *Smash Hits* cassette in a smashed plastic case. Broken teacups, ripped lingerie, an autographed cereal box. His precious stuff, all Donald's stuff. Strewn in the alley every which way, like trash.

All I can think now is, go see Granma. It's urgent, too, before this huge empty hole growing inside gets too big to find my way out.

19

Flowers poke out of this trash hopper at the back of the hospital parking lot, GOULD BROS. MORTUARY stenciled across it in yellow, right next to Mt. Sinai I guess, in case the doctors mess up. Shake *mortuary* out of my head, trying to imagine Happy Street instead. Lilac and love and bouquets of roses, heaven's perfume, Granma said.

But lifting the lid, the rot in the dumpster reeks—way worse than Goodwill or a bus station men's room. Still, I hike myself up, teetering over the edge picking the fresher flowers on top. When this gross-out thought hits me: is this where they throw parts of sick people out? Tonsils and appendixes and lumps of disease. So I don't look too hard or dig very deep to gather a bouquet together.

With the withered petals picked off, it looks okay. It's the thought that counts anyway, Granma once told me. Lopsided pinch pots or Mother's Day cards where the crayon went outside the lines, she still always gave me a kiss.

The asphalt sparkles in the sun, making my eyes squint and water. Debris crunches under these new cowboy boots, crossing the parking lot, up the curb and into the main lobby entrance.

NO VISITORS UNDER 16 YEARS OF AGE
PERMITTED BEYOND LOBBY

Man. I don't like hospitals or thinking about Granma being in one, even a new "medical center" like this. Arrows on wall plaques point in different directions. MT. SINAI SISTERHOOD GIFT SHOP. MORRIS C. GOLDMAN CAFETERIA. LEW MEYER MEMORIAL CHAPEL. RABIN ROSENBERG FAMILY PEDIATRIC CENTER—a tingle of pride in my chest about that. I tuck my hair all nervously behind my ears when the front counter lady asks can she help me. I nod at my grampa's name on the wall plaque.

"Can I go up to see her? Hannah Rosenberg, I don't know what room."

Her fingers run like a hamster over hundreds of index cards spinning on a wheel, till she finally stops it and looks up at me. "Mrs. Rabin Rosenberg? ICU 414. Immediate family only, hun."

My palm all sweaty and stuck to these stems. "She's my granma," I say, not wanting to hear the reason she rather I just went away. So I'm surprised she believes me and I'm sixteen. "That'll be the fourth floor, hun." She points down the hall to the elevators.

Stepping off the elevator I just feel numb. TVs flash behind curtains in glass rooms I pass, hushed voices, muffled silence. I don't look in any of the hall windows either, I don't want to know or remember the Memorial ICU or fourth floor, the whole hospital, really. Which room I was in when I tried suicide and Granma stayed at my bedside.

414

I take a deep breath and try to look normal. Take one cautious step into the room.

The blinds are shut so just a few wafers of daylight slip through. The rest of the room lies in shadow, so at first I don't recognize who's in the bed and apologize, turning to go. But her sunken eyes wake, sparkling and familiar, her parched lips on one side sort of flicker.

A sudden weight fills my lungs not letting me breathe, feeling like crying, actually. I look up instead overhead at the ceiling. It's splattered with agony the housekeeping crew never sees.

I should just go, that's like a refrain playing loud in my head, over and over.

"Jamey," she says. So I choke back emotion and step to her bedside. She's got like zero strength, taking my hand in her soft withered palm. But her touch only makes the hole bigger.

I don't want to move, or look at her, really. Or let go of her holding my hand.

"What have you brought...is that anthurium?" Her voice flat and dry like she hasn't been speaking for years. "Baby's breath...oh, and...a rose." She sniffs these flowers that reek pretty strong, well, they've been cut from their roots and they're dying. "Rabin won my heart with a rose," she confides and breaks into a lopsided smile.

It bugs me his name makes her smile. Rabin. He's nasty and mean, I don't get why she loves him. *Love's weird that way,* Tommy once told me. *You could fall in love with anyone, you never know who. Even a Capulet,* he said. But Rabin's not romantic, he doesn't deserve her, he's nothing like Romeo at all. He's not even here.

An indent rings her finger where her wedding band's been, the back of her hand's discolored where an IV's stuck in. Long hair hangs limp and loose on her pillow, not combed in a French twist or bun like before, and she's got on a shapeless hospital gown instead of a classy peignoir. Her hand's clasped on mine, all purple with veins and bones thinly draped in crepe paper skin. Which looks like it'd feel all leathery and rough, but no. It's the softest touch you can imagine.

"Granma?" Not really knowing what to say. "I...I'm sorry about before, in the park. I feel real shitty about that," I admit. "I'm gonna pay you back, I swear." IOU comes into my head. I. O. U. everything.

Her hand slips from mine, one eyelid half open, a glistening gray slit like a sleepy cat. "You're doing better, tatalah." Words that take effort to find their way out. "That makes me happy," she says. Half her face sags with tender wrinkles, serene and real peaceful. Like the beach at midnight with a million sandy footprints but nobody around at all.

There's a water jug on the nightstand next to her bed and I stick this bouquet inside it. Pick scattererd stray petals off her hospital blanket that lays pretty flat and not like it covers a person. And it hits me, she's shrinking away, hardly taking much space up anymore.

Flick my hair from my eyes. "I'm...I'm..." It's suddenly all wrong. I can't lie and say I'm doing better or on my way back to The Oaks. Exhale caustic air, straighten my smile, and face her. "I'm working stuff out," I say. Kneeling to gather the last fallen petals then dropping them into the trash can. Kneeling at her bedside, my chin on my folded arms so I don't have to hold myself up.

She asks, "Is Jesus helping?" It's my shirt that she points at, the pocket embroidered *St. James the Lesser*, the lesser that's me I'll never be more and why did I even buy it? "It's from Goodwill, it, it doesn't mean anything. Well, not to me."

She looks at me through eyes cloudy as courtroom glass. "Try something else then," she says, her voice hardly more than a whisper. "Go someplace else. But, sweetheart...keep your head about you. No matter what other people might do. Always keep your head." Her hand squeezes mine but just barely.

"I'm trying but I...I don't know."

"Did you call Daddy?"

Daddy. God, give me words to make her understand. "He doesn't want to talk to me, Granma. I know he knows what happened there, at Railton. 'Cause he listens to all his friends and lawyers and doctors.

He lets them say what they want about me. But not me. He'd rather pretend nothing happened."

She's quiet, real still and silent, lips loosely parted, eyelids half-closed and vacated. Not hearing. Or breathing. I don't hear her breathing. My heart skips, thinking what'd I do now? I jump back. Choking on panic, ready to scream for the nurses and pull the alarm—

"Tell Granma," she says.

Blinking, my heart calms just hearing her voice. But *tell granma*, two words like a dare where you'll carry the consequences with you forever. Like sneaking on an airplane without a ticket, or keeping what Ratachek did a secret, or going over the wall.

I shake my head turning away from her, but all I can see is a dying bouquet and everything ugly I brought here. I start to get up but her palm holds my wrist like a soft restraint. "You don't see your strength," she tells me. "But I see it, dolly. How strong you were there to survive."

Strong? Ha, she is so off, she has no idea. "Unh-unh, Granma. I...I..."

"You need to remember. You need to accept what happened to you. Sweetheart, talking about it will help."

Remembering doesn't take much. But I can't look at her when I say it. "Just...nobody stopped him. No guards, or like, trustees, or inmates, no one. I didn't do anyth—I just was getting lunch, peas and dogfood and peaches. And he, he just, like, picked me up out of the lunch line and got me alone in the library. And he tried to, like, rape me. Only he's too big and...and I..." Choking up this memory, the worst thing in the world, to be so weak and stupid. "I apologi—" My voice cracks just getting the broken word out.

Pulling away, I don't like her squeezing my hand. "I thought he'd just go away."

"But he did not," she whispers.

Shaking my head, make myself see the disgust in her eyes but no, it's just tears.

Her hand finds my cheek. "The world is full of unspeakable things. Oh, but, Jamey. Sweet angel, my darling. You are not one of them."

God, she has no idea.

It's peaceful in here. Quiet, with drapes drawn but not dark. Granma's asleep in a hospital bed with a hospital blanket and hospital tubes going into her skin like an experiment in Frankenstein's lab. On her table there's a tray of institution food flavored with Hospital you try not to taste when you swallow. Cottage cheese and lemon Jell-O. Canned peaches, I have to flush those.

Her hair drapes her shoulders like silver lace, her eyelids sunk deep in dark sockets, her lips cracked and colorless. What a lie, that's what I'm thinking, when you've seen her ballet picture from when she was young. Weightless on toe shoes, all slender and elegant in a hand-tinted black-and-white photo. Pink on her skin, her lips red, yellow hair, eyes blue with long-ago color. Now all that's gone, too. A whole lifetime gone, you only get one and what if you blow it completely?

"Once upon a time..." I know she can hear me even asleep when I sit down beside her and whisper. "Long, long ago in a beautiful land far away." Thinking about her being young or sixteen, I lay my head next to hers on the pillow. Recitals in gilded halls, society balls, and all her beaux or boyfriends who come courting. In the parlor on the love seat, stroking her long hair or kissing her cheek not wrinkled and old but still smelling like roses.

I wish she didn't have to be eighty. I wish she could just stay peaceful as this. Happily ever after.

Heaven's perfume takes over my dream and slowly, slowly awakes me. Take a last mellow breath of sleep then let go, opening my eyes to the day.

To bouquets of red roses *all* around me.

Blink my eyes a million times, but still, roses are all I see. Perfect red roses in full fragrant bloom exploding from vases filling the room. Raising to my elbows, prone on her bed, tossing her blanket off me. "Oh wow..." Try not to wake her sleeping beside me, slip my boots to the floor and sit up. "So trippy..." Man, there's got to be dozens of bouquets, a whole blooming red petal sea. I get up slowly checking it out, turning full-circle, all the way around, and stop, face-to-face with my grampa. Raging red as the roses and scowling at me. "Gramp—"

"Are you on dope?" His voice withers the petals and walls and any good things I was feeling. "What kind of person lies in his grandmother's sickbed? With street shoes on yet and a filthy coat?"

"No, I...I just..." but my shape fills her bedsheets and indents her pillow, her spic'n'span floor scuffed with bootheel marks, I struggle to take off the coat. Stirring now, Granma tries to sit up, her worried eyes wincing from Grampa to me.

He collars the bouquet of flowers I brought, rips it dripping out of the pitcher. "*This* is to cheer her? So she should, what? Give you another fifty dollars?" Rattling them right under my nose makes me sneeze and the petals shake from their stems to the floor. I don't look at him, only Granma when I recoil and my eyes open again. I think I'm allergic to roses.

"The *first* in this family to be in jail, is that not shame enough? Now *this* you stick in our faces?" His thick finger pokes at *St. James* and the cross on my shirt. "*This* is an insult. To me, to my Hannah, to six *million* dead! It's an insult!"

My head reeling, I turn away, kneeling in nice pants, gathering the petals that just crumble apart, messing the floor up even worse. "I—I know, but I..."

"Stop," Granma says in the loudest tiny voice ever uttered. So I stop and stand up just staring at her. But her eyes aim directly at Grampa.

I dump the petals into the trash where they should've been left in the first place.

"Bah!" Grampa snorts. "Bows he should wear in that hair, Hannah. Bows!"

So I'm pulling my hair back into a tail, tucking it behind my ears, down my collar, looking only at Granma. She stops me with two whispered words. *Don't apologize.*

I open my grip. My hair fans my back and falls loose on my shoulders. Grampa's clenched face turns even redder when I let it go.

"This is what he aspires to, Hannah. To be the worst he can be!" he bellows, so you could probably hear him down the hall. "A hippie bum! Hopped up on dope, doesn't go to school, doesn't work! Bah! Better you should still be in jail!"

"No, Grampa—"

"I bet you didn't say no to the other boys in there!"

It just blurts out. Two words, bursting off my tongue, the worst two words you could say to anyone. I say them to him, my own grampa. No apologies come from me either and I swear to angel *Never again!* I leave the mess wherever it fell and walk out to the hall in this gray space between peace and pain.

part five
richard

20

November 1970. That's the calendar page tacked over the register at Doreen's Fresh Cup Diner. With a photograph of a whole flock of turkeys, all black beady eyes and wrinkled red necks, not frantic or panicked or climbing the fences, just dumb to what happens next. *Compliments of Industrial Framing & Concrete,* that's what it says, with five days left to X off.

«everything's cool, breakfast and coffee, you're out of the cold and you're warm»

Doreen refills my cup, the strong coffee smell swirls into my head. Holding the pot, tattooed arms folded across her waitress dress, she nods at my empty plate. I ate it anyway, someone's leftover toast and cold gummy eggs. You can't complain about bad coffee after swallowing that.

She goes, "Friend of yours was in here early this morning asking about you."

A friend? This gulp of hot coffee brands his name in my tongue. Donald?

Doreen lifts the pot toward the picture of turkeys. "The calendar man. Big, heavy-set gentleman, blond, ruddy complected? Red and black plaid coat. Anyways. He left with one of the other boys instead."

So it takes a few seconds to digest that, *other boys*, and not who I hoped she would say. "Was Donald with him?" but I'm not very loud and my words float away unanswered.

"Hey! Doreen!" somebody shouts. "This coffee tastes like dirt!"

"Damn straight," she shouts back and winks at me, "it was fresh ground this morning!"

Making me smile and wish Donald were here, he'd probably laugh at that too. She scoops up a tip left on the counter and stuffs my egg-yellow dish in a pan underneath, clattering loud like she broke it.

I take this fresh cup to the one corner booth where you can drink it without getting hassled, pretty much. But soon as I sit down, the red and black lumber jacket slips in beside me. Richard. Mr. Hunt. The detective. The weight of him puffs the vinyl beneath me lifting me up a few inches. I put the coffee cup down without taking a sip. My hand's so unsteady, he's got to see that. How unsteady I am now.

«not unsteady. you just have some stuff to work out»

He slaps a five-dollar bill on the Formica before me. I flick my bangs out of my eyes, unsure what to say, thank you, or donate it to Goodwill, or keep it, just help me find Donald.

Richard rolls his palms open on the tabletop. "So? Obviously you're not in a mental hospital." He looks around, it's the dregs of society, the hustled and hustlers in here. Same patients, I'm thinking, just different walls.

He chuckles. "Obviously not at Grandma's." He lifts those sunglasses above his brow like he's peeking out a window at me. "Hope you at least got a decent home-cooked meal out of it."

I shrug, the reply stuck in my throat, what I wish would've happened but didn't. Around her antique dining table with hand-laced napkins, Friday night candles warming the room, the windows all steamy with smells from her kitchen, baking bread and bubbling pots. Sneaking me sweets before dinner, chocolate rugelach sparkling with thick sugar crystals that crunch in your teeth. There's chicken soup, rib roast, and baby potatoes, she picks out the onions, I don't like those. Pop bottles flowing, all colors, cherry and orange, even Green River, my dad fills my glass despite all the sugar and how crazy it makes me. Why is tonight different than all other nights? Tonight Jamey's with us, he says.

Richard shakes his head, he sees I'm pathetic and hands me a napkin. I flick my hair back and blink a few times. I don't need a napkin at all.

"My guess is you didn't get home-cooked squat," Richard says. "Hell, then the problem does not lie with you, James. You made a valiant effort, with the nice duds, fancy boots, cleaning yourself up. I were you? I'd say fuck 'em. With a capital F." His knuckle raps the Formica twice, he lifts himself off the bench. It deflates when he stands so I sink down even lower.

"What about Thanksgiving? You got plans? And don't tell me you're not hungry." He's pulled this brown furry wad like a pet from his red and black pocket, stretches half of it over each hand. Brown leather gloves with rabbit fur lining. "Hell, I know teenage boys, and there's two things you can always count on. They're always hungry. And they're always horny." He winks, nodding all matter-of-fact.

Shovel these bangs from my eyes, leave my hand on my forehead. Horny, I'm not that at all, well, not till he said it and I already ate.

Towering over me, he nods toward the door. "I've got a shitload of people coming by later. Big holiday shindig. What about you? I bet a nice kid like you already has plans."

Plans, well. Last year I got turkey sliced like baloney with canned gravy heated in ten-gallon vats but not this year, I did it just like he said, Fuck you with a capital F, so. No other plans, not for Thanksgiving, or, ever.

"Turkey, stuffing, pumpkin pie, the works. You in?" He checks his watch. "Gotta pick up the booze first, you don't mind tagging along."

He nods when I shrug.

"That a yes? I've got a turkey in the oven and a houseful of guests expecting a Thanksgiving feast. I gotta get moving." He waits though, the extra minute it takes for me to actually stand up and leave.

The sun's bright so it doesn't seem cold, but those mittens are lost so I stuff my hands in these Marlboro pockets. He points where he's parked the red truck, just up the street from the diner.

Walking with Richard, two steps behind his red and black Pendleton jacket. Lumberjack, I remember thinking that when I first saw him. Following him from The Fresh Cup to his red pickup truck. Just like Donald.

"Get out," he commands when we're at his truck and he opens the passenger door. But I'm nowhere near in.

"What the fuck for?" This snotty voice snaps back. There's already a kid in the truck's cab taking up the whole bench, really fat, with tousled rusty hair a lot longer than mine, and a red wool coat embroidered with Indian signs. A sun god or teepee, I think, or from Mexico. He takes a quick drag off a cigarette, looks at me full-faced and smiles. And I can see, well, *she's* not a fat guy at all.

A pink bakery box teeters and slips from her huge denim lap, she grabs it, shifting clumsily, and this weasely kid pops up on the bench beside her. In a torn army field jacket and flag-striped bell-bottom jeans, he clambers over her knees like a blond bony mountain goat and hops down to the curb beside me.

"You ride in the back, Zerotski," Richard tells him.

Black beady eyes dart in every direction landing a moment on me, then to Richard, the cab, the back of the truck. "Fuck," he says.

"I was here first, Mr. Hunt. Me and Cat were. Why don't Angel ride in the fuckin' back?"

"Guests and garbage," Richard mutters, ignoring him, nodding for me to get in. He signals the fat chick, Cat I guess, to switch places with me, so I climb up and around her huge mountain self and squish between her and the steering wheel. She's got combat boots on and big farmer overalls, she is big, there's hardly much room to fit in. She flicks her smoke out the open door, adjusting her red coat and the pink bakery box on her knees.

Richard slams her door shut from outside, it's like *whhoooomp* the winter air compressed in my ears.

"It's Dutch apple," she tells me when I'm settled beside her. "What makes apples Dutch? Do you know?" Her eyes smile but not the rest of her face and she pushes her long wavy hair from her forehead like she's surfacing out of deep water. "Maybe they pay for themselves," she mumbles, flipping the pink lid open. Inside there's a pie, all crumble-covered with cinnamon sugar. Except for a big drippy hole in the center where the silver pan bottom shows through. "Me and Zero had some. It's really good," she says.

Rand's friend Zero? I twist to see Richard chuck a blanket at the weaselly guy sitting in the truck bed, his pale stringy hair pressed flat against the rear window behind me. Still arguing, but it's pretty one-sided, just his snotty voice like Bugs Bunny, not Richard's deep baritone at all.

"Please stop talking, Zero," the fat chick Cat begs under her breath as if he could hear. "Before he gets pissed off and tosses us out."

Or maybe Zero does hear because he suddenly shuts up. Richard slaps his leather gloves together *WHOMP!* and slips into the driver's seat beside me. He slams his door shut, slamming himself against me, I have to lean closer to her. The pink box closed and balanced on her mountain lap. Her other hand caresses her belly.

Richard's voice in this tight space booms right in my ear. "You get close to your time, you make like pea soup and split." He's talking to her. "I don't want you around, that's understood."

"I know. Zero told me."

"Good. Glad to see one of you with a foot in reality." His hand shifts the gear, bumping my knee with his elbow. He downshifts, his leather palm lands on my thigh, he doesn't seem to notice but how can he not? My dad's warning voice plays in my head like a rule from last year at school. *He's an adult, you show him respect.* When I said how gross Mr. Ratachek was, sitting so close with his hand on my lap under the algebra book. My dad asked, Did you move over?

I can't move over or I'd be on the fat chick's lap and there's no room for me there at all.

I knock Richard's hand away. He looks right at me, his dark glasses just inches from my eyes. His shifty hand adjusts the mirror so it's my face filling the rearview. "Vanilla ice cream'll go good with that pie," he says with a nod. He leans over the wheel looking past me at her. "So what do you think of my new friend?"

"Angel?" She smiles, she's pretty when she does, not even looking so fat. "Everybody knows Angel," she says, "or wants to say they do."

So I look at her, too.

"Is that right?" Richard's hand's back on the stick shifter, changing the gear, engine revving. Passing a green highway sign up the I-90 on-ramp, merging with holiday traffic.

TO WESTERN SUBURBS it says.

21

Welcome to Westlawn Shopping Centre the parking lot entrance sign says, with center spelled "RE" like that makes it fancy or something. But it's just a drab strip mall, not fancy at all. A Shoe Repair, Western Union, Donuts, a beauty salon, everything closed for Thanksgiving. In some faraway suburb Richard drove to, I don't think I ever heard of.

Richard takes Zero with him into this storefront with *IFC* in script gold letters on the blinded window. Zero stays at his heel while he unlocks the storefront door. He leaves Cat and me in the truck with the keys and the engine running, keeping the heater on. He can trust us, he said. She's already knocked up and Angel's a guest, but Zero'll stab you the minute your back is turned.

At first it's just words then a punch line. When it hits me what "knocked up" means, which is kind of shocking. Flick my hair from my eyes to check out her belly, all big and round like a watermelon's stolen under her coat. She can't be much older than my little sister. But I've got no words or big brother advice, everything seems dumb or judgmental.

I hear myself say, "You're gonna have a baby?" See, really dumb.

"Looks like." She smiles. "Not right *now*, but. So how come you're here?"

"Richard invited me to Thanksgiving."

"Yeah, he said." She lowers her voice and giggles. "'Never turn down a free meal.' Zero's number one rule to live by."

I nod, I know about rules, that sounds like a good one.

Cat says Mr. Hunt's cool with her spending the night. "He said it's nice to have a woman in the house." She lights a cigarette, unrolls her vent window enough to blow the smoke out and ash it. "But once he pays Zero? We're splitsville, man. California. That's where we're having the baby. You ever been?"

I shrug, *California*. I don't even want to think about that, plane rides and airport police, waking my dad at four in the morning, making everything worse. Breaking a rule. Because I wasn't upstairs in my bed like he thought when he told me I'm grounded. *What the hell are you doing in Los Angeles?* he yelled at me over the phone. I didn't tell him I thought I was going to Berkeley. I didn't tell him Gary dared me to. I just said I didn't think they'd let me board with no ticket, but nobody checked at the gate or stopped me. *You never think!* my dad said.

"LA, man. That's where it's at," Cat says, twisting a strand of her long auburn hair around her finger. "Zero says it's always summer there. Man, you can pick oranges right off the trees so we'll never be hungry. Soon's he hitches to Hollywood and makes enough bread, he's gonna send me a ticket. Then, good riddance Chi-town, man. West until my feet get wet." She giggles, flicks her cigarette butt out the little vent window then turns the handle and rolls it shut. "Palm trees, man. Movie stars, swimming pools. You should come."

I tell her it's where my big brother goes to school. Berkeley, though. Not LA.

"Cool, a place to crash. Never say no to that."

I'm about to object but Richard's come out of the storefront with Zero, locking the door behind him. Zero's arms stacked with a case of beer, a carton with bottles clanking inside, liquor I guess, and two jugs of wine. Richard cradles a huge frozen turkey. He lifts it up like a trophy in front of the windshield.

"Hungry, kids? That's some go-o-od eatin' right there." Richard smacks his lips. His lips are thin and hardly lips at all, his mouth a small wavering hole ordering Zero around. "Get back there and hold the libations. Quit whining, for Chrissakes, we're a block away. Anything breaks, it's out of your pay."

Zero is pissed off, loading the liquor into the truck bed. Fuming at Richard, he doesn't climb back in the truck. Richard shoves him, cursing him out with tight lips and a warning, *get in the damn truck!* Zero protests, "What the fuck, man! Why're you dragging me into your shit? It ain't cool. You owe me, double time, Mr. Hunt. Triple time. Four-ple—"

BOOM! Richard drops the turkey in the truck bed, it echoes through the whole cab.

Richard drives slowly, one eye on Zero, one eye on the road, turning left at the corner a half block down, then left again and halfway up a neighborhood street. Shoebox ranch houses line each side, red or brown or yellow brick, the same house actually, just with different driveways between them, gravel or tar or concrete. Like in the cartoons on Saturday mornings, the same background houses repeat over and over behind Mr. Magoo or Huckleberry Hound. Richard turns left up a concrete driveway and stops.

There's a gate before us where the asphalt and sidewalk meet, one of those cyclone fence kinds, all crisscrossed silver wires that rattle so loud when you try to climb over. It surrounds a red brick shoebox house with a railed porch and front door that faces the street.

Richard sets the parking brake handle, opens his door, and steps out. When he does, Thanksgiving smells fill the morning air, so overwhelming I'm glad I decided to come. Turkey and all the fixin's. Cat knocks my arm and points at the key dangling in the ignition, the motor still running. "Wanna go to LA?" she whispers. I think she means steal the truck.

But Richard's got the gate unchained and wide open, he's back in the cab and behind the wheel. Shifting to go, he drives inside the gate, gets out, and re-chains it. Then hops in again, pulls up the driveway, and parks by the back door of the house.

Cat slides out backside-first, I jump down right behind her. Zero stands in the truckbed and hands her this big carpetbag, one like Mary Poppins had, well, in the Disney movie, I never read the book. He swings both legs over the tailgate in an Olympic leap to the concrete. "Angel," he hisses at me. "Help carry these."

"Hey! Leave Angel out of this!" Richard barks. "Get that booze inside."

Zero teeters under the weight of the booze in his arms, knocking into my shoulder. "*Here*," he spits under his breath, "*Take* this—" but Richard bumps Zero away from me, off the back stoop. Zero stumbles to his knees but doesn't drop the libations. He swears a lot, though.

"Don't make me regret you," Richard warns him. Richard holds the storm door open, selecting a key, his face tense and angry. Cat and her carpetbag enter first and I'm right behind her, stepping inside to a swirl of holiday warmth, roasting turkey, and spice. Richard hooks his keys to a keyring holder hung on the mudroom wall. He unlaces his size ninety-twos, setting them into a built-in shoe rack and takes the pink box from Cat. Zero and Cat kick out of their shoes, Cat struggling just to reach her laces. She racks both their pairs and stands waiting, inhaling, "Mm-mm," like a lullaby.

I take off my cowboy boots, too, slide them in the rack, then follow barefoot up these three mudroom steps and into a kitchen.

It's all dark wood cabinets and brown plaid wallpaper with a little brown rug at the double sink and matching plaid curtains on the window above it. Zero stacks both boxes on the kitchen table and those two gallon jugs. I doubt I could've carried all that.

Richard tosses a carton of Camels to Zero, he catches it against his jacket, one of those olive drab armyman kind like protestors wear or Sgt. Saunders on *Combat!* Zero's all slouched in a kitchen chair, tucking greasy hair behind his ears. He packs the cigarettes hard against the table.

"Hey! Useless!" Richard snaps his fingers in Zero's face. "We've got a feast to prepare! Who's hungry?" Richard pats his belly with both hands like paddles, then landing one so heavy on my head, he ruffles up my hair. "Take off your jackets, kids. Stay awhile," he says and takes his jacket off. But none of us do.

Cat's got the huge frozen turkey cradled all awkward and slipping in her arms. "Where should I put this?"

Richard opens the oven door releasing the smell of Thanksgiving, not last year at Railton, but Granma Hannah's the year before that. A fleshy mound browning in a roasting pan, sizzling and crackling. He pokes at it with a carving fork, checking a thermometer, spooning juices over the top, then glances back blank-faced for a moment at Cat, blinking at her or the mound that she's lugging. "That's for my girls, it goes down in the freezer. Let their bitch of a mother deal with it. Worst cook in the world!" he says with a chuckle, and shoos Cat away with one hand. "You'll sleep downstairs. Go. Make yourself useful."

"Angel? Come with me?" She makes that smile again, not really a smile but ready to be, and tips her head toward the basement.

Back down the three steps through the mudroom again, this time with her carpetbag in my hand, it's heavy. Following Cat, already a couple steps down in the dark. She stops and looks up at me. "Flip on the light. See? On the wall behind you."

I step back and flip this switch, the staircase brightens. Her half smile flashes then turns away, concentrating to even see the next step, even after I take the frozen bird from her arms. *Your Holiday Turkey Compliments of Industrial Framing & Concrete*, that's what the holly wreath label says. Still, it takes forever stepping behind her one stair at a time till we're all the way down to the bottom. There's another switch she flips on so the whole basement ceiling lights up.

It's paneled knotty pine, with a TV and built-in couch and cabinets and butt-ugly green tile on the floor. The other side of the staircase is more like a basement. Concrete floor, concrete walls, furnace, water heater, washer, dryer, and this big white freezer like a monument or tomb. Frigidaire. Cat lifts the lid, it's full with frosty boxes, cartons of whatever, perishables, I guess, from the faint smell maybe some are already perished. We exchange sour glances. She shrugs. "Leftovers, I guess." She takes the carpetbag from my hand. I let this turkey roll off my arms and into the freezer.

When the lid shuts, a poof of frost brushes my face. Cat shudders too, her arms hugging her red coat tight to her belly. "It gets pretty cold down here. I hate being cold. I hate being alone a lot worse, though," she says.

I nod, bite my lip.

"You stay with that fairy, don't you? We've seen you guys, like at the park and BK and stuff. Man, Zero had to tell me Donnie was a guy. I swear I didn't know. Pretty freaky, huh."

"Donald, he's Donald," I tell her. "I don't know where he went. I thought maybe here."

She shakes her head. "I don't think Mr. Hunt's into that. Only— one time? Zero told me he made him put on these, like, ladies' panties. Like a joke. Zero said he thinks they were his ex-wife's or something."

I don't get that, why Richard would make him or why Zero would do it, well, for five bucks, I guess. Donald would probably do it for free. This chick Cat's right, he is pretty freaky.

"Zero helped Mr. Hunt build a basement or something, like an apprenticeship, so we were staying here a lot. He's hoping to get a union card. Man, that would be cool." She drops her carpetbag on the couch next to a pillow and folded blanket. She sort of shivers. "I guess you'll get the daughters' bedroom."

I shrug. "I've got nowhere else, so."

"I hear you, man. But it looks like you've got Mr. Hunt now," she shrugs. "It's cool. He won't let us crash here when the baby comes anyways."

"Yeah, but you guys'll be in California, so." I say.

She turns to me and smiles like she forgot about that.

She's peeling potatoes over the sink, dropping the scrapings in the garbage, plunking the skinned ones into this big boiling pot on the stove. Making smashed potatoes, she says I can help smash 'em. She's reaching for a hit off Zero's smoke, but he twists away so she can't and sneers at her all nasty. Zero. Wearing lady underpanties, now I've got that picture in my head.

I give her mine, the whole pack Richard gave me. Newports. I don't really smoke anyway.

Ignore Zero's raised middle finger, taking a sip of this wine Richard pours me instead. In a real wine glass like restaurants use, tasting like alcohol mostly, the second swig making my tongue numb and fuzzy. My lips too, and the back of my neck, flowing through me, calming all the shaky places inside. Hands gut head neck. Groin. Richard raises his wine glass in a toast to us all and her big belly. "To the bun in the oven."

"To the bird in the oven," Cat says.

"To the boy in the basement," Zero says.

"Salud!" Richard says a lot louder.

"Quaalude!" Zero echoes, chugging his wine, so does Richard in a contest he lets Zero win. Richard puts his goblet down, it's not hardly drunk at all. He refills everyone, mine's just a few sips gone and her's with Coke, but Zero's with wine to the rim.

Richard dumps the pink box, pie and all, under the sink where the garbage can's hid, muttering something about never eating anything Zero stuck his fingers in. Never know where Zero's fingers have been.

"So how are you at pies, Angel?" Richard pats my shoulder. "You gonna bake us a pie?"

He doesn't use a recipe, just ingredients you make crust with, sugar flour Crisco, eggs he cracks squishing in this huge bowl with his fingers mushing it together in a raw yellow lump. He's cuffed his sleeves up his forearms like Popeye, then mine 'cause my hands are too goopy with dough. Rolling it out like he shows me, no different really than clay therapy. Pounding it down till it's this flat circle, "Just like a pizza," I say. Richard's brows rise, he's shaking his head. "Some other time, kid. Today it's a pie."

Three pies. One pumpkin, one apple, one peach, so I shake my head going, "Oh, no, no peach," just saying that word like spew in my mouth.

"What's wrong with peach?"

I don't say it's the flavor of rape. I just make a sour face.

"I *love* peach," Richard says. He nods at the drink that's undrunk before me. Bitter hard liquor like slugging medicine I rather not swallow at all. Richard chuckles. "What about oranges? You like oranges? Hey, Zerotski! Get the Triple Sec." Zero swears but disappears into the den.

I'm weaving dough strips like making a pot-holder, one of those loopy arts'n'crafts kinds. Crisscrossing a pie pan of slimy peach slices with Richard's instructions over my shoulder the whole time. "I can't believe you never did this before," he tells me. "That's gonna be fa-a-antastic." And I'm thinking it is pretty cool. I never baked a pie before.

But Richard takes over, his thick fingers move deftly despite their size getting my pie in the oven "sometime before Christmas."

"Try this instead," Richard says, setting a shot glass of amber before me. Richard waits till I taste it, this orange-flavored liquor. Sweet, thick, and warm down my throat. "Better?" he asks but he already knows when I finish the rest and lick clean my sticky numb lips. Zero brings the whole bottle and puts it down clunk on the counter so there it is, this shot glass, refilled.

The Beatles in stereo now, the "Blackbird" track fills Richard's house.

Oh the pie, I forget about the pie. Hearing that echo, *blackbirds baked in a pie* and wondering why I'm remembering that. *Four and twenty,* that's twenty-four, like a math story problem, how many blackbirds baked in a pie? All I can answer is, why?

The house is full with all these guys from each time the doorbell rang, so it's loud with gruff talk, cigarette smoke, and *The White Album* on the hi-fi. Richard keeps sending Cat or Zero to do this or get that, answer the door, more cups, more chairs, a serving fork, refill the ice bucket, more liquor, more beer. Weed, too, somebody fires up a joint and they pass it to me, marijuana. My head already spinning, still, I take a hit no longer feeling my lips, or the harsh smoke singeing my lungs. Just rising inside like an elevator ride away from my melting bones. Till I've taken the shape of this La-Z-Boy chair like James dough pressed into a pan.

Zero's talking to me, his features not quite in focus. He tries to fold something into my palm but I'm wasted and too numb to hold it. *It's from Donnie,* he says. A green plastic ring. Question words fumble to fit in a sentence. *What...where...when...*but they all come out lazy and garbled.

I blink once and Zero's not here and I'm too slow to turn in this chair to see where he goes. Squinting through the smoke and din, distorted faces moving in, chewing, talking, laughter. *Get Yer Ya-Ya's Out!* plays loud in stereo now, the Macy's parade on the Magnavox Color DeLuxe TV console, big balloon floats and raining confetti. I'm tasting puke, spinning, closing my eyes.

Warm puffs moisten my cheek from Richard's beery breath, his voice ebbs and flows through the chaos. "Why aren't you eating? For Chrissake get yourself a Thanksgiving plate, make yourself at home." But it's not my home or my aunt's pumpkin pie, Granma's hug or my sisters, my brother, my mom or my dad. I miss them.

Richard's face looms large before me, wobbly jowls, thin grinning lips moving too close to my ear. His hand dips into my lap and comes up with a green plastic ring. "Well, well. Where did you find this," he says.

Slurred tangled words barely crawl from my mouth. "Zero said it's from Donald. You said Donald's not here. You lied to me."

"You think Zero doesn't lie? Listen. Any guy who will suck another man's dick has got mental problems," Richard says. "Lying would be the *least* of them. You're a smart kid. So believe whoever you want." His grin folds, his heavy hand squeezes my shoulder. He stands up and turns to the room.

"Hey!" His big voice above me demands their attention. "Couple things before you goofballs chow down." The chatter subsides, the parade still moving across the screen, The Stones' bluesy vocals like sassy defiance, flames dance and flicker all fierce in the fireplace, sparks pop and crackle and twirl up the chimney.

"Turn that shit off," Richard says, so they silence Mick Jagger but the buzz is still there swarming my ears. "I know some of you pilgrims have actually got families and obligations later tonight, but isn't that the point of this goddam holiday? Guilt-free over-indulgences? So! Party hardy! Eat hardy! Say, where *is* Hardy?" Snickers and titters drown out Richard's voice with their din. "Quiet! Quiet. Seriously, you guys gotta hell of a lot to be thankful for. You got jobs. My day crew, here's to you finishing West Adams before 1971." His drink raises dizzily above me, they raise theirs too, *Here here!* paper cups cans beer bottles joints in a fleshy blur surrounding this swirling La-Z-Boy chair. "You got three days to sleep this one off and it's my dime. So! Knock yourselves out! Just make sure you're on-site and sober seven a.m. Monday morning."

Laughing low rumbles so I guess they agree. "Here! Here!"

"My night crew, just keep the mess down to a minimum. Some of you assholes are real slobs. You got that right, Dahnke, I'm looking at you. So!" His palms clap again loud by my ear. "Grab a plate, let's eat this bird, and put this goddam holiday behind us. Cheers!" Chugging whatever they're drinking, the music up loud again, the TV, everything spinning so crazy around me when sudden moist lips touch my ear. I pull away but then no it's Cat.

Her voice shrinking and growing like bad reception. "You should probably eat something," she says. But I can't, not one of the eggs she deviled or a cheeseball spread cracker potato chips and onion dip. God, no. My head swirling sunk deep in the leather headrest, the whole universe spinning if I close my eyes, I have to sit up. And when I do, just the smell of it, turkey in the oven or baking peach pie, it makes me throw everything up.

"Jesus fucking Christ—open the window—where's Zerotski? Zerotski! Clean up his mess, where's that goddam incense!" Richard barks somewhere above me.

"He can clean up his own goddam mess," Zero snaps.

"No, he can't. That's the difference between a guest and garbage. Which one are you again, Zerotski?"

Cat's hand takes mine, that's a surprise. It's all fuzzy though, leading me out of the den and the party, crowded with faces of guys I don't know, their introductions already forgotten. Holding on tight to Cat, moving away from the noise and confusion, down the hall lined with swayback doors, all closed the whole way to the end. Pulling me into a white room with green tile and wavering walls. An oblong toilet. Stumbling for it, vomit spills from my throat filling the bowl with runny eggs, I think those were Doreen's. Then after the roar, collapsed on the floor, tangled with TP, wiping gross slime off my shirt.

"It's cool, Angel," her words waver and fade in my ears.

Oh man, it's not cool at all. I don't feel good, angel. Barely balancing, missing the wall then the towel rack, grabbing the sink ledge tight. She starts at the collar unbuttoning this shirt, St. James the Lesser tuck in your tails my mom always says wear a belt if there's belt loops, tie your shoes, shoulders back, and stand tall. But I can't. I need her or this chick Cat to strip this wet pukey shirt off my chest and undress me, untangle my arms from the sleeves. Baring my wrists. Too drunk to hide it, object, or explain. How bad I messed up desperate to get out, I won't do that ever again.

"Oh Jesus, Angel?" her tongue clicks. Dunk my face to the faucet to rinse out my mouth and erase the bad flavor. She gathers my hair into a tail, tugging my head back to braid it. Stumbling on this uneven rug then out in the hallway the wobbly brown carpet, toddling through a dark doorway into black. Falling with Cat not letting go forever it seems mumbling don't leave me tumbling head over heels hugging her tight in a soft pillow landing surrounded by *buzzzzz*. Spinning out of control, no longer the navigator of this sinking ship, ha, if I ever was.

22

I wake to the world's worst migraine headache, so I wish I didn't wake up at all.

Everything's white. I just lie here not moving under the sheets, a jackhammer pounding my skull. The white of the ceiling is agony bright, the light fixture looks like a little glass table if that was the floor and this room upside down. But it's not.

Toss the sheet off confused at first just to focus on where I am. A little girl's bedroom, like a furniture shoot for a Monkey Wards catalog spread. White twin bed A, white dresser B, matching mirror C. White nightstand D beside me with framed photo E of Bozo the Clown with two white little girls. They wear party dresses, pigtails with ribbons, and posed camera smiles. One old as Beth, the younger one fatter than Cat.

Cat?

I flip to face the space beside me where Cat was last night. Empty now, she's gone.

The bedroom door is open. Sitting up, the pounding gets worse. I need aspirin so bad and my shirt. My schoolboy shirt, St. James the Lesser—where is my shirt? Bare feet on the rug, steady myself on the bedpost, zip up these schoolboy chinos. Where'd Cat go? Downstairs she said, where she stays with Zero. But it's blank about Zero or trying to think, Thanksgiving turkey, the party last night or what happened. God, what happened?

I'm thirstier than ever and need something to drink. A whole ocean of water, a bucket of aspirin. I drape the white sheet capelike on my shoulders. Stepping away, it peels off of the bed, trailing the floor at my heels.

All down the hallway the doors are shut so I don't know what room is inside. Except the first one, the green-tiled bathroom to get water and piss and I have to do that so I go in and do. But my shirt's gone. Not on the floor or the sink where you'd scrub it. Not in the bathtub either.

In the medicine chest there's a whole Walgreen's jug labeled 1000 ASPIRIN. Cup my palms under the faucet, guzzle down two bitter aspirin and water water water not even cold but I can't stop slurping it up by the palmful till my gut feels ready to burst. Still, my throat's dry and I'm thirsty.

But leaving this john, the doorway across the hall's open a slice so you see in the room without looking. Clothes on the rug, those stars and stripes pants Zero was wearing. His bony foot hanging off the edge of a bed, dirty and bare, one dangling thin arm, his stringy pale hair sunk face-down in a pillow. Or maybe not pillow. Richard's plump shoulder.

I jump when it moves.

Richard's head turns, his arm slides free so Zero's head flops to the mattress, then sinks under the blanket. Eyes squinting, Richard's wry smile grows at me and the bedsheet I'm wrapped in, too late to step out of his sight. One sausage finger to his small lipless mouth. *Shhh.* "Jesus, you're a skinny little shit," he whispers.

Clench the sheet tighter, blink back creepy feelings. I can barely find words to speak. "Where's Cat?"

"Party's over, kid. Guests have gone home. Only the garbage remains."

Zero's armyman jacket is flung over a chair, a shirt on the rug, and white underwear. *A fiver for a favor.* My headache versus aspirin, it's not a fair fight. "Zero's here," croaks out of my throat. "I thought they're together."

His whisper lowers. "Hell, you know how hippie chicks are. Free love. Hoochie-coochie." He looks down his nose at the lump moving under his blanket. "Probably found someone better than Zero. Not too hard to do." He winks. I feel my face redden.

Zero mumbles a muffled curse.

Richard lies back, relaxed. "What'd you think of last night?"

Last night's just a blur stirring this headache. Everything spinning, that's all I recall. In the bathroom with Cat, she took my shirt off, I let her do that, clean me up, put me to bed, lay beside me. Her skin touching mine, her big belly *or maybe not her*s, it's just blank.

Glancing down the hallway where the living room is, turn right, there's the kitchen, the mud room my boots the Marlboro coat and back door. Look back at Richard, then away, from the motion of Zero undercover.

My pants were unzipped. "I don't remember last night."

A sound bursts from Richard, a quick hardy chortle, so I look through the open door again. His eyebrows rise, he lets out a breath, his eyes open wide at me. He makes this movement like he's zipping his lips. "Gimme a minute to wake up here. You hungry? Of course you're hungry. How's turkey omelet sound?" He's not whispering anymore.

Turning from him, down the hall, passing the den with a quick glance inside—something flies straight at me, I duck but it lowers all harmless. A curtain. The wind sucks it back to its wide-open window. A faint vomit stink in the frigid air, I remember doing that. But not the mess scattered now, magazines, album covers, beer cans, toppled bottles, overfilled ashtrays, paper plates of dried cream and gravy, gnawed turkey bones. Not "party's over" and all the guests going home. Not Cat saying goodbye.

The kitchen's up-ended like a cyclone's come through, crusty pots, dirty dishes all over. The last piece of my pie in the metal pan. A toppled whipped cream can. An empty Triple Sec bottle.

My boots are in the rack, and I think Zero's too, but those combat boots Cat wore are gone. Down three steps to the mudroom, the space where she stuck them is empty. So my heart jolts, they're gone. The Marlboro coat gone from the hook where it hung, and her red coat, too. Unless they're downstairs. She said she hates being cold.

"Cat?" Dragging this sheet, holding the banister, fumbling down steps a lot steeper than yesterday. Down the stair shaft into the shadows and sour chill of the basement. "Cat?"

Slivers of sharp morning light leak in through a small covered casement window. The couch with a pillow and a folded blanket doesn't look slept on at all. I don't see her carpetbag, either.

Swallowing back the basement smell, musty or moldy, not like Thanksgiving last night. What happened last night? To get so wasted even angel can't answer. Retching waves rise in my chest with nothing but spit to gulp them back down.

The rafters above creak from movement upstairs. Two voices volley, muted and snarky, angry and gruff, back and forth, back and forth. Richard and Zero. Their footsteps, too, heavy and light, this way and that, like a dance. *Little shit. Pay up! Like hell. I quit!*

Hurrying now, fear or something urgent gearing my nerves, the cold green linoleum chilling my feet. There's a knotty pine door built under the staircase, a closet I guess, left partway open. There's clothes packed inside like a rack at Goodwill, I run my hand across all the sleeves. Blue denim, brown fringe, red cotton, black leather, plaid flannel. Dirty tan suede—the Marlboro coat!—I pull that one out with a wave of relief. And a Led Zeppelin T-shirt, which is pretty cool and not too big. A plaid long-sleeve flannel, I put that on too, then the Marlboro coat, and close the door that clicks when it latches.

Shivering so crazy with each button fastened, just all edgy to get dressed and go.

There's a basket with laundry on top of the washer, silky things and dresses, his ex-wife's I guess, and XXL men's clothes like Richard would wear, so I wind up the sheet and leave it in there. Padding barefoot back up to the top of the stairs, dressed a lot warmer but more queasy than ever. Pull on my boots, grab the back doorknob to let myself out—but the doorknob turns all by itself. I let go, stepping backward up to the kitchen. The door opens, a tall cowboy lets himself in.

He tips his cowboy hat at me and takes all three stairs in one stride. He's got cowboy boots on, a black leather motorcycle jacket, all zippers and chains, and battered Levi's. He nods at the pie pan on the counter, one gloppy slice left. "Peach pie? That one of Mr. Hunt's?"

I shrug. "I made it."

"No shit?" He lights a smoke, shakes out the match, flicking it into the teetering dishes all crusty and stacked in the sink. He scoops up what's left of the pie on a server, stuffs his mouth. Gulping it down, he gives me thumbs-up and hands the pan back to me. But I don't take it, just shoulder past him.

"Hey, where you going?" he asks, I don't answer. "Hold on, hold on. You need a ride?"

I turn from the back door to face him. He takes another long drag off his smoke, nods at the pie pan he's holding. "Help me tidy this place up and I'll drive you wherever you want," he says.

"Back to the city?"

He raises his hands, *sure, why not?* Pushing himself away from the counter, he stubs his smoke out in the pie, then opens the cabinet under the sink. He hands me a rag and bottle of cleanser and plastic trash bags from an industrial-sized box of a hundred. He shakes one open, holds the mouth wide, and scrapes the pie crusts from the pan inside. Then starts dumping other stuff in, emptying the pots off the stove.

I take the whole turkey platter, carcass and stuffing, dump it in. Spray and wipe the counter, the percolator, the toaster. Then the table, clearing that off, piling more stuff in the sink. When he moves into the den, I'm right behind him, trashing it all, paper plates on the bar, paper cups and beer cans, ashtrays and adult magazines, *Playboy* and *Fling*. I stop, though, at these other magazines. *Boy Love* and *Tenderloins* in red letters across two kids on the cover, all naked and touching each other and not looking too thrilled about it.

The cowboy snaps them out of my hand. "He's a twisted SOB. Here, gimme that." He stuffs them deep into the trash bag, then deeper. Then opening another ten-gallon bag, filling that up and two more. He's quicker than me, clearing the coffee table, leaving nothing but cup rings and spills on the armrests, the 8-track tape deck, the Magnavox hi-fi and TV console, the fireplace mantel and its display of framed pictures from Richard's life. A newspaper clipping, a cap and gown portrait, a young guy dancing outdoors in a black suit and tie. Richard, I guess, in thinner days with more hair and no sunglasses. Following at the cowboy's heels, I shoot it all with spray cleanser, wiping everything clean.

Moving slow, though, I admit, mostly because of those magazines. Thinking about why would they do that? The boys on the cover. Who are they or the hundred more posing inside? *Tenderloins*. Thrown out for the trash truck to haul to the dump. The faces of two naked boys.

I have to step out of the den. Take a deep breath, which doesn't help much. I need something else. Fresh air. The right drugs. Someone who cares.

Shaking, my headache shifts into high gear.

I lug these full trash bags down the three mudroom steps to the back door. He's loading the dishwasher, he knows how to do that, fill Electrasol powder to the red line in the cup, and what buttons to push to start it up. He checks his wristwatch. "Mr. Hunt's still asleep? You all must've really partied hardy last night."

Party hardy. I don't tell him Mr. Hunt's up and in the back bedroom doing whatever with Zero. Embarrassed to, almost, I'm looking around and everything's pretty much tidy. I just want to go now.

"Can't say I'm sorry I split. Not my thing." This cowboy leans back on the sink, legs crossed at his ankles, lighting a smoke like a pose for a Marlboro ad. "Help me haul this out to the trash and we'll hit the road."

"Does he pay you or something?"

"Probably a lot more than I'm worth." He laughs. "I'm his foreman on West Adams." He can see I don't know what he's talking about. "Construction site on a high-rise building downtown. Day crew," he adds with a wink.

The morning sky's dreary with misty rain falling so soft on my face I'm hardly aware I'm getting wet. We're lugging brown plastic sacks full of Thanksgiving trash, me and the cowboy foreman. Out of the house, down the walkway, across the backyard all soggy with dead leaves and branches. Then behind the garage to this little alcove surrounded by bushes and thick evergreens grown taller than the fence, high as the telephone wires.

A flicker of movement draws my attention back to the house. To a back bedroom window, Richard's bedroom window, I think, but soon as I turn, the white shade quickly snaps down.

A shudder flutters my shoulders even with this coat buttoned tight at my throat. I turn to the row of oversized trash cans lined up behind the garage and drop the full bags to the ground. The foreman guy nods. He's got leather gloves on and lifts one lid off, stuffs the can with the bulging brown plastic. He crams it inside and slams the lid on and it's done. His arms fly out wide and he takes a bow like it's the end of his rodeo show.

When I open this other can, it's practically full but, man, it reeks like bad cheese and peaches and I gasp, but not just from the smell. More from what's tangled under the layers of garbage inside.

My shirt. The schoolboy shirt and who threw that out? Cautiously lift it up by the collar, St. James the Lesser all crusty with puke so I drop it. But then floral purple snags my attention, buried deep under the trash. Making my heart skip and teeth start to chatter.

Lavender. The outrageous color. The color of lilacs and letters.

I get woozy, like fainting, so heat fills my head prickling the back of my neck and my fingers barely respond. My mind whirling for reasons why it would be here, but all I can think is: Donald got in Richard's truck.

"Hey! Planet Earth calling, come back, man!" Richard's foreman snaps his fingers in front of my face like you'd wake someone up from a trance. He turns toward the house, summoning me to follow. And I take one step toward him but then a step back, and quick dive my fingers into the can, reaching deep under the shirt through the trash for the lavender corner of paper. Snatching it, it's Donald's whole stationery pad—and I'm tugging it up through garbage and gunk into the light of the day. But my hand snags a sharp that rips into my skin, hooked like a fish or barbed wire. I blurt out, "Fuck—!" The cowboy goes, "What?" I let Donald's pad go, wincing to tear my hand free. *Ri-i-ip*, like torn fabric, I shake my hand out, then open my fingers to see. A deep gash splits my palm from the middle to my thumb, pooling with liquid red.

He's instantly on me like someone in charge. "Shit! You up on your tetanus shots?"

Two crimson rivulets drip down my wrist, that's familiar. It's bleeding and what did I do to get this? Stuck my hand in a can full of garbage and waste. A pukey shirt, dirty rags and magazines, the remains of a Thanksgiving feast. A lilac stationery pad. Thrown out so it doesn't exist anymore, buried without a trace.

Donald, where are you?

The foreman's talking about Band-Aids and Bactine, inspecting my palm in his. Mine trembling badly but not from the cut. I snap my ripped hand from his grip.

"There's a first aid kit in the house," he's saying as he goes around the corner. "You probably should get a tetanus shodjustobeshur..."

I don't follow, though. Thinking about Donald in Richard's red truck, in that ugly brown kitchen or bed. Blinking that picture out of my head, but it won't go away. Donald. His odd duck hair on Richard's white shoulder or under his sheets in ladies silk undies. For five bucks an hour or fifty minimum and his own room, first class all the way. Be something else, go someplace else. California or the Virgin Islands.

A dog barks so angry somewhere, making me jump. Tires on gravel pass by unseen beyond the tall hedges and backyard fence. In one swoop, I snatch Donald's notebook from the top of the trash and slam the lid shut.

JAMES JAMES JAMES. Printed in purple across lilac flowers and smeared with red, what from? Blood. *My* blood, my dripping palm.

"...ayman aryoo coming or no?" The foreman's voice approaches from around the corner of the garage.

Brain reeling, he's coming, I don't want him or Richard to take it from me. Quick! In my pocket, but the angle is wrong, the notebook catches and falls to the ground so I plow it instead deep in the branches all crackle and snap, and pull my hand free, standing up two seconds before he turns the corner and sees. *JAMES JAMES JAMES* hidden away, safe inside the evergreens.

23

"Let's not bother Mr. Hunt," the foreman says. He's running the tap on my palm, flushing this gash in a gush of cold water. Streaks of my blood swirl red down the kitchen sink drain.

He's Gus, he says, Gus Greenbacks (the Gambler) in parenthesis like the title of a top ten song, "Quick Joey Small (Run Joey Run)," or "Instant Karma (We All Shine On)." He calls me Angel, we met last night, but I don't remember that conversation. God, my hand stings, I try not to grimace and ask if he met Cat too. He says yeah, she had to split so he gave her a lift to some hippie crash pad in Uptown. Not Cat, "the feisty little knocked-up chick," that's what he calls her.

"That's where I want to go," I tell him. "Wherever you took her." I'm so edgy, I think that's what keeps my palm bleeding so bad. Real edgy to split now too.

He wraps a kitchen towel around the torn open skin. "Hold it up, above your heart, like this." He poses my hand in the air. "Give it a few while I warm up the van. Five minutes, tops. Hopefully, it'll stop bleeding by then. Or I'll be dropping you off at an ER somewhere." He pulls keys from his jacket, a whole set of keys on a metal ring shaped like a five-pointed leaf. He stops in the mudroom to zip up his jacket then pulls the door shut behind him.

The second he's gone, I'm thinking I should've went with him.

The towel's already soaked bright red with blood. I peek under, feeling queasy. The cut skin's peeled back, all slimy wet pinkness inside. Like a fish Grampa gutted one time.

BAM!

My heart skips and I jump at the loud noise under my feet—a door slamming or washer lid maybe—down in the basement someone, I guess Richard or Zero, moving around. More noises—a car door shutting, the cough of a sputtering engine, Gus Greenbacks (the Gambler) starting his van and the churning *whirr* the dishwasher makes cycling water through pipes in the walls.

I step toward the mudroom to look down the stairs, unwinding the towel. But it's still bleeding and before I can stop it, a drop hits this suede coat sleeve, a drop hits the floor. I quick bind the sting tight in the towel again. God, my hand's throbbing. Where's Gus and his van, what's taking so long?

Pull back the brown kitchen curtain. But the window's fogged up so there's nothing to see, not Gus or a van, just the top of the fence and the yellow brick house next door.

"Grienbach left, did he?" Richard says.

Whip from the window to face him. His frame fills the mudroom coming up the three stairs. Wet hair neatly parted, dark slacks, button-down shirt, and moccasin slippers.

"Good start," he says. He hooks a key ring on the key holder thing. "You can clean up the rest after breakfast." His eyes sweep the room catching every missed crumb or splatter. And the blaring red drip on the floor. "Whose goddam blood's on my fucking linoleum?"

At first I'm unsure of what I should do, get down on my knees and swab it or leave, he's staring me out like a dare. So I kneel down and wipe it with the dish towel wrapped around my hand. But he steps over me like a towering shadow, one thick thigh straddling each side of my neck. If I look up it's right at his fly.

His words fill my ears. "How'd you manage that?"

Clutching this dish towel tighter. "I thought it stopped bleeding."

He scoffs, a quick snort of breath from his nose. With two steps back he moves off me. "Let's see that," he says, holding my elbow helping me up off my knees. I jerk back from his grip and shudder. He shakes his head, like he's tolerating me but just barely. "Look, kid. I'm a trained paramedic."

"You already said."

He unwinds the towel, his towel, actually. Soaked red with my blood. My palm in his, he inspects it, pushing the coat sleeve and flannel cuff back. Then checks my other wrist. "Jesus Christ. You want to die?"

What? Shake my head. "It's not cut that bad."

"Christ. Take off your coat, would you? Let's see what you did. Besides helping yourself to my closet downstairs." He tugs at this flannel, pokes a hard finger in the Led Zeppelin T-shirt underneath. When I don't move to do it, he grabs the wool collar and in one movement strips the coat off me and onto a kitchen chair. "Taking what isn't yours. Is that stealing or borrowing? Some people might get really pissed off over a little thing like that."

Side-stepping me, bumping my arm, he steps from the kitchen and opens the first hallway door. It's a closet. He pulls out the black doctor bag, the one with the red cross he had in his El Camino.

Flick my hair out of my eyes. "Somebody threw my shirt out."

He brushes against me, opening the doctor bag on the counter next to the sink. He taps his forehead with one thick finger. "Yet you never thought to come to me and ask." He gets out a roll of white doctor tape and snips a piece off with a blunted surgical scissor but stops with it held up midair. "'Excuse me, Mr. Hunt?'" he says in a little mouse voice. "'I sicked up on myself. Would you have a clean shirt I could borrow?'"

"You were busy, or whatever. With Zero."

"'You were busy with Zero,'" he mimics, sounding more like a whiny little girl. He's squished gooey salve from a tube on this wound. "Zero," he mutters. "Useless excuse for a human being. Sniveling and complaining. Who needs that shit, right?"

I don't think I'm supposed to answer. He tapes both oozy edges of skin back together, wraps a long strip of gauze around my hand, the whole roll practically. Watching me while he does, like will I cry or unduly complain so I don't, though it's taped tight enough to be numb. He flicks on the faucet, rinses my blood off where it's splattered the sides of the basin. He pours bleach down the drain and drops the stained towel under the sink in the garbage can there. It's lined with brown plastic.

"You hungry?" he asks. "Or horny?" His big hand caresses his crotch, but the back doorknob turns and the door pushes open, and there, he's come back, Gus Greenbacks the Gambler, wiping his feet on the mudroom mat. Richard's hand swings from his nuts to his forehead, shoving his thick hair back. "Man, I could eat a horse," Richard says, both his hands patting his belly.

Relief eases my breathing, releases a smile that Gus Greenbacks returns with a nod. "Your neighbor's cool, Mr. Hunt. He gave me a jump."

"Jesus Christ, you back again, Grienbach?" Richard perks up angry or amused, peering over my head at Gus Greenbacks. "What're you bothering the neighbor for? Next he'll be over here wanting to borrow some goddam thing."

"He was pulling out of his driveway and offered to help. It's all cool. Cooool and copacetic."

"Goddam freeloading sonuvabitch." Grumbling about the neighbor or maybe Gus, the muscles in Richard's neck twitch.

"Just being useful." Gus Greenbacks leans into the counter, his arms folded across his black leather jacket, all poker-faced like a gambler. "Thought I'd stop by and help you clean up."

"Is that so," Richard says, more like a rumble escaping his chest.

"Angel here and me, we got your counters cleaned, the den cleared, got a load going in the dishwasher. Threw out most of the trash." Gus nods toward the backyard. "The cans are pretty full back there, might be time for a run to the dump. But unless you got anything else for me, I'll make like a pea and split."

I pull my coat from the kitchen chair, fumbling this bulgy bandage almost too big to fit down the sleeve. Turning to split but turning instead right into Richard blocking the way.

"You stay," Richard says. I start to object, I just wanna go now with Gus.

"Mr. Hunt?" Gus opens the storm door, a chill makes its way up the stairs. "Aren't your daughters spending Thanksgiving weekend with you? I thought you got a court order to make Midge comply. You're picking them up at four."

Richard's jaw tightens, he squints at the clock on the stove. Looking around at the rest of the mess, the kitchen, the den, and whatever was left down the hall. He grumbles, shoving my shoulder. "Get him out of here, Grienbach."

I step away from his reach. "Is Zero coming?"

Richard's eyes slit like he's angry I asked. "'Is Zero coming?' Ungrateful little shit. Zerotski's gone," he snaps. "And good riddance to bad rubbish."

Down the three steps in my cowboy boots, Zero's shoes gone and that army jacket, so I'm eager to leave now too, despite not getting breakfast. Gus holds the door wide so I duck under his arm, glad to be finally going.

"See you Monday, man," I hear him tell Richard. "Nice kid. Maybe I'll hire him on my day crew."

I don't hear what Richard grumbles. I'm halfway down the driveway to the open chainlink gate.

24

We're sitting on the curb outside The Fresh Cup Diner chucking pebbles into the street. She refreshes her makeup in a little hand mirror, lip gloss and mascara lashes, then drops it in the carpetbag at her feet, packed and ready to go. Waiting for the mailman, this is the third day we've come. Waiting for him to *"D-liver D-let-ter D-sooner D-bet-ter."* Cat laughs when I say it's The Marvelettes and sing it to her a cappella. She knocks my fingers away from picking the tape off this bandage. "Give it time to heal, man," she says, but I don't think it's healing at all.

She points out the last autumn leaf dangling from an empty tree. She easily distracts me. All the other trees look dead with bare branches. She hates that, she says, how everything dies here in winter. She can't wait to be in California, she asks if I think Zero's there now. He's going to send her a ticket to join him. He's going to mail it here. "We'll be like that poster at Head Land, man. The one with surfers and a Day-Glo orange sun, that says 'Endless Summer.'"

I shake *endless* out of my head. "Everything ends," I say.

"Man, that's the saddest thing in the world. Why would you say that to me?"

"It's not, though." So I tell her when bad things end, that's a happy thing, right? And just knowing they will end, well…I point at the postman like Exhibit A, heading this way with his mailbag full of letters. "Maybe that helps get you through."

She smiles and hefts her carpetbag up. She waits till the mailman enters the diner. She's right at his heels when he does. I cross my fingers and toss another pebble into the street.

From Rand's hotel window you can watch December take over Chicago. People hunch against the wind that swirls in off the lake, winding its way between city buildings, finding its way into his room. Icy fingers of cold whistle up my spine and down my shirt collar, but still. I'm not out in the street.

"Your turn," Cat says. We're playing Tic-Tac-Toe on a greasy pizza box. Rand, all wound up and smoking his tenth cigarette, passes his killer pot and a bottle of Ripple around. The second hit does it for me, so I'm not into playing at all anymore, or trying to teach Rand to read: *It's "E" not "I" when you read the word "PIZZA," it's "I" not "E" when you read "P-I-E."* When I write "C-A-T" in a heart, she corrects me. "It's cat with a K not a C."

Rand snickers. "See, yer not so smart."

"Kat," I say with a K, which sounds *exactly* the same.

She's sitting cross-legged on Rand's mattress beside me, one hand caressing her belly. Disappointment hangs heavy around her today, it's harder to get her to smile. The letter will be here tomorrow she'll say if you ask her. She flicks her cigarette ash in a BK cup, turns another page of her paperback novel. *Valley of the Dolls*. Rand knows all the names of the dolls on its cover. Doll, Donald called me, maybe he got it from the same book. So my last thought drifting off is of Donald.

Kat's sudden gasp pops me out of that dream.

"Feel! It's moving!" She grabs my palm, pressing it flat to her round denim belly under her red wool coat. *Ba-loop!* A bump like a shark fin swims under her skin.

"What is that?"

Her smile flickers but just barely. "A knee. Or elbow? I don't know, man. Maybe its dick." But she gasps like she's just been punched in the gut and sucks in a really deep breath, so I jump to her side and ask what's the matter? She shakes her head though, like it's nothing. She says sometimes it's harder to breathe if she's in a certain position. She doesn't like to complain. I quietly add, "Unduly complain."

"What do you mean?" she asks.

It is harder to breathe. *Rule #2. Do not agitate, unduly complain, or magnify grievances.* I tell her about the list of twelve rules at the state juvenile correctional facility at Railton. *The Directors Rules.* How they had mimeographed copies framed in metal screwed at eye-level to every locked door. So after eight months of waiting for doors to unlock, you know every rule by heart.

Kat mimes with her hands like she's ripping the list into millions of bits and throwing the rules away.

"America's a pretty big country," I say, when Doreen at the Fresh Cup flips through the mail and tells Kat again, there's no letter today. "LA's far away, maybe it's just taking longer to get there. Or something hap..." but I wisely shut up before the fear or despair in Kat's eyes gets any deeper. I really don't want her to fall in that hole. Ever.

Leaving the diner, she opens the door, the bell on it jingles. I follow Kat out, down the vestibule step to the street. I think she's upset and I don't want her to be. Something inside my chest flinches.

"The baby's supposed to be born in California," she says. "In the ocean, so it just swims out, and stuff."

"Really?"

"Zero said." She rubs her eyes with the heel of her hand, readjusts the guitar strap she attached to the big carpetbag to carry the weight on her shoulder. "Man, why did he have to split without me?"

I don't have an answer, I don't want her to cry. "You could go to O'Hare and maybe fly there to meet him."

"Really?" She perks up. "How much would that be?"

A lot, I tell her, I think a hundred. But maybe not, one time they let me fly free. Sort of.

Kat's smile reappears and she empties her pockets. A mitten, a Kleenex. A quarter. "Two bits," she says, and deposits it into her overalls bib pocket. "For California, man."

There's fifty-three cents in my pocket. The coins clink in her pocket meeting her quarter. Her fingers count in the air, her eyes circle up like she's thinking. "We just need ninety-nine twenty-two more," she says.

"We do?" I'm smiling at her sudden excitement, that she's including me in her plan, but mostly impressed she can do math so fast. And how I can get the rest for her faster. "My granma would probably give us the money. I mean, we could just call her and ask."

There's a phone booth at the corner. We look at each other for half a second then race down the block to be first dibs inside. It's a tie and we're laughing, squeezed in together, her packed carpetbag, her big baby belly. Her coat pressed against mine.

I call Granma Hannah collect. But it rings and rings and nobody answers. I don't feel good about that.

FLIP CITY

Rand kicking into my head wakes me up, I'm shielding myself and moaning, it's not the best welcome to a new day. But he's ranting again, unduly complaining, about rent-pills-pot and now my black Acmes. *His* boots he says because *Somebody* owes him, fergit reading lessons, that's bullshit not bread and he needs the bread *now*, man. Zero *always* paid up but Zero's not here, and now Somebody is me. "Cross my palm with green, or..." His thumb swings toward the door.

Kat shrugs at me and mouths, *They're just boots*, like it's no big deal. She pats the bib pocket on her overalls where the CA green is stashed. Spare change we panhandled yesterday, plus cash this morning, nineteen.

I kick these boots off and across the room—*his* room. And it's not so much giving them to him that pisses me off, it's more they were finally starting to fit okay without rubbing the skin off my toes. Rand kicks out of his worn Beatle boots and sails them over to me, which at first is like insult plus injury. But then I put them on and, oh, they just melt like butter around my feet, comfy as bedtime slippers. So I've got no complaints at all.

"Rule number one: Nothin's free," Rand says. "So where's the rest y'all owe me?"

25

It's got to be twenty-five or thirty stories, a tower of concrete and glass where Gus Greenbacks takes me to work. It's got hundreds of offices like empty boxes, each with a rectangle cut in the wallboard five inches left of the door frame. He gives me a carton of light switch covers, a thousand at least, a box of 5,000 screws, and a screwdriver. He'll be back at noon and treat me to lunch. He tips his cowboy hat.

I already know after doing two rooms I don't want to do this at all. There's other guys working, maybe ten crews of three or four each, moving together like chain gang pictures or sons of construction workmen. And a few stray guys I recognize, from early this morning outside The Fresh Cup. Gus said five bucks an hour so they jumped at his offer, and he drove us all in his old beater van to work.

Twist twist twist twist twist. Twist twist. It takes five twists to get the screw in then two more hard twists to secure it. Two holes on each cover, I follow the wiring crew office to office, attaching one to each wall. I'm not fast like they are and fall way behind. Break time they said is not till ten thirty, which feels like forever to come.

Twist twist twist so I just want to *shout!*... This one guy warns me I'm gonna be fired if the crew boss catches me sitting it out, but you know, I'm pretty much hoping he does.

FLIP CITY

I'm mostly thinking on Kat and the sweet way that feels, sleeping beside her on Rand's sleazy hotel room floor. Where I wish I was now and not doing this job, trading time spent with Kat for money. How many minutes already wasted, away from her and the baby moving inside? Then thinking instead, five bucks each hour and how much is that every minute? Whatever that is, I don't think it's worth it.

This tall lanky guy wanders in, supervisor, crew boss, maybe inspector, who knows. He doesn't say anything at first, watching me screw up another faceplate on the wall. I just wish he'd split, but no. He shakes two smokes from a pack of Winstons and offers me one. When I take it, his lighter snaps open and fires it up.

"She-it," he drawls—and when he does, you can hear he must be one of Rand's country cousins or cronies in crime—"hustlin' wuzza whole lot easier'n this." He yuck-yucks sort of shucking his feet, his body all fluid and boneless as Goofy, and shows me a hand-rolled joint in his palm. Bobbing his head like a cartoon or dope fiend, he nods for me to join him in the hall.

He's supposedly working with the restroom crew, spending his whole day bolting toilets into the floor. Commodes, though, he calls them. He steps in a restroom to show me, pointing out with the joint how perfect the commodes he installed are, and when I compliment him on a job well done, he beams like his life is worth living. I'm laughing, not at him really, more at feeling a whole lot better smoking his pot. He's got really good pot.

"Hey, yew bin to the top?" And when I say no, he races me up ten flights or more till we stop at the very top. I'm all bent over, catching my breath. Him too, we're both sucking air, heads down, hands clasped to our knees.

I follow him into this one corner office, over the raw concrete floor. You can see out the windows the frozen white lake below, the whole frozen city, the whole county maybe, spread wide like a live silent map. Somewhere down there is Doreen's Fresh Cup Diner, The Allnite Arcade, and Rand's seedy room with Kat asleep on the floor. Straining to find the orange HOTEL sign that flashes outside its window. Imagining her smile when I come in with BK French fries or maybe White Castle, and a bundle of cash for CA. When do we get paid? Inhaling more weed, it's really mellow, lightening my head and making the world not so scary. The burning end races to meet my lips, flaring hot and popping a seed so I'm laughing, passing it to him. This Goofy guy clamps it inside a matchbook he folds like a holder so your fingers don't singe. So I am impressed. He says he figgers if we jest keep movin 'round till quittin' time, well, yukyukyuk, how would they know? We jest punch out at four like ever'berdy else'n pick up our pay. I say that sounds ga-roovy to me and we slap hands high-five, sharing laughter.

I point out this one office building standing tall from the rest in the middle of the Loop.

He chuckles. "Wha'? That some famous landmark or sumppin?" Passing the folded matchbook to me, the roach in its grip just a small flaming paper. Sucking in smoke, it burns hot in my throat, making me cough and clouds my whole head up with magic.

"S'where my dad works," I say, hearing my voice all throaty and low, talking like somebody else. His face gets all puzzled at those two words, *dad* I guess and *works*. He takes a huge hit and passes the joint back to me.

His Goofy expression, his horsey teeth, I can't help it, his pot makes these giggles tumble like dominoes out of my heart, I can't stop them coming at all. Because it hits me how important it is that commodes get put in right, and I tell him, ha, it's probably the most important job in the world. More important than cops or lawyers. Or the president. This Goofy guy agrees. "Shit's gotta flush, man," and he's laughing too, quietly, but every once in awhile this loud hoggy snort honks out, cracking us both up again so bad, he loses his footing. He falls *BAM!* into the rattling window pane so my heart jolts insane—I grab his shirt, going "Whoa! Whoa, Nellie!" so we're cracking up all over again about that, *whoa Nellie,* holding onto each other like cartoon buddies.

The glass doesn't crack and he doesn't fall out. Just falls silent, swallowing his laughter all bug-eyed and suddenly pale. "Uh...catch y'all later," he says.

Ha, "Hope I don't have to—" I mean catch him later, laughing at that till the last of these chuckles dies and I take a deep breath, glad for his pot and that he didn't fall out, and I turn to wave him goodbye. It's when I freeze, too.

Richard's huge self fills the door frame. His head to the ceiling like some giant ogre, his heavy work boots take up half the gray concrete floor. Staring me down with sharp ray gun eyes.

"You're fired," he says. Two words left nailed in the air.

Richard nods toward the elevator and rides down it with me all twenty-three floors and won't break a smile when I do. His hand on my back, he hustles me out of the empty lobby into the cold of the day, stumbling over lumpy frozen mud to where his red Chevy pickup is parked.

"Get in," he commands, but I shake my head. "You wanna get paid? Get in the truck."

When I do, he slams the door shut, trapping me in the front seat.

Richard gets behind the wheel, pulls a thick envelope from his black leather coat, opens the flap. And he takes out, I swear, a whole bankwad of cash. Flipping through it, he starts whipping bills at me, at my face, at my lap, so I'm flinching with each one he throws. "That's what you get—forty bucks. I said I'd pay you five bucks an hour and if I hired a goddam hophead, that's my problem, that was my bad judgment, to treat you like anything more than a useless street punk in the first place."

I push his bucks off my lap back toward him and let my head drop to the headrest. Look at the ceiling, not feeling high anymore. "Gus Greenbacks hired me. I thought I was working for him."

His stare cuts into me, his lips tight like a rubber band and not a mouth at all. "Then you're both fired," he snaps.

Which is like being punched, and I practically jump off the seat. "How's that fair, if I'm the retard who can't use a screwdriver right? Forget it." Pulling up on the door handle to split. "Don't pay me anything."

"Whoa, whoa. Sit down." His heavy mitt traps my shoulder so I can't leave.

"Get your hand *off* me," I say.

His hand moves away, which I'm not expecting. He gathers the money and stares at me so hard I have to look the other way. Out the window. At construction workers, foremen, and useless punks off the street.

"Grienbach showed you what to do. Jesus Christ, it's not difficult."

When I face him, he scratches his head, runs his hand through his thick hair. Then bangs his palm hard on the steering wheel. "Listen," he says, suddenly calm like a teacher or somebody's dad. "Do you want a job? Do you want to actually work and earn a paycheck? Because if you're serious, hell, I've got plenty of jobs you could do."

Sitting straighter, I nod. "Just, no screwing," I say.

He grunt-laughs with a shake of his head. "No screwing," he says and starts up the engine, jams the gear in reverse, and looks over his shoulder backing up. The tires peel out in a skid and a hairpin turn, leaving the construction lot gate.

26

I'm thinking I'll just do whatever this job is he's got and get paid. I never have to even *see* him again, I just have to get through today. Then find a job someplace else where they pay you, a department store, BK, or maybe the diner. Someplace a lot closer than wherever he's driving me now. Up an on-ramp to the expressway.

«where are we going» Which is a good question.

"Crazy, wanna come?" Richard answers when I ask him.

I shake my head, regretting even getting into his truck, and scanning outside for an escape.

"Westlawn," he says, shifting gears, going faster. He raises his eyebrows at me. "You want to drive?"

"Me? I don't have a license."

"Don't need one. As long as you know the secret."

"What's the secret?"

Richard whispers, "Don't get caught." He flicks on the blinker, *click-a-click-a-click*, checks over his shoulder, then moves into the right lane, down the next exit ramp and pulls to the curb at the end. "Three on the tree. You do drive a stick, don't you?"

And before I can say I don't drive a stick, or a car, or a red truck, or *any*thing, he's stepped out of the truck and tosses the key to me.

In the driver's seat. Behind the steering wheel, of all insane things, to drive his red truck. Grip my sweaty hands around the solid steering wheel, looking over the dashboard out the windshield, sitting so high above the street. Feeling pretty grand, actually. Convincing myself I can do this. I mean if my mom can and Gary, how difficult, really? Even Granma Hannah can drive.

My heart pounds in time with the blinker. *Click-a-click-a-click.*

Richard climbs into the passenger side, adjusts himself closer beside me. "Your old man never taught you to drive?" He shakes his head when I say my dad doesn't trust me to drive, or live, or do anything. "Let's see how you do," he says. "Maybe go for your license next week."

"My driver's license?"

Richard nods.

"Clutch," he shows me, his hand moves my left foot to the pedal. "Brake," pressing my right foot on that. "Shift," his huge hand cups mine on the stick shifter knob, moving it back and forth in its channel, down, up, back, up, down. "Neutral, first, second, third." Back to first. "Accelerate." He moves my brake foot to step on the gas pedal. "Ready?"

Pressing my whole weight into my clutch foot, stepping down on it hard as I can.

"Up on the clutch, down on the gas." His hand on mine puts the key in the ignition and twists it. The engine rumbles, the truck vibrates just like when anyone drives. My sister in her Mustang or men in the night.

Richard nods. "Drive the truck."

Shift neutral into first. It grinds half a moment till I feel the gear fit and lock in.

"Check your mirrors, James," he says. "Always check those mirrors."

I nod, okay, look out the rearview, the side mirror, and over my shoulder, my heels all jittery just touching the pedals. Cars zip down the exit ramp really close, even Cadillacs and Mercedes. I glance at Richard.

"Don't hit the cars," he says.

Letting up slow slow slow on the clutch, the whole truck jerks-jerks-jerks—

"Gas, more gas!" Richard shouts.

Beside me his face is beefy and red and I try to do it like he said but it's so awkward with him hanging over my shoulder and I mess up, kill the engine. The whole truck shudders and dies.

"What the hell is so hard about this? I'm beginning to agree with your old man, kid. You're useless."

"Don't say that to me." I lift up on the door handle, stepping halfway to the street. A horn blasts, a Trans Am guns past.

"Whoa, whoa." His palms raise. "You're right. You're right, I'm sorry."

I'm sorry? Did he really say that? So I hesitate, one foot still in the truck. Looking around, nothing's familiar. Apartments, a store, a corner bar. I don't have a clue where we are.

"Jesus Christ, stop being so damn sensitive. Even your swishy friend Donald could drive," he says, and pats the driver's seat. "You wanted to know about Donald, didn't you?" Richard nods because he's got my attention. "Word is, he's in lockup on a morality charge. And loving it, I'm sure. Now come on. Get in the truck," he says. His gloves clap, rubbing together.

I don't get in, though. "Whose word?" I say. "Where's he locked up? I wanna see him."

Richard purses his lips. He looks away, at traffic passing on the highway above, then shakes his head and turns back to me. "Sure. You want to see him, I'll take you to see him, how's that." He offers his hand and when I take it, he helps pull me up on the seat. "You don't mind getting ID'd and fingerprinted and cavity searched, hell, go see him."

«no. don't open that can of worms» angel says. I make a face, shuddering, no thanks. But still, turning the key, starting the engine, I'm imagining Donald. Locked up in jail, driving this truck, sitting here beside Richard. Clutch, brake, shift, accelerate.

The engine purrs, there's this rolling kind of jerk, smoother though, and I've got it in gear and I'm driving.

I drove here, that crazy thought fills me, *I drove a truck.* Thinking of that like a miracle happened, and not about cleaning the rug in his den when I follow him into his house. Get out the wine and puke stains mostly, that's what he'll pay me to do. But I'm thinking maybe I could drive Kat to CA, how cool that would be and I'm not really paying attention. They're from his daughter's birthday party, he says. So I look at him like I've been listening, hoping I didn't piss him off or give him a reason to not get my license next week.

"Damn housewives can't handle their wine, their damn kids sick-up on too much chocolate," he says, going on and on about him and his neighbors as if it's something I wanted to know. He checks out what's left of the cut on my hand and gives me a kitchen glove to keep the scab dry. He brings me a scrub brush, solvent, and razor blades, he trusts me with those, then gives me this look like, *why shouldn't I?* He says the cleaning stuff is under the kitchen sink, no need to get anything from downstairs. In fact, I don't want you going downstairs. Just clean the rug, maybe take out the trash. The rest of the house is tidied and fine, everything neat in its place.

Black-framed certificates are hung on one wall. *Chamber of Commerce Contractor of the Year. 1965. 1966. 1969.* He's a contractor, not a cop. Why did I ever think he was? Detective, lumberjack, jack of all trades. Family photos line the bar and his fireplace mantel.

Checking out this one picture of Richard a whole lot younger and dressed in a suit, dancing on somebody's *grave*. RICHARD LEE HUNT, SR. carved on the headstone. A chill flashes through when his eyes meet mine.

"Happiest day of my life," Richard says. A quick smirk flicks one side of his mouth. He says his ex framed the pictures and put them there, he should toss 'em out, they're a reminder of past things he'd rather forget—which is *exactly* why she chose them. "Except this one. You see this? That's me with JFK. Bet that's worth money now."

I hold up the frame he's talking about, he nods at the yellowed newspaper clipping inside it. A photo of Richard shaking hands with a man on the Capitol steps. The caption says, **MEET MR. PRESIDENT: Westlawn City Council President Richard L. Hunt, Jr. and wife, Midge, meet Democratic candidate John F. Kennedy on a recent trip to Washington, DC.**

"That's you, huh."

"Ten years and twenty pounds ago," Richard says. He's proud about it though, you can tell.

I hold the frame up so I'm squinting, comparing the newsprint photo to him. "More like fifty pounds," I say.

"Hey, let me tell you," he says, patting his girth. "It's not easy keeping this boyish figure. Just wait till you're my age. You watch, some damn street punk'll be saying the same thing about you."

I shake my head. "Won't happen," I tell him. "I'm never gonna be that old."

"Don't be so sure," he says, going into the kitchen. He grabs his keys off the merit badge key hook, putting his leather coat on. "Well, I've got a business to run. You want to start dinner, I should be home around six. Unless something better comes up." Richard winks, slamming the door behind him.

I'm alone in his house after he's gone for hardly five minutes when this eerie feeling takes over, like someone is standing behind me. It's so creepy I don't look back over my shoulder, scared of what I might see. I don't know what, either. But the silence in here is so overwhelming its presence takes over the room.

I can't stand it and pick Led Zeppelin from a rack of 8-tracks on his Magnavox console, push the cartridge in, turn the volume all the way up. "Whole Lotta Love" zips between speakers set corner to corner, drowning the heebie-jeebies out. I'm screaming along with Robert Plant, faking a mic in my hand, down on my knees, scrubbing the rug or shaving the brown stains away. Like a rock star wailing "The Lemon Song" or a janitor singing the blues. *Down on this killing floor.*

Silence returns at the end of the album, slowly at first so I don't really feel it, but then even worse than before. I rock back on my heels, try to shudder the silence away. Checking around every inch of the rug, I think I got every last stain. So he can't say I've got a lazy work ethic or I'm useless and not worth being paid. Or as an excuse to not go for my license next week.

"It's cool," I say out loud to angel, breaking the silence and letting whoever's listening know I'm not by myself or helpless. "Cool and copacetic." I dump the bucket down the kitchen sink then rinse it, put the scrub brush and glove and razor away where Richard got them, under the sink with the waste can and cleanser and industrial-size box of trash bags. Another feeling stirs up inside, a cool feeling though, a sense of excitement like I got something new.

I drove here.

I can't wait to tell Kat. Come home from work with bucks in my pocket, I'm not sure how much, enough to pay Rand though, and ask her out. Like to a movie or real nice dinner. *Love Story* or surf 'n' turf. Or a plane ride to California.

Out the kitchen window, Christmas lights scallop the eaves of the house next door. It's holiday time, that's depressing. Another year not welcome home.

Ha, but if I *did* go home, I'd drive there. I'd pull up and park in front of my dad's house. Man, he'd probably ground me forever. Even *with* my license, he'd never let me drive his car.

Slip into this mangy Marlboro coat and my boots from the mud room and drag out the trash bag that's not even full. Open the back door and let myself out. Two steps down the stoop, through the backyard, turn left behind the garage. Trash cans, all empty this time when I open one lid then the others.

An icy wind rustles the trees with a whisper that bristles the back of my neck. *James. James. James...* From the thick evergreen boughs.

Jam my hand through the branches, despite sticker barbs that poke at the scab on my palm. Reaching deeper, till my fingertips bump the damp paper clump, the branches let go, and the lilac pad springs free in my grip.

JAMES. JAMES. JAME. Written three times on its ripped cardboard cover, streaked brown with Thanksgiving gravy or wine. Or my blood when I tore my palm open.

«because blood turns brown when it dries»

Crows flutter and fly off the telephone lines. A truck rumbles by rattling the tall backyard fence and the dense wall of evergreens that hide it. I'm shuddering too, clutching the notepad tight, one thought repeating loud in my head: *The secret is don't get caught.*

27

It's like I've brought Donald into the kitchen to sit at the table with me, and I flip back the cover eager to read what he says. The first page is missing the last ruled line, torn off in a strip at the bottom. And I flip through the pages to more disappointment. There's no message from Donald. Or letter to read. Or anything.

I just want to go. I just want to get out of here.

Richard said he'd be back by six o'clock and it's going to be six any minute. I can barely sit still, my knee jittery at like 200 beats. Waiting for the minute hand to click to twelve. Waiting for the rumble of his 454 V-8 in the driveway. His key in the back door. Counting out cash from the thick envelope to pay me. Then drive me back to the city with money for Kat and her CA fund or rent and more medication, and maybe to ask her out. I count on my fingers how many hours, a lot more than eight, you times that by five to get the amount you get paid. Thinking any second he'll step through the door, any second. Watching the back door but nothing happens.

The back door, where Donald came in.

Imagining that, Donald joking with Richard, *Well, call me a cab*, and maybe still laughing. Coming into the mudroom. Slipping his shoes off and into the boot rack, his penny loafers with shiny new dimes. Then his ladies fur-collared coat—no—*jacket*, he had on a red jacket, because it was my birthday, he dressed like a guy. In 501 Levi's like *Rebel Without a Cause.*

«red like the jacket in the closet downstairs»

I cram the notepad in the Marlboro coat pocket and jump up, barely stepping on the mudroom landing, leaping the stairwell three steps at a time down to the green tile floor. If it is Donald's jacket, then...but why would he leave it? Or his ring Zero had? Or his stationery pad?

I don't want you going downstairs.

Feeling my way around the corner into the dark, the basement smells musty and sweet, I remember that from Thanksgiving. The freezer against the wall, the big blocky furnace, the couch for Kat or where other guests sleep, the closet built under the stairs. Moving hand over hand along the knotty pine paneling, finding the closet. But the doorknob doesn't turn. It's locked.

«the merit badge key ring» Upstairs, he's got keys on that thing, so I run up, snatch the key ring, practically leap the whole stairwell back down. Finding the keyhole is like reading Braille, all these keys jangling and all I can think is why does he have so many doors? Inserting the right key, it easily turns with a click that unlocks it and opens the closet. Flail my hands overhead in the dark, till a hanging string tickles my palm. I catch it and snap the closet light on.

Instantly spotting red cotton fabric, parting the clothes with my arms, wondering whose are these anyway? They're not clothes that daughters or little girls wear. Grabbing the red zippered jacket, the jacket Donald had on. Frisking its two side slash pockets. One empty. One not.

I pull out a thick paper square, double-folded, which springs open like wings and flips out of my hand and lands on the rug at my feet. A lilac envelope, adorned with swirly handwriting in purple ink. Picking it up, my heart pounds.

"TO: MR. ROSS, ATT'Y AT LAW"

—that's my dad, it's addressed to my dad—but only his name, the two lines below it where you'd fill in the address are blank. Why didn't Donald just ask me? *#1 Blue Jay Lane River Hills Illinois.* I open the seal with unsteady fingers and pull folded pages out, three lilac pages filled with swirly purple cursive so perfect a teacher would probably show the whole class.

"A father & son: Everything one does, is done for the other one.'"

Tears come, reading that, or maybe the salutation:

"Dear Mr. Ross, (James's precious father)"

But a car's in the driveway, I can hear it pull up, the engine turn off, the sound of a car door slamming. My heart trips, my mind blanks. *I don't want you going downstairs.* I fold the rest of the sentence back in its envelope, click off the light, shut the closet, the lock clicks, I rip out the key, grab the rattling ring, and scurry around to the stairs.

Leaping them three at time to the top and into the mud room, hurtling up the three steps, past the back door to the kitchen above, hooking the keys, stuffing the envelope inside my shirt, calming my breath, somehow hoping that Richard won't notice. Blood, I swear, pulses so bad in my throat I can taste it. But when I peer out the window over the fence, it's the neighbors next door in their driveway. A mom and two kids get out of their car, the dad carries a baby inside.

Richard's gate's shut, his driveway is empty and dark.

I slowly sit down at the kitchen table, one foot tucked beneath me. Unfold the lilac pages again from the lilac envelope, smoothing them flat before me.

"Those were the wise words my mother sent me after my own rather melodramatic & thankfully inept attempt to end my own life. But I am passing them on to you because I know how painful it is

when someone you love slips out of reach & the difficulties between
you seem impossible to resolve. For WHATEVER reason. Believe me, it
is something I would never wish upon anyone, the failed expectations
between me & my daddy that so nearly destroyed me. Basically, that
I thought he would love me anyway, & I'd still be the son he was proud
of. You should know that despite whatever he's done to disappoint you
(I can only imagine!) James's love & admiration for you & his family
are so obvious it's painful to write about."

God, I wish my dad could read this.

"How you can tolerate even one day away from him is beyond
my comprehension! To be part of his life, oh, simply heaven! He is
funny, did you know that? & charming, polite & delightful. You have
fathered him well. How sad for you, one day he will realize he doesn't
need you after all, & fill the void you left in him with someone or
something else. (God knows if that someone were me, I would not be
writing this.) But he believes you hate him & hatred makes a really
bad bedfellow—"

Cars pass by outside, jerking my eyes from the swirl of purple
words. My heart's pounding, I get up from the table to peek out the
front window.

Christmas lights sparkle like holiday jewelry decking the
neighborhood houses, the whitened lawns glitter when headlights
sweep by. Muted blue squares glow behind draped windows where
TV sets flicker and silhouettes sit around dining room tables.
Watching *Carol Burnett* or *The Evening News* or eating supper
together. But Richard's driveway stays undisturbed, dusted in white
with small domes of snow on the gate posts.

Sitting back down at the kitchen table, I open Donald's letter
again.

"—& hatred makes a really bad bedfellow. It eats you away until
there's nothing to love. I can't imagine a man of your stature & integrity

wishing that hell on anyone, let alone your prodigal son. Please please please let James back into your"

Life. Family. Home. Turning the page, *"—heart."* It's so hard to read his last words. *"Love, Donald Griswold"*. Clearing his signature out of my eyes but I can't clear the longing that's burning my chest. I don't want his letter to end.

"PS James doesn't know I've sent this to you (he'd have never let me mail it.)"

The telephone's on the wall above the kitchen table. But what would I say? I want to so badly, just call my dad's number, River Hills 2 0779, because I miss his voice and how comforting it is just knowing he's there, even angry, even at midnight yelling, *You didn't think? You never think, Jamey!* Or, *Go to your room!* and his favorite two words, *You're grounded!*

The words Donald wrote are a million times better than anything I could ever think of to say. Still, I get shaky and hesitate, just imagining my dad finding the lilac envelope with the rest of his morning mail. Like, what he will think or the look on his face, reading the purple words.

«mail it. before richard comes back»

Glance at the clock, it's almost ten. Jump to my feet, cross the hall to the den. Rifle through his desk full of business stuff mostly, *R. Hunt, Sr. & Son Construction* business cards and match books, opened mail, a few wallets and IDs, payroll and bookkeeping ledgers. A whole roll of 6¢ stamps and Scotch tape in the top drawer. Lick it, stick it, first class, with a pen, I fill in the address, and seal it.

And I'm hurrying, before I change my mind or Richard returns and it's too late. Out the back door, down the driveway, to the mailbox mounted on his front gate.

part six
cleveland

28

My heart sinks. It's this other Richard that unlocks the back door and lets himself in, the Richard with cold distant eyes who rubs his crotch and mocks you like you're a girl. What took you so long? I'm about to say. You said six o'clock, it's way past eleven, and you better pay me for that.

But a swishy blond guy appears at his side and my heart ker-plunks even lower. I step back. From the sudden bitter cold air, from Richard, from why would he bring a queer guy here? From them both.

"Thanks, mister," this guy says, sort of shy and embarrassed. "I haven't eaten all day."

"Oh, don't thank me. Thank your host," Richard says, his hand toward me like an introduction. "Angel."

I step further back, shaking my head 'cause I'm not his host or angel. Richard just winks like I am.

Richard's quiet the whole meal. He's poured himself a shot and swallows it down, he's got a gallon jug of red wine and keeps refilling the swishy guy's glass. A whole pot of spaghetti with sauce Richard made from sautéed ground beef, chopped onions, and two cans of tomato paste. The guy helps himself to like two heaping plates full, half a whole garlic bread, scarfing it like his last meal. I had one bite but I'm no longer hungry. Just eager for work to be over and Richard to pay me and drive back to Kat.

Richard lights up a smelly cigar, sitting back in his chair like a boss. Tension or something winds tighter and tighter with each bite the queer guy swallows. Richards takes another puff, ashing it in the mound of reddened pasta on his plate. "Are you a boy or girl?" he asks.

"What do you mean?" The guy looks to me like I know the right answer.

"Some of you queers aren't sure." Richard turns to me. "Right, Angel? Boys with lacy panties on. Man, oh, man! First time I saw that, whew. Shocked the hell out of me."

He blushes. "Uh...well, I—I don't. I mean, unless you want..."

"Sure you don't," Richard says, and tosses a lid of pot on the table, a packet of ZigZags, and matches. "You're no full-time pansy. Just a screwed-up little dick who gets off dressing like his mother."

"If you say so," the guy says, but his voice is maybe not so enthusiastic now. "For five...ten bucks more? Sixty? Is that cool?"

"Hey, I'm cool. Ain't I cool, Ange? Whatever turns you on." Richard shapes his fingers round like a cylinder maybe two inches thick, round as his cigar. "Go on. Be my guest. Roll us up a cosmic doobie. See, Angel knows how cool I am."

But I'm not smiling. "I'm still on the clock, you know. Till you take me back."

Richard's whole face changes, not cool at all. "Good. You can clean up the mess when we're done."

I chug the rest of my chocolate milk and push back from the table. Richard refills his guest's glass with wine.

It's hard to get rid of the grease. The faucet pounds out steaming water, filling the sink with soapy bubbles but still, it sticks to everything. A coating of slick orange grease.

SOS pads help. Two just to scour the stove top, the sink. Down the disposal, what's left of his meat sauce, the rest of his uneaten meal. Flicking on the disposal switch, the grinding blades turn it to liquid disgust and gurgle it down the drain. But not loud enough to numb out the sounds coming in from the den down the hall.

Oh, so you're into jazz? Ahh. Hey! Just relax. No, it's not too tight. It's not tight at all.

Smooth FM jazz and wafts of pot smoke drift into the kitchen with Richard's words.

I can't believe a guy as faggy as you has never done this before. You're not duping me now, are you?

I should've had dinner ready and waiting when he walked in the door. I shouldn't have agreed to work for Gus Greenbacks. I shouldn't have got in the red truck.

Hold still! This feels great if you hold perfectly still. Relax! There, you just...doesn't that feel great?

Under the sink the trash can is full, I need to take out the trash, and pull a new bag from the industrial-size box he buys in bulk, that's what he told me, they're cheaper that way, he can give them to all his neighbors. He likes living on Summerland Road, if his ex thinks he's just going to give her the house, it just proves she's non compos mentis. Every neighbor here would agree. They all owe him favors. For discounted labor and cleaning supplies, for the work crews he brings by to paint and mow and shovel snow, for hauling their trash to the dump for free. For being block captain, watching out for their kids, collecting used clothing for charity. For getting them funding from City Council, for keeping their home values high.

Hey! Don't pass out on me! Don't you dare pass out on me!

Prickly noises seep through the wall, muffled sobs and please-don't objections.

In one step I'm across the hall jiggling the doorknob to the den. "I'm done," I say loud, slamming my palm against the wood, inching the door from its jamb, stepping in. "Richard—"

It's like a punch or a shock that just leaves me numb, a picture of pain hung before me. A naked guy prone on his elbows and knees, face down in the brown rug I just cleaned this morning. A white cord rings his neck, looping the claw of a hammer, the handle twisted, the cord ratcheted taut and deep in his throat with each thrust so he's choking, till Richard lets go of the rein that he's holding, glancing at me, and dismounting. The naked guy collapses, curling up in a ball, bound and blubbering and broken.

Richard scoffs. At me, at the brown rug, at this swishy guy struggling to pull up his Fruit of the Looms, at the bud of bright red blooming through the white cotton.

Even closing my eyes, it's burned in my eyelids, the shape of that bloody red blossom. Even stepping away, down the short hall back into the kitchen, the linoleum icy and hard. Whimpers surround me, defeated and desperate and coming from me. Stepping back, through the kitchen to the stove, the table, the curtained window, there is no escape. The taste of rape fills my throat warm and salty. *Swallow it, Ross,* Cleveland's voice fills my ears. *Or you'll lick every drop off the ground.*

"Hey!" Richard barks. "Angel! Get back here!"

Panic screams in my head, frantic for the ending or the best defense. The dish drainer stacked with the dishes I cleaned. Gleaming pots, pans, silverware, knives. Pick up a knife, *a serious knife,* the blade glints in the light when I step in the hall, then into the den straight toward Richard. He's buckling his belt under his pale bloated belly. He doesn't notice the knife, where it's aimed, his zippered fly, his floppy chest, the sagging skin cowling his neck. His double chin raises to face me. For a moment he's expressionless.

"Put the knife down," he says, walking toward me.

But I'm shaking my head, stepping back. Out of the den, into the hall.

"You aren't going to kill me. Put the knife down."

Something shrill screams in my ears, knowing he's right. I'm not going to kill him. Moving the knife without moving at all, the blade to my wrist. The dotted line's already there, it's just a matter of pressure.

«no» angel says, his voice rings in my ears. «don't do it»

"Put. Down. The knife."

Richard reaches for me, I can't move or think. Blinking my eyes a million times but panic blocks my vision. It's not the sting of the blade pricking my skin, it's just instant relief that I feel.

Richard's hands sandwich mine and take the decision away. His arms frame my shoulders and lock me against him, his mouth cups my ear. "Naw, shh-shhh," he whispers, moving me into his kitchen. "Why would you do something stupid like that?"

"You *raped* that guy!" blurts out, pushing away from his grip, my fist pounds his chest. "Why would you do that!"

He cuffs my wrist, twisting my arm to lock me against him, his gritted whisper hot on my ear. "Look. He got in my truck. He's a hustler. I paid him. That's *exactly* what he wanted." His embrace loosens, his hands fall away from my shirt. He lays the knife within reach on the table. "If that upsets you, well, boo-hoo."

Quick barefoot steps scuffle out of the den, thump the hall carpet, and patter the linoleum passing right by me and Richard. The guest like a ghost flies down the three steps and out the back door, half undressed. I don't look up till the storm door slams and silence replaces his presence.

Richard blinks when I step back, wipes blood off his hand on a napkin. *My blood.* "There. He's gone. No harm, no foul." He offers the napkin to me. "Come here."

But I'm shaking my head, the horror will not go away.

"Jesus Christ, kid. Fags hate themselves for the shameful shit they do, they want to be punished. Can you blame them? I was doing him a favor. Hell, he should be paying *me*." Richard chuckles, all suddenly lighthearted and sounding righteous.

"*Nobody* wants to be assaulted!" I shout in his face. "God, it takes away everything and makes you so small you can't function or trust yourself anymore! Why would you do that? Why would you want to destroy someone?"

Richard blinks at me, his mouth is a down-turned line. "Who the fuck assaulted you?" he says.

Turning from him, shaking my head, but tears escape anyway, from some locked away place, and words fill my throat, unspoken with sharp edges that leave scars behind.

"Aww, shit, kid," Richard says.

Wiping tears and snot down my sleeve and he lets me do it, he doesn't say calm down and quit crying. Between sobs and sniffles I tell him about Railton, how Cleveland raped me. How I came off in the middle of that—being raped—and how I just...I just lost it. That he could make me even do that, I couldn't protect myself even from coming off, how do you defend that? That you are so weak you let people even do that.

"Jesus Christ, who is this fuck Cleveland? I would've killed the SOB."

You can't, I say, because if you tell or fight back they just punish you worse, ground you, expel you, lock you in a padded cell, or place you in the loony bin forever.

"Fucking shits!" Richard shouts, and his fist pounds the wall leaving a dent in the plaster. "What the hell they expect you to do, lay back and take it?"

Ever since eighth grade when Ratachek touched me like it's so normal, my dad said, "Did you move over?" but it doesn't make him stop he just found this kid Kyle instead and probably more, probably a lot more, a whole Boy Scout troop or stupid kids that need to be tutored.

"And you're the one they put in a goddam nuthouse?"

I pushed Ratachek through a plate glass window, not on purpose, but I'm not sorry.

"Jesus Christ, you shouldn't be sorry! Except sorry you got nailed, sorry you got sent up to juvie, sorry you got it from a fuck like Cleveland. Sorry the system that's supposed to rehabilitate you fucked you up worse than when you went in." His palms hold either side of my face with thumbs like a sculptor blending tears into my cheekbones.

I'm supposed to just forget it, shake it off, be a man.

"Who the fuck told you that, some fucking shrink?" Richard scoffs. "When was this? Before or after the shock treatment?"

After. I say with no sound coming out. After.

"Jesus! Shock treatment? They really did that to you?"

My dad signed the papers. My dad wanted them to.

"What a shit! What an arrogant piece of shit. 'Just forget it'? 'Shake it off'? How many times were you raped, James?" Looking me straight in the eye. Demanding, How many?

I don't know. A lot.

"Don't give me bullshit, you know exactly how many."

Thirteen.

"'Just forget it'?" Richard shouts. "Listen to me! Every fucking day for the rest of your life—do you hear me? I don't care what else happens—you fall in love, the birth of your first kid, you meet the president, the best day of your life—you were *still* fucking raped! Get it? That don't *ever* leave you!"

Tears come so hard and out of control for all of it, anger and hatred and how good it feels, to be held in his arms and just cry cry cry cry.

29

I'm already sitting behind the wheel when Richard gets into the truck cab beside me. He rolls down his window, his red and black plaid elbow jutting outside as if he's too big to fit in the passenger seat.

The sun stabs my eyes through the windshield so brightly I'm squinting, and he gives me shades to put on. So I can see why you'd need sunglasses in winter. Or to hide any sign you've been crying all night.

I sit myself taller, adjust the visor.

Richard's got sunglasses, too. So I can't tell if he's still looking at me.

I'm grateful it's morning, for fresh air to breathe, glad to be finally out of his house and on my way back to the city. I've got Donald's lilac tablet under my shirt like smuggled treasure, safe in my waistband where I kept it and slept with my clothes on all night. In Richard's back bedroom. His daughters' bedroom, with the door locked this time, and the desk chair wedged under the doorknob. He didn't say anything about anything at breakfast, coffee and eggs and pigs in a blanket, just "Good morning," and "Hot bath help you sleep?" and "Why don't you take that toothbrush with you." Or after breakfast, when he chucked me the key to his truck and said I could drive.

Downshift. Punch in the clutch, shift into third. Up on the clutch pedal, down on the gas, hardly jerking at all, and kind of proud how quickly I learned. Driving the red truck. Checking the mirrors, steering the wheel, and picking the radio station. "Down on the Street" explodes from the speaker and sets me on edge, the raw squalling vocals *exactly* the way I'm feeling. Turning The Stooges up louder and louder to drown out whatever he's saying.

Richard snaps the radio off. "I said, 'What goes around, comes around.' Ever hear that expression? Hang a louie at the next light." His leather-gloved finger points which way.

The powerful song still rages inside me, I don't want to let it fade. But I nod and downshift, feeling the drag when the engine winds down, hand-over-hand like he showed me, turning left on the green with the left blinker clicking, keeping my eyes on the road.

What goes around comes around. Driving myself back to the city to Kat's endless summer and Rand's pharmaceuticals, the blue ones or red ones, before I completely flip out.

"That's what you call your 'poetic justice,'" Richard is saying. "Someone gives you a load of shit, someday a whole shitload comes back to that someone. Ten-fold."

"Like a boomerang," I say, just to let him think I'm listening. Switching the radio back on, but it's just some dumb commercial. *Bowling! We're all going bowling!* So I'm thinking of shit that comes back to you, like bowling balls, or the toilet at Rand's. "Or bad plumbing."

Richard takes his sunglasses off, facing me. "Like this asshole who raped you. He's got it coming. Or a poison letter—you mail it, it'll come back every time to bite you in the ass."

A poison letter you mail? Does he mean Donald's letter? For a second I freak out, a million fractured thoughts flash by me, almost forgetting I'm driving. Then calming myself because, no, I addressed it to my dad's house and mailed it. In Richard's mailbox with the red flag up. Unless Richard found it this morning before the mailman came. Stupid stupid stupid—I shift into third. "Well, not if you don't put a return address on it," I say. Out the corner of my eye I catch the odd look he gives me.

"Oh, believe me," Richard says, "there's a return address. She's going to make damn sure every asset I have goes to her. The house, the business, the girls, my goddam reputation. Man, oh, man, she better duck. Her and her kike lawyer. Making me pay her for the past fourteen miserable years? Duck and cover, honey. That woman will see a hole in the ground before she sees a penny from me."

What goes around comes around. I turn the radio louder but his message is already received.

"There it is," Richard says, like we're playing I Spy and he spied it first. Pointing his lit cigar out the window, ashing it over the cars parked on Center Street, where he told me to turn. For "one quick stop" he has to make before we drive back to Kat.

So I'm thinking Goodwill because of the trash bags he's dumped in the truck bed. We're on the main drag of some ugly suburb south of the city, sooty and sunless even at ten a.m. Driving the red truck at five mph, creeping past storefronts, searching for a Goodwill sign or for Richard to say where to stop. A five and dime, Illinois Bell, Executive Typewriter & Office Machines, Pop's Foto Shop & Film Processing. A hardware store with a saw on its awning and a sign that stops me dead-bang.

CLEVELAND BROS GLASS & HARDWARE

And it hits me, this *is* his quick stop.

"Cleveland?" Turning at Richard, "Is this—I don't want to see Cleveland. And, and anyway he's in jail, he's not even here."

"Oh, he's here all right." Richard grins. "Listed in the Yellow Pages. Under 'Hardware.' His directions were perfect."

Like he's already talked to Cleveland? "Un-unh, he's locked up, at Railton or Joliet—" Because you're sent to the big house when you turn twenty-one. My throat goes dry and I can't speak or breathe, hardly. Lowell Cleveland is here now? How did that happen? Who did he screw to get out? Shaking my head, my hands off the wheel, all buzzy and numb, I can't think.

"Park in front," Richard says. "And wait here."

Let up on the brake, my foot barely in my control, all stupid and more unsteady than ever. Steering the red truck hand-over-hand into the space where he points at the curb. What if I just drove away? I shove the gear shift into first.

Richard switches the ignition off and pockets the key, stubbing his stogie in the dashboard ashtray. He opens his door and steps out to the sidewalk under the awning saw. He helps himself to the hardware store entrance. He doesn't look back at me.

Through the front window, I can see him approach a cashier then turn where she points to the rear of the store. Then disappear behind displays of shovels and road salt and Christmas wreaths.

I scoot over to the passenger side. The vinyl's still warm from Richard.

Telling myself *be cool* but it's so hard to find enough air just to breathe.

I turn the handle rolling the window down, but there is no fresh air to let in. Cars crawl by in a dreary procession, spewing exhaust, adding more gray to the sky. The holiday lights just look creepy in daytime like strings of jagged barbed wire. Rust bibs the light poles and street signs like bloodstains. Rust stains the awning under the saw-shaped sign.

Cleveland Brothers. Plural, there's more than one.

I jump out of the red truck and *splat!* into a gutter of slush. Slamming the door behind me, static fills my head and takes over, blocking everything out. Sound, time, reason, soaked Beatle boot. Entering Cleveland's store, feeling all edgy with fight in my fingers, walking right by the cashier, following the way Richard went. Past towering shelves stacked with paint cans and hardware. Aisles of hand tools, tarps and tape, tubs of spackle and goop. Turning the corner to hammers and nails, a million kinds, bolts and glue, spools of rope and chain. Everything probably you'd ever need to put what's been broken together again.

I turn the corner into Aisle C—ELECTRICAL and stop.

It's Cleveland.

Screaming orange hair, you can't forget that, rippled like toilet water after it's flushed. Pale skin mottled with moles and zits and hygiene that clogs up your nose. *Break time!* when he comes up behind you, his knees digging into the backs of your knees till you crumble bent open beneath him. *Break time!* he tells you and takes you away. To a library tabletop, a broom closet or shower room, the mattress of his bunk or yours. Thirteen times. Till you don't even know who you are.

Anger like jagged rocks burns my chest and stinging tears refill my eyes, when you'd think after last night there'd be none left to cry.

He's on his knees unpacking a box of light switches, shooting each one with a price sticker gun *ka-chunka-chunka-chunka*, hanging them neatly on hooks in the pegboard. MAY I HELP YOU? I'M LOWELL pinned on the chest of his yellow smock.

Sweat beading up now. Under my hairline, armpits, upper lip. *Break time break time* stuck in my mind. Stuck because time is broken.

Richard stands behind Cleveland, towering bigger and more powerful above him. "Lowell here says he doesn't know any angels," Richard says when I approach.

Cleveland's head turns and he sees me, he shirks with denial but the smirk on his lips and his red blotchy flush say he hasn't forgotten a thing.

"Well, Lowell," Richard says with a cocky jerk-jerk of his head. "Could you get off your knees and help us find a few items? We're in a bit of a hurry."

Cleveland lumbers to his feet. "Yeah, what do you want?" His voice without malice or anything mean. And it's weird because I swear he was taller.

«what do you want» I want him to give it back, angel. Everything he took from me.

My mind's spinning, I can barely see anything I'm passing by. Walking the aisles with Richard and Cleveland, keeping two steps behind.

I want The Jamey Repair Kit, so what aisle is that in? I want him to fix what he's broken.

«how is he supposed to do that» I don't know I don't know but he's guilty he did it, he has to pay.

Trying to think of the right words to say, to nail him, like *Perry Mason*, so the whole courtroom gasps and Cleveland collapses, down on his elbows and knees. Like an offering before the jury and me, remorse, restitution, and begging forgiveness, sorry he ever was born.

I want him to unstick time.

Cleveland fills a cart with the stuff Richard tells him, he knows where everything is. Duct tape, a tarp, a fifty-pound sack of lime. Rags, he tells Cleveland, a couple of rags. And some sort of poison, the most lethal you've got.

"Depends what you're gonna exterminate," Cleveland says, his voice not like a rapist at all.

"Vermin," Richard says, one heavy hand on Cleveland's yellow smock shoulder. "Very large vermin."

A hundred stacked cans come into sharp focus. A red death's head warning on every black label. *B-GON B-GON B-GON Rat Rat Rat Killer Killer Killer.*

"Yeah?" Cleveland takes the can from me and adds it to the basket. "This ain't a mob hit, is it?" He chuckles and his hand lands on Richard's red and black jacket, guiding him to the cashier.

Watching Cleveland. The greasy stain ringing his smock's yellow collar. His pockmarked face, one cauliflower ear, his Adam's apple bobbing the length of his throat, his gaze piercing right through these darkened lenses. He looks me straight in the eye.

"Break time," he says.

Quick look to Richard and what will he do? But it's Cleveland who's got his attention. Cleveland, telling the cashier to go take her cigarette break, taking her place at the check-out counter, expertly pressing the register buttons, adding everything up. *Ka-ching!* when the cash drawer shoots open stopped by his yellow smocked belly. Counting change into Richard's open hand, packing everything into a brown paper bag.

It's not fair! That's screaming in my head now. Why aren't you in jail! Who let you out! What idiot gave you the key? You're supposed to be locked up forever, you're supposed to be punished for what you did, you *never* deserve to be free!

Rage burns seething hot, my arms crossed with two knotted fists, jaw clenched with gritted teeth. Richard bends to my ear. "Hold that thought," he whispers.

"Looks like you're the boss here," Richard compliments Cleveland with a nod of approval. "They must pay you quite well for that."

"Nope." Cleveland grumbles it's a family business, he works in the store for free.

"That hardly sounds fair," Richard says. "Hell, I'd pay you five bucks just to carry this out to my truck." Flashing a five from his wallet to Cleveland.

Cleveland hesitates for hardly a moment. "Sure, why not." His stubby fat fingers tug a key from the register, slam the cash drawer, and lock it. He hefts up the lime sack onto one shoulder, hugs the brown bag in the crook of his arm, clenching the key in his teeth. As if he's the warden or someone in charge. He waits till Richard pockets his wallet then follows him out to the street.

30

Cleveland's not even wearing a jacket, like he's so tough the weather can't faze him, but his fat pale jawline mottles in blotches with cold. Richard nods at the red truck and opens the passenger door. I climb up and slide to the driver's side as if it's my truck and I'm driving. Cleveland leans in, shoving the bag on the seat closer beside me, and just for an eye blink, I'm feeling his weight, the grease of his zits, yellow teeth, his bad smells. And the power he has to crush me.

It shakes me so badly, why can't I fight him, why does he make me so small?

He adds the lime sack to the trash bags in back, letting it roll off his shoulder into the truck bed, then turns, one palm open, to Richard, and plucks the key from his mouth. "That'll be five bucks, man."

"You ever work construction?" I hear Richard say. "I'm looking for a crew boss. Five bucks an hour."

Cleveland just stares at him, unblinking, his hand in mid-air.

"Five bucks an hour," Richard repeats. "That's what? More than three times minimum wage and five bucks more than you'll ever get here."

Cleveland's open palm is still empty, his other arm embraces his yellow chest, like he's starting to feel the cold. He shrugs. "Crew boss. Hell, I could do that."

"It takes a certain kind of boss to get respect from a crew. Make 'em do what you tell them to, no questions asked." Richard nods his head in my direction. "Make 'em earn their pay."

"People do what I say," Cleveland says. And his eyelids flutter, not letting his gaze land on me. "What kinda construction?"

"Demolition." Richard nods in some unknown direction. "Not too far from here." His brown leather gloves clap together, he blows into his palms like he's cold. "Look, why don't I just show you?"

Cleveland glances back at the store as if someone's watching.

"Hell, you said you're the boss," Richard says. "Make a goddam decision. I haven't got all day."

You can see Cleveland's breath fog the air when he talks. "Yeah, what do I have to do?"

"Get in the truck," Richard says.

The second Cleveland slams his door shut, Richard's hopped into the driver's seat, forcing me closer to Cleveland. So my coat sleeve's touching his yellow smocked arm, my thigh's against his and it's suddenly me with Cleveland again, trying so hard to stay calm. Hugging the bag on my lap. The bag full of extermination supplies.

Keep my eyes forward at the road ahead, the brake lights and streetlights and ugly holiday lights, blurry blobs of red and green, everything out of focus. Advice echoes in my head, *This is what you have to do*, from angel or Donald or Dr. Pauly. *You have to confront the people who screwed you up. If you want to be cured and normal again. Bite down on this and count to ten.*

Richard starts up the truck and pulls away from the curb, flooring it, shifting from first to third gear in seconds, catching the green light, and whizzing straight through the center of town. In just a few blocks there's only houses around us, and in a few more, just farms in the distance and endless dead fields dotted with skeletal trees.

Richard's shoulders unhunch as if now he's relaxed. Cleveland sticks a smoke in his mouth, his nose-picking finger presses the lighter into the dashboard as if it's been his truck for years. And sitting between them I'm just more tense and edgy with each passing minute.

"Angel's worked for me, what's it been, two, three times now?" Richard nods at me, like a confirmation. "He could probably teach you a thing or two."

I'm swallowing that like a lump of surprise, about to object, when the lighter pops up glowing red hot and ready.

"I doubt that," Cleveland mumbles, his gaze turns to the window and passing gray landscape.

"Fantastic. You know everything then." Richard pulls the popped lighter out, reaching across me to hand it to Cleveland. Cleveland lights his cigarette off it and snaps it back in its hole. Taking a drag, he flicks ash on the floor as if Richard won't mind or ashtrays don't matter.

"Where the fuck is this demolition anyway?" he says.

Richard's gloved hand shoots past my chin to Cleveland's jaw, grabbing it and catching us both off guard. For a moment Cleveland's just blank-faced and frozen.

"Here's how it works," Richard says. "I'm the boss. I ask the questions. Capiche?"

Cleveland jerks back, out of Richard's grip or maybe Richard lets go.

"Can't just hire you on the spot. What if you're a thief? Or a goddam liar?"

Cleveland mutters something.

"What was that, Lowell?"

"I said, what if I don't want your fucking job?"

It's like the world stops on a dime, *screeeeech!* whipping everything forward, all gravity gone and lift-off! We fly off the seat with no time to brace before impact. I'm saved, though, by the bag on my lap and Richard's gloved hand barring my chest from bashing the dashboard. But Cleveland's chin hits its edge and splits open, his forehead smacks into the windshield. He's cursing and spluttering when he sits back, spitting out blood and white bits of cigarette paper. Or teeth, his palms cover most of his face.

My eyes exposed now, I realize, the sunglasses flung off me and onto the floor at his feet.

Richard's big fists pound the steering wheel, the whole truck shudders, maybe the road below too. "Disrespectful little prick! No wonder your family won't pay you. What was I thinking, Angel? Wasting my time on a shitbag jailhouse rapist."

"Oh, is that what 'Angel' told you? I'm a rapist?" There's red soaking his palms when his hands leave his face, red twisting around his doughy fingers.

"Would he be lying if he did?" Richard says, like a challenge.

The look Cleveland shoots me I've seen once before, when I tried to report him at Railton. "Hell, yeah, if he said it was rape."

"You liar!" Two words and my fist fly toward his face.

"Hey!" Richard shouts or maybe that's Cleveland right in my ear as he ducks. But my fist stops mid-air, caught in the brown leather glove. Richard holds my wrist still so I'm struggling to strike out, he catches my other fist, too. So only my words hit Cleveland's warped ear and bounce off his rippled orange skull.

"Why'd you pick me?" I scream in his face. "What'd I *ever* do to you!" Jerking to break free from Richard. "Let me *go—*"

Richard's grip loosens but still holds me back. "Hold on, hold on. Let him answer."

Let him answer? Which ticks me off more, why Richard would even listen to him or *any* lie he has to say.

Cleveland turns from the window, eyes slit at me, blood colors his mouth like lipstick and outlines the shapes of his stubby yellow teeth. Blood spraying out makes his words hiss and lispy. "If it wasn't for me," he sputters, "you'd be dead, Ross. *Dead.*" He glances over his shoulder for the door handle or a quick getaway. "You come into Railton like a fuckin' princess, every dickwad in that shithole had it out for you. The stews and the screws," he says, then turning to Richard like they're buddies or something. "He's goddam *lucky* I felt sorry for him. He should be thanking me."

"That's your answer? He's goddam lucky you raped him? Jesus Christ!" Richard says, turning to me. "I'll hold him down, you wanna give him something to thank *you* for."

Cleveland scoffs. "Oh gee, I'm so scared," he says in a mocking voice, reaching to unlock the door button, his shoe stomps down on the sunglasses. Crack!

Richard releases my hands.

POW! like punching my fist in a padded cell wall only this time it's really his face. Bull's-eye, into his bull nose, rutted cheek, half ear, and then again, OW! hard as I can, striking bone or something so sharp my knuckles scream raw and draw back. "Here's what you say!" I shout like a lecture right in his face. "'I'm *sorry* I picked you! I'm *sorry* I fucked up your life! You did *nothing* to deserve it!'"

He cowers against the passenger window because I punched him, I hurt him, I made him bleed.

"Right," Cleveland blurts from behind his cupped palms. "You're an angel, nothin's ever your fault. A fuckin' angel with your goddam head in the clouds." Cleveland spits blood, one eye growing puffy and closed. "Fuck you, *Angel.* This sure don't look like heaven to me."

Something inside me shrivels up when he says that, something vulnerable and young. Me, I think, the me I used to be before angel. James Daniel Ross, who did nothing wrong.

Swallow tears back, clear my eyes quickly before he sees, but Cleveland knows me too well.

"You're pathetic, Ross. You go and pull that suicide shit, I coulda just left you to die. But I didn't. I saved your fucking life—"

A brown leather fist whips past my eyes and *BOOM!* Cleveland's head smashes the door. It hits the side window all skewed and distorted, like soft putty punched or a cartoon in slow motion. It rebounds and rolls back, loose on his collar, nose to ceiling. Snorting. Swearing. Done.

It's a shock to me how sudden it happens, and I draw back from them both, into the seat. The brown leather gloves tear open the bag on my lap and dive in, squirreling around, then pulling the rag out and the pint of rat killer, handing them both to me.

"Be an angel," Richard says, starting the engine, "and open that, would you?" First to third gear, flooring it forward, there's nobody else on this road.

In my hands there's a can full of poison. The most lethal they had with a cap that's a struggle to open. Richard veers sharply to a dust-raising stop on the shoulder so suddenly my head whips forward then whacks the window behind me. Cleveland, too, stops groaning mid-curse when the back of his head slams the glass. "Where're we," he moans.

Richard twists off the metal cap, pulling the can from my hand, and *glug-glug* drenches the rag in his glove. Then he's barreled across me, stuffing the rag into Cleveland's streaked palms where long gooey strings of dark blood keep pooling. "Here. Use this," Richard says.

Cleveland presses the wet rag to his gushing nose and gags, heaving once to catch his breath, but there's nothing he can do. The brown leather glove holds it there like a mask, over his fat bloated face until he stays still and Cleveland's whole body slumps forward.

How're you doing? Richard keeps asking. He's driving the truck all herky-jerky along some endless dirt path through a foggy gray field. With each rut or bump up we're swaying like rag dolls slung this way then that on the seat. Cleveland sinks down with each jolt and jerk, lower and lower and lower. Till he's filling the foot well, his stumpy legs twisted like roots of some heavyset tree, his yellow trunk slumped and bulky beside me.

"Mah-mee," Cleveland sputters, or maybe he's trying to breathe.

Richard chuckles, rocking along with the unsteady motion. "What a hot dog," he says. Bright yellow smock splattered red, like mustard and ketchup you'd put on a hot dog so that's in my head now, too. "Who'd want to hire a hot dog like that? Man, you were right on, James. At first I was skeptical, but you were right on about this useless shitbag. How're you doing?"

It's like a slow-motion movie, when the red truck stops moving and the last frame goes blank at The End.

You see Richard turn off the engine, the key left dangling in the ignition. You see his door open into the fog, his red and black jacket lumber out of the truck, stepping down. You feel the punch of his door slamming shut, hear the crunch of his boots on the frosted dead ground circling around the rear bumper. The muted thump-thump of his leather-gloved knuckles knocking the passenger window, his muffled command to unlock the door. You don't see much of the door or the window, just Cleveland all gurgling and leaning against it. So you have to reach over the yellow slope of his smock to pull up and unlock the door button.

You see the door swing away and Cleveland, too, disappearing into the gray, the thud of him hitting the ground. The rustle and snap of dead weeds and gravel, a garbled mouthful of threats. The struggle of Cleveland fighting back now. Or maybe he doesn't do anything, he's already learned not to object.

It's just me and Richard alone in the truck and I suddenly can't stop shaking. I don't want to be here or think about Cleveland or the question left drumming inside me. So I'm filling my head with Kat instead, knowing each bump and rut we jerk over is bringing me closer to her.

But Richard keeps talking about Cleveland.

"He was breathing," Richard says as we're bumping along. "Can't have him bleeding all over my truck...stupid shit...he'll find his way home to his 'mah-mee'... Man, oh man, is he gonna wake with one helluva headache! You got a good punch or two in there, I gotta admit I didn't think you'd do it, didn't think you had it in you. That's therapy, in my opinion. All the fucking therapy you need."

Richard's driving along like nothing's just happened, like we're on vacation or something, sightseeing and touring The Land of Lincoln. Taking the back roads, carefree and easy. Back to the city. Leaving all troubles behind.

"Hell, Cleveland might be one dumb fuck but he sure had you pegged right." He chuckles. "An angel with his goddam head in the clouds."

Covering my ears, I don't want to hear it, what Wills said my first day there, in the Illinois State Juvenile Correctional Facility at Railton. *Corrections Officer Mister* Wills, state employee, his catfish lips scowling, sun glinting off his tin badge. Standing above me blocking the sky, asking, "Does this look like fucking heaven to you?" Behind him the scarecrows moved in from the bases, the stews and the screws like faceless stick figures, hoping to get a good view. But all I could think was *He's an Official. He said the F word to me.* "I don't know what to do with you, Ross. We're playing ball and you're out here in left field like some fucking angel with his head in the goddam clouds. No—no, don't go giving me none of your 'I didn't do anything' bullshit, I don't give a fuck what your daddy is. You get the same choice as everybody else. Play the game or isolation. It's up to you."

I think that was the first time I answered to angel, the first time he surfaced to help me know what to do.

«just walk away» angel said. From the softball game? Because I didn't know I could.

«yes» From the yellow cluster of cinderblock buildings, from Wills' screeching whistle, from locks and keys and lists of rules I didn't think I'd ever keep straight.

«let's go home» angel said, turning us away and toward River Hills, he knew the direction to go. Away from Wills shouting, "We gotta runner!" Away from the distant blaring alarm, not really running at all, at first. Just moving toward the chainlink fence, impossibly high and topped with barbed wire. We got maybe halfway up.

«let's go home» angel says.

Traffic is stopped and backed up at a red light. In one motion, I've got the lock button popped and I'm pulling the door handle up. My right foot's practically on city pavement before Richard sees I'm half gone.

"Hey. Hey!" His brown leather hand clamps my left knee to the seat. "Aren't you forgetting something?"

If I move, my kneecap will snap. I'm stuck, holding still, frantically thinking what I'm forgetting, my jacket, my manners, a bag full of murder supplies?

"The money you earned. Your *pay*." Richard winks, freeing my knee, and pulls from his wallet a handful of cash that he dangles a moment before me. I just snatch the whole wad, bump the door open with my shoulder, and leap to the street in a mad dash to get far away.

31

Rand doesn't care when I give him the money, where did I get it or what I went through. Forty-two bucks, which is hard to let go of, but he snatches it up in a pick-pocket blur, boring right by me and slamming the door behind him.

The orange neon sign blinks night from the room then lets it back in so I'm blinded a moment and not sure where to step or who's crashed out on the floor. Till HOTEL blinks back on and the dark shapes around me ignite with fiery color. A box of dirty clothes in one corner. Rand's sleeping bag strewn on the bare mattress. Kat's big carpetbag. And Kat.

She's asleep, like a red lumpy island before me. The hardwood creaks when I tip-toe toward her, when I shake the sleeping bag out, draping it over her and her baby inside. She wakes, raising up on one elbow. Looking around, her eyes gleam with tangerine neon. Her brows rise with a question I don't think I can answer.

"I was worried you wouldn't come back," she says.

My voice cracks when I tell her I'm sorry, I wish I didn't leave her at all.

She capes the sleeping bag over herself and scoots her way onto Rand's mattress, adjusting her shape under the army green canvas. She beckons, lifting the plaid flannel lining like the entrance to a tent. "Come sleep with me," she says.

A noise like I'm wounded escapes from my throat. She touches my wrist and I realize how much I've missed touching. Slipping my feet under, my breath fogs the cold air.

"Angel? You're shaking. What happened?"

I just shrug, feeling edgy inside my own skin. I can't tell her what. It's ugly and not something you share with a friend, a bad gift you can't ever take back. Pulling the sleeping bag over my face, I want to shut out the whole world. Turning away from the pale shape that's Kat, the warmth of her breath and big belly filling this small space with her heat. So I'm shivering and sweating together.

"Man," she says. "My baby's going to be free to tell me *any*thing. Whatever happens, man. Without shamings or beatings or Hail Marys, none of that shit. Just hugs and love."

Hugs and Love. Two words I want to hold on to forever.

I pull the rest of this folded cash from my pocket and turn to show Kat, but she sets it aside. She helps me twist out of the Marlboro coat, her hands from behind pull my arms free, getting it off me, dumping it onto the floor. Then untucking my shirttails, her fingers slip under the flannel. Under the Led Zeppelin T-shirt too, I don't stop her. Her hands are warm on my skin, melting the shivers down the steps of my spine. To the small of my back, then around. To my sore gut so sunken and empty. Heading south. "Wait—"

But she doesn't.

Helping me out of these schoolboy pants down to my knees. Unzip the Beatle boots, kicking them off in a tangled blue knot past my ankles, tossing them aside, too. Wrapped in warm flannel so smooth on my skin, her cable-knit sweater scratchy, then gone. So it's just the soft milky shapes of Kat against me, shining in saffron then shadow. God. Closing my eyes more alive now than ever. Legs intertwine, her warm thigh between mine so I'm hardly breathing. Just everything flushed in a whirl down there, waking up and taking me over, making me set to explode. Her hand finds the trigger—how does she know?—unleashing a flood of crazy sensation. Which doesn't last more than a deep breath and shudder. Still, I would lay here forever, catching my breath till my head stops swirling. Turning to face her. Dreamy eyes, sleepy smile, twirls of her hair drape my shoulder.

Her embrace calms my jaw chatter down. Her arms holding me make me cry.

It's all chocolate milk, I think Hendrix told me. His magic guitar licks ripple the air, crisscrossing the ceiling speaker-to-speaker. I can feel Kat's heart beating with mine. She's combing my hair back from my eyes with her fingers just like my mom used to do. Or Granma at visiting time.

"*The Wind Cries Mary,*" Jimi sings, alive and cool as ever.

I don't want Kat ever to leave.

"Mmmmm," she hums, and the hum reverbs through me, then a trill giggle like bells. "I think my lady bits need you," she says.

Ha, her lady bits?

And I'm instantly giddy, ha, my fella parts need her, and when I tell her that, she's giddy, too. I look up face-to-face with her closed eyes, lips-to-lips with her soft kiss, and tumble deep into her mouth. Down down down like the rabbit hole spinning in freefall, entwined with majestic soaring guitar licks and her flickering tongue. Flashes of sweetness shoot through me like stars. Till her lips move from mine. She slips to one side "so we don't hurt the baby," filling my mouth full of creamy round flesh and a hard bud of nipple to suck. A sigh like harmonics vibrates her throat and her thighs open wide underneath me. Sliding right in and rocking inside her, plugged into Kat, that's what I'm thinking, how perfect we fit. How silky her lady bits feel.

Her lips brush my ear chasing chills down my backbone. "That's so much better," she sighs.

Love is good. Love is sparkling in my head like cherry cola. Sweeter and sweeter till the whole world explodes in this huge cosmic wave that crests in the stars and washes me over with pleasure. And for a long long time after. Laying together, Kat and me, elated, deflated, she has to go pee or I'd do it again in a heartbeat.

The Wind Cries Kat.

I know why you'd want to drape her in diamonds or surround her in sleep with a roomful of roses. So the first thing she sees when she opens her eyes is how precious she is.

Kat Kat Kat.

Just thinking of Kat I get goofy down there, I have to quick think of anything else, Zero, his letter, and why she'd choose him—when Doreen swoops in behind the lunch counter and refills my cup to the brim.

"Well, don't you look like the cat that ate the canary," she says. "Whatchya up to, Angel?"

I'm probably blushing, but I saw in the men's room, standing in front of the mirror. Close-up, you can see the hairs on my chin, I swear. "Feel," I say, and put her hand there. "I think that's my beard growing in."

Doreen laughs. "And a handsome beard it shall be. Some day."

Jingle-jingle, the mailman enters, which sounds like Christmas bells now.

She turns to the door to greet him good morning and returns with an armload of mail.

I try shaking sugar from the dispenser into my coffee but it's all clumpy and stuck inside. I have to slap the bottom to jostle it past the big chunks and stale soda cracker. Doreen puts those in to absorb the moisture, there's a whole carton under the counter. Two pale crackers wrapped in cellophane, she gives you two if you order soup or haven't eaten all night. Or if you're nauseous because you're having a baby.

"No letter," Doreen says, shuffling through the stack in her hand. She adds like five cracker packets into the bag and a few candy canes for Kat. "Maybe tomorrow."

I nod, and stand up, already dreading tomorrow, what then? There's not enough cash in the CA stash, it's easier to spend then to save it. But the letter could come and then Kat's gone and I don't want that to happen. The magic of blue pills pumping my blood keeps it all at a comfortable distance.

Overhead, tinsel and garlands are tacked to a shelf where a black and white TV's turned on, you can hang out and watch till Doreen closes up if you order a Coke or hot cocoa. The news comes on now, so I'm about to leave, take Kat's breakfast and split. But the lady's face on the TV screen is vaguely familiar so I stop to watch for a bit.

She's sobbing about her son who's gone missing, *"Lowell,"* she says is his name, so I'm listening. *"He wouldn't leave work in the middle of the day without his jacket. He wouldn't take off with the register keys."* His mug fills the screen, his name captioned in capital letters. LOWELL JASPER CLEVELAND, 21. So a million pin prickles swarm over my skin, and I'm blinking to tune it in better.

"We are asking the public and anyone with information about the missing youth and possibly others, to please contact lead sheriff's investigator Marc Gabriel at the West Division station." Black suit, white shirt, black tie, and fedora, he looks like a G-man in a film noir movie or an old black-and-white TV show. *The Defenders* or Eliot Ness. Breaking his way through the wall of reporters who shove their

mics in his face, his reply is the same to all of their questions. *The investigation is ongoing. No further details will be released at this time.*

Lowell Jasper Cleveland. Last seen. Last scene. End of story.

My heart pounds loud like he's here right behind me, his breath hot and beastly on the back of my neck. His orange-ugly mug smashed in and gory. His desperate gurgling in the thick fog outside the red truck.

I blink his face from my eyes, look toward Doreen instead.

She's refilling a customer's coffee and laughs. "It was fresh ground this morning," she says.

Something is evil out there. The nightmare replays on the ceiling and walls between flashes of Halloween color.

DAD! When Cleveland slams my back into the hard tabletop so stars spin above, that's all I see, a swirling universe. Panic to swallow the dizziness down and force my eyes to focus. Water stains like rusty clouds appear across the ceiling. Library shelves with a few lonely books talk to me from cinder block walls. We have no words, is what they say, our pages are blank, it's best that way. MOM! When the room wavers and I try to rise. He's hurting me, I realize. I try to tell him that. You're hurting me. He's glad and tugs the waistband wider, strips the sweatpants to my knees. Cold rushes in where it doesn't belong. Lifting me up, I weigh nothing at all, he flips me onto his pillow face down. ANGEL! When his hands pry my thighs apart, jerk my hips high, ram something that's too big to fit inside. The shock of it vibrates all through my skull to the core of who I used to be. I am being raped. The shock of it numbs me. The pain of it taken by angel. He's so much stronger than me.

I roll myself away from her, her warmth and scent and perfection, my arms wrapped around only myself. I'll never shake Cleveland out of my head, Richard's right, he'll be with me forever. Forget rage and shame and revenge and terrible things so bad you cry out for your mom. Cleveland's missing and that's my fault, he hasn't gone home to his *mah-me*. They'll find out and lock me away forever, or maybe I'll fry on death row.

Moving out of Rand's skanky room and into the moonlit hall, lowering myself to the floor. Winter floods through the cracked foggy window, freezing the air, the clouds of my breath, and any emotion with calm.

Kat sits beside me, not saying a word. She pops the snap on her overalls bib and pulls out the stash of trip money. Counting it out on the hallway floor between her legs splayed before her. Two tens, one five, two ones, a quarter, eight pennies. Minus food and the pot, the blue pills and whatnot, she gathers it up and snaps it safely away in her pocket. She leans into me, her cheek on my shoulder and that's how we both fall asleep.

part seven
kat

32

The phone rings three times before it's picked up, and I'm anxious about who will answer. If it's my grampa I'm going to hang up, but if it's my granma I'll ask her. "Cool," Kat agrees, squeezing into the phone booth beside me, embracing my waist while I'm dialing.

But it's not Granma *or* Grampa who answers. A smooth mellow voice says, "Hello? Can I help you?" Calm and familiar, like an FM deejay you fall asleep to at night, or my uncle who's always been part of my life.

The nerves in my neck twitch, my mind blanks, I forget what we planned I should say. "Uncle Shelly..." Holding the receiver away from my ear to let Kat hear my uncle. He's got really good drugs, I tell her.

"Jame-o?" In his same fond voice like when I was little. No words for a moment, just this weird silence on his end of the line. I don't really know what to say either.

"May I speak with my granma, please?" Polite as pie, I think. Kat agrees.

"I'm so sorry," he says, but not like he's sorry he answered her phone, more like he's sorry he's blocking my call. So *uh-oh* snags in my chest. Because it was his plan and my dad's to place me in The Oaks instead of Railton. Panic rising, *I have a better plan.* I won't go back, I hear myself stubbornly tell no one but angel. I won't.

"Grandma's left us," he says.

"Well, she never said *anything* about leaving when I saw her."

"Jay. Listen to me. Grandma's expired."

I'm not hearing right or something. Expired? What, like parking meters and Kodak film? Shaking *Expired* out of my head so only "grandma" remains. I turn away from Kat, plug one ear with my finger, the receiver pressed to my other ear tight. To block Kat out of the call. My voice cracks. "What, her passport?" Was she deported and left us? It's so crazy I'm thinking California, of course you'd go west if you're leaving. But everything fades like I've entered a tunnel and a shrill pitch grows loud in my ears. *Left Us* hitting me full force in the chest.

"The funeral is Saturday. I think you should be there," he says.

Shaking my head, my knees fold, I let go, the receiver falls from my hand. I can feel myself shrivel smaller and smaller into a ball on the floor. I suddenly hate her. For making me need her so badly right now. For not getting money for Kat. For making me promise to keep on living then ditching out and leaving me here on my own.

Kat retrieves the receiver, but the walls of the tunnel thicken around me, muffling her out with the rest of this world and whatever she says on the phone.

I realize Granma's been here the whole time, waiting for me to wake up. *Once upon a time,* she reads aloud, *there lived a handsome young prince.* If I peek through my eyelashes at just the right angle, she's a white silhouette sitting beside me. She turns the page, her mouth barely moving to the rhythm of the story she tells. She knows I can hear her, even asleep. She knows her words are a lifeline that keep me from floating away. Except for the last page, I'm dreading that, with its final two words I don't want her ever to read. *The End.* Two words to wake me and take her away forever. I'm not sure at all what happens before *happily ever after.* If it's a cool adventure or just more bad things not worth waking up for at all. She looks up from the book, combs my hair from my eyes with her fingers. *It's your story, my love,* she says. *That's for you to decide.* She holds up the pages to show me the pictures. So of course the pages are blank.

Granma? Inhaling a lungful of *don't make me wake up,* trying to untangle what's real from what's not. Questions I have for her burden my chest so crushing it hurts to keep breathing.

"It's Saturday," Kat says.

Is this where the story begins? I open one eye, then the other. Kat's rifling through her big carpetbag, pulling out clothes she holds to her shoulders picking what outfit she'll wear. It's too cold too early too bright to wake up. There's only two blue ones left in my pocket. Two sips of flat Schlitz to swallow them down. I pull her red coat over my head, close my eyes in the hideaway dark.

"Your uncle said she kicked from a cardial something-something. That's not your fault, man."

"*Fuck you* was the last thing she heard me say." Two words that hurt even worse said out loud. "So."

"I think you should go."

"I can't," I tell her. "I can't face those people, you have no idea." She goes, it's not for them, "it's for you," and peeks in at me under the coat. "What would Hannah want you to do?"

I don't have an answer except probably, "Go."

Kat gives the address to the cabbie. Adjusting the white maxi dress she's got on and her big carpetbag with all her stuff in it, we settle together into the taxi back seat. It's a long ride and the meter keeps clicking, each click adds a nickel or dime. My head heavy with blue ones rests on her shoulder. It's nice. "I wish we could just ride forever and never have to get out," I say.

She kisses my forehead, which I'm not expecting. "Everything ends, man," she says. "That's a good thing, right?"

The taxi exits the highway and turns down some side road into Solomon Memorial Park. This sinkhole feeling swallows me up and flips everything good inside out. It's just cemeteries, iron gates, and headstones with dead people buried below filling my head with *I don't want to go*, and how pointless it is to keep living.

We pass shiny cars parked on both sides of the road, then stop at the steps of this white chapel building where people in black head inside. Blackbirds swoop down, blackbirds in winter. There's a bird nest tucked inside the big Star of David over the chapel front doors.

The meter's stopped ticking. Kat reaches over the front seat to pay. Maybe their babies are still in the nest, that's what I'm guessing. Why the mother birds don't fly away.

I already know I'm losing my grip and I doubt even angel can help me.

I hike these jeans up by this wide leather belt, then tighten the buckle, but still, they ride low on my hips. They're not clothes you wear when your grandmother dies, no matter how cool Kat said they look. Who made that rule? she wanted to know. Her red coat's unbuttoned, her dress swirls loosely like gypsy clothing you mostly can see through—you mostly can't look away—her tits and round belly shrouded in gauze and embroidered red poppies, two perfect poppies, love beads, and trippy crystal-lensed glasses. Kat slips the glasses from her eyes to mine, so I'm looking through kaleidoscope eyes. Everything fractures into diamond-shaped prisms, all six directions at the same time. Six copies of Kat put on six floppy hats, I don't know which copy is real. Six Kats hold me steady not letting me fall climbing tumbling steps to the chapel.

Soft darkness drapes you stepping inside, all solemn with sorrow and dread. So I'm glad for Kat's glasses hiding my eyes and any pitiful tears they might shed. Rows of white chairs are lined up like headstones, way more than enough for each person here. Some seats have purses and coats or prayer books on them, saving somebody's place. A few random people already sitting, a few clusters mingling around. All tinted purple through crystalized glasses and multiplied a half dozen times.

"All these old Jews," Kat says in my ear.

I nod my head. "We should go."

One of them approaches from across the hall looking to me like a hexagon choir in long black robes and shined shoes. I clasp Kat's hand tighter the closer he gets with his baskets of black satin skullcaps. Yarmulkes, that's what they're called. His reaches to help when I fumble to put one on right, his six hands direct me to go through the chapel to a door on the sanctuary back wall. "Your family's there, gathered in the family room," he says.

Crossing the chapel with Kat, all crowded with relatives and cousins I mostly don't even know, dressed nice in black clothing with expressions times six, pinwheeling toward us when we walk through. Dozens of eyes wide with surprise and distain, mostly disdain, at me or Kat and the clothes that we're wearing or maybe the baby she's carrying that shows. Milling about, they circulate my name in hushed whispers. Fear takes my hand, like I'm lost in the woods or a fairy tale forest where evil spells and curses lurk behind the family room door. I just want to leave but first Kat has to pee so she takes off in search of a john, and leaves me defenseless pretty much, in a kaleidoscope forest of inquisitive trees.

"My, how you've grown, what grade are you in now?"

"Will we see you in the *Sears Christmas Wish Book* this year?"

"You and Hannah were so very close, dear. May her memory be for blessing."

"We're so sorry for your loss."

"Love is never having to say you're sorry."

I turn to my cousin who said that. Jodi Rosenberg, with a heart not a dot on the *i*. "From *Love Story*?" she says, beaming at me like a six-Jodi cheerleading team. "With Ali MacGraw. Didn't you see it?" she asks but behind her, there's Grampa. Repeated in these lenses a half-dozen times.

Harrumph! he clears his throat times six, parting a path like Moses through the trees. "What do they know of such terrible loss?" he croaks in an agony voice, so at first I don't think he's talking to me. His six fists pound six lapels all torn at his heart, a looped black ribbon pinned to each one with an antique pearl-tipped hatpin. "So much she gave, James. *Every*thing. Can you understand? And I ask, what can I do? Anything she wants, this I will do for my wife, my beloved. Anything." The line of six Grampas bows their heads.

I take the kaleidoscope glasses off, my eyes readjust, everything jumps back in place. His brown-spotted pate, his ghastly white hair, and his skullcap I think Granma crocheted. The skullcap rises, his eyes baggy and wet but not angry at me for the first time probably since I was ten.

"But to see you again? This!...this, I can't give!...to see her Jameleh. This, I robbed from my Hannah. Like a thief, I took. A gonif. You, I chased away." Tears break his voice, his trembling fingers touch mine. "So many things, James, I can never take back. My prayers beg God you'll forgive me." His white beard bristles the back of my hand with damp breath. "I'm a foolish, miserable old man."

It's not what I ever expected him to say. Begging God for me to forgive him. But he knows about God and religion, he talks to God all the time in his language and I never have, I don't know how to be Jewish at all. I try to say it out loud, *I forgive you.* But the words stick in my throat and clearing it *harrumph* they clear away too. I do forgive him though, I swear to God and I mouth those two words like a vow. *I do.*

He unpins the black ribbon from the lapel of his coat with trembly, unsteady hands, and slips Granma's hatpin through the flap of my flannel pocket, pinning it on like a death boutonniere. A looped strip of black satin with a triangle snipped from one end. His shaky fingers brush his lips with a silent kiss then touch the pearl and snipped black ribbon. "Cut," he says, "like her life from the living. To let everyone know you're in mourning."

So I don't think I'll ever take it off.

"Who'll Stop the Rain?"

Mostly the feeling of sinking inside numbs her funeral from my head. Not the long walk from the chapel with Kat to the gravesite. Not the bronze plaques in the grass with the names of dead people buried under your shoes. Not how you can't breathe under a canopy crowded with all that black clothing, or the haunting death psalm the rabbi sings. Not my dad standing tall, his eyes locked on Kat, how she's holding me up the whole time.

Before us lays an oblong wooden box, too small for a person you'd think, on a green drape of fabric that doesn't really hide the deep trench dug in the earth below. Or the metal rack with a hand crank to lower her down. The workers who do that wait up the road in the cab of a little bulldozer. Whiffs of exhaust wander inside here with the hum of their running motor. A faraway song escapes from their radio. *Who'll stop the rain?*

We don't really bury her. Just a shovelful each like the rabbi shows us, with the shovel face down so it's not how you'd normally use it. An upside-down shovel of freshly-dug earth sprinkled over a plain pinewood coffin. Then drop in one stem from a stack of cut roses with a few silent words of goodbye. Grampa's words go unheard in the canopy flapping from the wind leaching tears from his eyes.

Filling me with emptiness so overwhelming I wish she was back at his side.

He turns to pass the shovel to who's next in line. My dad, I guess, then Uncle Shelly or the old Jews who pray at his side. But, no. Grampa hands the shovel to me.

I doubt I'll remember my brother beside me, if he put on a skull cap or cried. Or my sisters either, what Laura was wearing or where Beth stood aside with my mom, their hugs and squeals to see me at first, then silence at Grampa's deep pain. But "Who'll Stop the Rain" and the grind of the bulldozer moving in, I'll probably always remember that.

Blackbirds caw and circle the sky. Blackbirds in winter.

Kat reads off the names stepping gravestone to gravestone, making our way down the hill. She crosses herself and says, "Rest in peace" to each one. And just reading them with her, or crossing myself, the heaviness inside me lightens.

Most of the parked cars are already gone by the time we get back to the road, and the rest are backed up in a slow-motion crawl heading out the memorial gates. Shiny new Lincolns and Cadillacs. Some honk and wave when they drive past us but I don't wave back. Kat does, but she won't let me carry her carpetbag or act like a gentleman toward her. And it's not like I'm gallant or trying to be, I mostly just wanted my family to see I can do stuff they never expected of me, despite being certifiably mental.

A black limousine glides to a stop at the curb. The back door opens and my father gets out, not waiting for the chauffeur. Impressive as always, he heads straight toward me like the president of his world. Sharply dressed, with classic balanced features you'd call handsome, but twisted now, his lips taut suppressing emotion.

Kat squeezes my sleeve. "Why's he so uptight?"

MARY BLUM. That's who I'm standing six feet above when my dad stands before us.

He brushes my hair from my eyes with one hand. So it's his gold wedding band and cuff links I see, his crisp white cuffs and stiff collar. Black suit, black tie. Pinned to his overcoat lapel, a snipped black ribbon.

"Jamey," he says, as if Kat's not here or doesn't matter, grabbing my arm he pulls me from her, off the mown grass to the asphalt. I turn back for Kat but he doesn't let go. "Who's the father?" he wants to know. "Because if you're not—"

"I'm *not*," I say. A slight nod of his head, relief probably but he sees how pissed off the question makes me, how ready to punch him or split. His hand moves away.

Kat's arm wraps my waist pulling me to her hip. "We came here for Granma, it's got nothing to do with you," she says, hiking her carpetbag up by the strap, she turns her back on my dad. Her arm then her hand slips from my coat, and she walks away, leaving me all disconnected.

I turn to join her, my dad's words unleash. "Jamey! Stop and think this through. You've got a whole life ahead of you! For your own good—get in the car! If not for me then for Mom, your sisters, Tom—for Grampa!"

She's moving faster. Near the park exit, she looks back for me, then goes out the gate to the shoulder along the side road. Thumb out, walking backward toward the street and the highway onramp. *Bee-beep!* A VW microbus pulls over and stops. Kat chats with whoever's the driver.

"My office can contact her family and—" My dad behind me argues his case. "Look, bring her with! She can stay with us while you serve out your sentence. At least until the baby arrives. Jamey, wait!"

But I don't wait, I'm suddenly terrified she'll have the baby without me.

"Running from the law is not the answer—. How are you going to take care of a baby?"

The side door of the microbus slides open, Kat shoves the carpetbag onto the middle row seat. A hand reaches out to help heft her up, then she turns back and motions for me. I take off toward Kat, breaking into a run till I'm past the last cars idling in line and out the memorial entrance. But my dad in his suit and fine Gucci shoes is only two steps behind.

I scramble up into the bus beside her, the smell of pot smoke in the air. The hippie driver's turned around in his seat, talking to Kat.

"Looks like," Kat is saying, caressing her belly. "Not right *now*, but." Her old man is sending her a ticket to LA, that's where the baby'll be born. We're heading back into Chi-town to get it. Then it's west until her feet get wet, I've heard that part before. She giggles, she's high, on life and the future, her eyes twinkle sparking my heart.

"Jamey..." My dad's voice cracks, standing at the open side door. He swallows back something searching for words, then grabs hold of my coat sleeve and for a second I think he might cry. "A father and a son...Jesus Christ...try to stay out of trouble. And...call me, if, well, if you...if you need me." He pulls out his wallet and hands me all of his cash. And it's weird when he hugs me, it's like déjà vu, like last year when he told me goodbye. Except, no handcuffs or Railton or useless advice. And he's the one crying this time.

33

A dime hits a crack in Doreen's countertop and spins out of kilter just when I'm ready to split. Clinking against my empty coffee cup, it falls flat and comes to a stop.

Flick my hair out of my eyes and look from the dime to the tall man who tossed it. Black fedora, the brim tipped over one brow. Black overcoat, black suit, white shirt, black tie. No black ribbon pinned on him like mine. Still, something about him's familiar somehow, I've seen his straight face and fedora before. He takes the hat off with a sweep of his hand. "Talk to me, Angel," he says.

"I'm not angel," I say.

"I know," he says, so a twinge of fear stirs in my chest.

He sets a briefcase down on the counter and a business card. *Marc A. Gabriel, Investigator. Office of the Cook County Sheriff.* Alarm bells go off in my head, I don't want to be under arrest.

"Marc Gabriel," he says.

"I know," I say back, trying my best to stay calm. But on his card there's the same State of Illinois seal that everything's stamped with at Railton. *Property of.* Rules, clothes, mattresses, library books, cafeteria trays, things you'd rather forget. And now here it is on Doreen's dining counter, staring at me like a threat. "I saw you on the news," I say.

"Lowell Jasper Cleveland," Marc Gabriel says. "You know anything about that?"

Just hearing his name makes me cringe, and for one dizzy second my mind hums with alibis. *I didn't do anything,* that's number one. Number two: *An honest day's work for an honest day's pay for breakfast and rent and daily medication.* Or number three: *I'm just here for Kat, to check if The Letter arrived yet from Zero.* Just thinking her name, this little thrill tingles all through me.

Kat Kat Kat.

Jingle-jingle. The bell over the door rings, somebody leaving with somebody else. Which is not an invitation to sit down at the counter beside me, like Marc Gabriel, Investigator, does.

His trigger finger beckons Doreen and her full coffee pot. Clapping a cup on a saucer before him, she pours hot coffee to the brim. Mine too, perfectly refilled. I nod thanks but I don't really want it. I just want to hurry back to Kat.

Kat Kat Kat.

Lighting a Camel then another off that, he hands the second one to me. His gaze catches my coat sleeve where a dark stain streaks the tan suede. So the twinge turns to guilt, or something you wish you had dry-cleaned.

Doreen puts a menu before him and asks what else she can bring. His hand waves again, this time cutting flat across the whole menu. "Whatever Angel wants."

Doreen already knows what I want. "Be just a few, darlin." Scribbling it on her pad, she turns toward the kitchen. *French toast whipped cream chocolate milk.* They don't have real fruit here, if you ask it's a glob of strawberry jam.

I'm smoking his cigarette, he's buying breakfast, he's the one in charge. "Thanks," I say, take a drag off this smoke, exhaling it toward the ceiling. "Except now I sort of have to talk to you."

He almost smiles, like I'm entertaining him or something. He nods at what's left of the scab marking my palm. "Is that how the blood stain got on your sleeve?"

Doreen sets a tall plastic tumbler before me. Cold choco milk dark as a Hershey's bar, triple shot of choco. I hang this smoke on the ashtray edge and chug, bottoms up, then clap the empty tumbler on the counter. "It's not my coat," I tell him. "This thief I met gave it to me." This thief, ha. And his stolen pharmaceuticals.

He crushes his cigarette in the ashtray. "How about hustlers? You meet any hustlers?" He slides something out of his inside coat pocket. A plain spiral-bound notebook, smaller than Donald's and not purple. Flipping it open, his thumb clicks the end of a pen. "'Doing dates' I believe they call it. You into that, too? Doing dates?"

"I don't, that's not true." I'm not queer. Just ask Kat.

"Cute kid like you would have no problem getting picked up. Make a few fast bucks?"

I just look at him. "Are you soliciting me?" Although...a few fast bucks, how much is that? Added to Kat's California stash. Eighty-something-something. Something.

He holds his gaze an extra long second. "I'm worried about you. You kids seem to think it's the hip thing to do, but it's not safe out here, my friend. Young men are turning up dead. The Summer of Love is over."

Ding-ding order up! Doreen slides a plate down the counter to me. Four yellow triangles of fried speckled bread topped with a rose of whipped cream. Sucking a mouthful of cream off my finger.

"I'm asking you to help idee sommov," Marc Gabriel says, "reported missing seela lab la bla..."

Tuning him out. Just eating my breakfast, two chewy bites of egg-spongy bread, then wrapping the rest in a napkin for Kat. It's not like gourmet that you'd get from a chef at the River Hills Inn or homemade with love like my granma's. The cook here's an ex-con whose menu pairs best with bad coffee and a Camel non-filter. Ashing it, I take a last drag and stand up to go.

But he's opened his briefcase, snapped a rubber band off a marked yellow envelope and he's sliding a photograph out. On the counter before me is somebody's picture.

"Recognize this guy?" he asks.

It's a snapshot from a family album of a boy in a front yard with a dog jumping up to fetch something out of his hand, a Frisbee or stick. The way dogs always do. But not just any boy. I sit back down. "That's Zero."

"What was that?"

"Zero, it's his name." Look away from it, at Doreen clearing the empty brown tumbler away, at my breakfast plate clattering into her dishpan. At the red rhinestone Santa pinned to her chest. At this coffee and my distorted reflection on the oily black surface. Look anywhere but at that picture. "The boy, not the dog."

"Zero? A.k.a. Charlie Zerotski. Eighteen years old. He's missing."

I squirm on this hard seat, not squirm, readjust. Zero's missing. Well, I hope he stays missing. For months or forever, I never want Kat to split.

"His mother's worried," Gabriel says. "If you know where he is, her prayers would be answered."

His mother? I crush the cigarette out in the full ashtray. Doreen hardly ever empties them, maybe that's something she'd pay me to do.

Look back up at this sheriff's investigator or whatever his grand title is, so poker-faced I've got no idea what he's trying to get at, hinting maybe I'm hiding Zero or the truth. Kat's going to have a baby, does Zero's mother know about that? But then it hits me, if Zero gets busted and brought back to Chicago, then maybe Kat stays here, too. So I tell him. "He split. Right after Thanksgiving, he went to California. The beach, I think. In LA."

His brows rise like he's surprised by my answer. He makes a mark in his notebook.

"What about him? Familiar?" He's suddenly got a different picture he wants me to look at, another smiling school portrait. I'm glad anyway he's all done with Zero, and it's not a.k.a. Charlie Zerotski's photo staring at me all wholesome and clean.

But he slides my coffee cup out of the way and starts putting down pictures face up, one by one. *Snap!* When they hit the pink countertop, he flips the edges so hard, *snap! Snap!* I don't know these anonymous boys, missing, or whatever he thinks, so after a while I stop even saying no no no. Especially Cleveland, when his mugshot pops up. I just let it go, as more faces fall, one burying the next, without any comment or reason to care at all.

Marc Gabriel tucks all his pictures away, secured in the clasped envelope. **Documentary Evidence**, it's stamped in bold letters. **MISSING PERSONS**.

Not Donald's picture, though. So I wonder, you know, who reports these guys missing? So that's what I ask him.

"Why do you ask?" he says.

Wresting it out of the Marlboro coat pocket into daylight, smoothing the pad on my thigh. *JAMES JAMES JAME* half torn away and streaked with brown on the counter before him.

"He's missing," I say. "That's his stationery pad. Donald, that's his name." *Missing*, that word stuck in my head like gum. Donald's missing and is that my fault too? I'm biting the inside of my cheek. "Or maybe he got busted?"

"Are you asking me?" The investigator carefully picks it up with a napkin between his pinched fingers.

"Well, you're the investigator," I say.

"You sure he wants to be found? He didn't just 'up and split' for LA?"

Looking at him, I'm starting to not like the tone in his voice, or that I even brought Donald up at all.

Doreen with her coffee pot gives me this look like she'll kick him out if I want, nudging the pot toward the door. I look away from her, too. "I don't think he would just leave me and not come back."

"You two are pretty close then."

"Well."

"Friends? Roommates? Lovers?"

Heat flushes my cheeks thinking of that. Lovers. I push these overgrown bangs out of my eyes to my forehead. "More like a brother. Or sister, maybe."

Gabriel scoffs. "When was the last time you saw him?"

Thinking back to forever ago, my voice cracks when I say it. "My birthday." Before he asks, I tell him. "October fifteenth."

He writes that down, too. "Over two months ago."

"I know the apartment where he lived before. If that helps." I'm toying with Gabriel's stubbed-out cigarette, smoothing it straight in my fingers, put it in my mouth. "The landlady might yell at you, though. Curse you to hell." Kind of miming how nasty she is, but Gabriel isn't amused.

Striking a match, he relights it and waits till I've taken a drag. "Tell me about the last time," he says.

Smoke streams out the chip in my teeth straight to the ceiling already stained from a million exhaled cigarettes. I doubt Doreen's ever looked up to see and maybe she'd pay me to clean it. "We sat like, right there." I point to the booth where nobody's sitting right now. "'Cause it's my birthday, you know, so for dinner and whatever, birthday cake. But then Donald left instead with this guy Richard Hunt to, you know, do whatever..."

Marc Gabriel stops me, his whole demeanor shifts, almost angry. "'Do whatever'?"

"Well, sex stuff, for money. That's what he does, anything and everything, that's what Donald told me. So the killer would have no reason to kill him. That's what he said."

"Because he's such a jewel in the sack." Marc Gabriel shakes his head.

Yes. Because maybe he is and still a good person. I don't say it though.

"But Donald never came back," he says. "The last time you saw him, he was with 'this guy' Richard Hunt. So why do you have his notebook?"

"I've been looking for him and I...I found it in the trash. It's how I got cut," I tell him. Sticking my hand where it doesn't belong, in somebody else's trash.

"You know his full name? Date of birth, home address, next of kin? Anything?"

Shaking my head. "Just, he's Donald. Donald, um, Griswold."

He's scribbling that down, I can't read what he writes, *Griswold*, I guess, so that's good, and my description when he asks: *Like Andy Warhol, if Andy Warhol weighed more. And wore dresses.* And was black.

Gabriel rips the page out and crumbles it into a ball. "Probably better to keep that out of the report. Nobody cares about blacks," he says.

What? But he shrugs at my stunned reaction.

"Sorry, that's just the way it is."

"What if he's not like *black* black, just a little bit black," I say, like an argument I've already lost. "With bleached hair. So he's blond."

His eyes flash, not at me though, even worse, at the door—uh-oh—and I twist on this counter stool to see two cops enter. They stand back like sentries, exchanging secrets with Marc Gabriel in a language that doesn't use words, and I almost laugh, realizing how the bell on the door has stopped jingling.

"So..." Gabriel says, turning back to me, "your gay, bleach-blond, dress-wearing sister was last seen with Richard Hunt. And you, of course." Looking straight at me, inside almost, like he already knows everything about me.

Get your lie right, someone once told me, but I'm hoping I don't have to do that. Maybe Gary said it, my best friend in eighth grade, so I wouldn't get detention or grounded. Or maybe it was Ratachek. "I thought Richard Hunt was a cop." Can he see the heat flood to redden my jawline and know how guilty I am? "He said Donald got busted when I asked where he was. He said he's locked up."

"Easy enough to find out," Gabriel says, so that's good and I'm anxious to know and not really listening when he asks, "Where is this trash can? Anything else in there I should know about?"

I slide my feet to the floor, grabbing a napkin and the breakfast I wrapped up for Kat. "Behind his garage."

"Richard Hunt's garage? You were at his house?"

Yes. No. I don't know! Trying to play the strategy out but I've never been good at chess. If this, then that, and what happens after, it's all scrambled eggs in my head. "Not solicitation though, I swear," that's what comes out. "Just at Thanksgiving and one time for a job, cleaning his kitchen and, and rug. Because I was looking for Donald and he went with Richard. I thought maybe Donald was there." It's all of a sudden important he believes me. The most important thing in the world. "Because I care," I add, but it doesn't change his expression. "I swear, you can even ask Richard."

"We'll do that," Gabriel says. He scribbles more in his little flip pad. "We'll go to his house, you and me. You can give me the guided tour."

Inside I'm flipping completely out. What did I stick myself into now? I didn't do anything. Two punches to Cleveland's face, that's all, not equal by half to what he did to me.

"Meet me outside here at six a.m.," Gabriel is saying. "We have a date?" He's straightening his overcoat collar but stops when I hesitate. "Or do I need to lock you up until then?"

"What? No, no, you don't need to."

Slipping his card off the counter, he hands it to me and waits till I take it, till I tuck it away in my chinos back pocket. He nods. "Good. Tomorrow morning." He adjusts his fedora, tipping its brim like he does, and gets up. "And James?"—so my heart stops and I feel my face flush—"Don't make me come looking for you. That would *not* be good." He turns, the two cops follow him out of Doreen's Fresh Cup Diner.

Jingle-jingle.

34

I'm wet, that's what wakes me. Soaked through the seat of these chinos, and freezing. Jeez, I haven't done that since Railton, pissed myself. Pissed *at* myself for taking too many blue pills—then panic. "Kat?" Because the space where she sleeps on my coat right beside me is empty.

Cold creeps in and around my ankles from outside this room, from the hall. Because the door was left open. She's gone, I don't blame her, who'd want a boyfriend who wets the bed.

Orange blinks out the night with the stark HOTEL light, flashing over the room. Rand's on his mattress, sitting slumped over, nodding out with a needle and spoon. Her carpetbag's here, her red coat tossed aside, her granny shawl and petite army boots.

My teeth chatter like crazy. I have to clench my jaw tight to speak. "Kat?" Stumbling to my feet, soaked chino fabric clings to my legs making it harder to stand.

I grab the Marlboro coat from the floor, but it's soggy and too wet to put on. I swipe her shawl up instead, swing it around my shoulders. Stepping barefoot toward the hall through leftover trash, last night's French fries, and breakfast remains from Doreen's. Past the mattress and Rand.

Rand stirs in his cowboy boots, his voice hardly there. "Shudda door," he grumbles.

I pull the door shut at my back, step into the hall like walking on ice with no shoes. Scurry quick to the john, the worst john in Chicago till me and Kat cleaned it. The door isn't closed all the way, the lock doesn't work, there's somebody in there, you never know who, perverts and junkies or rats, even worse. Closing my eyes but the words to apologize or beg for forgiveness don't come. "Kat?"

"James?" It's her voice all shaky from crying but she never cries, or I've never seen it. Her teeth chatter, too, chopping her words into pieces. "Some...something happened. A whole gush of water came out."

Opening the door, not sure I should but she doesn't object, just draws a deep breath like a hit.

She winces. "Oh, man, I don't feel good." And her face sucks in, every muscle pursed, panting *ooh ooh ooh ooh*. She's warped and misshapen, all hunched on the john. But you can't see the john, just her huge pale belly, the button popped out like the turkey is done. Her white knees spread wide poke out underneath, her pale legs streaked pink and ankle-deep in overalls puddled around her feet. She clutches the straps tight like reins. Then lets out a breath. Her eyes focus again, pooling with tears under tendrils of long, sweaty hair. "Oh, man, it hurts, make it stop. Please, please make it go away," she begs.

So I say okay okay.

In three steps I'm back in Rand's room. Two steps, right and left, into these broken Beatle boots, gather Kat's carpetbag, her mittens, her boots, her red coat. "Rand?" But he just grumbles when I shake his shoulder, all groggy and far away, riding his powerful drug. "I'm taking your jacket, okay? Mine got wet." I pick up the black satin Angels jacket where it's strewn on the mattress beside him.

He mumbles "fugkyew" or something you'd spell wrong. So I mumble "Thangkyew," back.

WALK-IN HOURS 10 A.M. TO 6 P.M.
MONDAY THRU SATURDAY

The free clinic's not far, just one block away but it's closed when we finally get here. I didn't think about that, they'd close a free clinic at night. So we're stuck on its stoop and locked out with no doctor on duty or medical help. Just chains on the door and thick metal grating that hurts through my boots when I kick it.

What to do in case of emergency? Come back in the morning at ten.

I don't think Kat can wait till then, she needs a doctor right now. The baby inside her's no longer moving, when you feel her taut belly, it's still.

"Oh God oh God oh God, I killed it," she says in a voice on the edge of a squeal.

Panic grows tenfold, it's hard to hide it and talk. "It's not dead, it's—it's napping," I tell her. "Babies take lots of naps." I don't really know, but her wide eyes believe me when I say so. And how it's not a big deal, babies get born every day, sometimes in a car helped by a cop or passing stranger who knows what to do, I saw that one time on the news.

But not now in Uptown at ten p.m., there's no help around at all. Kat's in pain that's awful to watch and looking at me like I know what to do. I just wish it was tomorrow and ten a.m., and this whole baby thing could be through.

I set her packed carpetbag down on the sidewalk and cup my face to the security bars on the window. Only the ghostly reflection of my own hollow eyes blinks back.

FOR EMERGENCIES GO TO COOK CTY HOSPITAL is scrawled on cardboard taped to the door. Kat collapses in the vestibule corner, like she just heard the worst news in the world.

"No! Not Cook County, I can't go there! Zero said they'll put me in Audy Home and take the baby away and if you're with me they'll bust you and lock you up, too—Zero specifically said do *not* go to County..." Curdled in the doorway of the chained free clinic, her bent knees spread wide, her overall straps unfastened so the bib flaps over her lap. Money spills out, clattering all over the concrete, and I scramble to gather it up. She says Zero talked to the doctor here and he said the baby won't come till next year after they're in California. What if she hitched? Maybe that's what she'll do, if we left right now how long would it take? Her desperate eyes look up at me. "Oh God, what should I do?"

The concrete numbs me sitting beside her, even cradling her wool coat, my teeth chatter louder than hers. In one of Rand's satin pockets there's a cigarette pack, in the other, his Buck knife and baggie of pills maybe blue ones, amobarbital whatever, I'm about to check, when Kat's face tenses all pinched up and painful so I have to bear down till her suffering passes. Her wet lashes flicker on flushed dewy cheeks. "I don't wanna do this," she whimpers. "I changed my mind, James. I don't wanna have a baby."

Leaning my head into her shoulder so the wind in my ear stops screaming, her trembling slowly subsides. Resting, exhausted, I think she's asleep. Her lips slightly parted with small gentle breaths. I keep still the whole time, huddled beside her. For maybe a moment I drift away, too.

"Fuck!" Her hand clenches the cuff of this black satin jacket, she squeezes my wrist, her nails dig deeper, she sucks in her breath like the biggest hit ever inhaled. "Oh God oh God oh God, Zero! Why didn't you take me with you?" she wails, but there's no answer.

Except we can't stay here. I get up, brush off the soggy seat of my pants, hold my hand out for hers. "C'mon."

But it hits her full force, the pain of the baby wanting out. Her whole face frozen in place like an agony photo in the museum of pain. Babbling apologies and promises to Jesus My Lord Of Lords, wishing Zero was here then cursing him out 'cause he's not. Cursing me out through chattering teeth 'cause I'm too fucking nice. "You're so good-looking you could have any chick you want, why would you ever want me?"

I could? Any chick I want? That's news to me. Wrapping both arms around her, well, halfway around that's all I can reach, in a hug like Scotch tape trying to keep her from falling apart. I can feel it, though, her whole body relax and go limp with her whimpers. She looks at me through teary eyes. "You really won't leave me?"

Which hurts that she'd even ask, so I'm feeling brittle and ready to crack. But it's worse probably for Kat, lifting her back to her feet, trying to get her to take the next step when she moves like a bowling ball's clutched in her knees. I'm trembling so bad, these wet pants chill my bones, holding her, I just want to be warm. "Kat, I would marry you."

She clutches my arm through this black satin sleeve so I guess she believes me. "Oh, God! It's coming!"

The baby, I realize she means the baby, because panic is already here. In the middle of the sidewalk with no heroes anywhere or cars to help. Her legs bowed and holding her lady bits down there, each breath like it's choking a scream. Me just all stupid and useless beside her. A useless excuse for a human being.

Headlights approach, blinding my eyes, splashing us both in a flash of white light but then just as quickly pass by. Kat moans, her face all sucked in and whimpering, "Oh hurry James I don't want it born in the street."

Thumb out, I'm shaking so badly, I step between parked cars into the street, walking backward. Flagging the few cars that pass us, warming one hand at a time in these thin jacket pockets. I'm actually thinking to steal a car, and wondering how you do that, when headlights slow down and pull over. "Kat! Here's our ride!"

Trapping us in brilliant headlights, I shield my eyes. A souped-up Mercury guns to a stop.

I grab the carpetbag and help Kat slip into the back seat, I hop in beside her and slam us together inside.

The driver is huge and decked out in black leather, like a Hell's Angel or hellraiser with tattoos on his face. I clutch Rand's Buck knife inside my pocket, just in case. It's for hunting, Rand said. Deer, I think, or squirrel for supper. But still. I've got one finger ready on the handle notch you have to press to unlock it.

But the driver's neck swivels, same as me, to Kat who's panting in quick puffs of air. Her knees spread, she cradles her belly, her hair cascades over her face. "Oh man hurry you guys," she gasps, "the baby's coming."

He jumps, facing forward, shifting the gear, twisting the wheel, and flooring it into the street.

Bright ember flakes flicker and swirl in the twin headlight beams that slice through the city before us, Uptown, Old Town, crosstown. The engine exhaust crackles and pops gunning through neighborhoods, but none of them look like the way I took when I went to Mt. Sinai before. And just when I'm feeling completely lost, he's swerved up a driveway where a lit-up white sign with a red arrow points. EMERGENCY ENTRANCE NO PARKING. The tires squeal to a halt.

I swing my door open, one arm around her but Kat can't move. "Ooh ooh," is all she can say, squeezing again, "no no no I don't wanna," stuck to the seat, eyes clenched and face gleaming with sweat. I don't want to leave her, but this hellraiser guy yells, "Go get a fuckin' MD!"

35

The warmth of it grabs me stepping inside, the stark lighting and rank human smell, it takes a quick moment to adjust from the chilled wintry dark. Till my jaw chatter slows, I don't have to squint, and I can breathe through my nose almost normal. But I've never been at this hospital before. Rows of seats fill the lobby where poor people huddle, waiting and weary and mostly not white, standing in line to check in. COOK COUNTY HOSPITAL—which hits me oh no, it's exactly where Zero said *not* to go, and I turn back toward the emergency door. YOU MUST CHECK IN FIRST the sign at the front of the line says, where a black nurse is working the check-in desk. So I cut in front just to ask her where else we could go. But she doesn't answer, just springs from her chair, rushing urgently past me.

I turn to follow, toward where I'd come in, where the last ER door slides all the way open, and a blast of snow blows Santa Claus in. Toppling over in a fat red coat with a carpetbag and long auburn tresses, it's Kat.

Before I can move, the nurse is beside her and an orderly guy with a gurney appears, the doors held wide open with the cold and commotion to get Kat inside. I don't even see her, just a red blur whisking by, when they wheel her away without me.

Hurrying to follow wherever they take her. Across this scuffed lobby, past a big Christmas tree with hand-made decorations, paper chains, doily snowflake charity donations, past a gift shop closed up and dark, through battered double doors that swing shut in my face, and when I push through, I'm already too late. They're in the elevator, the door closes them in, I'm just left on my own in a long eerie hallway without her.

I pound the button till the UP arrow lights, till the elevator dings and the door glides open and I step in and ask the hospital people inside, "Which floor for babies?" You want seven, they decide. Seven, that's what I push and it's where I jump off. LABOR & DELIVERY. Facing a nurse's station, but nobody's here. They're all laboring, I guess, delivering Kat's baby somewhere.

A nurse with gray kinky hair in a white uniform and pink sweater rounds the corner, we see each other the exact same time. She's wearing a stethoscope like a cheerleader whistle and hugging a chart to her chest.

She comes at me, wagging a finger. "Oh, no-no-no. You can't be up here. This is ladies' business."

"Where's Kat, I just brought her here, she's having a baby."

"The little white girl?" In two steps she crosses the hall and presses the DOWN arrow button. The elevator opens. "She's still got a while yet to go. Unlike you," she says, "who is going right now. Come back at eight, that's visiting time."

"No, no, no, wait," I say. "I'm supposed to be with her. She doesn't want to be alone."

She shoo-shoos me to step back. "Believe me, you *don't* want to be in there." But I don't believe her.

"The OB's on his way," she says, dismissing me.

"Obee who?" I'm starting to sweat and unzip Rand's jacket.

"The obstetrician." She shakes her head like she's talking to an idiot. "The doctor who delivers the babies."

"Oh. Sorry, I didn't know that." I scratch my head, thinking, an obee's coming, well, that's a relief, me and Kat could just leave in the morning. We could go anywhere. Hitch to California or a hippie commune, my mind already racing toward that perfect future. "Cool. No, really. Thanks," I tell her. "Thank you."

She's leaning one shoulder into the wall just staring at me, at my flannel shirt, at the toothbrush in my pocket, at the snipped black ribbon. "Condolences for your loss," she says. "Look, why don't you have a seat in there?" She points at this sign hung over a doorway down at the end of the hall.

FUTURE FATHERS it says.

There's a few decorations, Santas and reindeer and SEASON'S GREETINGS, and a stand with a TV set on, *The Tonight Show*, but without any sound. All kinds of magazines on the waiting room rack, *LOOK*, *LIFE*, *TIME*, but just one man in here waiting, one Future Father, I guess.

He's snoring. A bouquet of flowers wrapped in gold foil hangs loose from his fingers, chrysanthemums or maybe carnations and baby's breath—and *condolences* hits me because flowers are something my granma would know. I should do that, get a bouquet for Kat. I think roses, though.

Looking around at these snapshots they've got of mostly black babies tacked to the bulletin board, thank you notes and babies on greeting cards.

The future father wakes with a start, his bouquet drops to the floor. He rubs his face, stretching his features like Silly Putty, and yawns. His overcoat's open, his shirt's buttoned wrong. "Miss?" he says. "Hell. You're not the nurse."

I tell him I'm not a chick either.

"No offenses intended, you got that blond..." His fingers motion down the sides of his face like they're combing long hair, then swoop the flowers up from the floor. "What time is it," he asks himself, checking his wrist but he's not wearing a watch. On the wall clock it's twelve fifteen. Rippling his shirt so air passes through, he chuckles. "Sorry, be a bit stanky after ten hours." He tells me he's hoping his firstborn is a son, he's already picked out the name. Adam. "How about you? You prayin for the donut or the cigar?" He smiles a big apple-cheeked grin, making those shapes with his fingers.

I say I'm praying for it to be over.

Slowly, his chin sinks into his chest and he's snoring again, his lips slack and drooling, his porkpie hat over his eyes, arms folded. Poking from his pocket, his wallet and checkbook, full with money I bet for his new baby boy, for clothes and food and college. Or a mental hospital. Adam, his firstborn. So I already feel sorry for him and what he's got to live up to.

A father and son. Donald wrote that. *Everything one does is done for the other one.* What did my dad ever do for me? Or me for him. I shift in this chair, change positions.

"The Star Spangled Banner" plays on TV till the waving flag fades into a test pattern Indian.

I empty my jacket, Rand's jacket really, his black satin pockets. A baggie with pills. The Buck knife—how many bucks has it killed? A Marlboro hardpack, I flip its lid up to dump out a smoke—

But instead of a Marlboro, a thick rolled-up dollar pops out on my palm.

My heart starts up racing so crazy. I snap off the rubber band, unroll the top bill—it's a *hundred*. Then another $100, and when I peel that off, another, it scares me how much and where did Rand get it? Fifties and twenties and tens—I stop counting. And there's two more thickly-rolled bills in the hardpack.

It's not mine, that's what's ticking inside me. I flatten the unruly pile, my fingers too shaky to roll it tightly back up. I fold it instead, a thick wad of cash, guessing how much but then, what difference really? It's still not mine. The pills Rand's got too, just reds in this baggie I didn't pay for but swallow one anyway. Just one, okay two, that costs maybe a buck and he's got like...*a thousand.*

Someone passes the doorway, and I jump—not a cop, a man I think, a janitor. In a gray uniform, swaying a buffing machine down the hall. But still, I sit up, tuck my shirttail in, stuffing the folded wad of bills back in the box and everything deeper, deep as I can, the knife, the Marlboro pack, a baggie of pills, back into Rand's satin pockets. Watching the clock tick time away with slow hands and arms feeling heavy and stumpy. Sleep coming welcome and washing me over. My head heavy too, so closing my eyes, I lean back and let go, thinking, tomorrow I'll give back his jacket, and let myself sink into darkness.

I wake in the world's most uncomfortable chair, slouched low so I'm not really sitting. My head thick with something denser than sleep. Still, serious voices seep in. TV voices. I cover my ears and keep my eyes closed but there is no escaping what's coming.

"Mr. Jendrin?" A nurse in the doorway peeks in asking, but I'm the only one waiting here now. Hugging a clip-boarded chart to her chest, her white dress and white shoes walk softly away.

The daylight bites into my eyes. Blinking away sleep and trying to focus. Christmas cards and pictures of babies are tacked to one wall. *Leroy's first tooth! Maria's first Christmas! Jamal's first step!* The ashtray's been emptied, the floor's buffed, magazines straightened in a neat stack.

The morning news on TV, the anchor guy's face all somber and serious. Reporting the weather, the war dead, the wreck of some plane, and a homicide victim. I don't want to know any of it, even before the photo comes on. Familiar and awful, I've seen it before, the one of the boy with his dog. But not just any boy.

Icy tingles spike my arms.

"...the victim, identified this morning as eighteen-year-old Charlie Zerotski of Streeter, Illinois..." so I jerk up to see his yearbook face. Zero.

My mind ping-ponging one thought to the next, pictures names places, all stewed together. Except for two words the news guy says, two words like a caption or title. "The Victim." The victim is deceased. Deceased, that's like, dead, why don't they just say that? Charlie Zerotski is dead. God, my throat's dry, I need something to drink. I need to find Kat to tell her. Or maybe she saw the news too. Teenage remains found in the Des Plaines River.

Picturing Zero, hitching and picked up by a Country Squire station wagon, how would you know that's a car killers drive? You wouldn't, it's random, if you don't get inside, they just go pick up some other young guy. Another face in the stack on Doreen's countertop, but no longer Missing and filed in the folder marked Found instead. The investigator's got a lot more in his briefcase, so many faces, he'll never be done. The investigator's got—the investigator! Oh, crap! What time is it? The hands on the clock point to 7:54.

Seven. Fifty. Four. Wasn't I supposed to meet him at like six? Don't make me come looking for you, James—isn't that what he said?

Thoughts spinning all crazy now. He knows my name. Maybe my whole record, stowaway, assault with intent, and juvenile court, the juvenile correctional facility at Railton. My mental case file, slashed wrists and psychiatrists, and over The Oaks Manor wall. My address, my phone number. My dad.

I push myself up to my feet. Where's Kat? We gotta split. Vamoose. Exit stage right. Ten hours, Adam's dad said. I can't think straight to add the time in my head but she's gotta be done having a baby by now.

It's hard to breathe this hospital air all rancid with bleach and misery. The nurse at the counter is not the same pink sweater one. Her face gets defensive, she crosses her arms when I ask what room to get Kat.

"Patient's last name?" she asks me. I just shake my head. I don't know her last name, just she's Kat. Maybe Zerotski. But she says "Nope" to Zerotski without even checking her chart. Where's the nice nurse? I ask her, apparently the wrong thing to say. "Are you sure you're at the right hospital?" she snipes.

Turning from her, to the elevator panel, the button that takes you down. Slam it once with my fist, twice even harder, and dry my eyes on my palm. Stepping in when the door finally opens, into a car crammed with workers and doctors and visitors with flowers, but I easily fit, I'm a skinny little shit, I hardly take much space up at all.

LOBBY is already pressed and lit up, a few other buttons, too. "Hit six for us," a deep male voice says behind me. I glance over my shoulder but all I can see is *We Serve & Protect*, the Chicago Police patch on his wide leather shoulder, his crewcut, and Chicago policeman's checker-board banded cap.

Fear, that's what fills the elevator now, fear and not air to breathe. I hit the button marked "6," shutting the door and all of us into this box going down. I lock my arms tight around myself as if that's a disguise for not being seen, and keep my eyes closed, barely breathing.

"Audy Home'll be good for her," I hear the cop say to the lady beside him, and *Audy Home* catches my ears. I hear her agree, their whole conversation: "White folks are crazy. Disown their daughter but keep her baby? It makes no sense." "Well, the baby is the innocent one." "At fourteen years old? Honey, we're not talking about immaculate conception." "Well. She should've kept her legs closed." There's a sharp bump when the elevator stops, but the cop's still talking. "I'll deal with her. You let the nursery know the child will be picked up in the morning."

"The child?" she says. "You mean Mary Katherine or the baby? They're both children."

Spikes of heat prickle the nape of my neck, my forearms, the sides of my face. I know who they're talking about. *Mary Katherine and the baby.*

The elevator door wobbles open. Floor six, MATERNITY. I step out and let them walk past me, but still I can barely breathe. He turns down the hall in the opposite direction, a big macho pig I wouldn't want to mess with. So I follow her and the directory sign that points to the nursery instead.

All I can think is, *that's* the baby. That's *Kat's* baby. In this nurse's arms when she steps to the nursery window. A tiny pale bundle cradled in blue, a thatch of coppery fur on its head. Blue for a boy and she's rocking him gently on the other side of the glass. Three rows of small metal cribs are lined up behind her, like a market, as if you could choose. Napping and peaceful or terrified wailing you barely can hear through the wall.

The lady crumbles the paper she'd scrawled on that she'd first held up to the nurse. She's stumpy, sort of pig-faced in a pantsuit with high platform heels that don't really make her much taller. She wears a badge on a lanyard hung around her neck with her picture stamped COOK COUNTY DCFS and the great state of Illinois seal. She holds the badge up like proof she's official and someone you better obey.

She points to the nursery door and the nurse inside nods and walks out of view to meet her. The blinds on it rattle when the door at the end of the hallway opens, and I catch a few words that she says. Like *Tomorrow morning* and *adopted* and *protective custody*. Their conversation ends quick and the lady whisks past, scowling at me as she leaves. The paper she crumbled lays on the table, I straighten it out to read. *Jendrin, Boy.*

My heart pounding faster, Where's Kat? They can't take her baby and lock her away, I have to find Kat. Both palms on the glass but the nurse turns away with the bundle. On tiptoes, I'm watching to see where she puts him, which basket is his so I'll know. The card on the end with a stork and blue ribbon. *Baby Boy Jendrin*, it says.

Calm as I can, not too calm at all, my heart racing double-time with the weight of the future it holds. Walking away, turn the corner to the end of the hall, practically skating down the slick polished floor back to MATERNITY. Till there it is like a heavenly gateway under fluorescent light. The nurses's station. Leaning over the counter, it's the same snitty nurse, I just smile. "Mary Katherine Jendrin?"

The nurse checks her chart but doesn't look up when she points down the hall with her pen. "Bed B," she says.

36

I open the door to a ward full of hospital beds lined up on both sides of the room. There's white draped partitions wheeled between them but still, they don't make it private at all. Bed B's by the window, so I try not to look walking through, but the lady in A has a voice like a record singing a beautiful song. She cradles a baby, its brown fuzzy head pressed face-first in her chest so I'm jealous and kind of turned on. I hurry past that. To bed B.

Kat sits up when she sees me. Her wet eyes flare wide all fiery green and red-rimmed. "James!" I rush to her arms, I can't hug her hard enough or hold on any tighter. Clinging me into her hospital gown, my arms reach around her so easily now, that strikes me funny, my cheek fits perfect on hers. Feeling so sweet I almost start crying.

"You're here, oh, you're here!" She's sobbing and smiling at the same time. She kisses her fingers and touches the kiss to my black ribbon. "Oh...sweet Granma Hannah..." she says and buries her face in my shirt, shoulders bobbing. "Where were you? Why didn't you come?" Her fists clip my arm with tiny punches.

Choking any excuse back with tears, *Where were you?* in a bitter lump of betrayal. "You're Jendrin, see, I didn't know that."

"I thought you ditched me!" She's gripping Rand's jacket so tight I think it might rip. "I was so scared I had no one again!"

Tears come I can't stop. "I was here the whole time, I...I just... they told me to wait."

Her tears on black satin sparkle like raindrops. "They called DCFS, just like Zero said." Shaking her head, she tries out a smile, her eyes empty wells I wish I could fill. "A cop was just here. I'm supposed to be getting ready to go." Her smile sort of flickers, but she gulps it down, something much worse than bitter. "Look," she says, peering through her open white curtain at the whole ward. "Everyone gets their baby to hold. But not me."

It's true, all these ladies with babies, you can smell the powder and poo.

"Man, don't *ever* have a baby," she says. "The *worst* thing you can imagine." Her heart pounds through everything, her thin hospital gown, black satin, plaid flannel, Led Zeppelin T-shirt, and me. "'In pain shall you bear children,'" she says, "'and the Lord thus punished Eve.'" Warm sticky tears smear on my cheek, she wipes them away with the back of her hand and draws in a long shaky breath. "It got so bad I cried out for my mother."

Me too, I've done that so I understand how bad, what makes you cry out for your mom. But I shake all that out of my head and tell her, "Yeah, but Kat? He's perfect."

She's suddenly frozen, her eyes like black sinkholes, her mouth twisted into a frown. "What?" Kat shoves me back, her face full of horror. "He? He, a boy? You mean a boy, I had a baby boy? How... how do you know? James?" Her bare feet hit the floor, pulling away, she stands, gets her bearings, her gown falling open, she spins toward the window, the bedside nightstand, the ward, the way out. "You saw him? Where? Where, take me to see, I have to see him," drying her eyes on her forearm and the hem of her opening gown, showing her knees, skinny thighs, ginger fur, this thick wad of white padding strapped in between.

"They wouldn't tell me *any*thing! They just said to rest when I said where's my baby, can I see my baby? They said it's best if I rest and they gave me a shot!" Her words trip and sputter, turning to venom. "I thought it was dead, or, or born all retarded with its brains outside its head because of something I did. They wouldn't even say if it's a boy or a girl. Just, the less I know the better and, and it's time to heal and forget it ever happened!"

She spins, her stare pinned on me, I'm shaking my head. *No, don't ever forget.*

The IV goes into the back of her hand, I know about those. It's not easy pulling it out with fingers so slow to move when she's so overwound and not keeping still. And the nightstand too, I pull its door open, help tug her carpetbag out and dump all her stuff on the bed. She's talking fast too, how she's outta here, man, first get her baby then split to CA, west until her feet get wet, she can't wait to see Zero and how stoked he'll be.

The hospital gown drops from her shoulders, a wrinkled puddle of cotton on rumpled white sheets. Trying not to think about Zero, or the bed and how sweet to just sleep there beside her with a pillow and blanket and her jugs—God, I try to not see but that's what they are, two full balloons with dark erect nipples pointing at me. Her spread hands crossing over can't hide the whole things. "They hurt so much," she winces. "Like they need him, too."

I help her, tugging this T-shirt over her head, stretching it down to cover those twins. She flips her long hair out of the neckline, a twisted cascade of rust-colored waves down her back. Then the fisherman sweater over her head, all stretched out and big, helping her step into overalls. Hardest is tying her boots.

We pack her bag full with other stuff, a whole box of those white padding things. The toothbrush they gave her, a towel and washcloth and toilet paper, I throw that in. Till it's too full to latch it. Kat's jaw tightens, she digs to the bottom and pulls out a book with a shiny gold cross on a red leather cover. *Holy Bible* it says, and she tosses it into the trash.

Kat tries to go faster but she can't walk normal at all. Traumatized, or whatever they write on your chart when you're wounded down there, so anyone can read you've been torn. She gets in a wheelchair we find by the elevators, I can push her much faster. "Slow down," she says, then, "Hurry up!" when I do. I wheel her past visitors and nurses and the elevators, down the little maternity hall. Straight to the nursery window.

There's no one around. It's closed and dark, the blinds on the viewing window drawn tight. A sign with a cartoon bird feeding worms to a nestful of chicks says IT'S FEEDING TIME.

"I'll get him," I say, so her hollow eyes fill with something like hope, her fingers let go of my sleeve.

The door's not locked despite its warning, STAFF ONLY. I go in, then down this short hallway that leads to the nursery door, the blinds on its window pulled all the way up. It's twilight inside with no lights on, like nap time when I was little. There's just one nurse in a chair in the corner, gently rocking a baby.

I turn the knob and let myself in.

It's different in here, happy and peaceful and quiet as sleep. The front viewing window is only a few steps away. The cord's near my hand and when I pull it, the blinds rattle and rise. The nurse looks up in surprise, not pissed off but not saying welcome either.

I sort of wave at her. "You don't have to get up."

She *shhhes* me with one finger, maybe says to get out, I don't care, I'm just seeing Kat framed in the window like a Renaissance painting of the holy Madonna. She points all worried at the nurse. I point at the card on his basket, I can't stop smiling, reading his name. "Baby Boy Jendrin." Kat stands up, palms pressed to the glass. Tears glisten her face.

Looking over my shoulder at the nurse standing too, the baby she's rocking, pink for a girl, walking over to me on soft white nurse soles.

"She's his mom," I tell her.

The nurse has a smile a lot like Kat's. She signals her to come in.

I go to the basket, the last on the end. More scared of this bundle than any policeman, I never picked up a newborn before. Baby Boy Jendrin. His round pink face peaceful in sleep, bundled all snuggly in blue. "How do I do it, pick him up?"

The nurse holds the pink baby high up to show me. "One hand supports his head," she says. "Go on. He won't break."

Slip my fingers under, his whole head fits my palm, his whole little body riding my wrist up the crook of my arm. And I lift up. But there's nothing to lift, like he's not even there, he doesn't weigh much at all, I'm not expecting that. Holding him up, keeping perfectly still, like if I move I might drop him or do something stupid like trip.

Little cries like a kitten come from him, I woke him, I made him cry, that's my fault. I look at the nurse to apologize, but she just tucks the pink one into a basket, all sleepy and content, and comes over to me.

"Perhaps he's hungry." She gives me this little glass baby bottle, it's just sugar water she says, see if he'll take it. He takes my finger. The teeniest grip, teeny fingers, teenier nails hugging my finger. Hugging my finger so tight.

I never felt better my whole life.

The nurse smiling crazy and Kat here too, I didn't even see her come in. Waddling toward me, her face like wet sugar, her hands like a magnet pulling her closer, her stuffed carpetbag and red coat dropped at her feet. In my arms, I tell Baby Boy holding on tight, "Here comes your mom."

"Oh," Kat says. Just *oh*, that's all. She doesn't wait to learn how, just takes him from me, the most perfect thing ever created. Well, that's that. Kat looks up, not at me, at the nurse. She giggles like music or a lullaby. "Oh, man. I'm leaking out every hole in me." And you can see these two growing circles darken her overall bib.

The nurse gathers Kat's hair into a tail and twists it out of the way. "Your milk's come in," she says. "That's good! The more he suckles, the sooner your bleeding will stop. Your uterus will tighten and you'll lose that little tummy. Did they show you how to breastfeed?"

Kat shakes her head, almost crying. "They didn't show me anything."

"Sit here," the nurse says.

Kat eases into the rocking chair. Turning to me, the nurse puts him back in my arms. Baby Boy Jendrin. Just hands him to me, not cautious or scared I might drop him or trip. "Got him?" and yeah, I do if I stand perfectly still. Slip one finger in his palm and he does it again, clamps on. So this feeling takes over like peace on earth and how cool life is, plugged into her baby and calm.

Kat's eyes don't let go of him the whole time the nurse helps her, fluffing a pillow behind her back or slipping one under her butt. The nurse unbuckles Kat's overalls strap, pulls up her sweater, one side of her stained T-shirt too, so God, there it is again in all its full glory, Kat's balloon tit. I show it to Baby Boy. "That's for *you*. And she's got another one just like it." The nurse adjusts something or presses a button, a white stream shoots out.

"God!" I jump, the nurse laughs, so does Kat, they take Baby Boy back so I'm suddenly empty, and fit him just-so clamped to Kat. His little face buried in flesh, his own perfect pillow, smooth flexing cheeks sucking hungry and hard.

"My, he really took to the breast, didn't he?" The nurse has this sparkle in her voice, you can tell she'd rather be no place but here. "See? You're an expert already," she says. "I'll show you how to bathe and swaddle him. Have either of you changed a diaper before?"

It's when I step back and the nurse laughs again. She touches my arm so I understand why the babies calm down when she holds them. "You'll do fine."

Kat giggles. "Pay attention, James. So you can show Zero."

She has no clue Zero's dead, that they broadcast it over the news.

But the nurse is at another basket now, a blue one this time, a tiny live doll with a mouth crying wide as its whole pudgy face, a trembling tongue like a waving pink ribbon inside. And black tarry crap, which the nurse swabs away with a fluff of wet cotton, bending both tiny feet to his face. So his butt's clean and his little button dick, too. Something Charlie Zerotski won't ever have to do.

"Look!" Kat says. "I'm *breast*feeding." She looks up at me, all delighted.

Kat's in heaven, the glow on her face like the junkies' or Rand with a spike up their vein in a moment of bliss and perfection. So I'm jealous, wanting to feel that way too. I touch his soft cheek, his silky bronze hair, and the folds of new skin at his neck. A sweet newborn smell scents my fingers. Kat gently rocks him and hums.

But it's just for a moment or maybe two. Till the tiniest shudder prickles my heart and makes me aware of the future approaching. Outside the nursery, a big macho shadow darkens the hallway wall.

37

It's like seeing a thief, not a man of the law, just a villain in blue with authority, so my heart jump-starts with fear or bravado when he turns to look in this nursery. I lunge at the wall and release the cord so the blinds cascade down to the windowsill and he can't see inside here at all.

"We gotta go." I grab the carpetbag, hefting the strap on my shoulder. The nurse looks up from a baby she's changing, her eyes full of *how can I help you?* Kat tries to get up, she needs help doing that and the nurse is right there at her side. This time it's my finger touching my lip going *shhh*. "She's a good mom," is all I say, and the nurse stands a moment so still. Doubt on her face for maybe one second, till this hard *rap rap rap* of knuckles on glass turns us all toward the blinded window. Kat's eyes aching with desperate tears, her baby already attached.

The nurse blinks. "Let me gather a few things you may need," she whispers.

Pushing Kat in a wheelchair cuddling Baby Boy, she's got him bundled in a blue baby blanket double wrapped to her chest in the overalls bib like a kangaroo pocket or Indian papoose, that was my idea. Then her big red coat and her shawl around her shoulders hiding his head so you'd think she was fat or still big with a baby.

Her knees like a shelf balance her carpetbag and this sack the nurse gave her brimming with stuff you need for a baby, diapers, rubber pants and safety pins, powder and oil, a swaddling blanket, booties and T-shirts tiny as doll clothes. She brought us the wheelchair and showed us the back way out, the service elevator to the lobby. She put one gentle palm on Kat's pink cheek, the other on Baby Boy's too.

"Take care of each other," she said.

This elevator's padded with soft quilted walls, like a crib or a room where they let you be crazy. So you could bash your fists hard and still not get bruised. Kat laughs, but it's true.

"You're not mental, James. Everything's gonna be so cool, you'll see. From now on, man. Let's promise. Only good things." She kisses Baby Boy's tender forehead. Already so comfortable holding a baby, well, it's hers, she made it, that hits me now, how amazing she is. A human, Kat made one. I'll never do anything as incredible as that.

Watching her kiss Baby Boy, cooing or telling him secrets, I suddenly don't want the doors to open. I wish this boxed car was the whole world with just me and Kat living in it. "Kat? Can I kiss you?"

She smiles with this sound like a hum or a kitten or maybe it's the overhead light. She doesn't have to answer.

It's the best kiss ever.

That's when I decide I will do anything for Kat and Baby Boy. Anything. Keep them safe and happy forever. She says nobody can do that except Superman. And I stand akimbo as if there's a big red S on my chest. So she goes, yeah, but are you faster than a speeding bullet? Can you leap tall buildings in a single bound? Bend steel with your bare hands? Break all the rules?

Yes.

Kissing her again, so sweet and rich and better than any meds, making my heart soar and the thoughts in my head swirl like crazy. I want to do amazing things for Kat. Snuggling Baby Boy, she can't help peeking into the bundle. "Man," she says. "I never knew how much love I had in me. You know? It's like, *end*less. Every time I look at him, more pours out."

"I think that's milk," I say, and point out the two growing circles that darken her overall bib. Her eyes sparkle in the slits of her lids that close with her laughter.

"James?" She sort of chokes up, eyes flooded, shaking her head. "Thank you. I don't know, man. For everything. For making this the best Christmas I could ever imagine."

It's true and I want to say it to her, the word *love*, but she takes a deep breath and before I can fit it into a sentence, the elevator doors part open. So I just whisper, "Me, too."

The world's still here and it's pretty busy, at least in the hospital part, filled now with a feeling like Christmas. Visitors and medical staff and patients deck the halls, bearing gifts and poinsettias and good cheer. So only we hear it when Baby Boy cries his kitten song nobody else is aware of. We're laughing about it, Kat singing along, not to hide it but like a duet.

We cut past the Christmas tree through the main entrance lobby, a wheelchair obstacle course full of ankles and crutches, not easy to cross. She's heavy to steer or stop just in time and people step right in the way.

"Home, James!" Kat laughs, she's so high, just from the smell of his baby hair or the sweet soap the nurse used to wash it. I'm pushing her toward the lobby doors, so different than last night. And it hits me, success, like an A+ on a test, congrats-to-you-James, it's over, we did it, well, Kat did anyway, and now she's a mom. But I got her here, that was the plan I thought of myself without help from angel or anyone. And it's this sense that I did that fills up my chest. How helpless I felt in the scary night and how triumphant now. Like Superman, maybe.

Kat's got her chin tucked to her baby, kissing the hidden bronze wisps on his head. Telling him something, I think about snow or maybe California. "All you need is love, my Baby Boy," she whispers. "Aw, look, James. Look. He's got the cutest little face."

Squatting to peek into her hidden bundle, my heart melts to see him. Asleep, I think, little kitten eyes closed, not a care in the world. That's 'cause of Kat, too.

She smiles at me. "He's even prettier than you."

"Not possible," I say and her smile gets bigger. With one gentle finger I'm petting the silky soft hair on his head. "Good thing he looks mostly like you and not Zero."

Kat laughs. "Real good thing," she says. "Since Zero's not his papa."

I sort of fan myself like, *phew*.

But she deflects that like an insult I never intended. "Joke if you want, man. But he's one of the most decent cats I ever met. I mean, I was like, just some scared, knocked-up little chick with no place to go. But he cared about me when he didn't even have to, you know? And he's given me everything, man. More than just food and a place to crash. He's, like, let me be part of his life."

So I have to look away from her, seeing Zero suddenly through her eyes, like Zero The Hero who would do anything for her, and not creepy in ladies underpants and soliciting blowjobs. Or on the news labeled *Victim, deceased*.

Kat snuggles Baby Boy. "And, man, he's gonna be so stoked to meet you," she tells him. God, she doesn't know it won't ever happen, his trip to California, his unwritten letter, her ticket never purchased or ever delivered to Doreen c/o the Fresh Cup Diner. But there's no way I can tell her and Baby Boy now. I'm thinking I'll find a newspaper at the bus station or better, we'll sit together in one of those TV chairs and watch *The Ten O'Clock News*. So Walter Cronkite can tell her and I won't ever have to. We can be shocked and sad together.

We're near the payphones by the front lobby entrance, people coming in and out, healthy and sick ones you can't tell apart. A security guard—we both duck our faces and turn away. Flower deliveries, their guy in his uniform pushing a cart full of fragrant bouquets exploding with colors that could probably cheer anyone up.

I'm thinking it's too cold and far, the Hound station downtown, for a brand-new human to hitch to, I probably should just call a cab. *Okay, you're a cab.* God, Donald. He'd really dig this and probably'd wrap Baby Boy up in pink. I suddenly miss him and wish he were here, it feels like I've left him behind. Donald and Zero. Which opens the drain that sucks all the good things away. Hugs and love and my promise to be happy forever.

Looking at Kat, she's hiding a baby, I'm the only one in this whole world who knows. Well, me and the nursery nurse. She'd be haunted at night, that's what the nurse said, for the rest of her life if she kept a child from its mother. And it hits me—if we get caught that's just what'll happen. They'll take Baby Boy and lock Kat up and the nurse won't ever be trusted with babies again. I have to protect them from that. All three of them. And I'm thinking: the secret is don't get caught.

I pull the cigarette pack from Rand's jacket pocket and take out the wad of money.

Kat clutches my sleeve when she sees it. "Jeez, lou-eeze!" She laughs. "Where'd you get the bread?"

"It's Rand's, I don't know, drug money or something. I'm gonna pay him back." Even as I say it, I don't know where I'd ever get that much bread, I should put it back in the cigarette pack and bring it all back to Rand. But her smile at me grows, almost as wide as for Baby Boy. *Let's be happy forever.* "It's for, you know. California. So you don't have to wait for a letter."

"Enough for plane tickets?"

I nod, yeah.

Smiling at me, her eyes full and vibrant. "I love you, James," she says.

Pow. That's what her words do. Shut that sucking drain. Tears come up from some sweet place that opens deep inside. Words I've been waiting to hear my whole life. So I can't help smiling at her, at Baby Boy too, at how *good* love feels. I take the top hundred and hand her the rest of the wad. "Be right back," and when her eyes go sad I add, "I'm just gonna call a cab. I gotta get change for the phone." I hold up three fingers in the Boy Scout salute.

Across the lobby there's a row of payphones with numbers to call for a taxi. And the gift shop, with change and bouquets of flowers. I've already decided, red roses.

38

The taxi dispatcher said fifteen minutes. So I keep checking, glancing out the gift shop window for a yellow cab waiting outside. Trying not to, but there's holiday gifts and greeting card racks, candy and snacks and reading stuff, magazines and paperbacks, I easily get distracted. Potted plants, teddy bears, a refrigerated case of cut flowers. Tulips, baby's breath, roses, carnations, all in a mirrored display, it's hard to know what to pick.

Silver foil Kisses, the Hershey's kind, a whole bowlful on the register counter. I put change down and take one. Roses and kisses. Ha, just when I'm thinking life couldn't be much sweeter.

I step out again into the lobby and catch Kat's attention. She waves and blows a kiss my way. She beckons me toward her and points to the front doors. I hold up my finger, *one second*.

Taking another Kiss for Kat and one for Baby Boy, too. Sucking sweet chocolate off my front teeth, I'm thinking what else do we need? A few Snickers bars, I put those on the counter, then M&Ms, Twinkies, and Fritos. I nod at the saleschick and wait while she bundles the roses and baby's breath for me, cutting red ribbon, tying a bow. From the change on the hundred she already gave me, I hand her a twenty-dollar bill.

She pushes buttons on her cash register, it dings when the cash drawer opens. This time I tell her to keep the change, I've got no more room in my pockets. She thanks me and nods toward the lobby front door. "Y'all call for a taxi?"

I look between shelves of things you can buy, out the gift shop window to the hospital lobby and glass entrance doors, where a bright yellow taxi parks at the front curb outside. But turning back to the saleschick, a Chicago Police patch catches my eye, on the thick shoulder of a Chicago Police leather jacket—in the next aisle over from me. Crew cut and checkered band on a black-visored cap, it's that same macho cop from the elevator and nursery. In two strides or less he's rounded the aisle and towering over my head.

"Mskwiskdkls an ddkworu?" he asks me and I don't understand a word that he says, he's speaking a different language. Shaking my head to clear it, I'm not hearing anything right. Press my hands to my ears, I need Kat so bad and turn toward her in the lobby. Everything closes in on me, the hospital sounds or gift shop conversations, the saleschick, what's in the pockets of Rand's Angels jacket, people and time passing by. Everything whirling around me. The foil-wrapped bouquet of roses and baby's breath waiting for Kat on the counter. The candy and snacks for the long trip to California.

"Mary Katherine Jendrin," he says. "Where is she? You were seen leaving the maternity ward together."

Shaking my head, I don't know I don't know, wanting to beg, please don't bust her! The cop rips my hands from my ears. "Hands up, both hands. On the counter," he demands, like a reprimand or punishment, slamming both my palms flat on the counter, he kicks my ankles apart. His grasping hands all over my clothes, the seams of my chinos, the black satin jacket, stripping the sleeves off my arms and tearing Rand's pockets apart. Pulling out whatever he finds, tossing it all on the counter. A Buck knife, a baggie of red ones, a Marlboro hardpack full of money. A small folded white paper packet.

"What's that?" Because I've never seen it before and he tells me I'm under arrest. Cuffs out and rattling, twisting my wrists behind me, *click*. Possession of heroin, a felony, he says. I object and call him a dick. "That wasn't in there!" He bundles everything up in the jacket and grabs it, and I'm freaking out, but he doesn't care. "It's not mine, none of it's mine, it's not my jacket!" He shoves me in handcuffs out of the gift shop and through the lobby, pushing people out of his way, shoving me straight toward the lobby front doors and Kat. Kat! with her carpetbag full of baby stuff. Kat! with her milk jugs and those white pads she's got to cover her leaking holes. Kat with a secret in her pocket like a mother kangaroo, I can't reveal that.

God! I just want to go with her, protect her and love her and be Superman! But I'm not faster or more powerful or strong at all and I doubt that I ever will be. Screaming in my head, this is all my own fault! Zero said don't go to Cook County.

Aching so badly, I pull away, maybe two steps in the other direction. "You *planted* that on me!" I say, which distracts him, coming at me, not at Kat, draped in her shawl like a little old lady, hiding the bundle she's holding.

She pulls herself together, rising from the wheelchair, her embrace full with love and mine locked and empty behind me. I shake my head like a signal or warning at the look of horror warping her face. Then turn away in the direction he trips me, everything spiraling and gray.

Whisking me past her and out of the lobby, I'm smacked by the cold with no jacket to wear, steered through new snow to a NO PARKING ZONE and into the back seat of a squad car parked there. Locked in, looking out, not part of the outside world anymore, like facing the dayroom TV at The Oaks and all I can do is watch.

A Hallmark Christmas Special is on. A big yellow taxi is parked at the curb at the entrance of Cook County Hospital, a cabbie waits holding its back door wide open. A hippie chick ducks out the front lobby doors, her red coat hugged tight around her. There's maybe a close-up of the bundle she's hiding, of her Madonna smile, her green eyes looking right into the camera. *I love you,* she mouths, one finger to her lips like a promise her secret is safe forever. The cab driver settles her belongings inside, a big carpetbag, a sack of supplies, then helps her get in with her baby.

«shhh you can't say anything» angel says.

The squad car starts moving. I twist as far as I can in the caged back seat to see into the back of the cab. She's kissing her baby. She's going to California. She's no longer looking at me.

It's the hardest thing I've ever had to do, look away from her too. If this was the Oaks, I'd turn off the TV and go talk to Pauly instead.

BRAIN

part eight
jdr

39

Possession of a controlled substance. It's not mine. *With intent to sell.* It's not mine. *One thousand seventy-five dollars and change.* Evidence displayed on the table before me, none of it's mine. *Prison won't be kind to you, Ross. Think about that.* The macho cop's gone but still I'm not talking, my lawyer said don't say a word. For maybe an hour they leave me alone, handcuffed to the table in an interrogation room. Mostly I'm thinking about Kat. Where she is now and her ride in the taxi back seat. The sweet way her baby boy smells. Getting out at O'Hare in front of Departures. Her carpetbag on one of those luggage carts there. In line at the ticket counter or boarding gate. Or maybe she smiled and they let her fly free and she's already up in the air.

"James Daniel Ross," Marc Gabriel says, coming in, shutting the door behind him. Winter clings to his overcoat, he brushes the cold from his shoulders. He's got a yellow envelope in one hand and pulls a pack of Camels from his suit jacket pocket. "You wanted to talk to me?"

I asked for him, that's true. I'm not talking to anyone else.

"You want to tell me where you were yesterday morning at six a.m.?"

Yesterday? Man, it feels like a lifetime ago. Enough time to leave your old life behind and start a new life on the coast. So at first I'm excited to tell him, Kat had a baby! I had no clue, I got her to the hospital, the right thing to do, I'm supposed to be with her right now, let me go. But he nods at the evidence laid out on the table and the bar with my hand cuffed to it.

"In retrospect, you'd have been better off if I had locked you up." He gives me a dubious look. "Heroin?"

"He planted it on me. Investigate *him*, not me. He's dirty."

Gabriel tosses the cigarette pack on the table. "The charges are bullshit," he says, and when I agree, he goes, "What you're facing is a lot more serious," erasing my smile completely. He opens the yellow **MISSING PERSONS** flap and pulls out a snapshot of some missing kid. In color this time, so I look away. My heel's pumping the floor like crazy.

There's a knock-knock at the door, and Gabriel steps out so I'm in here alone again. One side of the room is one-way glass so I know that they're watching me. The dirty macho cop and Gabriel, probably, giving me more time to stew, until a uniformed cop comes in with a key and click!, the handcuffs are removed. As soon as he leaves, I'm out of this chair, looking anywhere except at that snapshot.

"Have a seat," Gabriel says, coming back in, and waits till I do. "Look familiar? Picture was taken on Labor Day. One week before his genitalia were found in a dumpster." He slides the snapshot before me, so that's where I have to look now. At a blond kid in a Cubs baseball cap, which snags my attention.

"The shirts," Gabriel says, his finger tapping where I should look.

A brown and blue plaid long-sleeved flannel like the one I've got on. Shirttails untucked and unbuttoned in front, same as me. So you sort of can see his white T-shirt underneath, the Led Zeppelin cover art from the LP. Exactly the same as me.

The chair tumbles backward when I jump to my feet, tipping over onto the floor. I can't get the flannel off fast enough, stripping the sleeves from my arms, ripping the T-shirt over my head, leave them rumpled where they fall. Doing a little shuddery dance, half-dressed in creepiness now.

Gabriel slips his overcoat off and capes it around my shoulders. It's warm like a tent or sleeping bag on me, but still, the heebie-jeebies don't leave. "They were in Richard's closet," I say, my teeth chatter. "I didn't know they were that kid's. I just needed something to wear."

Two detectives come in with detective stuff and seal the Led Zeppelin T-shirt up, then bag the flannel, too, with EVIDENCE tape and their signatures. But the black ribbon pinned to it gets taken too, and I'm all no no no don't take that! But they won't give it back. They don't care Grampa gave it to me, they don't care it's the only thing left from my granma, they don't give a shit I'm in mourning. *No sharps allowed.* "For your own safety," Gabriel says, stepping in, as if I'd kill myself with a pin. He puts a finger to his lips when I start to object. "Your lawyer's going to advise you not to talk," he says. "If you do, what you say can be used against you in court." So I don't say anything more.

It's a couple hours till my lawyer comes in, Jeffrey David Ross, Attorney at Law. He brings me a Big Mac and two Christmas scones from my little sister. Beth baked those special for you, he says. Oh, so I ask if a file's inside, and he smiles. "Please, no daring escapes," he says, and adds, "Not this time." He unzips the garment bag he's brought in, and takes out the suit my mom sent with him, all sharkskin black and tailor-fit for future auditions. Or funerals. "To look presentable," my lawyer says. My navy blue parka, new boxer shorts, socks, white T-shirt, crisp dress shirt, proper tie. In the restroom together he talks the whole time I'm in the stall getting changed, I mostly just nod at his questions. Did they read you your rights and other legal stuff a lawyer would ask. But straightening my lapels, buttoning my collar, knotting my tie, he's my dad.

He's already talked to Marc Gabriel and says there's a deal on the table. The felony drug charges will be dismissed in exchange for my cooperation. There's a much bigger bust that they're going for, and they want my assistance for that.

Mostly I'm a zombie doing what I'm told, the boy on the box again, posing. Face front, don't smile, turn left, turn right, *click click click*. Kat's desperate plea replays in my head: *I changed my mind, I don't wanna do this.* They give me a tissue to wipe off the fingerprint ink. "They need to eliminate your prints from the others," my lawyer explains.

Gabriel and two detectives in suits lead us into a windowless room, empty except for a table and chairs, two on each side, our side and theirs, divided across the table.

There's random stuff tagged in plastic or brown paper bags before us. Wallets, student IDs, a class ring. They belong to the others, Gabriel says. Teenage boys, most of them white. Nice-looking. Fair-haired. All missing.

This one detective takes the lid off a box. It's evidence, he says, found in Hunt's red truck and residence. What can I tell them about these things?

A prescription bottle. A Secret Spy Decoder ring. A cash register key.

My lawyer picks up the orange Rx bottle. *Rosenberg, Hannah* typed on the prescription label. Perplexed and blinking at me. So the next words I expect—*how the hell did Grandma's pain medication become evidence in a murder investigation?*—don't come. He doesn't say anything.

But I'm telling him anyway, because he's my dad, and I didn't do anything wrong. "I was waiting outside the bus station," I say, leaving out *like you told me to do.* My finger taps the snapshot of the Cubs cap kid. "He swiped Granma's pills, that whole bottle from me, before he got in the red truck."

My dad looks heartsick, I'm not sure about what.

Gabriel nods at the cash register key, and says it's from Cleveland Glass & Hardware, Lowell Cleveland's family's store. I try to stay calm but he's looking at me like he already knows what went down. "It was found under the seat in Hunt's truck. But the whereabouts of Lowell Cleveland are unknown. No victim, no crime," he says.

The detective picks up the small plastic baggie the Secret Spy ring is tagged in, which stirs up another whole bag of emotions, so I'm the one swallowing my heart. "That was Donald's," I say. "Where'd you get it?"

Gabriel nods at the detective now, a whole conversation in a glance.

"The Des Plaines River," the detective says. Another evidence package flops before me, muddied clothing flattened in plastic, so you barely can recognize what colors. An army field jacket. Flag-striped bell-bottom jeans. "The ring was found during the autopsy. Lodged deep in the decedent's throat. If you have any information about that, please, feel free to share."

"Those are Zero's," I say, to be helpful. "Were."

"Charles Zerotski. Blond, eighteen. Victim number..." he looks at Gabriel, "what are we up to here, Marc? Eight? Nine? Ten?"

"We're guessing he'd been in the water for about a month. Since sometime around Thanksgiving," Gabriel says, taking the seat across from me. "But we have no evidence to suggest he knew Richard Hunt."

"He *work*ed for Richard," I say. "That's where I met him, Thanksgiving at Richard's house. And Zero had that ring, I don't know why. But Richard took it. And the next day they were arguing, I *heard* them upstairs. When I got the shirts from the basement closet. Richard said Zero was gone when I asked. I thought he meant California."

"Arguing about?"

"Pay? I think, because he was—" but then, no, it's not my business to share what Zero does. Did. Or let his mother know. "There were lots of guests and liquor and Richard brought Zero to help with all that."

"Okay, help me out here. Why would Richard Hunt choke Charles Zerotski with Donald Griswold's ring?"

"I don't know! I didn't even talk to Zero, I only met him that day." But they're looking at me like I *do* know, even my dad. "Maybe that was their wedding ring and they were boyfriends or something, and Richard found out and got mad. That's how Donald proposed to me, with that ring. So maybe he proposed to Zero." I know that sounds crazy, I look at my dad. "I said 'no.'"

"Are you sure that's the same ring?" The detective asks.

"Just open it, he wrote me a note."

The evidence officer or whoever he is, takes the ring from the plastic pouch, with protective gloves on like dentists wear, or a surgeon, he snaps it apart. The plastic green band, the decoder dial, the green foil disc that caps the Secret Compartment. The tiny lilac scroll of paper inside it.

Unrolling it, they all recognize where it's from, the thin missing strip torn from the first page of Donald's stationary pad. And written across it in purple cursive: *I love James.* They don't need a decoder for that.

Here's another thing I wasn't expecting: Cleveland's family. But they're at the cop station when Gabriel leads us from Evidence past the front desk. The Cleveland Bros, making me cringe, all pale and orange in XXXL sizes, springing up off the benches when we parade through.

A few families surge toward us, all fair-haired with praying hands and anxious blue eyes. And a black woman too, in a car coat with pearls and a matching handbag. So I think it's Ms. Poole chasing me down with my MINS folder and medication. But her smile at me is so much like Donald, my heart jumps to my throat and I stumble.

Gabriel stops to put a hand on her shoulder, same as my dad steadies mine. He tells her he'll be back to update her later, but as of right now, he's got nothing new. He walks us downstairs, past file cabinets and vending machines through a smoky staff room where men wearing badges type at their desks, cigarettes in their fingers, telephone receivers crooked to their necks. Three, maybe four, join our parade, marching me and my dad to a brightly lit conference room.

My hands're still shaky. Eye to eye with Marc Gabriel.

"That woman looked like him," I say.

"His mother," Gabriel says. "See? I do care." He winks at me, then takes his place at the front of the room.

We need solid evidence, that's what Gabriel says. You can't just go into his house and start digging. "Hunt's got political connections throughout the county. Without new, conclusive evidence, the court won't sign off on another warrant." Gabriel passes stapled stacks of xeroxed pages around the room. "However…Hunt loves to talk about himself—these are transcripts of his interrogation. He believes he's invincible. And that's where he's going to slip up. We need to be there when he does, on his playing field with a tape recorder rolling." Gabriel steps behind me. "And that's where young Angel comes in."

Gabriel lets them direct questions at me.

A detective jumps up from his chair. "You were with Hunt the day Donald Griswold went missing. You were with Hunt the last time Charlie Zerotski was seen. *And* the day he picked up Lowell Cleveland. You were *in* Hunt's fucking house during the time they went missing. And you didn't think anything was *off* about this guy?"

I'm shaking my head that he'd accuse me. In front of my dad and everything. "He taught me how to drive."

"Oh. Well! Except for the raping and murdering, he must be a really great guy."

My dad grips my arm, his calm voice firm at my ear. "Don't say anything more."

"Look, Hunt is the bad guy here." Marc Gabriel steps forward, pointing at the wall behind him, or beyond it, at the whole city. "And he's back out there right now, roaming free."

The detective backs off, to his side of the table, accusing eyes aimed at me. "So he's after blond pretty boys, but this little puke is still alive. You don't find that a bit suspicious?"

"Maybe it is," Gabriel says. "That's a question you need to ask Hunt. But for whatever reason—and I am not claiming to know—Hunt has not harmed *this* pretty boy. He taught him to *drive*, for Chrissake. Maybe he's always wanted a son, maybe he's reliving his own failed childhood, maybe he's proving he can be a better parent than his own father was to him—I don't know."

Guests and garbage, that's what I would add in, if it was okay to speak.

"What I do know is this: Hunt trusts our pretty young friend here." Gabriel hands something to my dad. Legal papers, I think, with my name on page one. "And without 'this little puke's' cooperation, the case gets suspended. Hunt walks free." His knuckles rap the table, and he faces the rest of the men in this room. "And frankly, I'd like to stop him before we're pulling another kid's ballsack out of a dumpster."

My dad scans the pages and scowls. "He's a sixteen-year-old *kid*."

"And he's looking at another five years in juvie plus probation and a felony drug rap. If he helps us nab Hunt, he walks. Scot-free." Gabriel's hand lands flat on the table like a kickstand, so he's leaning into my face now. "I'm not asking your lawyer, James. Or your father. I'm asking you. Give me Hunt on a spit for Christmas."

"Give me a moment alone with my son," my dad answers. So everyone else leaves the room.

My dad thinks what Gabriel's asking of me is not something I should agree to. If what they suspect about Richard Hunt's true, it would be "leading a lamb to slaughter." He'd rather I stew in a cell a few years than risk losing me to a murderer. *You'll serve out the rest of your sentence in safety. We'll give you all the help that you need.*

I'd rather be dead than go back to Railton, that's what I tell my dad.

"It wouldn't be Railton," he says, reaching to straighten my tie, I don't let him. "The preliminary injunction we filed was granted because of what happened to you. That God-awful place is being shut down. Jamey, if this Richard Hunt is a murderer—"

"What?" I'm suddenly coughing, the Coke he bought me stinging the passageways right up my nose.

"A *multiple* murderer, if he's capable of—"

"Railton shut down?" All those dim yellow buildings zip through my head, the shower stalls, the library, dining hall, and padded cells. Cottages with empty bunks. Metal doors unlocked. Rules with no one to obey them.

"Back in October. Most of the youths were granted early releases. I'm sorry you didn't know."

Most of the *youths?* Rapists and liars and assholes? And Cleveland, it hits me. Released to go home and work at his family's store. Where he answered the phone call from Richard.

Because of my dad.

It's hard to look at him now, a million bad pictures flood into my head, of every bad thing I went through. Rug stains and blood stains and whimpers in the den. Cleveland's yellow smock splattered red, disappearing from the red truck into the gray, as if Richard could make it all go away, forever.

"Cleveland raped me thirteen times," I say. "You shouldn't have let him out."

For a second the color drains from his face, his eyes fill and blink maybe thirteen times with a glance to the door then to me. He nods, but doesn't ask. Thinking, I guess. Weighing each word on the scales of justice, balancing good and evil. *My* lawyer.

Lips pursed, he clears his throat and sits taller. "Scot-free will include any and all charges filed against you regarding Cleveland. Anything else?"

I cover my face with both hands, my elbows braced on the table. "I just want this nightmare to end," I say.

"Me, too," he sighs, one hand gently circles my back. "So, let's talk to Mr. Gabriel and see what he wants you to do."

Fair enough, that's in my head. Two words some stranger once said before he got hit by a truck.

40

They're listening in when I call Richard's number, all gathered around like mission control. To hear his admission, that's their mission, to arrest Richard Hunt, that's their goal.

Counting down with raised fingers, *Three-two-one…*the detective pointing at me, *Talk!* when Richard answers his phone. They click on their four-track reel-to-reel. Their plan is to record Richard confessing from home.

"'Richard, I have to talk to you,'" is what I read off the hand-written script that's before me. Gabriel's pen tip follows along with the words. "'I'm flipping out, man,'" it says. "'What if the cops bust me for murder? What should I say?'"

"It's after midnight for Chrissake," Richard grumbles. "Where are you calling me from?"

Just hearing his voice, a jolt of reality knocks the receiver away from my ear. Beside me, Gabriel mouths, "'Uptown. At a phone booth.'"

"Uptown," I answer. "At a phone booth. Man." I add that 'man' on my own.

Richard says, "Who did you murder?"

"What?" I look at Gabriel, I've got no idea what he wants me to say. "I didn't—"

"You've got nothing to worry about then," Richard says. "You're as innocent as I am."

"Wait! Don't hang up, please don't hang up—" Standing, the receiver pressed to my ear, I turn away from the table, from Gabriel, his officers, their tape machine, and my dad. Using my own desperate words now, and not the ones from their hastily-scribbled script. "I—I lied, I already talked to the cops, they busted me, God, now my dad's going to have me committed again, so today's my last day, Richard, tonight is the last night I'm free, before I'm locked away in the morning forever."

"Where are you?" he asks. Gabriel scribbles, "The Allnite Arcade" so that's what I answer. "Stay there," Richard says. "I'll come get you."

I am scared, it'd be the biggest lie in the world to say I'm not. Gabriel's stepped out "for a minute," he said, for a smoke or a donut, who knows, and these other detectives have no clue what they're doing, taping a miniature voice recorder to my skin under my clothes. I said to let me call my friend Gary, he's a whiz with mics and electronic things, he once made an eight-track tape of our band on a four-track reel-to-reel. They don't listen to me. This wasn't the way it was supposed to go down—as if it's my fault—but now that it has, they'll go to Plan B. They'll be tailing Hunt's El Camino wherever he takes me. And I go, well that doesn't sound like much of a plan, I don't want my balls in a garbage can. They say keep your clothes on if that's possible, and I say, well what if it isn't, what then? They say, you just get his voice on tape, his words, his guilt, his confession, you can leave your pants on to hear that.

My dad helps me slip my parka on over the hidden recording device taped under my black sharkskin suit. His hand on my back guides me aside, maybe to get me to change my mind or give me his last words of wisdom. But no. In his hand is the snipped black ribbon. He weaves Granma's hatpin through my sharkskin lapel, like pinning her over my heart.

Thanks is what I almost say but it's not big enough to hold all I mean and I don't know the right word that is, so I hug him. He hugs me too, and it's weird how he does it, his warm embrace, how the strength in it radiates through, like the good vibes between us are all that matter, and *it's all chocolate milk* is true.

"A father and a son," he says, his chin on my shoulder, hugging me still. Emotion or something cracks his voice, breaking his sentence in two. "I should have done more for you. Donald was right. I've let you down, Jamey. And I'm sorry."

It's *I'm sorry* that tips me over the edge, if I wasn't unbalanced before. Feelings for Donald flood in, too, his promise to get me and my dad back together *if it's the last thing I ever do. Scout's honor.* And now, here's my dad as if Donald *knew.* Boyish good looks, gray at his temples, blue eyes, and a movie star smile.

He hugs me again in this room full of men. "I believe in you," he says out loud. Which switches my confidence from zero to ten. The men turn away, look at their shoes, off-guard and soft for a moment.

"I want him watched every second he's out there," my dad instructs Marc Gabriel. And to me, "I'll be here waiting. If at any time you change your mind, you let Mr. Gabriel know."

I shake my head though. Because I'm not going to change my mind. I'm going to bring Donald home to his mom. *If it's the last thing I ever do.* I'm going to get my life back.

Gabriel is expressionless, smoking as he drives, speaking in code on his radio to the unmarked cops and detectives positioned around us.

Riding in the front seat beside him, I'm anxiously watching the city pass by, the storefronts and side streets and creatures who come out at night. Desperados and outlaws, milling about in the bright flashing neon in front of the Allnite Arcade. But Gabriel drives right past, too fast to recognize their faces. He hangs a ralphie at the first side street and pulls up next to a tavern. The motor still running, he 10-4s where we're at in a handheld two-way speaker. Blue light from a beer sign floods the car, dreamy and fluid like we're underwater.

He has me check the recorder a few more times, RECORD-STOP-REW-PLAY, just to be sure it's working, or maybe he's doubting I'll do it right. He pushes RECORD and checks it's securely taped to my side and my shirttails are retucked to hide it. He doesn't say anything about the black lapel ribbon and Granma's pin, he just straightens my jacket and helps get my parka back on. It's thick and fits loosely over my suit so you'd never suspect I'm recording you.

Gabriel nods. "You look nice," he says, and when I roll my eyes, he says something else too, one word of advice if the operation goes south. "Run."

It's cold outside, but just on my face, the parka and hood are windproof and warm. Walking fast, looking down at the sidewalk cracks, heading for the corner and then a louie toward the Allnite Arcade. But what if I just went a different way? Take the money my dad put in my pocket, call a cab to O'Hare... My heart's pounding crazy. I turn to glance back at Gabriel's car, down the dark side street somewhere among all the cars parked, so I'm not sure which one is Marc or unmarked, then turning, face front, I practically crash into Rand.

His look of surprise turns to anger. He shoves me hard, there's a knife in his hand, backing me into the tavern alley, so there's no time to duck or comprehend danger. Just an instant to gasp and freeze. He's wearing the mangy Marlboro coat and he's pissed, I can understand that.

"Where's my shit!" he says, pointing the blade at my face. "My stash, my fucking bank!"

I try pushing back. "I got busted, Rand! For your stash and your knife and your bank!"

"Well who the fuck said yew could take my jacket? Huh?"

I've got to go, that's all I know, before Gabriel shows up, his whole Plan B goes bust, and I land on *Go Directly To Jail*. "Here!" I say, taking my dad's money out, *emergency funds, just in case*. But even with all that money in hand and my promise to try and repay him, Rand wants my parka too. "Okay, okay just, put the knife down," I say, flipping the hood back, unzipping the parka and taking it off, looking frantically past him for Gabriel's car, or anyone unmarked who's watching.

Rand wriggles out of the Marlboro coat, checking me out, my suit and black ribbon, white shirt, and tie. His snarky grin cracks his acne-scabbed face, so he looks more like Rand on the day I first met him and not like someone who'd waste me.

"I thought y'all split fer California," he goes, emptying the Marlboro coat pockets and hidden splits in its seams, digging through holes in the collar and sleeves. Drug crap, bubble gum, cigarettes, cash, he stuffs the grimy coat at my chest. "Yew'n Kat, man, rip off my bread and head fer the goddam coast." Rand turns away for a paranoid moment, raising his voice in a bad falsetto of Kat. "'West until yer feet git wet.'"

Even bad, it sets off a pang of I miss her. Kat. Kat. Kat. I tell him she had her baby. "That's where we were. At the hospital, Rand. Having a baby," I say. Putting on the coat, the top buttons are gone, it feels spongy and gross and no way as warm as the parka. But better than having a knife at my throat. And he's right, I do sort of owe him.

"So Kat finally popped out her kid," Rand says, zipping the parka, the warmth of it brings out a smile. "Damn. Ain't that a helluva thang."

It hits me, Rand's safe because he's with me, they won't blow my cover to bust him. I can't tell him that. "I gave it to her, the rest of your roll of money. Except I got busted and couldn't go with her." Talking about Kat somehow calms me down. "But you could go, Rand. Be with her and the baby, you've got money. To like, make sure they're cool and taken care of."

His eyes squint like he's considering it for half a second, life on the coast with the baby and Kat. But Rand shakes his head. "People come 'n go, man," he says. "Yew gotta let 'em go."

Trying not to think about Kat, only that I've gotta go. There's a multiple murderer waiting for me, and I'm not going to mess up that.

I cut through the alley to the Allnite Arcade, faster now not to be late, regretting I'm back in this Marlboro coat—when a black Ford sedan pulls up to the curb and I see the driver wave. I'm thinking it's an unmarked surveillance cop car so I'm feeling pretty safe and protected. And I'm signaling them to drive down the block or the opposite curb to observe me, and hurry, before Richard arrives and detects them. But they don't move away. There's instead an impatient *honk-honk!* so I duck to the window to talk to who's driving and I practically choke 'cause it's Richard.

He pops the doorlock. I stand up, quickly scanning the street and the few passing cars, but I have no idea who's watching.

"Where were you?" Richard asks, when I'm settled inside with my back to the passenger door, the farthest from him I can sit. Turning the wheel, he looks over his shoulder, then at me, then the street, and pulls away from the curb. "I had to circle the goddam block twice before I spotted that coat."

"I thought this was an unmarked cop car, how was I supposed to know it was you." Looking outside at all the cars we pass by, as if I would know a cop's driving.

Richard turns at the next light, glancing at me with approval. "Hell, I would've had Grienbach rent me a limo if I knew this was going to be a formal affair." He lifts the lapel of the Marlboro coat, fingers the sharkskin fabric. His touch is a trigger that makes me jerk back.

"What?" He gives me a sharp look, like something's all wrong. You can see the sheen on his face in the passing streetlights. Sweat, I realize, it's thirty degrees and he's sweating. "Goddam pigs," he says, his glance ricochets mirror to back windows to mirror. "Tailing the El Camino all week, watching every goddam thing I did. What do you bet, taking notes. 'Dropped off Christmas gifts at ex-wife's,' 'stopped for coffee.'" He turns a dashboard knob and chilled sour air blasts out of the vents. "'Bought building supplies.'"

"Headed west on I-90," I say to my chest, under the loud whir of the A/C fan.

Richard confirms that with an odd look and nod. "Bumbling idiots," he says, turning onto the I-90 onramp, merging the Ford into traffic. "A rental car. That's the first thing I would've figured out if I were a cop tailing me." His gloved hand drops to my thigh. "Hey, don't be a stranger, get over here! I just rescued you from a lifetime of shock treatments, for Chrissake."

I don't scoot over though. He's picking up speed, white globes of headlights dot the highway, you can't tell whose. Gabriel's, I'm hoping, tailing behind. Wherever Richard takes me. «the faster you get his confession on tape the faster you get to go home»

"What'd the pigs say to you that got you so riled up you called me?" he says.

I point at his chest, his black leather coat, accusing. "You killed Lowell Cleveland and Charlie Zerotski," I say in a voice like Joe Friday on *Dragnet*. Richard's face blanches, he blinks at me wordlessly. "And Donald Griswold," I add, fishing for his confession, not knowing how many minutes the tape is, C-30, C-60, C-90, I never asked, or how long the batteries last. But Richard does not take the bait.

"They said that about you?" he says, amused.

"They have witnesses who saw me with you the last time any of them were seen. They found Zero dead. And that kid that went with you at the Greyhound station. They can't find Cleveland, though. Or Donald."

Richard scoffs. "Maybe they haven't looked in the right place."

I suddenly feel sick and hug the Marlboro coat tighter. But still, I ask him. "Well, where's that?"

Driving with one hand on the wheel, he looks straight ahead. "So you haven't been charged with murder."

I tell him they planted junk on me, that's how come I got busted.

Richard pounds the steering wheel, you can hear it shudder. "I'll sue those sons-of-bitches," he growls, cursing the county, the city, the cops, and state's attorney, every other word is the f-word. The f-cops pulled him over on a bullshit charge too, running a f-red light for Chrissake on his way to his f-ex's to dump f-gifts off for his girls. As if he had nothing f-better to do f-two days before Christmas than spend f-twenty-four hours being f-interrogated in lockup. While they f-ransacked his house on a f-trumped-up warrant and impounded his f-truck. All that for a few expired IDs from former employees, forgotten wallets, and personal things left behind by stupid little shits who worked for him so long ago he doesn't remember their names. As if keeping a Lost and Found is a f-crime—! Richard coughs, catching his breath.

Highway lights whisk past like eerie midnight ghosts. And I'm thinking, they all sat beside him on their last ride, anonymous guys he brings down this highway and home to his suburb, then naked maybe and whimpering on the brown rug. And then, *poof!* missing.

«in the right place»

When Richard says it again, the cops have nothing on him, they can search his house from now till next Sunday, they'll find nothing, I go, "Maybe you should be a cop."

"Hey, let me tell you, I'd have this case closed like *that*." His fingers snap. "I'd make Chief of Police in a week."

"They wouldn't suspect you if you were Chief."

"You got that right. Hell, they wouldn't suspect you either. You can bet I'd stop that first thing." He looks at the highway ahead for a moment then back to me. "And no nuthouse either, kid. You're no queer, I'd set your old man straight about that. What you did to Cleveland was justice served."

Me? But the words are already on tape. "Un-unh, Richard, what *you* did to Cleveland," then louder, my chin low to the mic, "you called him and picked him up and tricked him to get in the truck. I *never* asked you to."

"Hey! Who else is looking out for you? Huh? Mother is useless. You can't go to father, and we both know it won't be the cops." Wind whistles through the logic cracks. He's on my side, angel. He's looking out for me. He's the only one.

«he's the psycho killer»

"What you did, what I did—we're in this together, son! What matters is not getting caught." Richard checks his mirrors, the white sheen of highway lights sharpens his grin. "You don't deserve to go back to jail. I'd hate for that to happen."

"Well it's not going to happen," I say. "My dad—" «don't say anything»

"Oh—that's right. Your old man's a lawyer! A Jew *and* a lawyer. So he'll take care of everything, protect his darling boy from prosecution, get your whole criminal record tossed out." He chuckles. "Well, it won't be the first time he screws you over."

So I want to scream, Help me! Because it's true, if my dad had his way, I'd be in jail somewhere or The Oaks Mental Manor right now. All safe, in chains, or with a bite plate jammed in my jaws and a million volts frying my brain.

Richard's face blanches from headlights behind us that pass and exit the highway. "You and me, we've got a groovy thing here," he says, sweat from his hairline trailing both sides of his face. "Hell, if my old man was even *half* the father I am to you, believe me, I'd be a different man today." With a glance at the rearview, he flicks on the blinker and exits the highway. I don't see any other cars get off.

"And let me tell you, Railton was nursery school compared to what I got thirty years ago. What they did to me makes Cleveland look like goddam Mary Poppins." A wicked smile flickers at a passing cop car he sees or maybe a memory before him. "But, man, oh, man. Punching my old man's ticket to hell? More than worth it," he says, his chin lifted, shifting eyes watching whatever's behind us.

«he danced on his father's grave»

"You killed your dad, you deserved to be there, I didn't do any—"

"You threw your teacher through a fucking plate glass window. Did you not?"

No! I'm shaking my head, no no no. That's not what's supposed to be on the tape!

"Look, son," he says, "we're all born sinners. Assault, murder, lying, jerking off—so what? Three hail Marys, some horny priest gets you off and your soul is redeemed. That's the miracle of the Christ!" His knuckle knocks my knee twice. "If the idiot cops would do their job instead of wasting their time hassling me, hell, we'd be home now," he nods, glancing at me. "Enjoying your last night of freedom together. Not out here scrambling, for Chrissake, to cover our goddam tracks." Richard's arm lifts and slips around my shoulders, his palm cups my right ear, drawing me nearer, brushing his lips in my hair.

I duck and move over, out of his reach. "Cover what goddam tracks?"

Richard's eyes flash not at the mirrors or the new headlights beaming behind us, but at me. "Your little bunk buddy. Who did you think?"

Street signs fly by, names I don't recognize, I can't look back.

"Donald, I thought maybe—"

"Donald, fucking swishy Donald? Jesus Christ! You know what? How about I let *you* deal with Donald, you love him so much—" He suddenly jerks the wheel, hangs a sharp louie despite oncoming traffic, cutting into a parking lot, eerie and familiar and empty of cars. His headlights flash over the sign at the entrance, WESTLAWN SHOPPING with CENTRE spelled wrong, then his headlights switch off and it's dark. So I'm edgy to see if Gabriel's behind us and terrified what if he's not?

"What do you mean? Is that where you're taking me, where Donald is?" But it's like he doesn't hear my question at all, snarling "fucking Donald" over and over in a low voice to himself.

He passes Western Union, Donuts, the Shoe Repair shop, and Beauty Salon, the blinded window with IFC, the same storefronts closed at Thanksgiving. But this time he circles the shopping centre to the alley behind all the stores, past loading docks, dumpsters, and gated delivery bays. Spinning the wheel, looking over his shoulder, he backs up to a loading dock platform and stops, brake lights glinting red on a caged metal door.

First thing he does when he's out of the car is open the trunk so the hood's blocked him out of my view. He's shifting heavy things, the weight of whatever he's lifting out lightens the trunk so the rear end rises. Clanking metal on metal, the rankling sound of security gates unlocking and rattling open. The hard thunk of solid things hitting the ground.

Evergreens billow outside the windshield, telephone wires sway, icicles tinkle. Across the alley, a chainlink fence rattles. Behind it, there's backyards of dark sleeping houses. I look left and right but if Gabriel's here, he stays out of sight, I don't hear any cars coming. This edgy feeling revs up under my skin so I wish I took Rand's pills or something.

Then *CLICK!* a gun cocks, my heart shoots to my ears, but there's no gun or anyone pointing one. It's the voice recorder. Clicked off at the end of the tape.

Quick, tug my shirttail out of my waistband and reach up under my shirt. Rip the tape off my skin so the recorder falls loose in my hand. Sweating now, heart racing, fingering the boxy shape like Helen Keller or someone reading Braille.

Shadows bloom and retreat behind the raised trunk, the shadow of Richard hulking around, maybe coming back here and how would I ever explain? Fumbling to open the little flap window and flip the cassette to Side B. Twisting it, backward, sideways, down—till a s*nap!* fits the cassette into place. And here comes Richard, his workboots crunching gravel, three steps approaching. I press ON and RECORD or maybe ERASE when Richard opens the driver side door.

The dome light comes on, exposing everything. The open Marlboro coat and my suit jacket, my untucked shirt. My fingers spread like pouncing spiders over the recorder in my lap.

Richard's huge self fills the front seat, one foot on the gravel, one knee shoves into my hip. Reaching across me, all bulky and hovering, so I press myself deeper into the seat, breathing his smells, his leather coat and aftershave but mostly the stink of his sweat. He pops the glove compartment with a twist of his leather-gloved grip, pulls paperwork out, the Rent-a-Car contract, slams it shut, with his eyes on the papers and not my lap or the recorder under my hands. Hoping hoping hoping he won't notice, when I already know hope's no protection at all.

He looks at me, holding his gaze without blinking. Like he's thinking or confused that I'm here.

"You," he accuses. So I don't move or breathe or feel the next beat of my heart. "You going to make yourself useful? Or just sit there pulling your pud the rest of your life?"

I don't answer, just willing my hands to spread wider.

"Make a fucking choice." He backs himself off me and out of the car like a grizzly bear leaving his cave, slamming the door shut so the dome light blinks off and I'm alone in shadow again. Pavement grinds and crackles under his bootsteps moving around to the Ford's open trunk.

WHOMP! the trunk closes. A light from inside the building comes on, revealing the front seat, my lap, and the clear plastic window where the reels of brown tape slowly spin.

Twisting around to look out the back window. Richard's big silhouette lifts some bulky thing up, hefting it over his shoulder, with the shaft of a shovel gripped in one hand as he steps through the light of the doorway. And just for that instant, the night turns to color, his black legs to blue jeans, the black bulky thing to brown. Shaggy brown. *Den rug* brown—rolled up and flopping over his shoulder and halfway down his back. Till the door shuts behind him and night takes over again.

My heartbeat speeds up in my throat. What was that?

I scramble out of the car, sliding the recorder under my coat and into the black sharkskin pocket. Straighten my shirt, my tie, the sharkskin jacket, and Marlboro coat. Checking both ways down the alley but there's no waiting headlights or unmarked car. Where is Marc Gabriel? Anger at first trips me up, makes me stumble on the uneven pavement and the hard truth: *There is no one looking out for me.*

The security cage gate's left open enough for me to slip through. Crossing the concrete loading dock, the metal back door's unlocked too. Stepping in, it's an office, all knotty-pine paneled with gray filing drawers, a big metal desk, and a green linoleum floor. There's a phone and a calendar hung on the wall with a picture of mistletoe. *Compliments of Industrial Framing & Concrete.* Richard's black leather coat is on the desk, the shirt he was wearing, too, tossed over a toppled telephone book, business ledgers, POs, and receipts. The Rent-A-Car key on a Rent-A-Car keychain on top of a court decree. *Marital Settlement Agreement.*

"Richard?" I say, not wanting an answer, but it's creepy that he's not around. Or the brown shag rug either, that shovel he carried, where did he go? I peek out the office door into the storefront. Parking lot light fans through the blinds in shadowy stripes over all this construction work stuff. Stacks of fifty-pound sacks, folded tarps, metal drums, concrete mixing machines. Chemicals and nasty smells that send me back into the office.

There's a john, but it's full of cleaning supplies, a dolly, a vacuum, shop rags, TP. On the opposite wall there's an extra wide closet with double doors split by a thin line of light. An orange power cord runs from an outlet across the green floor, snaking inside it. So one door isn't closed very tight.

«wait» angel says, but too late, I ignore him. Turning the doorknob, pulling it open, to see why the light's on inside.

41

It's like a regular closet with a shelf and a floor but the back wall is slightly ajar like a door, with a strange amber glow from behind it. So this *danger* alarm gears up my heartbeat, ducking under the shelf to peer through. Six wooden planks descend like steep stairs to a square plywood landing and cinderblock wall down below. The orange cord's plugged in to a metal bulb cage hooked to a pipe in the ceiling, with a light bulb the color of butterscotch candy, tinting everything cellophane yellow.

I get one shaky foot on the first wooden plank and crouch low. Sewer gas hits the back of my throat and, God, it's so bad I have to pinch my nose closed just to breathe. A monstrous shadow flutters over the stairs and the two-by-four studs on the wall. There's an "Ugh" like gruff grunting, the sound of hard labor, the slice of a spade splitting dirt.

I lean forward maybe two inches.

Below me is Richard, shirtless and sweating, gripping the shovel with work-gloved hands, turning dirt over into a trench dug deep in the ground. Fixing the sewer, that makes sense, a pipe in the sewer line broke. He's filling it up from a mound of loose dirt, then drops the shovel and pours in white powder from a fifty-pound sack, which sort of covers the smell.

«it's a grave»

I shake my head to clear angel's voice but it doesn't clear anything at all.

«hurry go back before he sees you use the phone call gabriel take the rent-a-car key drive away» angel's chatter fills my head so bad I can't think so at first I don't hear Richard's voice. «don't think just go go go go»

"Sonovabitch!" Twisting his neck to glance up at me, his flab spills over the brim of his jeans, his sallow skin drips like he's melting. "Hey! Make yourself useful! Get down here!"

«run»

Pivoting to the door, my boot slips, my knee hits the top plank's sharp edge. "Good," he is saying, "I could use an extra set of hands." And then his are on me, cuffing my arm, how did his reach get so long? "C'mon, son." Pulling me down over six steep steps to the plywood landing, stepping me with him off that platform to the mud floor of this underground room.

«tomb» angel says.

Tomb.

Richard pulls my fingers away from where I'm pinching my nose. "Don't be a baby," he says. "Come on. The quicker we finish this, the quicker you put this shit behind you. Bury the past. Start anew. That's what you wanted, right?"

Wooden studs stripe the block walls like bars in a cell. Down at my feet where the earth's opened up, I'm not sure at all what I see.

Bright yellow fabric peeks through the poured powder, deep in the ditch Richard's dug. Wrapped in the shaggy brown rug from his den, with debris and dead grass stuck on. And some shriveled colorless thing, waxy and pale—a hot swarm of needles rankles my skin, the nape of my neck, down my spine—*a hand*, I swear, grasping fingers, mottled white flesh, reaching out of the loopy brown pile. I jump back, shuddering, puke fills my throat.

I turn for the steps, Richard's there.

"Good thing I got to him before the cops," he says, jabbing the spade in the ground. "You're looking at twenty-five to life, right there, son."

What is that, I hear myself say.

"You think it's easy, digging him up to bring him here? Hell, just finding where we dumped him was enough to make me ask myself if saving your ass was worth it. But I'd hate to see you go down for this piece of shit, after what he did to you. Hey! A little help here or what?"

The soft earth cushions my knees and I'm crying, my hands to my ears, trying to stop my guts churning. Swallow it, I command myself, and make myself obey. God I don't want to be here, I don't want to see. But shapes take form anyway, in living color, defining themselves to me. Spongy orange hair. Gaunt gaping jaw, a grimace of yellow teeth outlined in brown. Yellow smock.

"Hey!" I hear Richard say but he sounds like he's miles away.

Dirt tumbles over the white plastic nametag, *Hi can I help you? I'm Lowell.* Richard slings another whole shovelful in.

Weird sensations crawl up my skin I can't shudder away. I need to go now, angel's right. Take the key, take the car. Give Gabriel the tape. Tell him where Cleveland is buried. Proof Richard's guilty and deserves to fry. I'll happily testify.

Richard's pointing things out. The dark gash in the ground. The dirt mound, the shovel. The fifty-pound bag of lime. Cover that up. Pour on the lime, are his instructions. He's going to tidy the car. Then we'll mix up the Quickcrete and pour a new floor. No one will be the wiser. He hands the shovel to me.

«kill him, james»

What?

"Take. The. Shovel—" Richard says, annoyed.

«take the shovel»

"And cover this shit up."

«and stab the blade in his heart»

Richard lets go so it's only my grip on the handle and shaft, the blade tip aimed straight at his heart. A flicker of fear flinches his face for a second, like a dog you say *Bad!* to, bracing himself for the hit. He scoffs. "You want to see your swishy boyfriend again?" He shoves his hair back with one soiled glove, his voice more powerful than ever. "You plant this pansy first," he says, one foot stepping up onto the plywood platform, his back to the cinderblock wall. "Then I'll bring you to him. *Don*ald. You can rescue him. How's that." In two, three, four, five, he's up all six steps and gone.

The spade thuds with a dull metal clang when I drop it. Turning, as if Donald's here, but instead there's only the cinderblock wall with darkness looming behind it. I take a careful step toward it but the eerie dank soil slips under my boots, uneven in places with ruts and ridges in *grave-shaped* spaces, creepy and rank with body parts maybe, human remains, everything ghoulish in the stark light. Remembering the photos Gabriel had, maybe all of the Missing are rotting down here. Their faces and names forgotten.

Upstairs, water runs. Richard's turned on the tap in the john, then the squeak of the faucet turned off. Footsteps cross the floor overhead, a machine rattles wheeling behind them. Distant curses— Richard's curses—the creak of the opening metal back door, chattering wheels bumping over the threshold onto the concrete outside. Then the distant high-pitched hum of a shop vac turned on.

In three leaping bounds, I'm up the six planks, duck through the closet, across Richard's office, the wall phone receiver swung off its hook to my ear, the dial tone drone loud and steady. Flopping *The Yellow Pages* onto the desk, the cover flapped open, POLICE in bold letters on page one. Dialing all seven numbers, aware of the vacuum whining outside, the slam of the trunk, opening car doors, of every stray sound. Hurry and answer! is all I can think, what's taking so long? while it rings. Glance down at the paperwork strewn on the desktop, the ledger with file tabs dividing the pages. *Adjustments · Expenditures · Depreciation · Bad Debts* in Donald's perfect swirly cursive.

I jump when an officer comes on the line, and interrupt her greeting mid-sentence. "Where's Gabriel, tell him James called. Marc Gabriel, he—he's working this case, Cook County investigator... What?" when she says they're not part of Cook County, but she could look up that number for me. "Wait!" I go, "wait, can you just call Marc Gabriel—"

«keep your voice low»

Two octaves lower. "There's a dead, a dead body..." One frantic glance at the door and Richard outside, I could run past him, he wouldn't expect it, just outrun him, he's old, just run far away.

Some sergeant comes on now wanting my name.

"James," I say breathless. "Tell Gabriel it's James and I found, I found Lowell Cleveland," but just saying "Cleveland" chokes me mid-sentence, I have to swallow to get the rest of it out. "He's dead, he's dead! And Donald's here somewhere, I don't know where, I think maybe the house—please tell him to hurry!" At Hunt's business office, I say when he asks where I am. "In Westlawn. The shopping center. But centre, you know, spelled wrong with R-E—"

"ARE YOU FUCKING SHITTING ME?" Blasts the whole room and my ears like a bomb, the receiver ripped from my palm and *WHACK!* stuns my jaw. Holding the pain, turning away, I can't turn away, he's grabbed me. Richard's eyes like a hawk on its prey, I'm his prey, his talons hook into the Marlboro coat and I'm backing away but there's nowhere to back to, he shoves me hard into the wall. Help! is what I'm trying to shout but his palm mugs my mouth so nothing comes out.

He presses the receiver to his ear. "Who is this?" Richard demands, his voice clicks to calm. "My apologies, Sergeant," he says with breath heaving under a grin. "No, sir, no emergency here. Just my son making a phony phone call…Yessir…I'll take care of it, Sergeant…Right…I sure will. Believe me, it won't happen again," then *SLAM!* hung up so hard the bell in the telephone echoes.

His hand collars my throat, perfect fit, I can't breathe, I can't hear, a high C trills in both ears. Then tighter and tighter, choking me into absolute blackness so the last thing I see is a vision of him, wearing the grin of a killer.

Am I asleep and what was the dream? Life rushes in from a world somewhere beyond blackness. Aware of quick movement, of me hung in the air, my boots barely scraping the ground. Of his thick forearm wedged deep in my windpipe, controlling the air I can breathe. Of his faraway tirade rambling on, about parties and fun and fathers and sons who share interests and hang out together. "I did more for you than your old man ever did! I trusted you, for Chrissake, I defended you! I kept Donald alive, I got rid of Cleveland, taught you to drive, gave you a fucking *tooth*brush—"

«there, it's on tape» I'm ready to go now but terror takes over and pain enters too, he's dragging me through the back of the closet, back to the top of those stairs, rapid words pelting my ear—"because that's how you raise a son, you give him the best of what you never had!"—while trails of sweat streak his temples, the stink of it worse than peaches and sewer. His foot and mine hit the top plank at the same time. "That's what a father does!"

The frantic thought comes to trip him. Stick my foot in front of his ankle, make him stumble and fall, then duck when he loosens his grip and shove him, so he'll crack his head open on the cinderblock wall, landing half-dead six feet down. Like Ratachek. When I pushed him through the cafeteria window.

"This is the thanks I get? The both of you. Back-stabbers, the minute my back is turned," Richard is saying, and more words of judgment about who I am but the moment to trip him is gone. Forcing me with him, down step two and step three. The moment to *Run!* is gone too.

"What'd you do to Donald!" I spit out and the back of my head smashes into a wall stud, black lines weave before me, all my strength drains. I can't breathe, I can't push him away. My ears buzz so loud like an amp turned to ten, drowning everything out in the hum.

His voice is muted and far away. *Goddamit! Now look what you made me do!*

And then for a moment there's nothing beneath me, nothing to stand on at all. I'm out of my body, just weightless and free as heaven must be, everything peaceful and calm. Like Granma's touch and Kat's kiss and the sweet way Baby Boy smells. It's magic and how did that happen?

WHAM! When I slam into hard cinderblock, shockwaves shoot through from my bones to my hair. Heaven is gone if it ever existed, my brain shrieks screaming for air. Waves of pain rack my spine like a blade slicing through it, a rectangular saw with four searing edges that radiate through me like fire.

But Richard's hand is gone and my throat opens wide, gasping to refill my lungs. Sucking in air, all the oxygen around me, honking to hoard it like gold. My knees fold below me and bash into plywood, my elbow then shoulder crash to the ground. *Everything* hurts. He's going to kill me, he's waiting to do it, watching me shrivel and fall. I cross both my arms over my head, duck and cover, like the air raid drills at school for when the Commies drop the bomb.

Richard's huge sole, size forty-two, hovers above me, picking which target to crush, my teeth or nuts I feel that coming and whip to one hip so his stomping boot misses. Wooziness swirls around me instead in a mixture of pain and relief. Waiting for magic to happen again, heaven and happy endings, or just whatever comes next beyond this. Telling angel, I don't want to play this game anymore. Where is Gabriel to tell, or my dad? Merry Christmas, I quit.

I open my eyes, he's no longer here. Heavy footsteps retreat in a quick pounding rhythm up three-four-five wooden planks. Faraway there's a siren but six steps above me a heavy door's closing, scraping the floor until *pop!* instant blindness, the work bulb blows out, stealing my sight and the light when it goes. I try to move, but my bones aren't connected, it's agony each time I breathe. The door shuts in its jamb with a final click. All alone, lying here stuck in mud and thick silence. Entombed with the dead. RIP.

Nobody else knows I'm down here. Nobody's coming for me.

«let's go home»

Oh, man. I hear myself moan. I hate this, angel, I want to go home. But you'd think I was eighty or somebody spastic, in agony just trying to get off the floor. Groping the air till my palm touches concrete, I pull myself to my feet, hugging the cinderblock wall. On The Wall, shuffling slowly along it, till my toe bumps the step of the plywood landing. Step up on that, then the first plank, and each plank after, my bones out of whack, pain shoots through each time I move. Hand-over-hand, wall stud to wall stud, counting the planks to the top, nicking each shin one stair at a time till I count the sixth step and stop. Feeling for a doorknob but there *isn't* a doorknob, just thick solid metal like a cell door. Panic lashes my chest like a fiery rash, *I'm trapped.* Pound my fist on the metal as if someone's listening, Gabriel maybe, or the sergeant who answered my call. Shouting his name out but there is no reply, only "GABRIEL!" heard by deaf walls.

Clear the tears on my sleeve with one final bang on the door. I need to make noise, I need something heavy—the shovel—to clang on the metal, but dreading the pain to go down. One. Two. Three... counting each awful step, my whole self objecting, then stepping off six to the plywood landing, and seven, to the softer dirt floor. Keep my back to the wall, feeling my way stud to stud with one hand, inching around the room. Till I've got to be right where Richard was digging, where I dropped his shovel on the ground. By the grave. Cleveland's grave. Cleveland's dead body.

Nausea racks me just to kneel down. Feeling around for the spade, really creepy, just knowing what's down here. Touching a lump like a pillow—a body? Snap my hand back but it's the sack of spilled lime. My fingers brush past it and over the ground. Clumps of dirt, gritty sand, a hard metal handle—the shovel. Feeling triumphant, I hold the shaft up like that movie with Moses raising his staff to praise God. I smite thee, mine enemy!

Letting the shovel lead the way back to the steps like a blind croaker prodding a cane. But the platform's not there. Wait. Where is the wall? I turn back and *WHACK!* My forehead smacks hard on a pipe in the ceiling which fucking hurts but I stop myself crying.

Rule #2: Don't magnify grievances. HA!

Moving forward, reaching up with one hand feeling the pipe above, I think it's the one where the light bulb was hung. Following the pipe, trying not to think about pain or dead bodies, feeling my way back to the stairs. But there are no steps or wood platform there, no rough cinderblock wall to touch. Still, I keep moving, hobbling slow, using the spade like a crutch. One foot, then the other. Each step wrings my spine with a staggering jolt.

I count a half dozen steps, then a half dozen more, into the telescoping dark.

42

It's a tunnel, I realize, reeking of waste and decay. I'm trying to ignore the rancid air, but even breathing through clenched teeth I can taste it. I'm thinking, Quick! Joey Small! but I'm not quick at all, so I'm laughing at that, distracted. Sort of hobbling along to the refrain of that song, I try to move faster. But agony stops me dead-bang, even worse, like a shitty reminder of how much moving forward hurts.

Keep your head, that's what Granma said. And Kat, *I love you, James.* And Donald. So a different ache stabs my heart.

My eyes make believe or play night tricks on me, shapes form and shift in the dark, a bat cave, a deep grave, a gaping black rectangle like a door to *The Twilight Zone.* My heart's pounding faster, heading straight toward it, with hope that I've found the way out.

The dirt turns to concrete under my shoes, the shovel scrapes the hard floor. Feeling my way for four or five steps into a hallway, I think, with a low ceiling and cinderblock walls. Or maybe it's been like this all along. I keep one palm moving over the rough concrete blocks, inching the shovel before me. Till it clunks against metal and stops... *Another dead end.* Swallowing panic, flailing the air until my hand hits a pipe—a circular pipe, like a big steering wheel. I try turning the wheel like hanging a ralphie, but it doesn't turn right. Hang a louie instead—there's the tiniest squeak and a latch clicks, unlocked, and I hear angel cheer when I tug it, heave ho, and pull it open the tiniest bit.

Always go forward, Rand told me that. I keep tugging hard, again and again till it's open enough to squeeze through. And when I do, this feeling surrounds me like I've entered a much bigger space. A fan whirs above, and I'm hit with this rank male smell, like the first night in Railton you never forget, facing your new life in jail. One cautious step with the shovel ready, for what I'm not really sure. Another few steps—but my toe stubs and trips on the hard edge of something, a stoop or a platform, the shovel falls and I stumble, and for one weightless moment the ground slips away, in the next, it's me crashing down.

A loud *gasp!* escapes the pile I land on, lumpy and coming to life, it swells like a wave and erupts underneath me, bucking me up and over the side onto the hard gritty floor. Something huge and fluttering fans out above me, blacker than blackness, a bat swarm attacking or Cleveland rising from hell.

"Wait, wait—" I struggle to say, rolling onto my side—onto the shovel that jabs in my shoulder—I grab it with both hands then twist back around, like armor I'm wearing to shield me from harm.

"Oh, God! Help us *all* and Oscar Wilde," it squeals.

Relief rushes in at sound of his voice, all my defenses just melt and I let the shovel drop to the ground. But before I can say *It's me* or his name, he's gone. Fuzzy darkness wavers before me, with this fear that I'm hearing a voice that's not here and I've gone certifiably psycho. "Don't go, please, don't," I'm begging God or angel out loud. *Please let Donald be real.* "Donald?"

"Don't look at me," he sobs. "Oh, I'm a hideous mess. I don't want you to see."

I *can't* see. "Okay," I say, not sure where to *not* look, just relieved he really exists.

I take a deep breath and ease myself up. Squinting to make sense of this place, turning to look all around. A dim glow fans over the concrete floor defining the shape of a platform before me. A wavering figure rolls into the middle, curling up in its ghostly frame. *Donald Griswold*, 1970, flesh in darkness. I don't think he's wearing any clothes.

I look away.

Vague shapes emerge from the dimness around me, shy colors peer from the gray. The shovel, for one thing, on the dirt floor. The recorder, too, where it fell from my pocket. Agony grabs me when I pick it up, cursing myself for the pain. But despite one dented corner and the cracked plastic window, the cassette reels still spin on RECORD. "I found Donald," I tell it. "He's alive." Then add, "In this like underground tunnel or something. We're gonna find a way out." I slip it back into my coat pocket, the proof. For Gabriel, what a joke. He's the one missing or moved on to Plan C or maybe Plan Z by now.

"Who are you talking to?"

"Uh, a tape recorder. For like, evidence—."

"Turn it off!" Donald sputters. "I don't want anyone to know!"

I pull the recorder out, holding it in the direction of him and switch RECORD to STOP.

In the dim light beyond him a counter appears, and a cabinet. A half-size refrigerator. A toilet. The platform's a mattress or the bottom box-spring from a bed, with a floral fall pattern I can almost make out, in tints of golds, browns, and reds. But then—not autumn flowers at all. Stains. Dried smears and puddle rings too ugly to look at. I clench my eyes tight, glad for the blackness it brings.

I wish REWIND and ERASE were buttons to click in my brain.

«that's ECT» angel points out. So maybe that is what I need.

"It's a fallout shelter," Donald says, his voice cracking. "Unlike me, it's indestructible." It's stocked with enough supplies to survive a nuclear attack, that's what Hunt told him. "Won't that be lovely. Subsisting on canned bread and water in bottles. Oh, and let's not forget his tins of sardines." His sarcasm dies, choking on sobs instead. "'Reasons to Juliet Thyself'? Add dead oily fish to the top of that list."

"I don't want you to die," barely cracks out.

"He had me dig a...*grave*," he whimpers, pointing behind me at the tunnel where I came in. "I'm a *grave*digger, James. Dear *God*."

Something furry rubs my leg and I jump, wrenching my back out worse. But there's a wild *meow!* and when I turn around, there's a cat in his arms. *His* cat. My heart sort of calms. "A grave for who?"

Donald blubbers, "For Babsy," embracing the calico tight to his chest. "Apparently, his daughters are allergic. He doesn't want to lose visitation rights so Babsy has to stay down here. Or...or I could simply *drown* her. I would rather kill myself than kill my cat."

"How long have you been here?"

"How long, Babs? How long since Richard brought you to me?" As if the cat's talking to him. "Since Thanksgiving?" his mouth muffled in the fur between her ears. "Up until then, we all lived in the house. Richard didn't know they had allergies."

Donald opens his arms, Babs leaps to the floor. "I *am* a good wife, James," he says, like an opening argument, or a letter he's written to someone who's hurt him, *Dear James, (who thinks I'm disgusting)*. So I just shut up and listen.

"*I don't expect you to understand, being the handsome straight boy that you are.*" Sniffling, he wraps his arms around his chest. "*But he chose me! I was the one waiting for him to come home every night, to a tidy house with dinner ready & a passionate lover in bed...*"

I shake my head, I don't want to hear about that.

"*Oh, but it's true! I am his fantasy, James! (Can you imagine? Me, someone's fantasy?) I am the one he said 'yes' to after just two weeks together! I am the one he promised himself to: 'With this ring I thee wed,' in a ceremony I'd practiced so many times when I played with my Barbie & Kens. I am the one he honeymooned with when we consummated our marital vows—"*

I *really* don't want to imagine that. Or anything he's been through.

"Do you know what it's like to hide who you are twenty-four hours a day? Honey, it's exhausting! I didn't have to play that shame game anymore with Richard! James, it was heaven! I was living on Happy Street."

"Yeah, but you're hiding down here."

"Only until his divorce is final—can you imagine if anyone saw me with him? Dear Lord! His ex would destroy him & take everything— the girls, his house, his businesses! Thank heavens I'm a CPA. All we had to do was adjust his bottom line, turn his assets into liabilities. Because, honey, half of nothing is nothing, you know?"

I'm shaking my head, I'm not good at half math.

"Richard said he loves how we think alike. That's what a good wife does."

The cat grazes my pant legs, winding between my ankles. Picking her up is comforting.

"How quickly 'my one & only' turned to 'abandoned & lonely' again. Story of my life." Tears, I think, ride his cheeks and he sniffles, changing positions, like he's turned to page two.

"One night he brought home a newspaper clipping. The headline was simply horrid. Some poor soul was found in the river, & it...it was Allen. My dear, dear poet friend who'd gone missing. Oh, I was heartsick. But Richard laughed—Stupid kid falls off a bridge! & I said, how can you be so cold? & he accused me of always judging him— just like his ex!—& probably stealing from him, too. & he just...he just picked up & walked out the door." Donald swallows the sentence like a bitter pill. *"He started bringing street boys home late at night after that. As if our vows were a joke & the wedding ring just a worthless prize from a Crackerjack box."*

"Cereal box," I say.

Donald snorts snot up, a cry escapes him. *"Oh, James! I tried so hard to make him see how much he needed me! I spent two weeks planning his annual Thanksgiving 'shindig.' I cleaned the house, ordered the liquor, brined the turkey—the whole shebang. But he said all his financial statements had to be at her lawyers by the first of December—that was four days away! Four days to prepare ten years of ledgers! So instead of Thanksgiving, Yours Truly was dropped off at the IFC office. I was Cinderella NOT invited to the ball! I can't even tell you how crushed I was. I could barely see through my tears, let alone add & subtract."*

Babs bounds from my arms and curls up at his feet.

"I ruined everything! I don't know if he'll ever allow me back in his house. I just felt so rejected—oh, it was my whole life of heartbreak all over again! To top it off, Thanksgiving morning this cute hippie street boy Richard had picked up (talk about adding salt to a wound!) walked in the office & asked if there was a dolly handy & I said, 'Hell-o!' & he recognized me (from being with you!) & said you were right outside in the truck! Oh! My heart nearly flew out of my chest! I didn't know what to do! I gave him my ring & begged him to give it to you. I was not stabbing Richard in the back or trying to ruin anyone's life! I only wanted you to know I was there." Shaking his head, sobs drown his words. *"Because I have nobody else who cares."*

Love. Your Unconditional Friend. Donald Griswold. He doesn't say that but it hangs in the air.

He's quiet a moment and I want to say something or ask him a question, where's your clothes? or why didn't you leave?

Donald glances at the mattress, all the ugliness there. "He won't bring other guests down when I'm here," he says. "Just garbage. So." He wipes his eyes on the back of his wrist. "We don't see him very often, do we, Babs. Lately, not at all." He winces, as if *not at all* hurts the most.

"I loved him," Donald sniffles, but when I ask him why, he starts crying again. "He said he loved me."

I wish I could take his heartache away or knew how to make him feel better. But all I can think of is what he told me, *we hurt those that love us most.* So that's what I tell him.

Full-fledged Niagra Falls now. Between sobs he tells me that cute hippie street boy was dead, his body rolled up in a tarp on the floor the next day. "Right there," Donald points right behind me. "Richard said it was an accident. From playing the rope trick game."

I swallow back puke, a thick burning lump. "Charlie, that's who he was. Charlie Zerotski." I cross myself, *rest in peace.* "They...they found him in the river. With your ring, I think it was stuffed down his throat."

"Oh, God. Oh, God! It should've been me!" Standing up with bent knees, he's buried his face in his hands, shaking his head, his hair's grown to his shoulders all twisty and wild. "Oh, God, James! It's *my* fault he's dead!"

He switches a light on somewhere.

Where there was darkness there's instantly light, everything overexposed. Blinking my eyes until Donald's in focus. Hunched over, his arms crossed before him, covering himself, his fingers spread wide. "Look at me, James. What I've become," he says.

I step back from the lantern, averting my eyes, there's nothing here I want to see. "He wouldn't have picked you up if you weren't dressed like a guy." I confess, "That's 'cause of me."

I take the recorder out of the pocket and hand Donald the Marlboro coat. And my black sharkskin suit pants, I give him those, too, and the Beatle boots, that's fair, like half math, we're both half undressed. He shakes his head, but puts my stuff on and they fit. "Oh! My goodness!" he says.

"You look nice," I say. "Well, with a bath and a visit to your friend at Sassoon, obviously, but, still."

"I can't! I can't go anywhere! That boy is dead because of me! How am I supposed to live knowing that?"

I slip the tape recorder into my suit jacket pocket. "Well, if he's up there he'll probably kill us both anyway."

A squeal escapes him. "Oh, you shouldn't have come here!"

"I'm not the only one looking for you. I mean, mostly me. But other people too."

Donald, *odd duck Donald*, sort of brightens. "Like who?"

"Your mom, she's worried. Mostly your mom."

"Oh, James." Donald's voice falters with tears and he breaks, dropping to his knees on that awful bed, curling up into a ball again, sobbing and tangling his hair with his fingers. And I have no clue what Dr. Pauly would do, except give him a shot, or a bite plate.

Cleveland's riddle comes to me now: *You're chained in a cell with no doors or windows. How do you get out?* If I guess the right answer, he might let me go.

Look at yourself, see what you saw, take the saw, cut the chain in half, two halves make a whole, you climb out the hole.

How would I *ever* guess that?

Two halves make a whole. Donald on a mattress. And the hatch he points out, high above on the ceiling. Richard took the ladder away.

If I stand on the mattress I can open the hatch, that's my plan. If we lift the box spring on its end, if he keeps it steady, I'll climb up first and face Richard Hunt by myself. That's what I tell Donald, my mouth to his ear, lying beside him till his tears dry. Are you going to kill him? Donald wants to know. No—I don't know—but we can't stay here. Donald doesn't reply.

"Come on, Oscar Wilde. Help me lift it," I say.

You'd think it'd be easy to climb the wood slats that ladder the back of the box spring, tipped on its end and wedged against the concrete bomb shelter wall. But just straightening up, pain blanks my vision, just lifting my foot, my whole body complains. If not for Donald spotting me and bracing my back, I honestly think I wouldn't be moving at all. It's a really slow climb, one slat at a time, to reach the ceiling hatch, and shove my palms flat against it. Up it pops like a stubborn lid I have to wrench out of the way, flopping the rug on top aside. Uncovered, the square opens into the floor above.

Two halves make a whole. I climb out the hole.

I crawl off the top slat onto the rug, all ow ow ow getting sweaty, and take a few breaths to steady myself. I can barely stand up in the cramped darkness, draped by hung clothing and dry cleaner plastic I have to shove out of my face. Flagging my fingers high overhead till they snag a dangling string. *Click!* when I pull it, harsh light from the bulb floods my eyes. Puffy-sleeve dresses, princess costumes, vacation clothes stored until summer, I guess, or his daughters arrive.

I keep my voice low and call down to Donald. "There's dresses up here you could probably fit now." Ducking through clothing and tumbling hangers, I turn the doorknob, it's locked. For maybe two seconds defeat overwhelms me, but no. "Donald! The shovel—!" and after a moment, the handle pokes up. I lift it and fit the blade tip to the wood where the doorknob's screwed on. Then jam the blade down hard as I can, and jack it again and again and again, till the wood splinters, the screws pry loose, the doorknob thuds onto the rug. Breathing hard, but triumphant, the door opened a crack, and fear gears up at what waits beyond it. Peering into a shadowy basement. Knotty-pine paneled walls and a built-in couch, TV, and ugly green tile on the floor.

43

First thing, the marvel strikes me of this underground tunnel he's dug, and how it connects his IFC business to a bomb shelter under his house. Second, is, oh shit, I hear footsteps above, their quick *thump thump thump* on the ceiling.

The front doorbell rings, harsh and demanding, *Ding-dong ding-dong ding-dong!* loud pounding rattles the front and back doors. Glancing up at the rafters, the whole upstairs floor plan's mapped out in my head. The same heavy footsteps move quick down the hallway, squeaking the floor boards above, past the den, through the living room, to the front door. Muted shouts filter in from outside, orders and commands. Gabriel's voice and Richard's reply.

No, he's not with me. Do you fucking see him with me? Do you see him in the car?

Check my jacket pockets, the recorder's in there, Richard's confession, my card to Get Out Of Jail Free. I've got boxers on, but I don't care. I just want to get out of here. I call down to Donald, "The Cavalry's here!" and tell him I'm going up.

I leave the closet open for him and just when I turn toward the stairs, something rams the front door with so much force the whole house and me jump and teeter. Heavy footsteps rattle the ceiling, advancing and quick on the move. Thudding back through the living room, down the hall, tapping across the kitchen's linoleum floor.

Richard hollers above, "Hold your fucking horses! I'll open the goddam door!" moving quicker, down the three steps to the mud room at the top of the basement stairs. Maybe opening the back door to give himself up—I'm crossing my fingers, but no. He's turned in the mud room and is heading down here.

My heart pounds faster and panic sets in, a split-second of rational thought fills my brain, turning everything into a weapon, a pillow, a chair, the hangers spilled on the closet floor, and the shovel I left inside it.

But twisting to get it, my legs go numb, my heart in a race with Hunt's gait, here he comes. Pound pound pound down the staircase, his shit-kicker size forty-twos step into view with just the wood banister between us. Pound pound pound, his pant cuffs and pantlegs, his knees then the hem of his black leather coat, his black leather shoulders, disheveled thick hair, rounding the stairwell, boots on green tile, and the killer is standing before me.

Richard Hunt. Agitated, with frantic eyes slit, quickly reading the room, the splintered door, the open closet, the light on inside it, scattered hangers and clothing, the doorknob dead on the floor. And me.

He scoffs with a grin like he'll easily take me. "Come here," he says, his right hand extended at first I think to shake mine. But then past my palm, he's clenched my wrist and twists my back into his chest, his forearm across my throat. He hisses, "The secret is *not* to get caught," his mouth in my hair, while his left hand frisks me, my crotch and my jacket, mangling my pocket fetching the tape recorder out.

"What the fuck? You *sneaky* little son of a bitch," he says, holding it before me, his proof. My throat cinches tighter, locked in the crook of his elbow, he's got the recorder in both his big hands. *Snap!* he breaks the little window off and pops out the cassette.

No, not the tape! God, don't let him destroy it!—but I can't move without choking, or stop him from pulling a tangle of brown tape from the cassette.

Glass breaks upstairs, the smash of a window, the clinking of shards shattering on a hard floor. His grip on me loosens, glancing up. I swing my fist at his face like he's Cleveland, and pow! it connects, but not forceful at all. His jaw tilts up slightly, his double chins wobble, his eyes aim like ray guns right at me. His chokehold tightens till everything's spinning, a kaleidoscope nightmare of knotty pine paneling, Hunt's lipless grin, beady eyes, flabby chins. I pull my hand back to hit him again but it catches instead on the death boutonniere with a scratch that draws blood from the hatpin. Granma's heirloom hatpin, there's comfort knowing that, from the Rosenberg family tree, and I slip the pin free, the flab of his jowl just inches from me with only her hatpin between us. He turns or looks down but he can't see the pin when it pierces his skin and jabs up the side of his throat. He jerks and nods to break away, which just stabs the pin even deeper. His huge slab of palm slams upside my jaw, the ceiling arcs back in a blur of dizzying motion. A shriek fills my head, shrill and deafening, like the A-bomb's been dropped, or the end of the world, but I open my eyes and it's Donald.

"Don't you touch his face!" Donald squeals. There's a *whoo-oosh*! from the ceiling when the shovel swoops down then thwacks with a clangy dischord close behind me. The thrust of it jolts me and caves in my knees, Hunt's arm drops away and my throat opens free, he collapses chest-first on top of me, but I twist to one side when we hit the floor, so it's only my legs that get pinned.

There's a grunt, "Ugh," and the cassette tape hits the floor, his hands grapple his throat, grasping to find what stuck him. Blood streams down his face through a split in his head, a piece of his scalp flopped over one ear, a slice in one eyebrow gushing. He blinks once, wide eyes bulging in disbelief, maybe in more shock than me.

Oh God what'd I do? I'm taking in big shots of air like painkiller, and try to get up, but a huge wave of pain steals my breath and stops me from moving at all. "Donald..." I start to say.

The bloodied shovel clatters hitting the tile floor, and Donald kneels beside me. His cat purrs when he pets her in his arms and lays the cassette on my palm.

There's other sounds now. Doors, it seems everywhere, opening and closing, footsteps flooding the rooms overhead and pounding the stairs in a rush coming down here. Whole swarms of uniformed men take over, their faces around me all blur together. Blinding lights flash from the pictures they capture: knotty pine walls, built-in couch, sarcophagus freezer and what's frozen inside it, the closet open, the hatch exposed. The killer lifted up and taken in chains on an ambulance stretcher. Donald surrounded in a circle of men, telling his outrageous story. And I'm shaking with pain that clings like raw lightning, waiting to be taken away, too.

But Officer. Gabriel's here. I'm not sure how long he's been standing above me, I'm not sure if he knows what I've done.

"Get a stretcher down here," I hear him say. He points at the closet, the shovel, his voice recorder cracked on the floor. More blinding flashbulbs, they jump to obey him wherever he points, like he's the director in charge of this set, The Man they want to impress. But it's my shoulder his hand grips, it's me he congratulates, I'm the one earning his smile. "Couldn't keep your pants on, I see," he says, crouching beside me.

Marc Gabriel close-up. Black suit, white shirt, black tie, hat brim tipped over one brow. He takes the cassette tape out of my hand.

"You did something tonight no other man in this room could have done. And we all—this entire city—owe you a debt of gratitude."

No other *man*, that word hits me so hard I don't know what to say. Except, "Merry Christmas."

Tears come, I couldn't tell you why. Maybe for all the boys buried here, or relief that the cavalry's arrived. Or just knowing this time *I did do something* and me and Donald survived. He's in the arms of two dashing policemen, and he is pretty shocking to see, a rat nest of hair he never would wear, the fuzz of his beard and mustache grown in, and freckles without any makeup. We look at each other for maybe an instant. And I want to say something, *I still think you're pretty. Hug your mother. Don't kill anybody.* Or maybe just, *Have a nice day.* But they turn him away, a flash of high-heeled boots and black sharkskin pants, a suede shearling coat, and a calico cat, disappearing up the stairs.

«he knows you care» angel assures me, in a voice that's never really been there. And I say, hey, angel? Go with him now, Donald needs you a lot more than I do. And in my head, peaceful silence for that wise decision. In my heart, a calm rhythm and cool harmony.

Like James Daniel is back, except perfectly sane.

I'm suddenly trembling, my teeth chatter loud, my arms wrapped around me can't stop it. Colors wash out till there's no colors at all, everything fading to white. But he's here when they lift me, walking beside me, holding my hand as we go.

"Let's get you home," my dad says.

His smile, that's the last thing I see. He's calling my name like to stop me from leaving but I'm already long gone. All the pain falls away in a last floating moment, no matter how tight I hold on.

AFTERWARD

"Manic Depression" plays in my head like a welcome-back kiss, crazy guitar licks and lyrics I silently sing to myself. Much better, I think, than Tofranil-PM or anything you'd cop off of Rand. Jimi HendRx, the only Rx I need.

Music, sweet music, keeping me sane.

White-capped blue waves splash over the breakers on my left off of Lake Shore Drive. On my right, the Chicago skyline winks between light poles and leafy green trees in the park. Heading south into the Loop, my dad at the wheel of his baby blue Mercedes looks straight ahead as he drives. Bright spikes of sunshine burst off the windshield making him blink his eyes. His jaw moves releasing his last words of wisdom or maybe he's singing too, verses of lyrics in his legal jargon that end with a happy refrain. About acquittal and pardons or paying the judge off, who knows.

The Prosecutor may ask the Court to grant the witness immunity from prosecution for any criminal conduct the witness may reveal by his or her testimony

My dad goes over the Oath of Witness, it's what I have to repeat or they won't believe me. In exchange for my testimony, I won't be prosecuted no matter what I confess.

If the Court grants such immunity, the witness
is required to answer completely the questions asked
by the Prosecutor or grand jurors, but the witness
may not thereafter be prosecuted for any crimes that
testimony reveals

He's not allowed to go in with me, I have to face the grand jury on
my own. "I'll be waiting right outside," he says. "I promise."

Hearing those two words, knowing how fragile a promise can be.
So it's not that I don't believe him. It's more that I think the promises
you make are not in your control. All you can do is take care of
yourself and make sure you keep moving forward.

My dad turns off the Outer Drive and into the towering city. Any
last questions? he asks. Any concerns?

I'm playing with the dial on my transistor radio, clicking it OFF,
then back ON. I pull the earphone from my ear, unplugged. He nods
his approval.

I lift my shades from my eyes to my forehead. The opening chords
of "For Your Love" vibrate in my palm. "Just, what if what I say gets
the whole case thrown out? So he's set free and clear. Like Railton, all
those criminals out on the street, that's because of me."

His hand leaves the steering wheel for a moment then grips it.
"Hunt had body parts wrapped in his freezer, James. Corpses were
found in that tunnel he built connecting his house to his business.
We may never know how many young men he murdered or where
he buried the dead. But we do know the killing is over," my dad says,
turning toward me as he drives. "And that's because of you. James
Daniel Ross."

He nods with pursed lips not hiding his pride. "As far as your
testimony today goes? My advice is to take your time with each
answer and tell the truth to the best of your recollection."

I nod, okay. But still. A million thoughts buzz in my head of the
truths I've collected and what's the best one to tell, but he's already

driven underground and given his keys to the parking attendant, gathered his briefcase and me from the car. And honestly? I don't know what truth I'll say. Walking beside him into the courthouse, he has a question for me. "Why do you think all those boys got in the red truck?"

It takes a while recollecting that answer. All the obvious reasons. Five bucks and breakfast, a bed off the streets, and someone who wants to be with you. And the truth. "I don't think when you're sixteen you think you will die," is my guess.

What shakes me the most is the look on my dad's face when he hands me over to Gabriel. Like he's watching me turn into somebody else and it's the last time he'll ever see James. So I try to let him know I'll be fine but I've already said that like fifty times. Still, he just looks defenseless and small watching me shake Gabriel's hand in the hall, and tell him it's good to see him.

Gabriel tells me I'm looking much better than last time he saw me. I'm thinking he looks a lot shorter. Well, his hat's off, that fedora he wears even in April, he holds it by the pinch in its crown. How're you feeling? he asks me. He's glad I'm no longer down and in pain. Drugs, I tell him, and maybe therapy helped. He goes, I meant your broken back. I say, I know what you meant. He nods at the paperback and my finger bookmarking page two. He checks out the title. *The Catcher in the Rye.*

"Good book?" he asks, and I say my sister gave it to me, so far it's okay, but he doesn't really want a review. His hand finds my shoulder and leads me away before I can say goodbye to my dad, which is the only thing left to do. Out of the hallway into a little room. A waiting area or maybe holding cell.

"I have something to give you as well," Gabriel says. And he slips some bright orange thing out of his jacket but stops before handing it to me. "Listen, I want you to know. If you ever need anything—"

But I plug the earphone into my ear and switch the radio ON, volume dialed to ten. "This Time Tomorrow" by the Kinks fills my head. I swipe the orange card from his fingers.

It's a picture postcard like a tourist would send, from their vacation or someplace they've traveled, The Statue of Liberty in NYC, or The Art Institute of Chicago. But this one's from an even better place, maybe the best place in the world. The Endless Summer, a postcard just like Kat once described it, a brilliant orange sun with silhouette surfers. GREETINGS FROM SANTA MONICA. And flipping it over, I read the address she's written. *To: James, c/o the Fresh Cup Diner.* Her message forwarded to me.

Wish you were here, that's all it says. With a smiley face dotting the "*i*."

DIRECTORS RULES

To develop in the inmate self-reliance, self-control, self-respect, self-discipline and the ability and desire to conform to Accepted Standards for individual and community life in a Free Society. To this end, this set of Directors Rules has been established which every inmate is expected to Obey.

1. Always conduct yourself in an Orderly Manner.

2. Do not agitate, unduly complain or magnify grievances.

3. Promptly and politely obey all Orders or Instructions given by State Employees.

4. Do not use profane or obscene language.

5. Do not boo, whistle, shout, or make other loud or disturbing noises.

6. Do not participate in any sexual or immoral act. Do not place yourself in a position which might lead to such an act.

7. Smoking, Drugs, and Alcohol of any kind are Prohibited.

8. Be Attentive and Respectful toward all State Employees and Officials. Address any such person as "Mr.", "Mrs.", or "Miss", followed by his or her last name or by there proper title followed by there last name. Do not speak unless personally addressed.

9. The Clothing issued to you is State Property. You are responsible for it's care and condition.

10. Be properly clothed at all times and keep your Clothing and shoes as neat and clean as conditions permit.

11. Bathe frequently. Keep your teeth clean, keep your hair neatly cut and groomed.

12. Be clean shaven and wash your hands when needed, particularly before meals and after using the toilet.

13. Do not laugh do not tell do not sit on the bunk they forgot to put those down.

Oh, and:

14. Don't give up hope.

1970 MEDIA AND PLAYLIST

(by chapter, in order of appearance)

Forward **Music:** "Quick Joey Small (Run Joey Run)" First release by Kasenetz-Katz Singing Orchestral Circus; "Purple Haze" Jimi Hendrix; "Gimme Shelter" The Rolling Stones; "Whole Lotta Love" Led Zeppelin

1. **TV:** *Adam-12;* **Music:** *Electric Ladyland* and "Crosstown Traffic," Jimi Hendrix

2. **Music:** "The Firebird Ballet Suite" 1945, Igor Stravinsky

3. **TV:** *American Bandstand; General Hospital; Let's Make A Deal; I Love Lucy*

4. **TV:** *Dragnet; Hawaii Five-0*

7. **TV:** *The Beverly Hillbillies*

9. **Movie:** "Staircase," quote from a play by Charles Dyer

13. **Music:** *Smash Hits,* Jimi Hendrix; *On a Clear Day You Can See Forever,* Barbra Streisand; **Movie:** *Rebel Without a Cause*

18. **TV:** *Marcus Welby, MD; Ben Casey; Dr. Kildare; Dragnet*

21. **TV:** *Mr. Magoo; Huckleberry Hound;* **Movie:** *Mary Poppins;* **Music:** "Blackbird," The Beatles; *The White Album,* The Beatles; *Get Yer Ya-Yas Out!,* The Rolling Stones

23. **Music:** "Quick Joey Small (Run Joey Run)"; "Instant Karma (We All Shine On)," John Lennon

24. **Music:** "Please Mr. Postman," The Marvelettes

25. **Music:** "Twist and Shout," The Beatles

26. **Music:** "Whole Lotta Love" and "The Lemon Song," Led Zeppelin;
    Movie: *Love Story*

27. **Movie:** *Rebel Without a Cause;* **TV:** *Carol Burnett;*
    The Evening News

28. **Radio:** Smooth FM jazz

29. **Music:** "Down on the Street," The Stooges; **TV:** *Perry Mason*

31. **Music:** "The Wind Cries Mary," Jimi Hendrix; **TV:** *The
    Defenders; The Untouchables*

32. **Movie:** *Love Story;* **Music:** "Who'll Stop the Rain?," Creedence
    Clearwater Revival

35. **TV:** *The Tonight Show with Johnny Carson;* **Music:**
    "The Star-Spangled Banner"

37. **Music:** "All You Need Is Love," The Beatles; **TV:** *The CBS
    Evening News with Walter Cronkite*

40. **TV:** *Dragnet*

41. **Movie:** *The Ten Commandments*

42. **Music:** "Quick Joey Small (Run Joey Run)"; **TV:** *The Twilight
    Zone*

Afterward **Music:** "Manic Depression," Jimi Hendrix; "For Your
    Love," The Yardbirds; "This Time Tomorrow," The Kinks

ACKNOWLEDGMENTS

To publisher Tyson Cornell and the team at Rare Bird Books for giving *Flip City* a home and allowing me the time I needed to deliver the most polished novel I could. A huge thank you to editor Hailie Johnson, who kept James's journey moving forward each time it wandered off course.

To my writer's group, the Oxnardians past and present, for their story notes, encouragement, and invaluable feedback through years of rewriting these pages: Jack Maeby, Roger Angle, Sharon Sharth, Bob Shane, Jamie Diamond, Patricia Smiley, Jonathan Beggs, Matt Witten, Craig Faustus Buck, Bonnie MacBird, Andrew Rubin, Terry Shames, and Harley Jane Kozak, who asked only that James be home for Christmas.

To Anne Edelstein, who believed in the boy on the box from the beginning.

To Toddrick, Maggie, Salinger, and Jon, the cogs in the wheel my life spins around. To the moon and back! I couldn't be more proud of these humans.

To "all the crumbs in the Burrows breadbox" as our dad used to say, and what loving crumbs we turned out to be: Bob, Betty, Dan, Deana, and Mom. Especially Mom. How blessed we are to grow up and old together.

To talk show hosts Oprah Winfrey and Phil Donahue, whose TV interviews with Survivors of Terrible Things planted the seed of this novel in me. How could I protect my sons from a madman? What would they need to survive?

To Linda Swartz and Holly Faulconer for keeping me sane when long nights of rewrites overwhelmed me.

To my Rag Dolls and Dirty Martinis, the SCRs and Team RL for the miles of smiles shared on trails and paseos while scenes and dialog worked out in my head.

To the stylists at Paul Mitchell Innovation Center for asking about my book's progress every six weeks, and working their magic on the sleep-deprived writer in the mirror.

To my BFs from 1970 whose memories may be sharper than mine: Claudia Sainsot, John (Jeffo) Walté, Deb Reis, Stu Leviton, and all the suburban bad boys whose stories sparked life into James.

To the artists and musicians of my generation: Thank you.

With apologies that I couldn't write fast enough before you left the party: Dad, Mary, Lynn, Nerida, Lisa. All of you are in these pages.

And yes, to my care team at Kaiser Permanente, without whom I may never have finished this book.

Printed in the USA
CPSIA information can be obtained
at www.ICGtesting.com
JSHW030611080224
56925JS00003B/3

9 781644 283493